Also by Victoria Heckman
In the Elizabeth Murphy Animal Communicator
Series:
Burn Out

In the K.O.'d in Hawai'i Series:
K.O.'d in Honolulu
K.O'd in the Volcano
K.O.'d in the Rift

In the Coconut Man of Ancient Hawai'i Series:
Kapu

Stand Alone Mystery:
Pearl Harbor Blues

Wet Work

Victoria Heckman

For My Family
and Pet Owners Everywhere

This is a work of fiction, a product of the author's imagination. Any resemblance to persons or events or persons living or dead is entirely coincidental.

Acknowledgments

Gratitude to a great many people for their support in creating this work. My editors, Sue McGinty and Margaret Searles, my Beta Reader Deb Roy, WHAR wolf hybrid and rescue for the tour and the patient answering of my questions, Yoshi Honda for vetting Japanese culture and customs, Clarke Koi of Toronto, Canada, for the great cover koi, and yes, it's a real fish! And most of all, my family who supports my writing adventures, both far and near. Special thanks to my friends in Cooper Landing, Alaska, Lorraine Temple and Mike Amos and the Cooper Landing Library.

WET WORK

BY

VICTORIA HECKMAN

One

They're too big to eat. What good are they?
Teddy, Elizabeth Murphy's rotund tabby said.

They both stood at the edge of the koi pond that Elizabeth's husband, Tig, had built for them in the backyard. Four feet deep and twelve across, its kidney shape took up a great deal of the yard. The tinkling of the waterfall was lovely and attracted many birds, especially hummingbirds. Much to the delight of Teddy and especially Edward, the small black cat Elizabeth had rehabilitated as a kitten and they'd kept. Elizabeth had warned the birds, so Teddy or Edward rarely were successful. She'd had many a talk with them about this issue, but they were cats, after all--stubborn and independent at times, needy and loving when they wanted to be.

Elizabeth was dicing fresh tofu into her hand to toss to the exceptionally large fish. "Jewels" they were sometimes called, and brilliant gems in the water they were. When they saw her standing at the edge, it usually meant good things for them. Most often food, but sometimes a little pat. Not enough to take off the slime coat, but they did enjoy hers and Tig's attention. It made it easier on the rare occasions when one was ill or injured and needed to be removed from the pond for medical attention. That was an unpleasant and stressful task for all concerned.

Hey, want to hurry it up, there? came a muted, sort of—well—watery sensation in Elizabeth's mind as Princess Keiko, the oldest and largest koi sent a picture of the tofu dropping into the water. High in protein and an excellent food source, they loved tofu in addition to their regular koi food, along with whatever bugs and creatures fell into the pond.

A clamor of similar sensation came from the other koi and Elizabeth dropped the cubes in, a few at a time. She enjoyed this ritual, but it also served a purpose. It allowed her, or Tig, to check them when they surfaced to eat. Anyone of the eleven who didn't come might be sick or hurt. Keiko had the most experience 'talking' with Elizabeth. Tig loved his fish, but he was more of a plant guy, and after all, Elizabeth could communicate with animals. She was at a loss with plants. Or a plant murderer, as she sometimes put it. Unintentionally, but still she left the garden and pond care to Tig.

He was a firefighter, but on his days off he did landscaping and pond building to make extra money. She used her animal communication skills to create additional income and word of mouth brought her enough business. She had briefly worked with Tig at the fire department doing temp work—data entry—but that had lapsed when the job was complete. Just as well. She'd rather be with animals than in a cubicle tied to a computer all day.

Tig's business had done so well in fact, that last year he'd hired an assistant, Karl, to help with the maintenance and big jobs. Once Tig built a pond, it was solid, but ponds did require cleaning, liner repair and anything else the homeowner wanted. He was often called to fix other pond-builders' mistakes. Waterfalls were his least favorite to diagnose and repair, and he had trained Karl and let him take most of those.

Lately it seemed that people really wanted koi ponds, and koi, so he had begun a small koi nursery pond. The babies were so cute and their mental pictures so quick and abstract—probably like toddlers, Elizabeth mused. At the moment, it was empty, Tig having placed the most recent batch.

She and Tig were going to start "trying" to have a baby soon. Well, as soon as they felt they had a nest egg to cover the extras, plus the time Elizabeth wouldn't be able to work as much. She could do telephone conversations with pets via owners, but she much preferred to 'speak' to the animal in person. More fun for her, and more successful. She hadn't quite mastered the phone as a reliable form of help.

Mom, this is boring... Teddy's sturdy body sat next to her. He gazed into the pond with disdain. *Those are not fish. I don't know what they are, but they don't smell anything like my food. But the water is delicious.* He crouched and stretched all the way down to the water level to drink. Elizabeth always worried when the cats drank from the pond. She had tried to get them to stop to no avail. She worried that their bodies would overbalance and they would fall in. She had seen it before with other pond owners and it often ended tragically. In their pond they had floating rings with nets that doubled as shade for the pond and as rescue areas for errant cats. Once a sparrow had made its way to a safety ring. Tig had picked it out of the pond and given it to Elizabeth. She'd calmed it and placed it in a shoe box covered with a towel until its wings dried. When it was able to fly an hour later, not only were no thanks in the offing, but she'd received the sparrow equivalent of some four-letter words.

Centered in the pond was a huge, heavy-duty planter of water taro that also could serve as a resting place. She had tried to get the cats to drink from the waterfall as a safer option, but that only earned her looks of disdain.

"Where's Edward?" she asked Teddy. Teddy, like many animals who had lived with and around humans, sent her sentences as well as pictures. Wild animals often just relied on pictures from their mind to hers, and certain species, like insects, she had real trouble understanding. She had encountered a rattlesnake on a hike once and got nothing but the cold shoulder from it as well.

Waiting for a bird, Teddy said.

Elizabeth knew what that meant. She sighed and crossed to the glorious jungle of tropical foliage framing the waterfall. Sure enough, Edward was scrunched deep in a bed of ferns, invisible to a seeker, or a bird. He was grown now, but remained a small, thin cat. His lovely green eyes and pointed chin were adorable.

Hi, Mom, Edward said. *What are you doing?*

"Feeding the fish, as you well know. You're not supposed to be here, stalking birds. We all agreed that rodents were okay, but not birds."

You *might have agreed,* came from Teddy.

Sorry. I just can't help it, Edward answered. She picked him up and nuzzled him. He immediately went limp and began to purr.

"Come on you guys. It's time for breakfast."

About time, said Teddy. *I'm starving.*

Elizabeth eyed his girth and sighed. The vet had put him on diet food, but that made him cranky and he hadn't seemed to have lost any weight. Edward, on the other hand, was the one who needed to eat all the time. He favored canned food, and although dry kibble was available most of the time, he often just waited for Elizabeth to open a can. Teddy, however, would eat all the kibble in a show of contempt for his new diet, and Elizabeth and Tig were nonplussed to resolve the fat-cat vs. skinny-cat issue.

She opened two cans, one diet, one regular and received a look of scorn from Teddy and sweet gratitude from Edward. Then she had to stand guard or Teddy would muscle Edward away from his food.

Tig was on a twenty-four hour shift that began last night and would return after six PM tonight. Then he was off for a few days and would continue on a new pond-build he had begun with Karl. The clients were wealthy and lived in 'the heights,' an area a few miles but many dollars away.

She had already done her morning meditation so she poured her second cup of Peet's French Roast coffee—her favorite. She checked her calendar: one client visit. She also planned to see her godson, who happened to be the child of her and Tig's best friends and lived across the street.

Garrett was nine months old now, pulling himself up to standing and getting into trouble. Already he was a redheaded, blue-eyed lady killer. Their dog Buster was an ancient black pug who took his role as uncle and child-minder seriously. Nearly blind, he could find Garrett by smell, but that was no feat really, most days, given that he was still in diapers. Buster dutifully and arthritically followed Garrett around the house, barking if Garrett needed human intervention.

Her cell phone rang. Tig. "Hey, I was thinking about you," Elizabeth answered.

"Guess what? I got a referral from a customer. Someone called wanting me to help buy koi for his pond. He sounds like money. He'll pay me to shop for him! He, well, his assistant or something, sort of told me what he wants, but I basically get to buy all my dream fish!" Tig said all in one breath.

"Wow, that's exciting. When does he want them?"

"Yesterday of course. I told him I'd have to see his pond first and make sure it was ready for a lot of large fish. No point in spending money on fish if the herons are going to wade right in and have lunch." That was why the sides of their own pond were vertical. Predators had a harder time. Kingfishers, egrets and herons could stand on the side and do a lot of damage by puncturing the fish, but they couldn't wade in to hunt. Raccoons were also a problem, but again, the steep sides helped.

"Do you want to come with me? It sounds like an amazing property. Out by the airport in the winery area."

"Sure. When are you thinking of going?"

"Tomorrow, first thing. Then Karl and I are heading to the heights to continue on the Masuka's pond. But you know what this means?"

"No, what?"

"We get to go to the big koi farms and shop. I might even get to import some from Japan if this guy's serious."

"Sounds fun. What about the koi shows? I've never been to one."

"That customer wants them ASAP, so assuming his pond is ready for that much fish poop," Elizabeth had been amazed at how much waste their own eleven large fish made, "we won't be able to wait for the koi show."

"Next time."

"For sure. This might be a great sideline; as a koi buyer for the discerning client. If it works out, I can be the middle man since we can't keep that many koi here."

"Plus, we get to shop for koi." One of their favorite places was in San Jose, and the most recent trip had garnered number eleven. Casper was a ghost koi. Lovely, luminous white scales; he was a 'butterfly' koi with long flowing fins, and two dark rings around his eyes. He was only about ten inches long when they bought him, but he'd grown a lot since then. One interesting thing about koi, Tig had told her, was their 'growth hormone.' If they had a large pond or place to live, they would grow a lot. If not, their bodies regulated the growth.

Elizabeth was skeptical. At least eight of the current were battleships.

"That sounds great." Elizabeth scooted Teddy back from Edward's food with her foot. He seemed to know, just like kids, when she was on the phone and less able to deal with him. "I'm free tomorrow."

"Okay, I'll see you tonight. Want me to bring anything for dinner?"

"Nope, I've got your favorite chili in the crock pot and ready to rock."

"Love you. Kay, bye," Tig said.

"Love you, too. Kay, bye," Elizabeth replied. They had started using this abbreviated closing after hearing some pre-teens on their phones at the mall one day. They'd found it so abrupt and funny they'd immediately adopted it.

Elizabeth saw Edward was done with his plate and lifted it to the windowsill where chubby Teddy could no longer fit. Teddy's eyes narrowed. He knew that ploy. He settled to eat his own food now that Edward's leftovers were out of reach.

"You don't have to eat it at all, Teddy," Elizabeth said. "Doctor's orders. I'm thinking of your health."

Whatever, Teddy mumbled.

Elizabeth ran her hand down his back and he raised up, still pleased at her touch, despite her shortcomings as food prep and wait staff.

She did a quick mop of the tiled and fake wood floor areas. With cats it was best to leave carpet just to the bedrooms. Almost time to see her client. She hoped to have lunch with Garrett and company. He was always so much fun to watch. He'd begun insisting on feeding himself and she didn't want to miss any of the pre-show set up which involved a painter's drop cloth.

This morning's client was an older disabled woman whose service dog was acting strangely. She'd taken Jato to the vet of course, to rule out illness or parasites, but although he'd been given a clean bill of health, he was still not himself.

Jato and Millie lived across town, so barring any unforeseen circumstances she should make it back easily for lunch. Elizabeth had asked about Jato's unusual name. Millie's late husband, had been a colonel in the Air Force. JATO was an acronym for Jet Assisted Take Off, and that certainly applied to the dog, although his in depth training had channeled it.

19

She pulled up in front of Millie's cute little corner house. Banana trees and large ferns bordered the property along with flowering plants, (Tig would know what they were, but she had no idea), giving it a tropical look.

From the street she heard Jato barking. That in itself was unusual unless Millie was in trouble. She hurried to the door and turned the knob yelling, "Millie, it's me, Elizabeth! I'm coming in. Are you all right?" The barking continued so she followed it to the laundry room in the back of the house.

Millie used arm crutches to get around unless she was having a really bad day and needed a walker or her wheelchair. Today, she leaned on the washer, crutches dangling from her forearms. Jato stood barking at her, tail wagging slightly.

Elizabeth hollered over the barking. "Millie, I'm here. Jato! Stop that now." Jato stopped but did not take his gaze from Millie.

Millie worked herself around and repositioned the crutches. "Whew! That was like to drive me crazy. I don't know what's gotten into him."

Jato was a black lab, rescued from the humane society and trained as a service dog. He and Millie had been perfect partners up until a week or so ago, when he began barking, whining and pushing at Millie in ways that were inconsistent with his training.

Millie looked haggard and Elizabeth said, "You go sit down. Let's all calm down. Shall I make some tea?"

"That would be nice. Toby's gone to the store for me, so I haven't had any yet." Toby was Millie's college-student handyman/helper. Toby did errands, drove her to appointments and provided company several days a week. She also had a nurse's aide every few days to help with bathing.

Elizabeth put the kettle on. Jato settled next to his mistress, eyes never leaving her face. But at least the barking had stopped. "Jasmine or PG Tips?" she called, naming Millie's two favorite teas.

"Jasmine I think; thanks."

Elizabeth brought two mugs with tea bags into the little sitting room that overlooked a tiny backyard.

"Anything you can tell me would be helpful. Vet's report?" Elizabeth began.

"Absolutely nothing. Perfect health. I mean, to look at him he seems fine now. I checked his feet of course right away, to make sure he hadn't stepped on anything. I did all the usual until I just had to take him to the vet. I don't know, Elizabeth."

"Anything going on with the neighbors? New people, animals, activity in the neighborhood?"

"Not that I know of. He won't leave me alone, doesn't follow commands to sit and stay when I need to do something. That's not like him. Do you think his hearing is going?"

"I'll find out. What about his hand signals? Does he respond to those?"

"Sometimes, but not like he should. He's been. . ." Millie searched for a word. "Clingy.

Needy, I suppose. That's what made me think he might be sick. His blood work came back fine."

"All right. I'll see what I can find out." Elizabeth closed her eyes and grounded herself, listening to her breathing, feet flat on the floor, connecting with the energy that aided her. It helped that she already knew Jato, because when she finally asked permission to talk to him—silently with words and pictures--a barrage of images and emotion washed over her immediately, instead of the usual coaxing and trust establishment.

Mom's sick. Mom's sick. Mom's sick, came the instant flood from Jato.

I know. You know that, too, Jato. What's happening to you?

No, she's really sick. She doesn't know. I can smell it. She's worse. Something's wrong. You have to help.

Okay, I will help. What can you tell me? She's worried about the way you're behaving. She needs you and you're not listening to her properly.

I know. I'm sorry. I need to be with her all the time. Close close close.

Do you know what is wrong with her?

Something bad. More than her hurt legs. In the middle of her.

Can you show me where?

Jato sent picture of Millie's chest.

Okay, Jato. I know what to do. But you have to help, too.

I know. That's my job. Help help help Mom.

You have to listen to her in order to help her. Promise?

22

Okay.
I will take her to a human doctor like she took you to your doctor.
A picture of the vet's office from Jato.
Yes, like that, but for people.
Jato sent a negative feeling.
I know it's scary, but they are very good and this is important if you want to help your mom.
Okay. Help.
Thank you, Jato.

Elizabeth roused herself and said, "I know what's the matter with Jato. He's worried about you. He says you're sick. How have you been feeling aside from your arthritis?"

Millie suffered from extreme arthritis, debilitating and painful.

"I've been really tired. More so than usual. I attributed that to getting older, sleeping less well. I guess I feel okay. My appetite's a bit down, I suppose."

Elizabeth noted she hadn't even touched her tea. Unusual. "I think you should have a check-up. In fact, I promised Jato that you would. In return he promised he'd obey you better, but you have to take care of yourself or he'll go back to barking. He feels he has to take care of you. I know that's his job, but it's more than that. He says you must listen to him."

Millie laid her hand on Jato's head which now rested in her lap. "Okay, boy. You win. Pass me the phone, will you, Elizabeth?"

Elizabeth helped coordinate a doctor's visit. If Toby was unavailable to drive Millie, Elizabeth said she would.

They hugged and Millie pressed money into Elizabeth's hand. That part always felt awkward to Elizabeth and once again, she thought maybe she should get a website where people could pay instead of handing it to her. She knew nothing of constructing a website, but Tig had one for Precision Landscaping and Ponds, so he could help her. Some of her older clients like Millie would still do it this way, they preferred it, but she was getting many new, younger clients and figured they'd rather do it online like they did everything else.

Elizabeth sat in her car for a moment. What she hadn't told Millie was what else Jato had seen. A dark mass on one side of Millie's chest. Still small, but there. And when Jato had shown her that, she felt all his terror—beyond fear—for Millie. Something was terribly wrong with her friend and only Jato had known. She hoped it would be in time.

Two

A little shaken, Elizabeth arrived home to Teddy and Edward complaining about imminent death from starvation. She rectified that with two types of food. Teddy grudgingly ate his, keeping a watchful eye on Edward and her—in case they forgot to guard and he could invade.

The cats and their quirks always seemed to center her when she'd had a bad read or got bad news.

"Hey, guys, want to see Buster? I'm visiting Janie and Garrett and you could hang out with Buster. He loves you."

The cats' relationship with Buster was interesting. He was much older than either of them, but they both tolerated him despite being a dog. Dogs were gross; everyone knew that, as Teddy liked to remind her. She thought that secretly, the cats actually liked Buster. He came over often with his mistress, and periodically she and Tig were called on to dog-sit, as when Janie was in the hospital delivering Garrett.

Teddy's main concern was his food bowl. Of course. Elizabeth put it up on a too-high-for-an-old-pug end table. Problem solved.

Occasionally, despite Teddy's protestations, she'd find them all sleeping together, snuggled in a noisy, snoring ball. Usually on someone's bed. Not sure how Buster managed that, but hey, points for ingenuity.

Janie and Elizabeth had become friends because Janie's husband Terry and Tig worked together at the fire department. They'd started together and hit it off, although now they were assigned different stations. It was a bonus that their wives also became friends and when the house across the street had come on the market, Janie and Terry snapped it up.

Cats' appetites sated for now, she picked each up and gave them a hug and kiss. As per usual, Teddy stiffened, claiming not to like the attention—until she set him down of course, and Edward went limp and purred so hard he rattled.

"Well, guys? Coming?" she asked them.

Is that noisy thing there? Teddy asked.

"If you mean Garrett, yes he is. And he is a baby, not a thing."

Fine. That baby human thing. That will be there, too?

It was true that Garrett loved the cats and squealed shrilly when he saw them. The same thing happened when he'd first gotten a real look at Buster, when he was three months old. However, Buster was almost deaf. No problem for him, but lots of fun for his parents.

Eventually, Garrett got used to Buster and they worked out their relationship when Garrett began to crawl. Now that he was pulling up and working on walking, the cats were even more leery.

"Guys, it will be lunch time for Garrett. You know how you like lunch time over there." Elizabeth shamelessly tried to bribe them. She enjoyed the dynamics of the baby with the animals. Teddy was smart and moved quickly for a large animal. He could dodge chubby fingers with a magician's sleight of hand. Edward was younger, and although he took his cues from 'big brother,' he still got nabbed occasionally. However, Teddy thought with his stomach and that proved the deciding factor.

Okay. We'll go, but I'm not promising to stay.

"You guys can leave any time you want. Just say the word and be careful crossing the street."

Elizabeth laughed, grabbed her cell and keys and locked the house. She crossed the street tailed by two cats. She and Janie pretty much had an open door policy for each other, so she knocked, then opened the door and called out, but not too loudly.

"Hey, it's Elizabeth. Safe to come in?" She wouldn't want to interrupt private time with Terry, or worse, naptime for Garrett.

"Sure, come in if you dare," came the response. They all trooped through the living room to the kitchen/dining nook.

The scene was quite impressive. A painter's dropcloth covered the floor. Centered on it was the high chair, Garrett already imprisoned. He, too, was swathed in a bib/towel arrangement, much like when one goes to the barber or a salon. Only his head and two little hands were visible. He shrieked a greeting and Elizabeth bent to nuzzle him and give him a smacking kiss that made him giggle. Buster lay strategically under the table, at the ready.

"You are just in time," Janie said, and put a big plate with compartments on the tray of the high chair. Each section held a small amount of something, but Elizabeth wasn't sure what.

Garrett gurgled in anticipation and said something like, "mom mom mom mom."

"Is he talking? Is he saying mommy?" Elizabeth asked. "That's so sweet! His first words!"

"Nope. He is talking to and about, his food. I wish it was me, but no. It's food. He's cutting a tooth or six, so he's gnawing on everything including me. I'm still pureeing most of his food, but see a few whole peas. . ." She didn't get to finish because the 'few whole peas' came flying out of the tray. Buster was prepared. For an old guy, he moved quickly.

"Buster doesn't like broccoli, no matter what I do to it, but most other vegetables he's good with," Janie said.

"Aren't you going to feed Garrett?" Elizabeth asked.

"Maybe later. Right now is self-serve time, which is what Buster prefers. As do your guys, from what I can tell."

"That's for sure."

Teddy and Edward were patrolling the perimeter because Garrett had dropped a fistful of, uh, something delicious that oozed down the leg of the high chair and onto the drop cloth. Then his little fist went into his mouth for suctioning and it started over again.

"This is amazing," Elizabeth said. "You do three shows a day?"

"Nope. More like six. Plus nursing. I'm exhausted by the end. At least now he's sleeping through the night. Mostly."

She rubbed her son's curly head and he beamed up at her, completely happy, completely at ease with his eating skills or lack of them.

The meal continued, such as it was, and Janie served Elizabeth a tuna sandwich with a small salad.

"This is great, Janie, thank you. I had no idea it had gotten like this. Next time I'll bring you lunch. Wow, you ate yours so fast!"

"Have to or I don't eat." Janie swabbed off Garrett and put a limp spaghetti noodle on the tray. "Watch this. It's hilarious."

Garrett did his best to pick it up, brow furled, scowl in place. He finally managed to get it between his chubby fingers, but just before it made it into his mouth, he dropped it. Instead of crying, he renegotiated and tried again.

"Oh, that's so funny. Why don't you give him a bigger noodle?"

"Couple reasons. One, miss all this? I don't think so. And two, he can't really chew well, so I don't want to give him something bigger he could

29

choke on. When he gets more teeth he can graduate. This kind, when it does make it in, he can gum it pretty good. It's kinda mushy anyway."

Elizabeth saw that was true. The noodle was pretty well smashed into its original ingredients. Janie sensed when Garrett was ready to really eat, and she scooted her chair over and fed him with a tiny spoon. Soon Garrett insisted on taking the spoon himself and Janie relinquished it and began to clean up what Buster and the cats had missed or refused.

"Is the show over?" Elizabeth asked.

"The fun stuff is. We're going to the park after I clean up. Wanna come?"

Elizabeth checked her watch. Nothing 'til Tig came home after six. The chili was well in hand in the crock pot, so why not?

"Sure. Let me take these guys back home and grab my purse. Walking, right?"

"Yes, to the little park down the way." She was already mopping Garrett and the kitchen looked pretty good.

"Okay. Back in a few. Come on, guys." She herded the cats across the street. They declined to come in the front door with her, but rolled on the warm concrete of the porch.

They had their own door to come and go, but preferred the large doors with staff in attendance. Elizabeth checked their dry food and water, grabbed her purse and locked up. It was a lovely day for the park.

*   *   *   *

Elizabeth returned from the outing to find both cats passed out on the bed. Nothing unusual there. The house smelled deliciously of chili. She made a salad and some garlic bread to throw in the oven just before Tig got home. He was off at six and they lived close to the station. He would arrive soon so she jumped in the shower so it would be free for Tig. He always showered at the station if they had a call, but he would want to again when he got home. Nothing like home. Even after two showers he sometimes still smelled of smoke. She was used to it; it was part of him.

After her shower, the oven beeped indicating the right temperature. She put in the bread and as she closed the door, she heard him call, "Hey," from the front room.

They met in the kitchen and kissed hello. He didn't smell of smoke. The town was so small that fires were uncommon, and 75% of their calls were medical, but she still felt a tingle of relief.

"How was your day? Hungry?" she asked.

"Easy. Couple medical calls. Took the truck for donuts; the usual. I'm starved."

Tig was always hungry, so having food ready for him was part of her day. She even froze single servings of meals so he could nuke one anytime. Not that he was helpless in the kitchen, but he always moved so fast, she knew he wouldn't take time to make something healthy. It made her feel good to do it.

She ladled out bowls of chili and put the salad on the table as Tig set out plates and silverware.

"The garlic bread will be warm through in a few minutes, but we can start now if you like," she said.

"I like." Tig served himself a mountain of salad. He topped his chili with cheese, sour cream and diced avocado. She did the same.

When they'd finished the salad, she checked the bread. Done. She brought it to the table and the fragrances of garlic butter and chili were irresistible.

A few spoonfuls in Tig came up for air. "So good," he mumbled. "How was your day? Who did you have today?"

Elizabeth told him about Millie, and Jato's discovery. "I'm sure it's some kind of mass, but I hope just a cyst. Jato said he could smell it, so I don't think that's good."

"That's rough."

"If her helper Toby or the medical aide can't take her to the appointment, I said I would."

"Okay." Tig sat back and sighed. "So good," he repeated.

"Your turn. Anything new today?"

"Not a thing. Oh, we might get a new coffee maker. We debated for half an hour about the type and the old guys were like, 'Mr. Coffee's the best there is,' and the young guys like me, wanted the kind where you make an individual cup whenever you want. That way the pot doesn't turn to tar or we waste it. You'd think from the grumbling we were talking about world peace or a rocket launch."

Elizabeth laughed because she knew most of the guys Tig was talking about.

"We tried to tell them it was really easy, just put the kind of coffee you want here," he pantomimed, "and that it comes already packaged, and then you put your mug under the spout and push 'go.' Not that hard."

"Well, that certainly sounds exciting," said Elizabeth as she rose to clear the dishes. "I also had a kitchen incident of sorts today."

"Really? What?" Tig looked around the kitchen.

"Not here. Had lunch with Garrett across the street. So fun. It's something to see. I took the guys to help mop up. It's almost more than Buster can handle on his own at the rate Garrett slings his food around."

"Sounds like a good 'sharer' to me," Tig said. "I'm going to water for a while, okay?"

Elizabeth knew 'watering' was also a code for decompressing from his day, checking the plants and fish, and planning his next day. She did the same thing but mostly when she was with the cats. For some reason, petting a cat was soothing and healing and excellent for thinking. Teddy and Edward encouraged this strategy.

She kissed him again and he went out the back door. Now that it was summer, the pond and landscaping clients were rolling in, and it stayed lighter later, allowing Tig to water/think to his heart's content. She knew he was working on the big build in his head, and how best to use his assistant Karl. Karl was a little younger and very strong. Smart but inexperienced in the pond-building game, he was learning fast. They seemed to get along well on jobs. She cleaned the kitchen and put away the meager leftovers. Out the window, she saw Teddy supervising the watering while Edward played with a dried bamboo leaf.

Tig came in an hour later. "I've got to load some stuff for tomorrow because after you and I look at that pond in Edwina Valley—you're still going with me, right?" She nodded. "I'm meeting Karl at the heights job. I'll just drop you off on the way there, okay?"

She could see his mind was already on tomorrow. "Sure. You don't even need to stop, just slow down and I'll roll out and you can be on your way."

"What?" Her words sank in and he laughed.

"I'll be ready." Elizabeth hugged his solid frame. "Wanna watch something?" That meant time for NetFilms--an internet based service with an endless variety of commercial free TV shows and movies. Elizabeth's brother had introduced them to it and they were skeptical at first. Sounded too good to be true, but now they were addicted. They both loved movies and 'good' television—they had slight differences of opinion on that one—but they despised commercials.

The cats loved NetFilms too, because two semi-comatose humans meant lots of petting and cuddling. Sometimes they got kicked off the bed for no reason at all, and the door was closed to them for a while. But usually, the room was reopened to

them later, and NetFilms resumed for a bit. Life
was good.

Three

Elizabeth almost always woke early, before Tig. Not before the cats, however. She made coffee and fed them their first of many meals. By the time she'd finished her morning meditation Tig was up and pouring his coffee. On his days off he liked to feed the fish and she joined him by the pond. Well, they all joined him.

"Hey," he said, and kissed her.

"Morning. What's the schedule like? Do we have an appointment to see this guy's pond?"

"Yup. I made it early because Karl's meeting me in the heights and we have a lot to do today. Actually, Karl should see this pond too, maybe." He re-thought while they watched the koi slurp at the surface.

Elizabeth loved the kissing noises they made and had been surprised at their range of sounds. She'd always thought fish were quiet, based on her childhood experiences with goldfish. She'd learned they were much like cats, especially in their personalities, but made sure no treasonous thoughts like this leaked when Teddy was around.

"If this pond is right for koi, I'll have Karl come help me when they arrive, that is, if I order. Or maybe if we like any in San Jose, he can help me then."

"You just want to order some giant sumo koi from Japan, don't you?" she asked.

He laughed. "You know I do. But it's better to get them small and let them grow. Cheaper to buy, cheaper to ship and safer for them. Sedating and handling them when they're large can be risky."

"I'll help."

"I'm counting on it." He put his arm around her waist. Edward sat on his shoe, so he released her for a moment and picked him up, tucking him into his arm. Edward immediately went limp and began to purr. Tig repositioned his arm around her.

Hey, what about me? Teddy asked.

"You know you don't like to be picked up. Especially near the pond," Elizabeth said.

I know. Still. . . it's not fair.

Elizabeth laughed and knelt to pet him. He immediately purred, flopped on his back and exposed his stomach.

That's more like it.

"Silly," she said. "Want some breakfast?" she asked.

Yes, I do, Teddy said.

"Yes, thanks," Tig said.

"Not you," she said to Teddy. "Waffles?" she asked Tig.

"Perfect. I'm going to shave. Leave right after we eat?"

"I'll be ready."

The cats followed them inside. Edward went to help Tig shave and Teddy watched her warm the waffle iron and make batter.

After breakfast she dressed and was ready when Tig finished double checking his supplies for the day. He always tried to load ahead of time, and then re-check.

"Since this job is so close, it's not a problem to come home and get something, but when a job is far, it wastes time and gas," Tig said.

"I remember." Elizabeth had met him "half-way" on enough jobs to convince him to make a list and 'pre-load' with a re-check. Far fewer errors since then.

She kissed the top of each cat's head and locked up. "How long do you think this will take?"

"Half hour each way and maybe fifteen minutes there. Depends if the owner's there and wants to chat. Why?"

"If I get a client call, I need to know when I'll be free. I don't have one now, but just in case. I was going to grocery shop when I get home."

They chatted about the heights job on the way to Edwina Valley. Out by the airport just past industrial parks and arid-looking land, Edwina Valley had become an elite corner of the county, with vineyards and expensive homes on large estates. The dump was just a few miles past and Elizabeth enjoyed the irony of that.

Tig told her the address and said they were hunting for a 'large torii gate' connecting a six foot high stone wall. Addresses were few and far between, but they finally found it. Everyone had a high stone wall, but there was no mistaking the Japanese torii. Two twenty-foot tree trunks (Elizabeth had no idea the variety) upheld a top cross piece that dipped in the middle and rose on the ends. A second cross piece under that was straight and shorter and connected to the upper one by a vertical piece of wood. The highest piece was black, but all the rest, including small flower decorations was bright red. Hard to miss in this part of the county. An actual, closeable iron gate stood open inside the torii. The drive wound around some native oaks, after which the landscaping became quite Japanese.

Elizabeth gasped and even Tig, who had seen some of the loveliest properties anywhere, was struck silent.

She felt like they had been dropped in Japan. She knew nothing about Japanese gardens except for a few samples on trips to various botanical gardens, but this felt like the real deal. A large area of gravel, separated by a rock border, met them. They parked and got out. The other side of the rock border was dotted with three large rocks that appeared to be randomly set; she knew they'd been carefully placed. Gravel was raked into patterns of swirls and lines reminding her of water at tide pools ebbing and flowing around the shoreline. A walk of misaligned blocks of stone, each about two-feet square, led to the house. They passed red Japanese maples, myriad other plants Elizabeth could not begin to guess, a dry stream bed with fist-sized rocks leading to larger rocks representing a dry waterfall. It all seemed to funnel them toward the front door. The house was clearly of Japanese architecture and they stepped up onto wooden decking that ran across the front and disappeared around both sides.

Not a human sound could be seen or heard. Breeze blowing leaves, rustlings in the shrubbery, and she caught a slight sound from the airport. Easily ignored, so she did. The place simply oozed peacefulness--feng shui—she thought, and then restrained a giggle because that was Chinese, not Japanese. Well, whatever, it was heaven here.

Tig knocked and they waited. The door opened and a slight Japanese man in a white shirt and black pants greeted them. "Yes?"

"Mr. Tanaka?" Tig asked.

"No, Mr. Tanaka is not here. I am his houseman, Goro." He looked enquiringly.

"Oh. I'm Tig Murphy and this is my wife Elizabeth. Mr. Tanaka hired me to buy koi for him and I made an appointment to check the pond and see if it was ready for fish?"

"Yes. Come this way." He opened the door wider and they entered an anti-room with low shelves and two benches, all of beautifully carved wood. "You may take off your shoes here." He indicated they were to leave their shoes on the rack. "Would you like slippers?" He pointed at rows of new, packaged slip-on house slippers.

"Uh, no thank you," said Tig. Elizabeth shrugged. She was out of her depth on all levels here and took her cues from Tig.

Goro nodded and when they had put their shoes on the rack, he led them through the house which was a series of large open rooms with sliding doors. The halls and living room were of dark wood, smaller rooms were floored in tatami, and most were nearly empty. This puzzled Elizabeth since Mr. Tanaka was obviously a wealthy man. They passed a living room with couches and tables and western-style art displayed. Elizabeth felt a little shame at her relief in seeing something familiar.

Goro stopped at another sliding door, glass this time, and indicated they should put on rubber slippers in yet another rack discreetly tucked in a corner near the door. "We are going to the pond now," he said. "You don't want to wear just socks there." His English was perfect and melodious. Almost a British accent. Goro exchanged his own house slippers for a rubber pair.

"Not to worry. All new slippers for guests." Goro smiled.

"No it's fine, Mr. Goro. We've just never seen a house like this," Tig said. "It's beautiful."

Elizabeth added. "I'm overwhelmed. I feel like I'm in Japan."

"It's not Mr. Goro. Just Goro." He held the door open for them once they'd managed the slipper issue. "You have been to Japan?"

"No, but I feel. . . I feel like this is what it would be like?" she ended on a question. She didn't want to offend the man and have it get back to the boss and ruin something for Tig.

Apparently it was the right thing to say. Goro smiled. "That is Mr. Tanaka's wish. When he is here, he wants to feel like he has a part of home with him. That is not to say, of course, that he does not love it. That is why he built here, and not in Los Angeles."

"How is it that he doesn't have any koi?" Tig asked, following 'just Goro' outside.

"This house was finished not long ago, and he did have koi. They got sick. They died and now he needs new ones."

Tig and Elizabeth exchanged looks. "I will need to check the water and filters—make sure that whatever made them sick isn't still present," Tig said.

"I understand. Of course. This way." They followed Goro on a path through extensive landscaping only to circle back to where they could see the house. Between them and the house lay a huge pond. Really huge. Elizabeth saw the living room from here and realized that from that room, one would have a perfect view of the koi pond. Probably the point. The pond curved out of sight around the house.

"What's on that side of the pond?" she asked.

"Mr. Tanaka wishes to see the pond from his private rooms so he had it extended past this side of the house. He likes to feed his children from there. Even though he had not had them here very long, he had become quite attached." Goro seemed upset at his boss' loss. Perhaps Goro was in charge of them when Mr. Tanaka was out of town and missed them as well.

Elizabeth understood. Each of their koi had a distinct personality and she and Tig had been devastated last year when one died.

Elizabeth saw the wheels turning in Tig's head. "Want me to get your pond bag from the car?"

He nodded.

Goro jumped in. "Bypass the house and just follow this path." He pointed to a small gravel footpath extending toward the side of the house, "and through the bamboo gates. It will take you to the parking area and you don't have to change your shoes." He smiled, understanding their confusion with the shoe-slipper issue. Elizabeth thought perhaps he didn't want her in the house unescorted. That made sense.

"Thank you." Elizabeth had kept her purse with her, so she had a set of keys to Tig's truck. She slopped down the gravel path in the rubber slippers. They weren't the beach kind she was used to, with a thong between the big and little toes. These just had a big, two-inch wide band that crossed mid-foot. Felt strange, like her feet were going to shoot out the front at any step. Not uncomfortable, really, they didn't hurt, just felt weird. The two little bamboo gates she encountered were works of art in themselves. She saw no nails or screws, just pieces of bamboo woven through and then tied at cross-hatchings. Even the 'hinges' were tied. She took a quick photo with her cell phone for further study. Tig would need his test kits and maybe other things. She wasn't sure. Things with fur and feathers were more her area.

She returned the way she'd come and saw the two men kneeling now, in conversation at some sort of valve junction nearly hidden in the bushes.

As she approached she heard Tig ask, "Can I see the pumps now?" He turned. "Thanks," he said to her.

"Of course. This way." Goro led them around the house to a door she hadn't noticed on her way to the car. He unlocked it and they went down some stairs and she knew they were at the bottom of the pond, but next to it. It felt very odd. The pump room hummed with electricity and water moved and bubbled. Huge cone-bottomed sediment tanks took up most of the space. She knew from Tig they were very expensive. She wasn't surprised. She had expected top of the line equipment once she saw the house. Tig wandered around checking gauges and tubing.

Elizabeth lost interest. She also wandered and at the far end, found a little surprise. A section of the wall was clear Plexiglas and she could see into the pond itself! What a great idea. Too bad their yard was too small for something like this. What fun. No fish to see at the moment of course, but the water gave off a lovely luminous green glow.

This part of the pond must be near Mr. Tanaka's rooms, she thought. She was a little turned around. She couldn't see above the surface so it might even face the living room.

"We're going back up now," Tig called. She hurried to catch up. Goro locked the pump room door behind them and Tig asked to take a water sample.

Goro led them back to where tig could access the water itself without disturbing the landscaping. Tig got his samples and checked the water.

"It all seems fine now. I'm going to take some water back for more testing to be sure. We don't want to put thousands of dollars' worth of koi in here just to have them get sick. Did Mr. Tanaka have a necropsy done on any of them?"

Goro shook his head.

"So, you're not really sure what they died of?"

He shook his head again, but seemed more hesitant.

"What?" Tig asked. "Anything you tell me will help. Even if you're not sure. Bacteria can get in, well, all kinds of things."

Goro shook his head again. "Nothing."

"Well, your water looks great now, and all the equipment is the best and in good shape. I'll test this sample for a few things to be sure and then I'll be in touch. Can I talk to your current pond guy?"

Goro shook his head. "No pond guy."

Tig elaborated. "I mean, who does your pond maintenance? I'd like to talk to him, or them. Whatever the company is."

"No one now. We would like you, if this all works out with the koi purchase. Of course, Mr. Tanaka would meet you and have the final say. I wanted to meet you first and then report to him. I did a reference check on you Mr. Murphy and you are highly recommended, so that is why you are here."

"Well. Thank you." Tig seemed at a loss and Elizabeth enjoyed the moment. "Thank you very much. I'll let you know today what I find. When should I start looking for koi?"

"As soon as possible. I will vet your selections, but all choices are up to Mr. Tanaka."

"Does he have an idea of what he wants? Type, size? Does he have a breeder he likes to deal with?"

"No breeder. Not anymore. I will email you his choices, but he would like to start with seven. That is a good number for us."

"Us, too," said Tig. "Lucky number seven."

Tig stuck out his hand to shake and Goro took it, familiar with western culture. However, once they had done the rubber-to-cloth slipper (or in their case, socks) exchange and gone back through the house to put on their shoes, Goro bowed to Tig and then a smaller one to Elizabeth. They bowed back awkwardly.

"Thank you for your time, Mr. Murphy. Mrs. Murphy. I think this will be an excellent arrangement. I hope you feel the same."

"Please, call me Tig."

"And me, Elizabeth."

"I will. Except when Mr. Tanaka is here." He smiled and they understood they now shared a private joke.

"Great. I'll get you those results by this evening."

Tig tossed his pond bag in the back seat of the truck and then drove out carefully, to avoid leaving a rooster tail of gravel and dust.

Elizabeth said, "You think Goro takes care of that whole place himself?"

"I don't know. I don't think it's possible. Maybe it's like "Downtown Abbey." One of their favorite shows. "You know, only a small staff until the place has to be opened and cleaned because the rich owners are coming?" Tig glanced her way.

"Maybe. I know nothing about Japan or its culture. I'll try and read up if you're going to do business with him. He might recommend you to other Japanese clients. It'd be a shame if you offended him just by being you. Or American."

She laughed and he said, "Thanks a lot," but his smile said he knew she was kidding.

"Isn't your pond job in the heights a Japanese client? Didn't you say Masuka?"

"Yes, but I don't think they are Japan-Japanese. Maybe the father or grandfather is. Maybe they are part of the vegetable growing empire in the south county."

"Oh, of course. I've seen the signs. They have little roadside produce stands, right?"

"Yes, but I don't know if the Masuka's house in the heights are part of that business."

"I wonder why they live so far from relatives, way up here?"

"Maybe they don't. Maybe it's not part of that family. I don't know that I've met the owners.

I think I saw them once, coming or going, but it was a while ago. Now that you mention it, a houseman, sort of a Goro, but much less formal, was who I dealt with getting that job. He handed me drawings and a deposit and has checked on the progress regularly."

"Maybe you could talk to him about etiquette?" Elizabeth rolled up the window as they crossed into the chillier 'fog zone,' an imaginary line between the 'big city' and where they lived near the coast. Fog always hung at the border and they often joked that their little town didn't really exist, that it had disappeared or been invaded, like the haunting tale, *The Mist,* by Stephen King.

"If I get a chance. Usually I'm covered in dirt and it's not conducive to chatting."

Elizabeth laughed, knowing exactly how he looked mid-job. They enjoyed the rest of the drive back.

Four

Tig dropped Elizabeth at home and went off to his job in the heights. Almost lunch time. The morning had flown. She fed the cats a little canned food before they starved to death and made herself a sandwich. She realized that Tig probably didn't have any lunch because of their early morning meeting. She certainly hadn't packed anything for him, and it was unlikely he'd taken the time to fix something, or she would have seen him.

She made more sandwiches, gathered some fruit and bottled water and threw them in a cooler with a blue ice pack. Karl probably didn't have lunch either.

Tig had described the house and where it was, but she didn't know exactly. She wanted to surprise him so she didn't text for directions. Portola Heights, or the heights, as it was referred to, was a housing development on a hill above the town with steep streets and expensive homes. Lots were often small but houses loomed. She wondered how a pond would work there with many of the houses on lots that fell away behind the houses. Stunning views of the coastline and towns to the north, Cove and Cuyamaca Beach, were the tradeoff for a tiny, sloping lot.

The good part was there weren't too many streets to check. She started at the bottom where the slope of the land was less and she thought there might be room for a pond. No luck. She wound her way up the main road and turned off. It was a little like a fish bone, with one main up and down road, and a number of streets teeing off. Some of them connected in 'S' turns so she was able to go back and forth and continue up without too much going back. It quickly became tedious. She was about to give up and text Tig when she decided to go all the way to the top and skip the rest of the middle bits. It was so high that the lots were actually flatter here, at the mesa-like apex. She now was above the clouds and unable to glimpse the ocean near the shore. But she could see far out to sea which was a little disconcerting and surreal. Floating, sort of, above the marine layer. At the dead end, or the 'tippy-top' as she said when she was a girl, sat Tig's truck. Of course, the property would be the farthest from their house.

A Spanish-style house, one-story, red-tiled roof with a spiked iron fence and an uncompromised view. The ornate gate was open so she entered into a large central courtyard where she saw Tig and Karl hard at work. Spanish-style homes often had a courtyard, usually with a fountain in the middle. This courtyard, however, had a big hole where Tig and Karl wrested to lay out yards of pond liner. Flexible, black, and heavy, the liner did not want to lie flat. At least it was warm and sunny up here, so the liner was soft. Tig had told her tales of pond building in cooler weather when moving liner around was like unfolding cardboard. Tig always used pond liner in this earthquake riddled area--also as many flexible parts as possible so repairs would be minor. They had little tremors every day in this area, most of which they never felt, but plumbing joints and walls did.

The pond was large, with only a few feet between it and the house on two sides. The third side, by the street would have a small waterfall which housed the pump and tanks. The waterfall served multiple purposes; to disguise the works, to be a lovely addition to the pond seen from the house, and to aerate the water for the fish. The fourth side was set six feet from the walkway that led from the gate to the front door.

"Hey, you guys," she called. "I brought lunch. How's it going?"

"Great," Tig answered. He seemed happy enough. He did love to create.

"Hey, Elizabeth," Karl greeted her. "I'm starved."

"Let's break for lunch, Karl." Tig climbed a ladder set inside the liner. The ladder had 'socks' and padding at its feet and they had taken off their shoes to make sure the liner didn't get punctured while they worked.

Tig put on his shoes and came to give her a peck hello. "Thanks for remembering. I'm hungry, too."

Elizabeth handed them each a sandwich. "I also brought fruit and water. There are more sandwiches, too."

Tig opened a water bottle and drank half immediately. Karl inhaled a sandwich and opened a water, drinking deeply. Elizabeth handed him another sandwich. In seconds, it seemed, only crumbs were left. The apples, the grapes, even the bananas were gone.

"This is a nice house," Elizabeth said. "How's the view?"

"Amazing. Go around back and look if you want. The owners aren't here."

"I will before I leave. How's it going here?"

"Pretty good. I wanted to get the liner in today and seated with the first line of border tiles. They asked to keep the Spanish Saltillo look so I'm having a load delivered and I hope it arrives in time." Tig pulled out his cell to check the time. "Anytime now, I guess. We still have to get that liner to cooperate. We're going to have to pleat it to get it to lie flat. I expected that."

Karl got up and stretched. "I'm going to stack the old tiles we can still use. I'll put them close to the edge so they'll be easier for us to grab. Should I get the mortar mix out of the truck while I'm at it?"

"Sounds good. Thanks," Tig said.

"How's Karl doing?" Elizabeth asked quietly.

"Better than I thought. He catches on quick, and as you heard, is getting good at anticipating what we'll need. I think it's going to work out."

They watched as Karl returned carrying a bag of mortar mix over each shoulder. About six feet tall and not overly muscular, he was quite strong according to Tig. He seemed bright and caught on to the differences in land and pondscaping versus construction, which he had said was his experience. Tig had found him on Biglist, an online classified ad service. He'd never hired a person from there before, but both he and Elizabeth had bought and sold items.

Tig and Elizabeth had discussed the hiring of an assistant and the usual routes hadn't turned up any candidates. It was hard physical work and Tig couldn't pay a whole lot, plus it was part time. They had decided to try Karl. Tig ran an online background check--which had turned up nothing. He felt he needed to do at least that, since it was his name on the company and they were going to people's homes.

Karl had seemed fine with all the job parameters and besides telling them he was returning to college, also part-time, they hadn't discovered much personal information beyond what was on the standard job application form.

He seemed nice enough to Elizabeth and Tig had no complaints. He said Karl worked hard, didn't talk a lot, and was eager to learn. Tig mentioned it was possible that Karl might open his own pond business someday, but it was just as likely he'd change his mind after he saw how much work it was. Elizabeth agreed. There was plenty of business in the county for two, Tig had told her.

Elizabeth packed up the sandwich wraps, empty water bottles and fruit remains. "I'll leave the extra waters in the cooler with the blue ice for you guys, okay?"

"Great, thanks," Tig said and kissed her good-bye.

"Thanks for lunch Elizabeth. Don't forget to check out the view," Karl said as he descended into the hole once again.

"Will do." She picked up her bag of trash and headed around the house using the Saltillo tile walk. Her cell rang.

"Hello?"

"I need some help or advice or something for my cat. Is this the right number?" a woman's shaky voice asked.

"Yes, it is. How can I help?"

"My cat has disappeared and I put up posters and asked at the vet and Animal Services. I know," she broke off and Elizabeth heard a sniffle. "I know when small animals disappear it usually means coyotes around here, but I just have a feeling he's still alive and looking for me."

"I base my business on feelings," Elizabeth said, "so let's get started." She quickly interviewed the woman and discovered that she was going through a bitter divorce and although her husband did not want the cat, he knew she loved it and may have taken him just to be spiteful.

"Email me a picture of your cat and I'll call you back when I get home. I need to be in my own space to do my best work."

The woman, Rachel, agreed and Elizabeth went to her car to head home, waving to Tig and Karl on her way out the gate.

As Rachel had described her cat, Yuki, she had begun to get some sense of connection to him so she wanted to get home as soon as possible and start. Pulling in the drive, Teddy was waiting for her as usual. He always knew when she'd arrive and she was heartened to see him.

"Hi, baby," she said as she unlocked the door. "Lost kitty emergency. Snacks later, I promise."

Teddy didn't answer, but walked to his dish of hard food, tail twitching, and began to eat. He was sympathetic to lost animals, knowing how good he had it here, despite his complaints to the contrary.

Elizabeth booted up her computer and looked at the picture from Rachel. Yuki was a handsome black and white tuxedo cat with a startled expression. She went to her 'meditation' chair, sat, feet flat, and grounded herself. She relaxed into her breathing and began to cycle energy. She concentrated on Yuki and Rachel and their connection.

Yuki? Are you there? she asked.

Yes, came a faint reply. The energy was weak and afraid. From Rachel she knew he'd been gone almost a week before a friend had suggested she try Elizabeth. After exhausting conventional means, Rachel had acquiesced.

Are you hurt?

A little. Who are you?

55

I'm a friend of your mom's. She's very worried about you. Where are you hurt? Will you talk to me?

A pause. *Yes. I had to run fast away from dogs*, here Elizabeth got a jolt of terror and a flash picture of a coyote. *I hurt myself getting away. I'm afraid and hungry. I was hunting but now I can't. My feet hurt.*

Show me, Elizabeth said. A picture of torn pads and shattered claws.

I'm going to help you, okay?

Okay.

Do you know where you are?

By water. I drink from a stream sometimes. He showed her a picture of a stream near a road. She thought she knew where he was.

But I don't know where this is. I rode in a box in a car and then I got thrown out onto this road. He showed her the same road. *I was a little hurt then, but I ran and hid.* He showed her a picture of a place she knew well. She and Tig had mountain biked there several times. She also knew why he hadn't been able to find his way home. The stream was more like a river, and connected to the estuary so there was tidal ebb and flow. In either case, he would not have been able to cross it to get home. It lay between their town and Cove, the next one over.

I think I know where you are. I'm going to bring your mom with me, and we're coming to look for you. Will you come out if you hear us call you?

Will it be dark?

No. You are close to us. We'll come right now.

Will you bring food?

Yes. Your mom will bring food. I'm going to get your mom now, and my energy to you will be less, but I'll still be here, okay? Elizabeth likened this to mental hand-holding. Her remote connection would fade when she had to concentrate on talking and driving.

Okay.

Stay safe. We'll be there soon.

Elizabeth called Rachel and explained the situation. The woman was crying by the end and Elizabeth barely understood the address of her house. She lived on the other side of town.

"I'll be there in five minutes, okay? Yuki is hungry, so bring some canned food in a bowl he can smell and eat right away, okay?"

Rachel waited on her porch with a bowl held tightly in both hands. She ran for the car when Elizabeth pulled up. "Thank you. Oh, my God, thank you."

"We haven't got him yet. He said he was hurt so he might not be able to come to us. His feet looked pretty bad and I think he hit his head escaping from a coyote."

Rachel looked at her. "What do you mean, 'his feet looked pretty bad'?"

"I communicate with pictures as well as words, depending on the animal. Yuki sent me a picture, from his head to mine, of his feet. I think you'll need to take him to the vet for a checkup."

"Okay."

57

Elizabeth could tell this was the tipping point for Rachel. It had gotten weird and very real. Elizabeth only hoped Yuki would come out to them before it got dark.

She pulled onto the rural road and stopped where she and Tig had previously accessed the bike path. "There's a trail from here and I think he's hiding up there someplace. Bring the food. We'll call him and see if he can hear us and smell the food. He's pretty hungry and he's been too afraid to hunt much."

The trail began steeply but then leveled off and Elizabeth led them on a smaller deer trail. She had felt Yuki was elevated, on this higher section where he thought he could keep watch, as opposed to lower, near the stream. He had to cross the road every time he wanted a drink, so he was probably dehydrated, too. She had water in the car.

"Go ahead and call him," Elizabeth said. She resumed her internal connection with Yuki.

Hey, we're here now. Help us find you. Listen for your mom. She brought food. Your favorite.

I'm here.

Can you call to your mom? So she can hear you?

They heard a faint meow. If they hadn't been listening for it, the sound would have been lost in the wind.

Elizabeth made her way through manzanita, sage, dry grass and what she and Tig affectionately called the 'maple syrup' plant. She prayed she wouldn't encounter a rattlesnake sunning itself. She didn't have much luck talking to snakes.

Keep calling. We're coming. If you can walk, you can come to us. Do you hear your mom yet?

Yes. You're close. But I'm afraid.

It's okay. Can you at least come out of hiding so we can see you? I promise you're safe.

Okay. I can see you! he said excitedly. He'd begun to walk toward them on obviously pain filled feet.

Stop Yuki! We'll get you. Don't hurt your feet more.

Rachel had seen him too, and ran to him. She picked him up, her tears wetting his short, dirty coat.

Elizabeth looked at his feet. They were pretty banged up and needed professional attention. "Do you want to let him eat now?"

"No. I'm not putting him down."

Elizabeth got the bowl and held it in front of Yuki and they all stayed like that for several minutes while he ate ravenously.

I have water for you in the car, okay, Yuki? We're going back now. Yuki was still in pain, but relaxed and content now that Rachel was there. "Let's get him to the car and then to the vet, okay? Who's your vet?"

"On Eleventh Street." Rachel nuzzled Yuki. They reached the car and Elizabeth poured water into the food bowl. Rachel set Yuki in her lap with the bowl and he lapped industriously.

"How does he look?" Elizabeth asked.

"A little thinner. Except for his feet, he seems okay."

Elizabeth began to drive. "Do you want me to take you to the vet, or do you want to get your car and take him yourself?"

"I can drive. Maybe take me home and I'll get his carrier and use my car. I can't begin to thank you. I never would have believed. . ." she trailed off.

"I know. I hear it all the time." Elizabeth laughed. "I'm just glad we had a happy ending. Remember to tell the vet he may have bumped his head. He seemed pretty lucid but you never know." She reached over and gently petted his head. "I don't feel a bump, but still, have them check."

She pulled up at Rachel's house. "Let me know how he's doing. Call me later and I'll fill you in on what else he told me."

"Okay," Rachel said absently. She stroked Yuki lovingly and a rattling purr emanated from him. She got out and carried Yuki up the walk. Elizabeth waited until they were inside and then pulled away.

What she hadn't told Rachel was that her suspicions were correct. The soon to be ex-husband had taken Yuki and tossed him for spite. She would have to tell her, for her own and Yuki's safety. She didn't understand some people. But, today had a happy ending and so often, they didn't.

Five

The next day, Tig's cell phone rang just as Elizabeth finished her morning meditation. She heard Tig mumble a greeting. They'd had a late NetFilms night, including a cat-free break. Most satisfying, but it had caused them to sleep in a little. Well, as much as Teddy would allow.

She poured herself some coffee and got another mug for Tig. When she heard the mumbling stop, she took it back to where he lay in bed.

"Morning." She handed him the coffee.

He was sitting up against his pillows. "Thanks. Morning."

She leaned in to kiss him.

"That was Goro on the phone. We have the green light to koi shop!" He smiled. "He's going to email me Mr. Tanaka's choices. I can't believe I'm being entrusted with such an important task. We may not be able to find what we want locally. I may have to reach out to Japan."

"We might go to Japan?"

"No, I don't think so. But Japanese koi are such quality. Do you remember the koi show I went to in Los Angeles a couple years ago?"

"Yes. The time I couldn't go."

"That one. There were buyers and breeders from all over the world and I made friends with a one from Japan, Yoshi. He said if we ever got to Japan, he'd show us around the koi world, and he's also a top breeder there. I think I could work with him long distance. If he doesn't have what I want, I bet he'd know who does."

"That sounds good. Are we still going to San Jose at some point?"

"Of course! How about my next break?" Tig meant the following week after his twenty-four hour shift.

"Sounds good. Those baby koi are so cute."

"I should have the heights pond up and running by then. It can season while we're gone." Tig referred to letting the concrete cure and for the water to be drained and refilled several times. "There are a lot of good koi out there; but also a lot of bad koi. This isn't just any backyard pond we're stocking. This is a businessman from Japan who could go anywhere he wants. I still wonder why he doesn't go through a Japanese breeder himself."

"Goro made it sound like he'd had a bad experience with his breeder. Or the breeder is no longer in business for some reason."

"Yeah, I got that, too. Still seems weird, but I'm okay with that. I'll get an advance to shop for fish, plus a commission."

"Maybe you can get fish for that heights pond, too, while you're doing Mr. Tanaka's."

"I don't think those owners want to spend the kind of money these koi can cost. Goro said Mr. Tanaka wanted some medium and large koi; top quality. I didn't talk price yet, but since he's already had koi, I bet he's aware of the cost."

"How much are we talking?"

"A large koi, which can live for years by the way, can cost thousands of dollars. A few can run a hundred thousand."

Elizabeth's mouth hung open. "For a fish?"

"Yup. A fish that can drop dead at any minute before you even know it's sick."

"Holy cow. I can't quite wrap my mind around that."

"I know. People are funny. I'm pretty sure Mr. Tanaka isn't talking a hundred thousand dollar fish, but he has worked hard to make the house here be a little piece of home for him. I imagine he wants the best Japanese koi, and not koi from the US or Israel. They are both excellent, too, but since he's Japanese. . ." Tig sipped his coffee. "I'd better email Yoshi and see if something can be worked out."

"I take it the water tests for Goro came out clean?"

"Clean and beautiful. Ready for fish."

"Good. So, we'll go to San Jose to shop for the heights pond?"

"Sure, and if we happen to see anything we can't resist. . ." Tig smiled at her. "Besides, they do buy stock from the same trade show I went to and they may have something from Japan already. We'll just have to see."

"Sounds like a plan. What's up for today? The heights pond?"

"Yes, we finished the border and the rest of the tiles came in after you left. I'm going to check all the plumbing and seals. We did that yesterday, too. Karl's pretty good with the tiles, so I was able to put together the lines from the pond to the pump and settling tanks. We have the bottom drain done. We did a lot. We still have a lot to do, but he's a good worker. Plus another strong back to carry the heavy stuff."

"Yeah, you should have been a balloon animal designer. Not so heavy to carry around." Elizabeth gently slapped his thigh and stood. "All right, get yourself up. Want a scramble for breakfast?"

"Absolutely. What's up for you today?"

"I'm going to check on that new client I told you about yesterday, Rachel and Yuki. See how he's doing." Elizabeth had filled Tig in last night. "I also have another client to see and I want to catch up on the groceries."

She fixed their breakfast and saw Tig off to work. This time she packed a lunch for him and Karl.

After he was gone, she booted up her computer and hit her search engine for 'koi.' She got a million hits and had no idea where to start. She changed it to 'show koi' and that narrowed it down some. She also looked at 'how to pick koi.' That gave her lots of information on body shape and skin quality and fin proportion. Too much information. She had no idea there were so many types of koi: *sanke, showa, kohaku*—she couldn't keep them all straight. Of course Tig had told her a lot about koi over the years, but she didn't remember the specifics. She remembered their names and personalities. Like the Princess Keiko. She was a *kohaku,* a red and white koi, and queen of the pond. She was sweet and mellow and usually laid eggs every year when the weather warmed. She was by far the largest of their collection, but Jack Dandy, who had turned out to be a girl as well, was quickly catching up.

Not all their koi were top quality. Sometimes a baby koi which showed potential when young just didn't meet it as it grew. They had also rescued some koi on a trip and kept the few who survived. They were mutts as far as the koi world went, but Elizabeth liked their rascally personalities and the toughness they showed in surviving.

Goldie was a lovely gold-scaled sparkler; her scales reflecting light and her lovely eyes wise and luminous. She was a little ditzy, which goes to show looks can be deceiving. Elvis had a glossy cape of black that began in a widow's peak just behind his eyes.

She switched to the *images* part of the search engine and was impressed by the number and variety of fish displayed. She also discovered koi clubs and breeders everywhere. She closed her search windows. She'd had enough for one day. Her stomach rumbled and she was shocked to find several hours had passed while she was lost on the internet.

She warmed a bowl of chili for lunch and made out a grocery list. She called Rachel to see how Yuki was doing.

"What did the vet say?" Elizabeth asked.

"His feet will be sore for a few days, but he's in pretty good health otherwise. He hasn't left my side since we found him."

"He's very happy to be home."

"What happened to him, do you know?"

"Yes, he told me that a man, I think it was your husband, had taken him from the yard. He went willingly because it was someone he knew. Is that possible?"

"I really didn't think Tom would do that to an animal, but he was very bitter when I filed for divorce. He knows I love Yuki so I suppose that was the first way he thought of to hurt me."

"Well, Yuki said he was put in a box and driven to where he was dumped. He couldn't get across the river and back to you, so he hid. He wasn't really sure where he was. I mean, that spot is between here and Cove. He's never been there before, right?"

"No. He's not a cat I want to take on casual car rides into the country. The ten blocks to the vet is enough yowling for me," Rachel said.

"Since he was in the box he couldn't see how he got there. Maybe that's just as well because if he'd tried to cross South Bay Drive, he might have been hit by a car."

"Oh, that's terrible."

Elizabeth heard Rachel sniffling. Then she felt a warmth and knew that Yuki was trying to console his mother.

"Can I do anything? I mean legally?" Rachel's voice was strong again.

"No, I don't think so. We can't prove it was him. Keep Yuki inside for a while. Let me talk to Yuki for a moment."

"What do I do?"

"Nothing. Just a sec." Elizabeth connected with Yuki, which was easy now. He was open to her and trusted her, so the link was immediate.

Hi, Yuki.

Hi.

How are you feeling?

Great. Happy.

You need to be careful now. That man who took you could come back.

I know. I am staying inside now. Mom put a box of dirt for me! In the house! It's amazing. Dirt in the house. It's so fun. Elizabeth saw a picture of a litter box.

I'm glad for you. You may want to play outside again sometime—

No. Never. I'm never going out again.

In case you do, just be careful. No cars. Stay away from the street and people you don't know, and that man, okay?

Okay! The connection was broken and she sensed contentment.

"Rachel?"

"Yes?"

"I've spoken to Yuki. He doesn't want to go outside now, but that may change."

"I know. I've put a litter box in the spare room and closed the pet door."

"He was an indoor—outdoor cat before, right?"

"Yes."

"That is kind of hard to undo, despite how he feels now. When and if he decides, and you decide, to let him resume that, I've given him some instructions. However, cats aren't known for their great long-term memories, especially if he's hunting, so maybe let me talk to him again when the time comes. Okay?"

"Absolutely. Thank you again. I'll mail you a check, okay?"

"Fine. Thank you. Call anytime."

They ended the conversation and Elizabeth felt the familiar sense of accomplishment that accompanied a satisfied client, but more importantly, a happy animal.

A quick trip to the grocery store and she was ready for her new client. This one lived near Tig's pond project in the heights. Maybe she'd drop by after her consultation. She never tired of watching Tig's strong arms work. Large hands that could also be so gentle—she was getting distracted and stopped herself.

Her new client would be interesting. The heights backed onto the same open land their own home did, just a little farther toward the coast and much higher on the hill. That meant, for all of them, living side by side with nature. That was great, until nature did something that people didn't like. Usually, nature lost.

Elizabeth and Tig loved walking out there; they called it 'the outback' and always saw something new—a flower, a horned toad--rare but adorable--sometimes a snake. Once Elizabeth had seen a bobcat and was absolutely breathless at her beauty. She was hunting among the stacked picnic tables at the campground and jumped atop one with her prize, a limp rabbit. She proudly carried it across the campground road, not twenty yards in front of Elizabeth.

Night brought out the coyotes and mountain lions, which is why their cats were locked in at night. Sign after sign posted on power poles and at the vet's office asked about 'lost' animals. Elizabeth knew what that meant. The coyotes hunting cries still gave her the willies, even though she knew what made it. Shrill ululating howls, traveling across the eucalyptus-dotted hills, filled her with dread. *Must be primal,* she thought, because she was nice and safe in her home. She'd seen an occasional coyote out and about and that never bothered her, but at night, with mist drifting in from the sea, the maniacal noises never failed to shoot adrenaline through her.

Today's client was unique. Because of the proximity to the outback, people's yards were fodder for not only the hunters, but the hunted. Gangs of raccoons, skunks, possums, rabbits and deer came to feed on the luscious contents of landscaped gardens. This family had found a fawn, alone in their yard. Deer were crepuscular, feeding at dawn and dusk, bedding down in between. Elizabeth often came upon their sleeping places, little flattened circles in the long veldt grasses that filled in the outback between groves of eucalyptus, manzanita and oak.

Does often left their babies while they went off to feed, but once the babies were big enough to graze, they stayed close to the mother, traveling from yard to yard, eating the buffet of blossoms and other tidbits.

A fawn in a yard alone was unusual, and this area had many deer vs. auto accidents. Usually neither party fared well. The local mule deer were quite large and hitting a buck would be like hitting a horse. Deadly.

When the family had first seen the baby, they had quite wisely left it alone the first day, waiting for the mother to come back. She hadn't. Then they had asked around the neighborhood but no one had seen a stray doe or had any ideas. One neighbor suggested Elizabeth. The family didn't want the fawn to end up at animal services or worse, so they decided to call her first.

She easily found the house in the lower section of the heights and rang the bell. She was welcomed by a middle-aged couple with two teenagers, a boy and a girl.

"Thank you for coming. I'm Bruce," the man whispered. "This is my wife Susan, and Amy and Brock." Elizabeth nodded.

They beckoned her to the living room whose picture window overlooked a lovely garden. In a flower bed lay a fawn. Still spotted, however, it was certainly old enough to follow its mother to eat solid food.

"Nothing new?" Elizabeth whispered back.

"No. It's just lying there. I think it got up to eat early, because it's in a little bit different place now," Susan whispered.

"We have that fountain for it to drink from," Amy added.

"Isn't it weird that it's still here? And by itself?" Brock whispered.

"Yes, that's not usual behavior. I think you may be right, something happened to the mother. I'm going to check in with it." Elizabeth said. "You're welcome to stay and watch, but I'll need absolute quiet for a while, okay?" Solemn nods. The family sat around the living room, eyes glued to her like she might levitate at any moment. She was used to pet owners watching, just not quite so many at once.

She sat in a straight backed chair facing the window, feet flat on the floor and closed her eyes. She quickly grounded herself, cycling her energy and sending it to the little fawn. She felt its surprise at her energy's presence. It was afraid, but not overly so.

Since it was wild, she sent pictures and colors to it as well as words. It would not be attuned to human speech, but she would do the best she could. She mostly sent calming waves as she communicated.

Can I talk to you?
Who are you?
I want to help you. Where is your mom?

71

I don't know.

Can you show me where you saw her last? A picture of a doe, the mother she assumed, grazing in the front of the house. The proximity of the mother indicated the fawn had been close, but lying down, perhaps hidden in the bushes, resting.

What happened? Where did she go? The fawn showed a car careening down the street toward the house. The curve on which the house sat, allowed the car to come close to the curb as it swung wildly, the driver fighting for control.

The frightened doe leapt as the car jumped the curb, hitting it a glancing blow. The fawn relived its terror as it heard its mother cry out and hobble away from the car and the danger. Perhaps attempting to lead the 'predator' away from her baby?

Fear pinned the fawn to the ground and the mother disappeared into a grove of eucalyptus in a canyon across and up from the family's home.

Elizabeth took it as a good sign that the doe was able to move, but that didn't mean its injuries weren't life-threatening or that it hadn't died later.

Little one? she called to the fawn. *I want you to think of your mother. The way she looks, sounds smells. I'm going to look for her but I need your help.*

Images of the mother came rushing to Elizabeth, she in turn used herself as a speaker of sorts, a satellite, to send those images and thoughts out toward the eucalyptus grove and beyond.

She used all her 'sight' to look and listen for a response. It was day now, and it took several minutes for an answer. The hurt doe had been asleep. Her injuries had kept her from seeking her fawn but she was not dead, not dying. Elizabeth felt relief wash over her. She sent those feelings to the fawn.

The doe was wise and understood Elizabeth better than she had anticipated. Elizabeth 'felt' her, checked her wounds and general health. The doe had been badly frightened and bruised by the car. Her instinct had been to lead it away from the baby, but also to get herself to safety and seclusion where she could heal. Or die. Her pain had been extreme and she had been unable to get back to her fawn. She still had not arisen to feed herself and felt weak.

Elizabeth was grateful no bones had been broken. That would have been another ending. She connected again to the mother.

I don't want you to move. I will bring your baby to you. She sent a picture of herself, along with warm, gold light and energy. Then she sent a picture of herself with the fawn, bringing the baby to her.

Stay, she told the doe. *I will bring her to you. Don't be scared when you hear me; when you smell me. I will have your baby with me, and concentrate on her.*

She felt affirmative energy back.

She passed the same message to the fawn. The fawn was less sure about the upcoming adventure, but trusted Elizabeth.

I'm going to come into the yard where you are, okay? She sent that picture to the fawn. She sent a picture of it getting up and following her to her mother. The fawn agreed.

Elizabeth was not at all sure how this would work out. It entailed the fawn following her across two streets and into a canyon and she wasn't clear exactly where the doe was. She would have to keep contact with both the doe and the fawn if there was any hope at all of reuniting them.

She slowly 'returned' to the living room. All eyes were upon her, and Amy and Brock's mouths were agape.

"Okay," Elizabeth began.

"That was so cool," Amy said.

"Weird," Brock said. "Your eyes were closed, but they like, moved back and forth, like you were looking at stuff."

Elizabeth smiled. She had no idea what she looked like when she connected.

"What's next?" Susan asked.

"The plan is for me to take the fawn to its mother. She was hit by a car," this elicited gasps from Amy and Susan, "but she's okay. I'm going to take her water. She hasn't been able to move since the accident, but it's just deep bruising and nothing appears to be broken. I'll get her some food once I'm there, but do you have something I could put water in for her to drink?"

"Sure." Bruce rose and went to the kitchen. He looked a little stunned.

"He thought this was bunk," Susan whispered.

"I get that a lot." Elizabeth smiled. "Next I'm going into the yard to get the fawn to follow me."

"Can we come?" Amy asked.

"Not this time. I'm sorry. They are both pretty skittish and I just want to reunite them. Wild animals can be touchy. If this was a domesticated animal, it would be different."

The kids looked disappointed. "You can watch from here, though. She's used to seeing you at the window."

"Really? She saw us?"

"Yes. She knows this is your den. She knows you've been watching her. She is glad you never came into the yard. You did the right thing in giving her some privacy."

The kids looked a little cheerier. Bruce returned with a Tupperware bowl and a bottle of water. "Will this do?"

"Great. Thanks. Leave it on the porch for me and I'll take it when I go." Elizabeth put her purse in her car but her phone in her pocket after making sure it was on 'silent' mode. No strange noises to startle anyone. She hoped this would work. No plan B. She was working blind here, since she'd never attempted anything like this.

She reached out to the fawn. *Ready? I'm going to come around the house now.* She walked slowly to where the fawn could see her. *Let's go. Mom's waiting.* The fawn obediently stood and walked behind her and out into the front yard. Elizabeth gathered the bowl and water bottle and continued across the streets and into the canyon, and the fawn remained about twenty feet behind her. She felt like the Pied Piper. She prayed for no traffic, backfires, or any startling noises. She glanced back and saw it carefully picking its way down the little game trail after her, tail wagging, heart lifting as it got closer to its mother.

Elizabeth reached out to the doe. *We're in the canyon now.* She showed her where they were and she showed her a picture of her baby coming toward her. *Where are you? Help me find you. Can you smell me yet?*

No. The doe sent a picture that told Elizabeth she was inside a cave of pygmy oaks. The low-growing oaks made perfect nests for animals and forts for kids. They also all looked alike.

Can you show me how you got there? Any special trees? Anything to help us find you?

Silence for a moment. She felt that the doe hadn't been able to travel far but didn't know which way to pursue. Up the canyon or down? Up was farther from people, but would have been harder on the doe in her condition.

The doe had continued up. Elizabeth turned uphill and trudged along, her charge happily trailing. Suddenly the baby stopped, lifted its head and squeaked. Elizabeth had heard nothing, but the baby sure had. It took off like a rocket up the trail, past Elizabeth. Elizabeth jogged to keep up. A few more turnings and she just saw the flip of its tail as it disappeared into a large grove of oaks. If she hadn't seen that tail, she never would have known.

Hey, I have water for you. Can I come in? she sent to the doe.

All she felt was happiness. Mom and baby reunited. *Can I see you? I don't think you should get up, but I have water, okay?*

A warm wave of assent. She parted the oak branches and entered a cozy, dappled glade. The doe was bedded down and the fawn cuddled right up next to her.

She carefully opened the water bottle and poured it into the Tupperware. She wanted the doe to smell the water before she approached, just in case the mother became afraid. She was big enough to hurt Elizabeth with those sharp hooves even if she was injured.

However, all Elizabeth felt was gratitude and thirst. She slowly moved forward and put the bowl in front of the doe who lapped eagerly. Her shoulder and legs were blood-spattered but appeared to be whole. The skin had been torn but was now scabbed over and seemed clean.

Can I touch you? Elizabeth sent a picture of her hand on the injured shoulder.

Yes.

Elizabeth gently laid her hand near the wound and felt only warm skin, not the heat of infection she was afraid of. She tenderly ran her hands down the doe's forelegs. The doe trembled but didn't move. She only felt warmth and happiness, speckled with minor pain.

What do you eat? I can bring you some.

Elizabeth got a picture of flowers and moss along with greens. None of that was in the glade with them. *I'll be right back.*

She found what she thought the doe had showed her and returned as quickly as possible. The fawn was licking the last of the water out of the bowl. She offered the food to the doe who ate it immediately. She was as large as a pony and must eat a lot, Elizabeth thought.

She couldn't resist. She petted the fawn who stilled under her hand. She didn't indulge as much as she wanted. She wouldn't want the fawn to grow up to seek humans. She also lay a hand on the mother.

Rest today. Do you think you can feed by tonight? Do you think you'll be able to get up?

Yes. Now that we are together, I can do that, the doe responded. She licked her baby who happily submitted.

Elizabeth gathered the bottle and bowl and backed out of the glade, a wave of warm energy and gratitude wrapping her as she left.

In minutes she was back at the house. She knocked and when Bruce answered the door, she relayed the story, the whole family clustered around her. As she returned the bowl, Bruce pushed a hundred dollar bill into her hands.

"That's too much," Elizabeth started.

"I've never seen anything like that in my life. You keep it young lady. Do you have business cards? I'm going to tell everyone about this."

"Um, no I don't have cards. You can just pass on my cell number to anyone who's interested."

"Well, you might think about cards. You'll be getting some calls."

"I've already posted it on Facebook!" Amy said.

Elizabeth took the hundred, and her leave. As she drove up the hill toward Tig's job site, her mind swirled with ideas. Business cards? Facebook? Wow.

Elizabeth was amazed at the transformation of the courtyard. Where the hole and recalcitrant liner had been, now was a glistening pond and trickling waterfall. Tig and Karl were industriously planting around the cascade to give it that 'been here a hundred years natural pond' look. Most of the plants were xeriscopic, meaning they didn't need a lot of water, but they sure looked lush. She only knew because they had a lot of the same ones in their yard. She loved the tropical look, but this Central California beach area was deceptive. It was really a coastal desert, and many tropical plants were not fooled. They knew it wasn't Hawai'i or Santa Barbara. They never got the required heat, which is one reason Elizabeth loved the coast, and also the nights were seldom warm. Annual rainfall was, well, like the desert. Most of the native plants got half their moisture from the daily or nightly mists that rolled in from the sea, absorbing it through their leaves. *As opposed to a 'normal' plant,* she thought, as she looked at the paradise before her.

One great thing about a pond Tig pointed out, was you always had a water source for fire and for watering plants. With fish, you had to make water changes, and as long as you didn't salt the water—she had learned that salt for koi was a form of medicine and very good for them—when half the pond was drained, that water was excellent for plants. In fact, the settling tanks where water filtered out stuff, well, fish poop, was some of the best fertilizer anywhere. Orchids in particular loved fish-water as she called it, as did their other plants.

"Hey," she called. "It looks beautiful!"

Tig's head popped up from behind a large fern. "It does, doesn't it?" His broad smile showed pride and happiness with her praise. "Let me just finish this guy and I'll show you what we've done."

She stepped down onto the walkway and Tig met her. "What are you doing here?" he asked.

"I had a new client nearby and thought I'd drop in. Wow, you have worked fast."

"Who's the client?"

"Long story. For later. I want to hear about the pond." She knew he really wanted to tell her first, so she indulged.

"We're cycling the water, letting the concrete bleed out and cure. You know the water is going to be alkaline for quite a while, but we should be able to put some fish in here in a couple weeks." Tig had told her that as concrete cures, which it needs to be wet to do best, it leeches into the water and raises the alkalinity. Not so good for fish. She nodded.

"So far the waterfall is looking good and holding up. We had a tiny leak, a rivulet I wasn't expecting, but I adjusted the stones and it's doing what it's told now." Tig much preferred to build a waterfall from scratch rather than try to troubleshoot an existing one. Homeowners rarely were willing to let him tear it all out and build up, even though in the end the cost would usually be less than him testing and patching for days.

The cascade was lovely, not too loud, and the meandering path of the water soothing and natural where it fell into a short false riverbed to trickle gently into the pond. Occasionally people wanted a waterfall to be loud to drown out noisy neighbors, but she much preferred this soothing sound.

He took her around the fall to the pumps and tanks. "Here's the neat part. When this handle is lifted, the tanks empty into a pipe we've run around the house. There's a natural fall that allows gravity to drain it into two places, a holding tank for watering and we've also set it up to automatically water the flower garden. I also had a sign made to remind them not to do that if they use salt. I put a side line in for emergencies; they can drain water into another area for that.

"Wow, you've thought of everything," she said.

"We try. We're just finishing up the plantings so the tile guys can come and finish the pavers tomorrow. I'll be checking the pond every day for leaks and water quality. We've got the pond on a timer so it will refill, but it's adjustable so they can reset it if they're on vacation or we get a heat spell and more evaporation. They are going to be surprised at how many critters will drink out of this. Their caretaker said that was okay, but they are right here in the wilderness so I made sure they were aware."

Elizabeth looked again in admiration at all they'd accomplished. She called to Karl, "It looks wonderful, Karl. Good job!"

He smiled his thanks but kept right on working.

"I'm going to get going and let you get back to it. Any ideas for dinner? Barbecued burgers?"

"Perfect. I should be home soon. Another hour to clean up here. Karl's almost done with that border and we have to sweep and pick up our trash. Put stuff away."

Tig prided himself on leaving a clean job site on a daily basis.

"Have the owners seen this?" Elizabeth asked.

"No, but the caretaker, Mike, comes home around the same time we're leaving each day. He's passed on our progress and they've seemed pleased, according to him. I reminded them through Mike that we needed a couple weeks before fish could go in, but they were really nice about that. I know how hard it is to wait. If we get them fish in San Jose next week, we can keep them at our place 'til this pond is ready."

They had a little emergency pond set up behind their house. Frogs loved it, and in case they got new fish or rescued any, it was an area of quarantine. New fish were never just put into a different pond. They had to get used to different temperatures, salinity, quality, a lot of things. But, the main reasons were to observe for health issues, and to protect any existing fish. Especially in their own pond. A new fish could have diseases or parasites and they loved 'the girls' as they called them, even though they weren't all girls, as evidenced by annual egg frenzies followed by tiny hatchlings. They would never put their fish at risk; there was enough they couldn't control, like predators or things blown into the pond.

"Okay, I'll see you at home, then." She kissed him good-bye and waved to Karl. She drove home, her busy day replaying in her mind. A good day.

At home she fed the starving cats and lit the barbecue to warm for Tig. She made the burger patties and prepped condiments. All the while, she couldn't get the idea of Mr. Tanaka wanting Tig to buy fish for him out of her head. Something seemed odd about it, but she couldn't put her finger on it. Maybe the idea of it being so 'big time' and Tig's business was so local, so well, 'small time,' not to sound unkind.

He did design flawless, beautiful ponds in the area. He did have a website. He was getting more business. "I suppose it makes sense. I'm worrying about nothing," she told the cats when she heard the truck in the drive. Edward ran to the front door and sat, tail curled neatly around him, like a tiny statue.

Teddy stayed with her, in case any burgers fell. *Just helping,* he said.

"I'm sure you are." She knelt to give him a chin scratch which always made him smile. Irresistible. She kissed the top of his head, then rose to wash her hands again as she heard Tig come in. He was home; the cats were here, burgers for the grill. All was well.

Six

The next morning was 'business as usual' until Elizabeth turned on her cell phone. She had six new messages, an oddity—she never had six messages. Even Tig at his most excited might only leave one, but mostly they texted. Five of the messages were potential new clients, and three of those five had discovered her on Facebook. Since she didn't have a FB page, she decided it was due to Amy. She thought Amy was kidding, but clearly she was not. Perhaps she would get a Facebook page. Kids did it. How hard could it be? Two messages had been referrals by the family yesterday, and the sixth was from Susan herself.

"Hi, Elizabeth. It's Susan with the doe and fawn? That sounds like an English pub. Anyway, I just wanted to thank you again, and let you know they both came back to browse or graze or whatever you call it. They were here last night after dinner, and I think they may have slept in the garden. Not sure, but they were also having breakfast in the garden. I'm an early riser so I saw them just as they finished up. Mom looked pretty good although she was moving slowly, but baby looked perfect. Anyway, you're a marvel and we're singing your praises. Have a good day."

"Who was that?" Tig had staggered out in his PJs for coffee and overheard the last bit.

"Remember that family with the fawn in the garden I told you about yesterday? That was the mom thanking me and giving me an update. Looks like all's well there. They have been referring me, even the kids apparently, so I have a few phone calls to return."

"That's great." Tig had prepared his coffee and took a grateful sip. "So good. I'm a little sore from yesterday. Karl and I really pushed ourselves to finish the heavy stuff. Today's my last day off 'til next week. Want to do anything?"

"Don't you have to work on that pond?"

"I am going to check on it, but the tile guys are there today. I'm going to do a water sample— double check my seals and the pumps, etc. Should all be fine. I have time after that. Any plans?"

"Nothing I can't get done in the morning. I want to return these messages, but I won't schedule any clients unless it's an emergency."

"Great. Maybe lunch at the Thai place? And a walk along the bay?" Edward had discovered Tig and was already tucked in his lap.

"Sounds perfect." Elizabeth began to make waffles, one of Tig's favorites. His cell rang.

"Hey, Yoshi, how are you?"

Elizabeth had wondered who was calling so early. Well, relatively early. She recalled that

Yoshi was Tig's koi breeder friend from Japan. Was he calling from Japan? What was the time difference? She had no idea. She tuned in on the conversation.

"Let me get my notes." Tig grabbed a spiral notepad he left on the table and flipped a couple pages. "Okay, I have list of koi the client is interested in, but I want your input too. If there's something else out there you think he should see, let me know. I think this might end up being a nice side thing for me."

Elizabeth sipped her coffee while Yoshi answered, but she could only hear Tig's end. "Showa, maybe 20 inches. Female. Kohaku, same. Um, lessee, how about a Kin-Rin. But I'd look at a silver, too. A tancho for sure—what?" Elizabeth had been immediately lost in the flurry of koi types. She knew a few from their own koi, a butterfly koi, for example had long flowing fins. Their ghost koi was white with black circles around his eyes, but most of the Japanese terminology was new.

"Seven," Tig was saying. "To start. Probably around fifty grand for now."

She could not have heard that right. Fifty thousand dollars? For fish? Mr. Tanaka was willing to spend that much on seven fish? How much had he spent on the first batch? And what did he do for a living? *Well, that was uncharitable*, she thought.

"Okay. Email me some pictures and I can take them to Goro and he can vet them with Mr. Tanaka. Who's the breeder here? Kodama?

They're good. Who else? Nishikigoi? Yeah, I know them. Okay. Let me know. Thanks, bye."

Elizabeth brought waffles and sausage to the table. "You have to fill me in. Fifty thousand dollars for fish? Did I hear that right?"

"Yup. And that's not unusual. These aren't even the most expensive. I think these are around seven thousand each, give or take. We could go up or down depending on size and color. A better color or pattern costs more, so sometimes you buy a smaller fish and hope it stays that way as it grows. Mr. Tanaka wants larger fish to start with, so the coloration will remain stable. Fifty thousand was just a starting point. Goro said we could use that as a base, but to let him know if I found something amazing." He ate as he talked. Edward's pointed little nose stuck up above the table and Elizabeth saw his nostrils working. Tig slipped him a morsel of sausage and the nose disappeared.

"This is incredible. I never knew any of this stuff."

"It was kind of a non-issue with our koi budget, so I didn't really talk about it."

"What about San Jose? I don't think I've ever seen a koi that expensive there."

"They don't keep their specialty koi out with the rest. You have to make an appointment and the really big guys of high quality are kept separate under lock and key."

"Well, it's not like a burglar is going to come and steal one." Elizabeth saturated her own waffle in syrup. "Is it?"

"You'd be surprised. There's a lot of stealing in the koi world. This is a valuable commodity and collectors of prize fish are like collectors of anything: fairly unreasonable and a little wacky, in my opinion." The nose was back and Tig passed on another bit of sausage.

"I think I'm stunned." Elizabeth took a bite then added more syrup. "What about all the Japanese? Do you speak enough Japanese?"

"The only words I know relate to fish, so far. But I like it. It's an interesting language." He took a bite and continued. "Those were types of koi Mr. Tanaka is interested in and Yoshi has a couple breeders in Japan he deals with and they are reputable. Their shipping and arrive alive ratios are excellent."

"What's a showa?"

"A black koi with red and white markings. But there are lots of mini-categories and definitions within that. A tancho means a red spot on the head. It can have other colors on the body, but I'm looking for a white body with the red spot, like the Japanese flag."

"They come like that?"

"Sure. They are bred for all sorts of qualities; that's just one. You know, like horses or dogs are bred for certain characteristics." Tig pushed back from a spotless plate. "That was delicious."

He rose and plopped Edward to the floor. "Thanks." He put his plate in the sink and kissed her. "I'm going to get dressed and get going."

Elizabeth was still only partly done with her waffle. The whole koi discussion had given her a lot to think about. She sure knew more about koi now than she had an hour ago. She also wanted to see the special koi in the back room when they went to San Jose. She made a mental note to ask Tig in case an appointment was needed. She couldn't imagine what a five or ten thousand dollar fish would look like.

She had finished her own breakfast when Tig was ready to leave for the heights.

"I should be back by noon or so," he said. They kissed good-bye and Elizabeth cleaned up from breakfast and settled down to return her phone messages. Lots of food for thought.

She got a bit of dry koi food and went out to the pond. The morning sun hit it obliquely and she could see right to the bottom. The koi also saw her and rose to the surface as she sprinkled the koi kibble. Teddy and Edward also thought koi kibble was delicious so she put some down on the flagstone for them.

Hi guys, she said to the fish.

As usual, Princess Keiko was the first to respond with a warm-bubbly sensation. It sort of tickled the way something can itch or tickle at the same time.

How is everyone today? She sent out her mental feelers to check each fish. They were used to it, but Casper was the newest and still skittish about responding to her. She waited until he stopped zooming around the bottom and sent him a warm enquiry. He nibbled at the water taro roots and let her. He seemed healthy and happy; he'd adjusted well to his new pond.

She checked everyone else and they burbled at her like a crowd of people. *More.*
She tossed a few more kibbles on the water. She watched them Hoover them up like little vacuums. They just opened their mouths and water and food flowed in. She loved their barbles, only she called them whiskers, because it added an element of personality and whimsy to each. She thought they were very cute, but that energy met some resistance when she sent it to the fish. When she told the cats they were cute, they took it as their due, and frankly, worked that angle. However, the koi, were more dignified and Keiko had spoken for them like a union leader at one point.

We're not cute, she had sent. But her feeling-image for cute had a negative undertone that Elizabeth didn't understand. She had tried to explain but had only received an image of, well, how to put this? If fish had arms and could fold them and tap their fins in impatience and solemnity, then that's what Keiko sent back.

Okay, Elizabeth had said. *You're not cute. You are regal, imperial and lovely.* She sent images of palaces and queens and a feeling of ritual and pomp. More out of frustration than because she thought Keiko would have any idea of royalty or palaces. However, Keiko had been pleased and had passed that onto the rest. A feeling of satisfaction rose from the pond.

"Oh, for Pete's sake you guys," Elizabeth had said. After thinking about it, however,

Elizabeth remembered that Keiko was one of their few koi who was actually bred in Japan from a top breeder, and from a long line of classic koi. They had had to buy her when she was small, since small fish were cheaper. However, her lineage and status were clearly part of her make-up, and although all the koi weren't directly from Japan, Keiko was the matriarch of the pond and often spoke for all.

How is it in there? Teddy asked, squatting to look. He lapped at the water, since he was there.

They are fine, Teddy.

Edward also squatted to have a drink, but he couldn't reach the pond.

Still a baby, Teddy said.

Am not. I'm just small. It smells funny anyway. Edward rose to drink out of his water bowl just inside the back door.

Teddy took a few more spite laps of water. *Ahhh. Delicious.*

Elizabeth had to laugh. She bent to pet him, then picked up the fish food container and returned it to the shelf in the 'cat room.'

"Okay, guys, fun's over." She got her cell and listened again to the messages, jotting down the names and numbers. Two of the three calls mentioned Facebook and were just congratulatory and hadn't left numbers or names, although the senders' numbers appeared on her phone. The voices were young, and the messages in the "that's so cool," vein. She discarded those. One of the FB calls also said how cool it was, but mentioned wanting to ask a question. She returned that call but had to leave a message. The two remaining calls were recommendations from the fawn-family, as she thought of them, and seemed to want her services.

For one she left a message, but the other picked up.

"This is Elizabeth Murphy. The. . ." she blanked on the fawn-family's last name and changed gears. "I'm the one who helped the fawn and doe reunite. I'm returning your call."

"Oh, yes. I called because my wife, Emma, and I have a little problem with our dogs. They keep jumping up on us and when we come in from outside they race ahead. They're pretty big dogs and the wife and I aren't young anymore. The funny thing is, they've both been obedience trained and this has just been happening the last few months. I'm afraid they're going to knock poor Emma over one of these days."

"Has anything in the household changed since this began? For example, have you moved, or has anyone left the household or moved in?"

"Not that I can think of. We live on a ranch out in Cuyamaca and we have a lot of coming and going anyway with the ranch and farm, but nothing new. We run a bed and breakfast sort of thing, but that's not new either. We have managers for the avocados and livestock, but no one hangs around our private house or us, really. We are just at a loss. I was talking about it to Bruce and he mentioned what you did for them, and before we make the dogs take a refresher obedience class, I thought I'd give you a call."

"I'd be happy to schedule an appointment for tomorrow or the day after if that works for you."

"Perfect. How about tomorrow at 10AM?"

"Fine. Give me your address and some directions, if you would."

He complied. "My name is Fred Leahy, by the way. I don't think I mentioned it."

She hung up and checked the time. Almost noon. Tig would be back soon and probably ravenous. She looked forward to a little quiet 'couple time' with Tig. Their favorite Thai place and a nice walk along the bay would be perfect. He went back to work tomorrow, four days of twelve hour shifts, then his twenty-four hour shift and then three days off. Recycle, repeat, she thought. On his next three days off, she remembered, they would go to San Jose Koi. Fun.

Seven

The next day, Elizabeth sent Tig off to the fire station with clean uniforms and a kiss. In that profession they ate well, so other than occasionally sending a treat *for everyone,* she didn't pack lunches for him. When he worked a landscape job, he often forgot to take something, since in the other parts of his life, food was provided.

Now she found herself looking at her hastily scribbled directions while she drove the narrow, winding Cuyamaca Creek road out to Fred and Emma's ranch. She warned herself not to say 'Fred and Ethel.'

Addresses were few and far between out here, and most land parcels were huge and looked to be working ranches or farms, often with names visible instead of numbers. He had mentioned a fork in the road and a bridge, but she wasn't sure if *this* fork was *the* fork. She took it but didn't see a bridge. She would give this road a mile or so before she turned and took the other fork. No bridge. She turned around in the next wide-ish spot in the dirt road and went back to the fork, taking the other branch. Over a rise she came upon a bridge of sorts over a small, dry creek bed. Cuyamaca Creek? Maybe it wasn't a real creek, or perhaps it was 'seasonal' as they were fond of saying in this area. However, just bit farther she saw an iron arch proclaiming "Leahy Ranch" and gratefully turned in.

The long unpaved drive rose gradually, so when she reached the large ranch house and circled to park in the dirt turnaround, she had a lovely view of the avocado groves she'd passed and of cattle dotting the hills. She let the dust settle before she opened her door and as she waited, two bouncing dogs flew out of an out-building to greet her.

She sent them calming energy as soon as she saw them, and by the time they reached where she stood beside her car, only sniffing and tail-wagging occurred. They had stopped barking. A man in his late fifties or early sixties followed the dogs, much more slowly, from the building. She made the dogs' acquaintance and Sadie and Ben, as evidenced by their collar tags and not her abilities, were happily seated and dusting the ground with their feathery tails when Fred caught up.

He stuck out his hand. "Fred Leahy, nice to meetcha."

"My pleasure." She returned his shake.

"I see you met." He indicated the smiling dogs. "You're already working miracles. They always jump and bark at new folks, sometimes even at my foreman and workers, and they know them."

"They are very excited."

"Let's go up to the house where we can sit. Should they come with us?"

"Yes, it's better for their focus."

Fred turned and led the way to the larger ranch house. A smaller one sat slightly behind it. Both were painted bright yellow with white trim, rockers and a swinging love-seat on each of their wide porches. The smaller house looked identical to the first and she wondered if it was a guest house or for the workers. Fancy for employees, but maybe. Seemed like Fred was a good guy so maybe it functioned as a bunk house.

"Your homes are beautiful," she said as they stepped onto the first porch. "Is that a guest house? It's just like this one, but smaller."

"It used to be a guest house a long time ago, but now we've gotten into that thing, what's it called, that's so popular? My wife Emma thought it would be a good idea. Um, working vacation?"

Elizabeth shrugged. He held open the white painted screen door for her. "With the economy and all, we agreed to try it, Ishmael—my foreman— and I. Folks want a vacation on a working ranch, so they pay us money to come and work. I know crazy, right?" He saw her face.

"It's not my idea of a vacation," she began, but she didn't want to offend him.

"Mine, either. Nor the wife's. But it takes all kinds. We signed up with a service that specializes in that sort of thing. It's worked out pretty well, so far. That little house is for the guests. We feed them and train them and most of them are pretty good workers. A few older folks come, too, and they do the best they can. Most of them underestimate how hard it is."

"It seems like very hard work to me." Elizabeth sat where he indicated, a high-backed chair with a needle point design on the seat. Surprisingly comfortable.

"It is. I've had the same foreman for years and he hires good people. We had to hire another one just to take care of the tourists, but that's okay, it's added to their fees."

"So do they work all day? What's it like?" The dogs settled between Elizabeth and Fred, flat out on their sides panting like they'd run for miles, tongues lolling.

Emma appeared in the doorway. "Hello, I'm Emma. Coffee will be up in a minute and I've got some pastries too."

"Thank you very much. I'm Elizabeth." She tried to stand and step over the dogs to greet Emma, but Ben sat up just as she stepped over him so she straddled him, his head bumping against her middle. Big dog. She was trapped against the chair.

"Ben," Emma scolded. "Don't worry; we don't stand on ceremony here. I'll be right back."

Ben, lie down, Elizabeth sent just as Fred said, "For Pete's sake lie down Ben before she does the splits. Sorry about that," he said to her.

Ben complied and she settled back into the chair. Her hips were not as flexible as they used to be. She felt a little twinge as she sat. She assessed the dogs. Ben was possibly the largest black lab mix she'd run across. The feathers on his tail and legs flew like flags when he ran. His glossy fur shone with health and youth. Sadie was a golden retriever-looking, with long blonde hair any woman would love. She was more placid than Ben, and sent to Elizabeth that they were mother and son. Maybe his long feathers came from her side of the family. Sadie felt Elizabeth communicating with her, and her tail thumped contentedly. She remained on her side.

Emma bustled in with a tray of mugs and a carafe of coffee. A double-tiered plate held a variety of baked goods. "This should hold you for a while. No!" she said to Ben as he sat up again. "I'd love to stay and chat but I've got the guests' morning snack to finish--more of this—she indicated the coffee and pastries, "and then I've got to get lunch started for them. Can you stay for lunch, Elizabeth? You're more than welcome to."

Elizabeth thought fast. Tig was at work all day and she didn't have anything scheduled. She was curious more than anything else about this 'working vacation' concept. "I'd love to, thank you. Would it be okay to talk to the guests at lunch? I've never heard of this kind of tourism. I'm interested. Would it be rude of me?" The last thing she wanted was to upset these gentle, hardworking folks.

"Not at all," Fred said.

"Have at it," Emma agreed, and went back the way she came.

"Thank you," Elizabeth said. "Now, let me focus on the dogs. You told me the basics yesterday, but let me see what the dogs have to say. They seem fairly calm right now. Is that typical?"

"Not lately. They don't come in the house much, especially during the day. They have free run of the ranch and barns but I've had to curtail that some since they've started jumping up. I don't want them knocking over any of the guests. Or us," he added.

"Okay. I'm going to talk to them now. You won't see or hear anything, but give me a few minutes."

"Should I go away?"

"Not at all. This won't take long." She settled into her meditation—connection pose, feet flat, hands relaxed in her lap and connected with the earth energy. She sent out a greeting to the dogs. First she asked Sadie to talk to her, figuring correctly that Ben would follow what mom did.

Hi, Sadie. So Ben is your son?

Yes. I'm very proud of him. Her language skills were excellent; clearly she had been around humans for a long time.

Your Dad, Fred, is worried about you two. Do you know that?

Yes, I can tell.

Do you know why?

No.

You and Ben are behaving differently to them. Do you think so?

What do you mean?

You are jumping on them. They are frail humans and you could hurt them.

I would never hurt them.

You wouldn't mean *to hurt them, but you could. You and your son are very large.*

100

Yes, we are.
You are also barking a lot more than you used to.
We're talking.
Who are you talking to?
Ben's father. He's back. Elizabeth was surprised at that. Ben was obviously unneutered but for some reason she'd assumed that Sadie had been fixed after the litter. Maybe not.
Sadie? Do you know if you can have more puppies?
I am. Hmm. Interesting answer. Maybe she didn't quite understand. But she wasn't spayed and that was new information. *So, Ben's father is back. Is that why you and Ben are barking and more excited lately?* Elizabeth didn't send out a specific time reference because animals didn't measure time like humans. Short spans, like a night or two, she could communicate to Teddy, and Edward was learning about measuring nights and days, but Teddy was disinterested as it had no bearing on his life. Until she explained that sometimes she and Tig would be gone, and wouldn't it be nice to know when they were coming back? Teddy had allowed that it would and grudgingly participated in learning how humans measured time. *I will never understand people,* was his succinct assessment of the process.
Sadie? Can you show me Ben's father? Elizabeth noted increased excitement in Sadie, her heart sped up and she was immediately alert.
An image of a wolf. Not a coyote, but a wolf. Oh, my. This changed things in so many

ways. Elizabeth didn't know there were wolves in California. She often saw coyotes, but this was definitely a wolf, and not a husky or Samoyed or any other dog. It was wild. That might explain Ben's size. And increased aggression as he grew. Also, Sadie's heightened excitement. Oh, boy.

Sadie, I need you to concentrate. You can't jump on people any more. At all. And you need to control your barking. Talk to Ben's father. It is dangerous for him to come around here. The ranchers will hurt him if they see him. Do you understand? You have to tell him to go away. North, far north where it is safe. She sent a picture of the wolf traveling with the sun moving across him. She hoped that would mean north to an animal. Elizabeth had no idea if 'north' would be safer, but maybe where there were more woods? Tahoe, maybe? The locals freaked out enough about the resident predators they knew about. She couldn't imagine what would happen if a new hunter showed up. It was fortunate that he hadn't been seen yet. *What about packs?* she thought. *What about a wolf pack? Or what about the lone wolf?* She knew nothing about wolves she quickly decided.

Do you think you can do that? Warn him? Get him to leave and control your behavior?

Probably.

What about Ben? Will he listen to you?

Uncertainty. *I don't know. He is very like his father. He has wildness in him.*

That's what Elizabeth was afraid of. There was one thing she could do. Just as she was about to break off her connection, she got another picture. Sadie was pregnant. She hadn't thought to ask about the rest of Ben's litter, but now she didn't have to. Sadie had only one pup. It was big, like Ben, and it was part wolf. Elizabeth understood Sadie's answer. Sadie had spoken perfectly. She was already pregnant.

She roused herself from her relaxed state to find Fred watching; a worried look on his weathered face.

"Are you all right?" he asked. "Want some coffee? You look a little, uh, spooked, I guess. Do you always look like that when you talk to animals? I would." He handed her a mug of coffee without waiting for an answer. He nibbled a Danish.

"Okay, Fred, here goes. On the bright side, Sadie says she understands about the jumping and barking and will stop. She thinks she can get Ben to stop too, but maybe not. The bad part is why all this is happening."

"They're not sick are they? Poison or some such?" He looked worriedly at his dogs. Ben was completely relaxed now, but Sadie was alert from their conversation.

"No. Sadie is, however, pregnant again."

"Oh, is she okay?"

"Yes, but I have some disturbing news. I have never dealt with this before, so bear with me. It seems, as unlikely as it sounds, that the father of Ben, and of Sadie's current puppy, is a wolf." His jaw dropped. "I know. There is no mistaking it, however."

"We don't have wolves here."

"We do now. So far, it's just one wolf. I tried to get Sadie to tell him to move north and not bother any ranches but I don't know. I don't know anything about wolves. I'll research it, but for now I can only make some suggestions."

"Shoot."

Elizabeth wasn't sure if he meant 'go ahead,' or 'oh, no.' Maybe both. She went ahead. "Ben may not be able to exert any self-control unless you neuter him. He has a lot of wolf in him. He may look like Sadie, but he's all wolf inside. It will get worse as he grows, so the sooner the better."

Fred looked like she said he should be neutered himself.

"Fred, this is important. The wolf started coming around a few months ago, when all these behavior issues arose. It's communicating with Sadie and Ben, maybe trying to make a pack with them. I'd keep them on the property for now, if you can. I've heard of domestic dogs forming packs. The puppy is due soon, from what I can tell. Sadie needs to be kept here. That puppy should be fixed, too. I wouldn't trust a wolf hybrid around my family or tourists. I don't see this getting better without some intervention. If you can control Sadie and Ben for a while, the wolf may go away. Especially if Sadie has told it to. I don't know."

"What about the ranch? The animals? Are they in danger?"

"Maybe, but if it hasn't attacked anything yet, maybe it's getting enough to eat from the game around here. That won't last forever. I want to give it a chance to leave on its own. Can you give me some time for that to happen?"

"How much time? If a ranch gets hit, I'll have to tell someone."

"I understand. You haven't seen it, though?"

"No. I never woulda believed it. A wolf." He shook his head.

"I know this is hard, Fred. Take care of Ben first thing. That has to be your priority if you want to save your dog. If he hurts someone, Animal Services will have no choice. It's in your power now."

"I see. Well, thank you very much. I'll walk you." He rose and she followed out the door. The dogs leapt to their feet and trotted out.

She admonished the dogs once more at the car. She shook Fred's hand. She felt sad, being the bearer of bad news. Bad for all. Maybe she'd try to contact the wolf herself. She'd never been very successful at remote 'calls' and wild animals were skittish and often unresponsive, but she had to try.

She suddenly remembered Emma had asked her to stay for lunch. She'd forgotten. Fred had too, she supposed. She wasn't in the mood for fun anyway.

Eight

After the wolf discovery at Fred and Emma's, Elizabeth was a little down. She'd tried to contact the wolf with no success. She'd keep trying. The cats consoled her the best they could; their own interests superseded hers in terms of food and affection. That was fine with her. She had a lot to do; she just didn't feel like doing it. Around five she put in a roast and potatoes and made a salad. Tig should be home about 7:30 from his twelve hour shift. She made a cup of tea and took it out to the pond, sitting on the 'viewing port,' a raised platform Tig had constructed next to the stairs that led to the 'outback.' She sat in a lovely hand-made wooden love seat and sipped with a perfect, unobstructed view of the pond. It wasn't long before the cats joined her. Teddy immediately jumped up next to her, not much of a lap cat, but Edward detoured to look at the fish and try to drink from the pond again. She tuned in on them.

You're too little. You shouldn't even try, Teddy said.

I am not trying, said Edward, who was clearly trying to reach the water level, *I'm just looking.*

Elizabeth scritched Teddy under the chin just the way he liked. His lips curved up in a smile. *You shouldn't tease your brother.*

Why not? It's fun.

Because it's not nice.

Nice shmise. She wasn't sure that's what he said, but the tone was clearly dismissive.

Speaking of mice, I'm going to look under the plants in the other yard. I'm sure I smelled them. Teddy jumped off the seat and sauntered down the steps, tail flicking. Edward waited until he passed and then ran to Elizabeth, immediately draping himself across her lap. She petted him absently while she reviewed her afternoon's findings. She watched his thin ribcage rise and fall, his boneless body limp with contentment. From his traumatic childhood when he was rescued from under a burned out house and brought into their home, he had certainly adapted to a pampered pet lifestyle. He had some Siamese, she was sure. He didn't have the yowl, just the triangular head with an unbelievably pointy chin and almost no lips one could see. He was coal black all over so eyelashes, lips, everything, blended invisibly.

She finished her tea and stepped inside to check on dinner. Edward was very forgiving about being ousted from her warm lap. Although it stayed light late in the summer, here on the coast, the evening fog often obscured the sun, cooling the land quickly. Nearly 7 PM and dinner was done. She removed the roast to cool and set, covering it lightly with foil and then a towel. She showered so the bathroom would be free for Tig when he arrived.

She had just finished setting the table when she heard his truck pull in. On a hunch, she peeked out the window facing the drive and sure enough, both Teddy and Edward were already there, seated, tails curled, waiting. They had been there a while. *How do they do that?* she wondered. The cats did that for her, too, but she figured it was because she sent out thoughts of arriving home or something subconscious. Tig didn't have any ability that she knew of, but maybe the cats were just tuned to him, too, and could pick up those things. She had asked Teddy about it, but he wasn't interested in the *how* of things and had said blithely, *I don't know how I do it, I just do it.* She figured if she opened a can in exchange for information he might be more forthcoming, but she wasn't willing to stoop to blatant extortion just for that. Yet.

Tig burst in—that was how he usually entered and it didn't mean anything in particular—followed by two cats, tails waving. They had smelled the roast cooking, too.

"Wow, it smells amazing in here." He dropped his things near the door and kissed her. She hugged him and took an exploratory sniff. No smoke.

"No fires today?"

"Nope, three medical calls and a whole bunch of brass-shining. Really fun day." He didn't look disappointed, and she knew that was how most days went--mostly medical calls, rarely a fire, and lots of training or housekeeping.

"Dinner's ready."

"Great, I'm starving." Tig was always hungry, and it was nice to cook for such an easy audience.

They sat down to eat and sure enough, a small black nose emerged. Elizabeth had stopped trying to tell Tig it was a bad habit. From not being much of a cat person when they met, he'd come a long way and she was grateful he had his own cat. More or less. She could tell he loved the extra attention Edward paid him, always near him or on him. If Tig was not available, however, Edward was just as happy to drape his limp self on her.

She listened to his day, waiting for her turn. When it came, she took him through her visit to the Leahy ranch to the unnerving discovery of the wolf, just the way she'd experienced it.

"You're kidding!" was his satisfying response.

"Nope, a real, live wolf. I saw it myself."

"You *saw it*, saw it, or just in your, you know, head?"

"Sadie showed me. I'm not sure what to do about it. I tried contacting the wolf directly, but didn't have any luck. I'll keep trying."

"Are you going to tell anyone? That could be dangerous to kids, too." Tig took more salad.

"I know. I'm torn. Since no one's seen it or talked about it, I think it's keeping a low profile. That's good. I'm going to do some research on them tomorrow, but maybe they're kind of shy. I don't know."

"Me neither. So the rancher, Fred? He's going to get the half-wolf fixed?"

"That's what I'm trying to talk him into. He seemed really opposed to it. Even though he's seen the danger of wolves and the changes in behavior in his own dogs, he is still reluctant. I hope he does. Also, I hope he fixes the new pup as soon as it's old enough. That one might be aggressive, too. It's kind of a mess and I'm not sure what my duty is. I want to wait and see if Sadie can get her boyfriend to move along, but I wouldn't forgive myself if someone got hurt."

"You want my opinion?" Tig didn't usually ask if she wanted it, he just gave it.

"Sure."

"Try to contact the wolf. Give it only a day or two and try Sadie again. Check in with Farmer Fred, too, and see if anything's changed. If nothing has improved, you'd better report it. I'm the last guy to want to see a wild animal hurt, but we're talking livestock and people who are unprepared for this predator here."

Elizabeth sighed. "That's a good idea. I'll give it two days and then see where we are." She wasn't hungry anymore and Tig had eaten voraciously through the telling of her story so he was full. Even the owner of the nose was full from the bits Tig kept putting below the table.

They cleared the dinner things together and put away leftovers. Tig wandered off to shower followed by his little shadow and she loaded the dishwasher.

Teddy flopped in the middle of the small kitchen and she had to step around him to get anywhere. He was sure he was perfectly safe and that no one would hurt him. *Teddy, I might accidentally step on you. I wouldn't mean it, but you could still get hurt.*

Nah, was his response. No one said cats were reasonable. *So, what's a wolf?* He used her word since he had no picture.

She showed him a picture, the same one Sadie had shown her. The wolf slightly down from the ridge, so no silhouette, head lowered, eyes intense, focused on Sadie and the ranch.

She felt Teddy's fear spike. *That's not a coyote?*

He knew those since they heard them almost every night, and occasionally they appeared in daylight. She had taught him and Edward well, she hoped, since so many pets were 'lost,' with owners posting notices all over power poles and at the vets' offices. She knew they weren't lost. Well, not most of them.

No, it's much bigger and heavier and we don't have them here. This is the first one I've ever heard of outside that rescue place in North County.

Maybe it got away from there? Teddy was familiar with animal rescue, both from her work she shared with him, but also the odd time she helped foster a litter when the local rescue group became overwhelmed in 'kitten season.' And, rescue was how they got Edward.

That's a good idea. Maybe I'll call them tomorrow and see. She instantly rethought. If something had escaped, it would be in the news immediately. If nothing had escaped, she would be the one to set off the alarm. But, calling them might still be a good idea in terms of getting information on wolves.

You're pretty smart. For a cat.

Ha ha.

She started the dishwasher and headed to the bedroom, along with own shadow, tail flicking, tummy rolling side to side.

Tig was exiting the shower when she flopped on the bed. Teddy jumped up beside her, the bed making an ominous creak. She looked at him, eye brows raised. *Diet?*

She didn't know how he did it, but he shrugged. Not a human one, but the cat equivalent. Then he turned his head and stared blankly at the wall. Subject closed.

Tig checked his cell. "Message from Goro. Let's see what he has to say." He turned the speaker on so he could towel dry while he listened.

"Hello, Mr. Murphy," Goro began. "Mr. Tanaka is pleased with the fish you have chosen. He agrees to transfer funds to your account and you make the purchase, if that is acceptable? Or he can send the funds directly to the dealers. He would prefer you handle it, however. Plus your fee we discussed, once the fish arrive. Let me know how to proceed and where to transfer funds."

"Well, that's great," Tig said. "I've got to give Yoshi a finder's fee or something. That's got to come out of my end, I guess. He's doing the leg work over there with the dealers and physically checking the fish. For this kind of money, I don't want to rely on just pictures over the internet. At least for the first purchase."

"Yeah," Elizabeth said. "The internet can be so deceiving." They both laughed because it reminded them of a friend who was exploring internet dating. A couple of times he'd been burned when meeting the first time. He discovered the woman had posted a picture of herself taken ten years earlier and at least ten pounds lighter or one time, it wasn't even her photo at all. Their friend was no Greek god, but at least he was honest about what he posted.

"Why does Yoshi's fee have to come out of your end? Isn't it a reasonable expense that you found a broker in Japan you trust? Especially since Mr. Tanaka hasn't used his own person. It sounded odd to me that he didn't. Bad blood from the last buy, maybe?"

"I don't know," Tig said, pulling on a soft tee shirt and sweats. "I guess I should run it by Goro. Especially if I decide to be a fish monger."

"I don't think that's right. You're not going to eat them, just sell them."

"Okay. Whatever," Tig said absently. He picked up Edward and lay on the bed next to her, setting Edward on his chest. Edward stretched his paws under Tig's chin and closed his eyes, letting out a contented sigh with a slight whistle at the end. Tig and Elizabeth laughed.

Teddy stopped looking at the wall and nestled into Elizabeth's side. Edward wasn't going to corner the market on cuddling.

"I'll call him back and we'll figure out the nuts and bolts." He dialed but the call went to voice mail. "Hi, Goro. It's Tig Murphy returning your call. Everything sounds good. I'll give you bank transfer information when I speak to you in person. I'll handle everything for Mr. Tanaka, that's fine. I want to run something by you, though. I have a reliable friend in Japan I sent to vet the fish personally and I'd like to give him a finder's fee. Would that be okay if I billed his services to Mr. Tanaka as well? He's knowledgeable and honest, and I want eyes on those fish before I commit that much money. He's also willing to be there when the fish are shipped. For this first buy at least, I think that's a valuable service. Let me know what you think is fair. Talk to you soon."

"That was nice," Elizabeth said. "I know you'll do the right thing for Yoshi even if Mr. Tanaka doesn't want the extra expense."

"I think I'd like to keep Yoshi as a friend and a buyer." Tig smiled at Edward as his little chest rose and fell. His entire body fit on Tig's abdomen and probably always would. He had stopped growing, and although his legs were long and deer-like, he was still a small cat. "What should we watch?" Tig asked, just as his phone rang again. "Sorry, it's Karl."

"Hey, what's up?" Tig listened for a moment. "That's great. Do you want to meet with them first since it's your find? The soonest I'm available is next week. You could do the preliminary meet and show them the contract. I could meet you after work in the next couple days to go over it and I meet the client next week."

Elizabeth laid her hand on Teddy's substantial body. So strong. So sturdy. He rolled onto his back at her touch exposing an acre of tan belly fur. She called it 'down' because it was so soft. Teddy had not been amused since it didn't fall into his definition of a flattering description with his knowledge of the word. She explained how soft and lovely down was and showed him a picture of a duck and the feathery 'down.' He liked that immensely, but wanted to know if the duck was okay to eat, and if so, when he would receive a bird.

Tig hung up. "Karl got a new pond client. He was buying parts at the pond store and another customer started asking him questions. One thing led to another and they'd like a consult. I gave Karl the go ahead to meet with them at their property."

"That's great. It was good of Karl to tell you. You know, not take the job for himself."

"I think so. I also think he knows he's not ready to go off on his own yet. I've been thinking about that, though. He may not stay with me forever, once he knows all about pond building. He's smart and capable and could start his own business."

"I thought you said there was enough business for both of you?"

"Oh, yes, there is. But if he goes off on his own, I'll lose my assistant. Good helpers are few and far between."

"Cross that bridge when you come to it. Or, look at it as doubling your business on large jobs. He's going to need someone to help him, too."

"True. What do you want to watch?" He adjusted Edward's flicking ears so he could see the TV screen. After they all dozed off mid-movie several times, they gave up and called it a night.

Nine

The next day dawned gray and wet, typical coastal California summer. June Gloom, as it was sometimes called, could last on and off for months. Residents joked that the best summer weather came in October. Fall was warm, lovely and clear most days.

Elizabeth sighed and opened her eyes as she felt Tig moving about the room, getting ready for work. She had slept in a little. No cats, so he must have given them the first of their typical sixteen breakfasts. "I'm awake. You can turn on lights or whatever." She rolled over and stretched.

"I'm sorry," he said. "I forgot to put my shaving stuff into the other bathroom."

"It's fine. I'm usually up anyway."

"Coffee's ready and I'm out the door. See you tonight." He bent and kissed her good-bye and in moments, the whirlwind was gone and she heard his truck back down the drive.

She flipped back the covers, rose and opened the blinds onto the dark day. She could already tell from the darkness of their bedroom, but it was a depressing sight, nonetheless. She heard toenails clicking down their hardwood hallway toward the bedroom.

"I'm coming." She met both cats, tails waving, mid-hall. She side-stepped, made it to the coffee maker and poured the last cup. Teddy flopped in the most central, inconvenient spot in the kitchen. Edward sat near the wall, tail curled, an adorable statue. Eyes unblinking, no facial expression visible—inscrutable. She tuned in.

Hey, Edward.

Hi, Mom. Enthusiastic welcome. She knew that look was just a facade.

Hungry?

I could eat. Teddy.

Not you. Edward is a quarter your size. He needs to bulk up.

I'm sturdy. That's what you say. Is that bad? Real concern.

No, Teddy. You really are perfect just the way you are. And she meant it. *We just want to keep you healthy. And sturdy.*

Warm, loving waves from Teddy. *Me, too. What's for breakfast?*

Elizabeth laughed so hard she had to put her coffee cup down. Puzzlement from both cats. When she got control, she gave them each another breakfast; Teddy a tablespoon of diet food, and Edward a good serving of regular.

After guarding Edward so he could eat unmolested, Elizabeth meditated and then dressed.

She sat at her computer and put in 'wolves in California' in the search engine. She got several hits but clicked on the department of fish and game first. She discovered that wolves had been destroyed and hadn't been seen in California since 1924, until recently. Wow. A single male wolf had entered California from Oregon in 2011 and left quite a trail. A tracker had been placed on him and a corresponding map showed his territory, which was vast. They noted that the information wasn't current to protect his location. *Well, I got news for you guys,* Elizabeth thought. *I know exactly where he is.*

Apparently their wolf was of the lone-wolf variety. Wolves are not a danger to humans and were federally protected should one enter California, she read.

After rummaging on several links and sites, she decided to call the wolf rescue place in North County. She wasn't sure how to broach the subject of a wolf sighting, and gee, did one of yours escape and you're just not telling? *That* conversation would go over well.

She saw from the website that they did tours and she figured that might be a great place to start her search. *A little covert op,* she thought. How spy-ish of her. The site said she needed a reservation and to bring raw, bone-in, skin-on chicken legs for the 'feeding tour.' She substituted 'frenzy' in her mind, but erased it. She should at least give the wolves a fair shot. Besides, since they've been around humans, they might 'speak' to her. Now she was energized and inspired. Witness interviews! She laughed thinking how Tig was going to respond. He knew enough about her gift to understand its accuracy, but they both knew that kind of information usually did not go over well with the general public.

She quickly got a reservation for both herself and Tig. She could always cancel his if he had to work. She made it for his next day off. San Jose Koi would have to wait a day. This was more important. Speaking of, she called the Leahys to see how the dogs, Sadie and Ben were behaving. Although it had only been a day, she wanted to check in and also to remind Fred of the importance of neutering Ben. She had an idea that might convince him and outweigh his reluctance.

"Leahy Ranch." Elizabeth recognized Emma's voice.

"Hi, this is Elizabeth Murphy. I came out to your ranch yesterday?"

Emma's voice went from business to pleasure. "Well, Elizabeth! How nice to hear from you. What can I do for you?"

"First, I want to apologize for not staying for lunch after your kind invitation."

Emma made a sound like pshaw, and Elizabeth could not recollect an instance where anyone else had said that. Somehow it fit, though. "No apology. It gets really busy at mealtimes and honestly, I forgot about it myself! But a rain check, okay? We're happy to have you visit anytime."

Emma sounded enthusiastic. Maybe Fred hadn't passed on all the information to Emma. Maybe Emma didn't know about the wolf or that Sadie was pregnant again, by the same Alpha male wild wolf who was also Ben's father.

Elizabeth took a breath. She didn't really have time to vet this all with Fred. Let the chips fall where they may. "Emma, did Fred tell you what is going on with your dogs?"

"He mentioned that they were bothered by wild animals coming near the ranch. That makes sense since they can hear and smell so much better than we can. He also said you talked to Sadie and Ben about their behavior!" Emma was clearly tickled by this. "Talked! Well, whatever you did, they aren't jumping up any more. Still a little barking off toward the hills, but like I said, that's okay. They're protecting us, right?"

"Emma, it's a bit more serious than that. I need your help convincing Fred to get Ben neutered." She expected some resistance, but Emma surprised her.

"I've been telling that stubborn old man the same thing. And to fix Sadie, too, for Pete's sake. I let it go because he was so set against it. We've been married a long time, gotta pick your battles, you know?"

"I think the time may have come for you to insist. I spoke to him about it yesterday because it's directly linked to what's happening."

"Really? Oh, let me turn off the kettle; it's whistling. I want to hear all of this." A clunk as Emma set the phone down but it was picked up again almost immediately. "Okay, shoot."

"First let me say that Sadie is pregnant again." Elizabeth took a breath to continue but Emma interrupted.

"Oh, I just knew it! When she was pregnant with Ben, we were so excited. We expected a cute little litter, but out came this giant pup! I guess I'm glad for Sadie's sake he was the only one, but that's unusual, isn't it?"

"Not necessarily." Elizabeth was grateful for her research. "Since Sadie is not a large female, compared to a wolf, perhaps that's why. However, in the wild, litter size is often determined by available food."

"What do you mean, compared to a wolf?"

Oops. Not the best way to disclose potentially alarming information. "The father of Ben, and the father of her current pup, who is also a single, is a wolf. This wolf has been hanging around the ranch again, communicating with Sadie and Ben. They aren't just barking, they're talking to the wolf."

Vast silence. More silence.

"Emma? Are you all right?"

"That's amazing," Emma said quietly. Almost reverently. "I didn't know there were wolves in California."

"Well, there aren't. Not really. One wolf has made his way into the state. Fish and game know about him because he's wearing a tracker. I assume they could find him if they want, but for now at least, they don't. Maybe something happened to the tracker. Anyway, that wolf could become a problem, so that's why it's really important to get them altered. Ben immediately of course, but after Sadie safely delivers, her too."

"Why? Can't we have more wolf puppies?"

Well, that was a surprise. "It's not a good idea. Ben is a lovely dog, but inside, he is mostly wolf, and as he matures, those traits will further manifest. That is why he's become more aggressive. Neutering can help, but it may not be enough. I think the male wolf is trying to recruit him, or even both of them, to make a pack."

"A pack? Of regular dogs?"

"It's not unheard of. Don't forget, Ben is not a 'regular' dog. He's half wolf biologically, but more wolf than not behaviorally from what I can tell. While I was talking to the dogs yesterday he made it very clear that he was an Alpha, and let Sadie lead because she was his mother. That may not last as he reaches adulthood."

"Oh, my. What about us? Will he turn on us?"

"That is unlikely but possible. You need to neuter him. Also, right now, since wolves and 'regular' dogs are still pack animals, he considers you and Fred his pack. Fred is the Alpha male and Ben accepts that. It's important that both you and Fred retain your rank. You will always have to watch his behavior. He may change as he ages and be less reliable around small animals or children-- even the elderly or what he may perceive as a weak animal."

"I've caught him chasing the chickens, but I never thought anything of it."

"Right now, he is interested in joining his father. You can't let that happen. Not only will you never get him back, but he could get hurt. He is not a pure wolf and doesn't have the wild savvy that his father does. If they join together and something happens to that wolf, it's unlikely Ben will survive."

"What about Sadie?"

"If Sadie joins the pack, their odds for survival go up, but again, Sadie is not a wolf. Not even part wolf. I know she could join the pack, but she would probably want to stay around here and be a part-time pack mate. I've heard of that before. In Colorado, my friend's dogs were part of a pack led by a hybrid wolf. They didn't even know until it was almost too late."

"What happened? How did no one know?"

"She lives in a rural area; everyone has large lots, acres, really. Ranches and farms, like here. All the dogs run loose like here. This hybrid, also someone's pet, would make the rounds and gather all the domestic dogs she could find—"

"She?" Emma interrupted.

"Yes, it was an Alpha female. She made her own pack. My friend didn't find out until she got a call that her dogs, along with a wolf cross, were on a ranch killing chickens. It didn't end well."

"What happened?"

"Fish and game got to the hybrid before the owner could. My friend's dogs had left the ranch by then, but neighbors confirmed that her dogs had been there, too. She called me in tears and told me the whole story. Very sad for all. Her friend had noticed some behavioral changes but nothing huge."

"You're saying this could happen to Ben?"

"It's possible. But you have information now and that is your best ally. If we can get the wolf to move on, and then do our best to protect Ben and Sadie, it should be fine."

"All right. I'll see that Ben gets fixed even if I have to take him myself. The same for the new pup I suppose." A heavy sigh. "Thank you Elizabeth. I'll let you know how it goes."

"I'll keep trying to talk to the wolf. Get him to move. He has a huge territory. If I can convince him that Ben and Sadie are off the market, that might help."

Elizabeth had been on the phone so long that the morning fog had lifted. Her spirits had too, a little. It was up to the Leahys now. From her research she felt pretty secure in the knowledge that the surrounding farms were safe from the wolf. She was saturated in wolf information so she decided to try talking to it once more.

Hey, what about us? A little something? She looked down, and Teddy lay flopped out, his usual position, but his junior assistant lay next to him. In a show of solidarity of weakness due to lack of food, she figured. She smiled but didn't want to leave her mind place of wolves at the moment.

I have to talk to someone. Don't eavesdrop because you won't like it. I have to talk to a wolf. She wasn't even sure they *could* tune in, but caution was the word. If anyone could listen in on her, it would be Teddy. They were linked even when she didn't intentionally create it.

The cats understood. They rose and went out the pet door to the yard, then instantly rethought the wisdom of that and retreated to the bedroom, where even from here, she heard the bed creak signaling Teddy's launch. Maybe time for a new bed, since a new cat, or even a thinner old cat, was out of the question.

She sat in her meditation chair by the window and grounded herself. Feet flat, hands relaxed. She was already mentally focused on the wolf so it took no time at all to send her calls to the ridge where Sadie had seen the wolf. It helped to have a mental picture of him, which she had received from Sadie, and also a location—she'd seen the ridge above the ranch herself.

Hello? Are you there? I am a friend of Sadie. She actually sent the thought of pack mate and not friend, although that was not strictly true. Wolves didn't seem to have 'friends.' Packs were comprised of family units and relations of some degree or another, so at least that was plausible.

She had so much more information this time and had also connected remotely with both Sadie and Ben, albeit unconsciously, while talking about them to Emma, and she got a stirring in her mind right away. She was surprised, and not sure it was the wolf, but she called again.

The way she explained it to Tig when this happened before was like seeing movement out of the corner of your eye. You're not really sure what you've seen, or if you've seen anything, so you try to focus on it. Sometimes it works, sometimes it evaporates. This time it worked.

Not even a word, though. A questioning that filled her mind.

It seemed this animal spent no time around humans. At least not on purpose or during consciousness. She knew the wolf was tagged with a tracking chip. However, the wolf had no recollection of the event and was not bothered by it. Good news for science. Although it had started its journey in Oregon and made its way this far south, it had almost never been seen, and had rarely stayed for any length of time where humans were. A smart creature. She got all of this in a flash. She sent a few random pictures of ranches and humans and was met with a distinct lack of interest. It, well, she'd better call it a he now, wasn't afraid, he was disinterested. Bored even. He had no problem hunting--his territory was vast and full of food--so ranches and farms were not something he sought. He didn't like the smell of mankind and the noise that came with that smell, so was successful in avoiding both. What he did want was a mate. He was the only one of his kind and continually looked for a companion. Why he picked Sadie she would broach another time, but the fact that he chose her, not once but twice, might make convincing him to relocate difficult.

He let her be in his mind. His lack of fear at her probing surprised her. She decided this was to her advantage and just stayed there, out of sight more or less as he moved about. He drank from the creek, caught and ate a rabbit. She made her presence as neutral as possible and added pleasant, warming waves, much as she would for a frightened domesticated animal, or even a feral one. He was unfamiliar with all of this, but seemed comfortable with it. She decided to let him go, considering this first contact a success.

Good-bye, thank you. She sent waves of gratitude and contentment, probably interpreted more as fullness from eating, but still positive, and she left him. One thing concerned her--he was never more than a mile from the Leahys and within that mile lay dangers for him in the form of several other ranches.

When she came out of her communicative state it was getting dark. She was shocked at how much time had passed. Tig would be home and where was dinner?

More importantly, two angry cats, well, one angry cat and one sweet, passive copycat, awaited a scoop of canned food. She complied with lots of pets and kisses. A little guilt for taking so long, but a full dish of kibble told her just how close to death from starvation they had been, since they didn't deign to eat a crumb.

Ten

"Good news!" A door slam heralded Tig's return from work that evening. Two escorts, tails waving, followed him to the kitchen after the traditional thump of his belongings hitting the floor near the door.

Elizabeth put a rack of ribs, garlic mashed potatoes and rolls on the table as he breezed by and kissed her on his way to wash up at the sink. The salad was already on and he automatically pulled utensils and napkins out as he spoke.

"Schedule change. Because of summer schedules, they're changing us to two 12 hour shifts, then our 24 hour shift. We still have three days off. Feels weird, but I'm fine. They said it was an experiment with our station and if it works, others would pick it up. Anyway, that makes my 24 tomorrow and my three days off start the day after."

Elizabeth smiled at his enthusiasm. He loved his job, but he also loved his time off which he instantly filled with pond jobs or work around the house. He spent a little time with his best friend Terry, but now that Terry was a father, that time had shrunk.

"That's great, honey. I have news, too. Not that good, though." Elizabeth started to serve. Tig sat and the little black button nose appeared.

"What's your news? We can go to San Jose Koi sooner now." Tig put hot sauce on his ribs.

"Yes and no." Elizabeth filled him in on the wolf sighting and her need to get to the rescue place. "Do you want to go with me? I made the reservation for both of us, but I can change it."

"Sounds interesting." Tig scooped more mashed potatoes. The black nose apparently liked BBQ sauce and hot sauce as evidenced by more rib meat slipping under the table.

I could never get away with that, came a crabby voice from the floor.

Let's start with how you could never fit on my lap under the table, Elizabeth replied, *and move on to how you don't like laps, and then go back to Edward is a stick compared to you, and finish with my concerns for your health.*

Fine. I was just talking about behavior.

Sure, you were. Elizabeth smiled lovingly at Teddy, whose normally still tail twitched with irritation.

He gets away with everything.

Stop it Teddy. Want to taste hot sauce? That's what Edward's eating.

Of course I do. Cats love hot sauce.

Elizabeth sighed and rose. "Just a sec. Teddy's crying favoritism. I'm going to give him some BBQ & hot sauce."

Tig said nothing, mouth full, but eyebrows raised.

"I'm practicing for having kids."

The eyebrows went higher. "Whaaa?" was all Tig could manage.

"Not literally. There, Teddy. Happy now?" She had put a dollop of the sauces on his plate and one drop on his wet food. She returned to the table. "He sniffed and rejected. Of course."

Cats do not like hot sauce, was the surly rejoinder.

"Sorry about that," Elizabeth continued. "I'd like to visit the wolf sanctuary on your first day off and then go to San Jose Koi. Will that work? Do you have anything going on with that heights pond?"

Tig was finally able to speak. "That was so good, thank you." He always thanked her for cooking. She appreciated that. "No pond stuff unless Karl calls me about his new client. The pond is seasoning right now. Yoshi has shipped the fish from Japan and they should be here soon. I just need to be ready to receive them."

"That's so exciting. They're from different dealers, right? How are you going to quarantine them?"

"I've got some mini-ponds I'm going to fill with Mr. Tanaka's pond water and separate them by dealer. I may have to have more mini-ponds if I have to separate them by their original holding areas. I just have to wait and see."

"Can't you put the shipment with the most or biggest fish in Mr. Tanaka's main pond? Then you won't have to have as many little ones."

"I need them in a small, contained area where I can see them and keep checking them for stress or illness. In that giant lake they can go to the bottom and I'd never know if there was a problem. If they need salt or anything, I need to know right away."

"Oh, yes. I forgot about that." Elizabeth started to clear. "Oh, so that means tomorrow is your 24 so you start at 6 PM, right?" Tig nodded. "So we can see the wolves tomorrow?"

"Sure. I need to check in with everyone, Karl, Yoshi, Goro, but yeah, that should work."

"I'll see if we can go tomorrow." At his questioning look she said, "It's a rescue place, not a zoo, so you need a reservation."

Tig finished clearing while she loaded the dishwasher. She noted that Edward now lay on Tig's chair, a wave of smug wafting toward Teddy, whose sour face showed what he thought.

"I'm going to water a bit." Tig lightly smacked her bum and headed out the back door. She wiped the counters and when she turned around, both cats had abandoned her and followed Tig outside to the pond and the bamboo jungle, all animosity forgotten.

She texted the rescue place about the change and was pleased to get a quick response that her choice was available.

She followed the troop outside to tell Tig the plan but saw he was on the phone. She sat on the edge of the raised deck and scritched the cats who had joined her.

Mom, mom, roll on your back! It feels so good! Teddy lay upside down in ecstasy.

Why not? She lay on her back and the warm deck felt wonderful. It *was* relaxing. Edward climbed on her chest and lay bonelessly, purring. She could still hear Tig on the phone, although from her prone position, she could no longer see him over Edward, flat as he was.

Tig ended his call. "Oh, hey, that was Karl." He must have turned and seen her, but she still couldn't see him. The deck felt too nice to move just yet. He laughed. "That would make a great picture." She figured he took one with his phone since he was still laughing.

"The wolf place is a go for tomorrow," she said, eyes closed. "Noon. We should leave by 10 since I have to stop and get raw chicken legs."

"Raw chicken legs?"

"For the feeding. Bone in, skin on. They were very specific about what to bring."

"Okay." She heard the watering move from the far side of the yard to the upper bamboo bed. "Everything okay with Karl?"

"Yup. He was updating me on his new client. It sounds good. I'll meet with them and Karl with a contract maybe tomorrow after the wolves if there's time or the next evening after my 24."

"Do you think Karl's up to the job?"

"Sure. At this point, he's just coordinating. We're going to do the job together. It's kind of nice having a job I didn't have to scrape to get, or have after a long wait between jobs."

133

"Sounds good. I'm going to shower."

"I'll be right in. NetFilms?"

"NetFilms." It was like a command for the cats now, and they both leapt up and trailed Elizabeth in to assume good viewing positions on the bed.

Eleven

Bright sun greeted them as Tig and Elizabeth attended to individual morning routines. Tig's schedule change threw them both a little off. The cats were never thrown off schedule, unless it had to do with food distribution.

"Elizabeth!" Tig called from the bedroom. "I just got the call. The fish will be here tomorrow!"

She followed his voice. "That's great. When?"

"Morning flight. They will have cleared customs and be put on the first out of LAX. I can pick them up mid-morning. I'll get a text advisory."

"Wow. Then what?"

"I think it's best if I set them up at Tanaka's. Goro already cleared it and the property is so big it's not like it will look bad to guests. I thought about doing it here in the outback or side yard, but even though that is more convenient for me, I decided not to." Tig sat to tie his shoes and Edward oozed into his lap.

"That means you'll have to go into town at least once a day, right?"

"Yes. I know. I think it's better for the fish. Less transport time and one less trauma. If they're already on the property, then I just have to adjust their water to the big pond. It'll be easier to use that pond water if I'm near it. Plus, when the time comes, we just heave ho from the minis to the big pond. No driving or worrying they'll hurt themselves."

"Sounds like a plan."

"You'll help me with transfers, right?"

"Of course. I can check them at the same time." Although Elizabeth wasn't great at 'fish reading,' if she touched or held them, she got reliable results. These fish probably were not exposed to humans much more than a handful of food tossed in every day, and perhaps less than that if an automatic feeder was used. It might be her only chance to double-check their health.

"Karl hasn't been trained yet, so it'd be great if you could help me with that."

"Of course, but you know I love doing it."

"I know. I just think the more people who know how to do it properly, the better." He stood slowly and let Edward slither to the floor. "Who knows, Precision Landscaping and Ponds may get so big that we'll have lots of ponds going and you'll be 'fishing' on your own."

"Ha ha. I get it. Fishing. You're hilarious."

"I know." He gave her his best rascally smile and a kiss. "I'm ready when you are."

"Me, too. I'm so excited to see a real wolf. I know I saw him in my head, but to see one for real, not in a zoo! I'm taking a cooler and ice to keep the chicken cold on the drive. I bet it will be hot up there."

"Close to a hundred by the time we get there."

"Let me get a hat and some water bottles. Sunscreen?"

"Done."

"Okay, let's go."

Of course, 'let's go' didn't mean right now. Elizabeth petted the cats and checked their water. She had to explain to them where they were going and when they'd be back. Tig was trapped into one more feeding. It was quite a production but finally they were on their way.

They stopped at the store for chicken legs as requested. The drive north was easy, traffic-free and lovely. They kept an eye out for bears on Old Creek Road, but of course, they never saw one. Almost every one of their friends had, but alas, not Elizabeth who would have given a lot for that treat. Even Tig wanted to see one. Every time they drove this way, which really wasn't that often, Elizabeth sent out her 'feelers,' but no one ever answered or even seemed close to the road.

They stopped for cold drinks at a convenience store since they were a little early and the heat slapped them in the face. A thirty degree difference from their little coastal town to this one over the mountains.

"Wow. I'm not good at this," Elizabeth said as she raced back to the air conditioned comfort of Tig's truck. "This is why I didn't want a house up here. It's gorgeous with the rolling honey-colored hills, but sheesh, half the year I'd either have to be inside with the A/C or driving madly to the coast."

"Oh, my delicate little flower," Tig teased as they got back on the road. "I love heat, but this a little much, even for me."

They found the wolf rescue center easily and parked in the dusty lot. As soon as they exited the truck they heard barking. Elizabeth was surprised it wasn't howling, but it really sounded like a regular dog. Maybe that's why the Leahys didn't know there was a wolf. It was barking to Ben and Sadie, and just sounded like another of the ranch dogs in the area.

A number of large, high-fenced pens surrounded a huge, old oak that provided a bit of shade. Other small trees dotted the grounds, and where trees were absent, shade structures provided relief from direct sun. Some of the pens had two wolves, but some only had one. Those who were singles, had at least one adjoining fence section. For nose-touching? Elizabeth wondered.

A woman was cleaning a pen with a giant scooper and shovel. Another was filling water troughs. A young man came to greet them.

"Hi, I'm Eric."

After introductions and hand-shakes they were relieved of their chicken and the first woman came over.

"Hi, I'm Kristi. Nice to meet you. Thank you for coming." Kristi's engaging smile and firm handshake welcomed them. She was short, strong-looking, and bronzed from hours of working outdoors in the north county sun. "Eric will take

138

you around and answer any questions you have. I need to finish these pens."

Eric led them to the first large pen containing what he said was a large Arctic wolf and a smaller wolf-malamute hybrid. He showed them an underground den the wolves had been building, but now it was too dry for them to dig. "The ground is like concrete now, so they'll work on it again when it rains."

The Arctic wolf paced and ran in circles along the fence line. "Why does he do that?" asked Tig. "Is he okay?"

"He's fine. That's his normal routine. He's hot and shedding now but healthy."
The wolf was thin but strong and long strips of fur dangled as he ran, trailing like streamers.

"Why is an Arctic wolf out here?" asked Elizabeth.

"He was actually bought as a pup from a roadside stand in Texas. The owner brought him illegally to California in Orange County. He was never wild so he can't be released into the wild. He ate the guy's couch and destroyed the backyard."

"Probably making dens," Tig said.

"Probably," Eric agreed. "Anyway, he's got a home here for the rest of his life." They all watched the wolf lap the pen several times before he settled under the shade structure. "It's a similar story for most of the wolves and hybrids here. Someone thought it would make a good pet and found out differently. Depending on the wolf content of the hybrid, the behaviors and temperament determine if it can be rehabilitated to be fostered out or adopted. Hybrids have special requirements."

They moved on to another area that had four wolves in several contiguous pens. All gray wolves or gray-wolf hybrids, they looked as different from each other as any dog. "I thought gray wolves were gray?" Elizabeth asked.

"Gray wolves come in lots of different colors and looks. These two are brother and sister, but they are completely different."

True, the male was white, much like the Arctic wolf, but much stockier compared to his thin, streamlined cousin. The female was mostly black with a little gray-white mask that made her look shy.

A sudden spate of howling and barking began from the far side and the wolf in the pen next to the siblings joined in.

"What's going on?" Tig asked.

"We have two females who are discussing bragging rights to the Alpha position and they just have to chat once in a while," Eric said. "They can't be together because the females will fight harder than the males. Every day they have a discussion. If a wolf is behaving in a way a higher ranking wolf doesn't like, even from afar, the dominant wolf will settle the other."

"That's interesting. I didn't know that," Tig said.

"There's a lot I didn't know," Elizabeth added. They continued around all the pens and visited with each resident including a four month old puppy, Klein, and a coyote-dog mix. Kristi joined them at her pen.

"I didn't know anything about coy-dogs 'til I got her. I thought there was something wrong with her because she didn't act anything at all like a wolf. The more I worked with her, the more I changed my mind about that, but I still didn't know what was going on. One day Fish & Game was here on a routine inspection and said, 'where'd you get the coy-dog?' Everything made sense after that. I learned a lot then and still am from her. She's a sweetie, but just so different from the wolves. She isn't interested in the pack and has a lot of coyote behaviors. She can never be in someone's home or in the wild." The coy mix sat in her over-sized water bowl and looked adorable. Elizabeth squatted to take a photo and the coy-dog immediately got out and backed into the shade.

Elizabeth tried to read her, but all she got was caution bordering on fear. The dog wished for a better place to hide—a den or cave in her pen would be welcomed. The mix did understand Kristi was here to help her and had bonded to her as much as a coyote can, but she still wished for something different. She just didn't know what.

"Okay, time for chicken," Kristi said and led them back to the little office mid-compound with refrigerators outside. She emptied the chicken legs into a bucket and Eric took Elizabeth and Tig around to feed. Elizabeth could tell from Tig's face that he was surprised that they would be able to feed the wolves themselves. Eric gave directions on how each wolf was to be fed, and specific ones in the case of two wolves sharing a pen. Elizabeth was thrilled and each wolf took the proffered chicken leg politely and then asked for a second. Seconds were distributed and Tig's face showed the same joy she felt.

In the air-conditioned office they were introduced to the office manager, a hybrid bobcat named Neem, and Elizabeth exchanged internal greetings. Neem often talked this way to Kristi, although Kristi was less-aware of the concreteness and accuracy of their exchanges.

Neem did not mind living among wolves at all. Elizabeth presumed it was because Neem was half bobcat and used to wildness, but even Neem didn't know. Some cats just get along with dogs and visa verse. Teddy and Edward not only got along with Buster, but really seemed to care for him. Sort of like an elderly uncle.

Kristi was more than willing to talk wolves but Elizabeth was nervous about bringing up the wolf in the county. Kristi opened the door herself by mentioning the lack of wolves in California and laws regarding wolf ownership in different states.

"I read on a website that one wolf has come to California from Oregon. Have you heard about that?" Elizabeth asked.

"Oh, yes. OR7. He's a lone wolf. Quite a wanderer. He started in Idaho. They think he left Oregon because a rather large pack, twelve or so, I think had already established territory. He's in California now, but might go back."

Well not for a while, Elizabeth thought. *Not unless I can get him away from Sadie and Ben.*

"What makes him travel so far?" Elizabeth asked. Tig was scritching Neem just perfectly, according to Neem.

"Not sure. Probably a mate. If he finds one, he'll probably settle as long as there isn't another pack close by."

Uh, oh.

"Thank you so much for your time. We really appreciate it. We brought a donation, too." Elizabeth handed Kristi their contribution. "Can I call you or text you if I have more questions?"

"Of course. Part of our purpose is to educate. Anytime."

On the drive back over the mountains, Elizabeth and Tig chatted about their individual experiences with the wolves. Elizabeth's mind wandered a bit to her own wolf problem. If OR 7 won't leave Sadie, then what?

When they got home it was only 2:30 so they grabbed some leftovers and Tig left to meet Karl and the new pond client. Tig had to be at work at 6 PM for his 24 hour shift. They would have an early dinner and she wouldn't see him again until dinner the next day.

"Oh, no! The fish." Elizabeth remembered the koi were coming tomorrow. Tig would be at work. Karl couldn't do it on his own; he didn't know enough about koi yet. She couldn't lift the fish herself. It could be dangerous for the fish to keep them in the travel containers any longer than absolutely necessary.

She would have to discuss it with Tig at dinner. They had to resolve the issue before he left.

She could meet the plane and sign for the fish. She was an employee of Precision, at least on paper. She and Karl could get them to Mr. Tanaka's—that was just down the road from the airport. The problem was setting up the mini-ponds with aeration and pumps, and oh, man. So many details and those fish were worth thousands. She started to sweat.

She called Tig, but he didn't pick up. She didn't expect him to if he was in a consultation. She left a voice mail. "It's me. We have to set the ponds up before you go to work tonight. I can't do it by myself, I don't know how. Bring Karl with you and we'll do it all as soon as you're done with the consultation. I'm pulling all the pumps from the garage and your big pond kit. The mini-ponds are behind the house but they're too big for me to get to the front myself. I found four aerators, too. I don't know what else you need. Call me when you get this. Love you, bye."

She then made good on her comments. It was much easier helping Tig than it was thinking of all the things he did. She just hoped to get a head start and save some time. She cleared a path from the back where the ponds--like heavy duty above ground pools--were stored down to the driveway. She heard her phone ring from her pocket and wiped her grubby hands on her pants.

"Hey," she said breathlessly.

"Hey, honey. Thank you so much for the head's up. I don't know how all that slipped my mind. I guess the schedule change threw me. Karl and I are on our way. We're almost there and we can finish. Can you help at the Tanaka's? It will take all of us I think if I don't want to be late for work."

"Of course. Have you called Goro to let him know you're coming? Did you explain all this to him?"

"Crap. Not yet."

She heard the truck pull into the drive and she hung up as she came around the house. They all met on the drive where she had spread everything so he could see what she might have missed.

Karl drove a truck, too, which was fortunate because the formed ponds were two different styles and would not nest in a single pile.

"I cleared you guys a path and wiped out the ponds a little. No black widow spiders. I figure we'll have to wash them out anyway before we fill them, so I didn't want to do it twice."

"Thanks." Tig grunted as he and Karl brought the first two ponds through the side gate around a tight corner.

"Is four enough?" Elizabeth asked. "How many groups of fish do you have?"

"Two dealers, but four containers. I'm going to keep them separated in the ponds the way they were shipped. That way if any are sick, it's contained to the one pond. How many pumps did you find?"

"Four, plus four aerators. I didn't know what you wanted. I can do a water change if I have to."

"I'm sorry about this. The first few days are critical. You'll need to check the water and the fish pretty often for changes. You know fish, by the time you see they're sick, sometimes—"

"It's too late," they finished together.

"Really, it's fine." Elizabeth put a soothing hand on his arm. I can get you by phone if you're not on a call. It'll work out. Maybe they'll tell me they're sick." She smiled.

"If they do, it'll probably be in Japanese." Tig kissed her smudgy cheek.

They finished loading both trucks. As much as Elizabeth wanted to ride with Tig, she took her own car. If the set up ran late, or into difficulties, she and Karl could stay and Tig could get right to work. He kept clean uniforms there (well, she *gave* him clean uniforms to take there) and as he liked to joke, there's nothing like getting paid to take a shower. Full facilities awaited the fire fighters, not only to clean up after a fire, but to make it as homelike as a work place could be. After all, they spent whole days there, trapped in the fire station. No one could leave unless they all left. Sometimes they took the truck and went grocery shopping or to get take out or ice cream. Like any family, too much togetherness led to problems.

The caravan headed into town and traffic was light going in, most of it was heading the other way after work.

Elizabeth had helped Tig set up enough ponds, both regular ones and quarantine ones to know how to get started. Karl was a beginner, but very strong. Almost as soon as Tig made a request, Karl had the part or the hose or held up the end of

146

some heavy thing.   They made a good team, Elizabeth observed.

Tig called Goro on the road and he was there in the gravel drive to greet them. He opened a side gate and they were able get the trucks very close to the pond in the pump room area. That was fortunate since they needed access to the pond itself as the main water source and to electricity for the pumps.

"Karl, we're going to fill these ponds with water from the main pond. That will give the new fish the temperature and salinity they need. They'll sit in their bags of water in the new pond to let both temperatures adjust—maybe 20 minutes--and then we open the bags a little and let them out. By keeping it shallow for now, we can observe them for changes or problems."

"Sounds good. How do they survive a long plane ride in a little bit of water?"

"The water temperature is kept colder and they're anesthetized with a little oil of clove before they're shipped. It keeps them sleepy and they are calm and use less oxygen. It's easy to make a mistake, so I don't use it but I also don't ship thousands of dollars' worth of koi across the planet."

Water from the big pond was pumped into the mini-ponds and Tig quickly hooked up different pumps for filtration and aeration. He threw a net over each one.

"What's that for?" Karl asked.

"Koi will jump out of their ponds sometimes, especially if they are transferred from one place to another."

"They'll also jump if they're sick or injured," Elizabeth added.

"That seems counter-productive to the species," Karl said.

"I know. Tig, remember when Keiko was flashing and jumped out? Thank goodness you were there."

"What's flashing?" Karl asked.

Tig finished fastening down the edges of the nets. "It's when they dart around the pond and sort of rub themselves on something. Usually it means a parasite and it can be serious. Keiko was swimming sideways on the bottom of the pond. If it's an external parasite, they may be trying to physically rub it off, but it can be internal too. It's just instinctual."

"I tried asking her why she jumped and she couldn't tell me." Elizabeth started to help put things back in Tig's truck.

"What are you talking about?" Karl asked. "You asked the fish why she jumped out?" Karl's expression was somewhere between sure that he was being played and alarm that she might believe she talked to fish.

Elizabeth forgot that Karl didn't really know what she did. He knew she 'worked' with animals, but she and Tig agreed to let him think it was more like training them. Ha. Training Teddy. Karl had become so valuable to Tig so quickly, and then working with him in such a frenzy today, she had dropped her guard.

"Uh, sort of," Elizabeth hedged. "I am really good with animals and sometimes they sort of let me know when they're hurt or sick."

"Oh, my mom is like that with her cat." Karl looked relieved. "So, you don't really talk to the fish, right?"

That was so, as far as it went. Keiko was her biggest success, but still she was harder to read or interpret than just about any mammal or bird. Even the wild wolf gave her clearer signals. Something she decided this minute to work on. If Tig was going to buy thousands of dollars in living inventory, she'd better up her game.

"No, fish don't talk to me," she replied with complete honesty.

Karl had tossed the last of the large items in his truck since Tig was going to work. "I gotta get going. Anything else?"

"Elizabeth will be in touch with you tomorrow. Can you be on call? You're checking the heights pond, right? The water quality?"

"Sure, and yup. I'll be writing up the estimate for that new client. Should I show it to you first before I give it to them?"

"No, I gave you all the notes, just double check that what we talked about is in the contract. That waterfall they have is going to be horrible to fix, but if they want it fixed, they have to be aware of the potential for a rise in costs."

"Will do, boss." Karl got into the truck and drove carefully out, not raising any dust.

"He's pretty good," Elizabeth said. "I put my foot in it, though. If he stays with Precision, I guess he's going to find out. I'll think on what to say."

Tig laughed. "I say, if he can't handle it, too bad." He glanced at his watch. "Oh, man, I'm going to be late if I hit any traffic at all.

Goro approached them. "All set for tomorrow? Mr. Tanaka is very pleased with how quickly this has come together. He thanks you." A slight bow.

"You're both welcome, but let's see how the fish shipped and what they look like before we celebrate too much."

"Of course. Would you like some tea?"

"I have to get to work, but thank you. Elizabeth and my assistant will be bringing the fish over tomorrow from the airport."

"You will not be present?" The tiniest frown of displeasure creased his brow.

"No. I have a 24 hour shift which starts in 25 minutes. It was a last minute change I couldn't get out of. However, Elizabeth is the expert with fish. I am with ponds and water, but she is the one you want at the head of the transfer process."

Elizabeth worked to keep her face neutral and immobile. That was news to her. If he wanted a conversation with the fish, maybe she was the expert. But she would do her best. She could call Tig, too, she reminded herself.

"Goro, I've done this many times and it will be fine." Elizabeth tried to reassure both herself and Goro. "You can watch me the whole time. This is what we do, so not to worry. Those fish are in good hands."

What a liar. Those fish better be perfect or they were all screwed. Her legs felt a little weak.

"Well, Goro, as I said, I have to get to work. Elizabeth will call you when she gets word the fish are ready to be picked up." Tig stuck out his hand and Goro took it.

"Yes. Tomorrow, then."

Elizabeth added. "Goro, Tig will be right over after his shift ends at 6 PM tomorrow to check on things personally, all right?" That little gem had just occurred to her. Genius born of desperation.

"Absolutely," Tig added. She could tell from the heartiness of his reply that he hadn't thought of it either.

Elizabeth bowed to Goro and to her delight, he bowed back. She finally felt like it was going to be okay and they took their leave. She watched in her rearview mirror as Goro shut gates behind them and watched them in turn.

Twelve

Elizabeth passed a quiet night alone with the cats. It was always strange when Tig had his 24 hour shift and didn't sleep at home. It was almost easier when he rotated into the night shift since then he was gone every night and it was worked into the family routine. Almost easier.

She woke to find both cats snoring on the bed. When Tig was gone, she left the door open and they slept with her. The door was closed when Tig was there. Teddy had complained but in reality, two cats took up an awful lot of square footage on the bed. She and Tig had made the hard call when they had awakened one too many times with cramped muscles and had been pushed to the edges of the bed while the cats stretched luxuriously down the middle.

As she made her way to the kitchen she heard the telling thump as Teddy jumped off the bed to follow. Edward would be there too, but was too light to make a noise on the carpeted bedroom floor.

The overcast day had let her sleep in a little. She fed the cats and got her coffee, then sat at the window for her customary morning meditation. As she grounded herself and focused, she flashed on baby Garrett and realized she hadn't touched base with Janie in a couple days. Mental note, then she slipped into her meditation. She checked on Tig and her clients. Tig's energy was happy, as usual. She moved on to Rachel and Yuki, the cat nabbed and abandoned by Rachel's ex-husband. Nothing jumped out, so he must be healing well. Millie and Jato. Must check in with Millie, since Jato might be too emotional to get medical information. Sadie and Ben. Ben was very distressed and she was momentarily concerned until he showed her where he was. He was awaiting neutering at the vet. He had not been fed since midnight because of today's anesthetic, and so was very hungry and nervous. She made another note to call the Leahys later and check on him, and them. She sent him calming waves and reduced his hunger. He settled. She checked in with Sadie and she was anxious too, since it was the first time they'd been separated. She was still at home, and had been fed and so was less physically uncomfortable. Elizabeth checked on the pup. A female, much smaller than Ben had been at this stage. That was good. Elizabeth already found the pup to be less wolf-y, for lack of a better term, than Ben. More good news. She knew that could change, but for now, things were about as positive as they could be.

She mentally wandered over to the canyon where she'd left the doe and fawn. They weren't there, bedded down for the day, which surprised her a little. Maybe they change sleeping places every few times? She didn't know but that made sense in terms of the predator-prey relationship. She looked for their energy, which in this state was best described as a trail of glitter, and discovered it led back down the canyon.

When she'd been a little girl and seen the 'glitter trail' she always thought it would lead to fairies or something other-worldly. She was always slightly disappointed to find it only led to some animal or another. Now she appreciated the visual, but she enjoyed the potential for magic it always created in her.

She found the doe and fawn camped out at their rescuers' house. Bedded down for the day in their backyard garden, all Elizabeth felt was calmness and security from both the animals and the household. They must have reached some agreement she figured.

She let herself drift up out of the canyon and north to the ridge above the Leahys. She searched for the wolf. She felt him, but couldn't 'see' him. It almost felt like he was 'cloaking' himself in some way, to use the Star Wars vernacular. That was unusual for her. If she could feel an animal she could usually 'see' it, too. However, she had never seen the wolf in the real world before her visit to the sanctuary. When she had been with him before, he had let her, and she had only seen him through Sadie. Maybe it was time to find him in Cuyamaca canyon for real. A little shiver ran up her spine at that. Maybe not. Cross that bridge later. After her experience at the wolf sanctuary, she thought she'd feel more connected to them, and maybe to OR7, than she had before. It didn't happen that way. They were very closed animals. It wasn't like the fish, who didn't seem to think like she did. Keiko did her best, but it was just different, and she was quite open and happy to 'talk' to Elizabeth. But it was water, fuzzy, like hearing it far away, or in a language like English, but not English. Hard to explain. The wolves though, were just not really interested in her. She was not of their pack; Kristi was their human pack leader, so they didn't really see the value in even a temporary relationship with Elizabeth. Kind of rude, really.

Elizabeth smiled in her meditation and continued to probe for the lone wolf. She connected with Sadie first, who was asleep and used her to help find him.

Instantly he was there. She saw him near the creek again. He was digging a den, apparently something he did to help pass the time as well as from instinct. He dug near the creek where the earth was relatively soft. Winter rains had been scarce and the ground was hard all over the county. The farmers and ranchers were having a tough time as were all the rural fire departments.

Hey. She sent.

A questioning feeling. He knew she wasn't Sadie but was connected to her.

How are you? She sent a series of feelings and pictures with the words: for hunger she sent the feeling with a picture of the rabbit he'd caught; for health she sent a feeling of energy along with a picture of himself looking hale and hearty.

He seemed to grasp the concept and sent back positive waves along with some pictures of what he had seen--a mule deer leaping away, far too healthy to be dinner for him, a rattlesnake wriggling away swiftly when they'd met on a game trail, a whiskey jay screaming at him as he passed through its territory.

He raised his head and looked right at her. He sent a picture of Sadie with her. He knew who she was. A little scary. No animosity with the picture, though.

She experimented. She sent a picture of him with Sadie, and then moved them apart.

He didn't like that picture and barked. Just like a dog. Or the wolves at the sanctuary.

She moved them back together and he relaxed. Interesting. She showed a picture of Ben.

He sent back that he knew Ben was his pup, part of him. Building a pack.

She didn't want him to read her anymore. For a wild animal, he was certainly skilled at this. She separated herself from his energy and showed herself moving away from him. He dismissed her and continued work on the den.

She returned to her living room, both proud of her growing ability, and anxious about how to use it to help the Leahys and their dogs. This was the first time in her practice she felt she might be out of her league to help an animal. This was big and had several down sides, not only for Sadie, Ben and the Leahys, but also the wolf. She felt he was her responsibility. Time was not on her side, before he was discovered. If the wolf was determined to

156

create a pack, she wasn't sure how she could prevent it without human assistance and often that did not go well for the animal.

The airport could be calling anytime now with the delivery of the fish. She decided to go to Mr. Tanaka's and re-check the ponds. She wanted to be absolutely sure the water was ready. She grabbed the spare pond bag from the garage and checked to be sure it had temperature gauges and chemical tests. She knew she'd need to check for ammonia after the fish arrived. They often dumped ammonia from their bodies into the water and she needed to neutralize that right away.

She texted Karl to let him know she was going to check but that the fish hadn't arrived yet. She wanted to be sure he could join her at Tanaka's. The airport people could help her load them, but unloading she would need help.

He sent back that he was at the Masuka's pond in the heights doing a water change, but that their pond should be ready for fish in the next couple days. Great, since Elizabeth and Tig were buying from San Jose Koi soon. That was exciting. She loved going to the big fish dealers and seeing hundreds of beautiful fish. The babies were so adorable, and the battleship-sized ones so regal. He would be ready anytime she called.

Last, she phoned Goro. "Hello?" he answered right away.

She wondered what she would have said if he'd spoken in Japanese. "Hi, Goro. This is Elizabeth Murphy."

"Yes. Are you well?"

"Yes, thank you. I would like to check the ponds one more time before the fish arrive. Is now convenient? You don't need to be there, but I wanted you to know. I expect a call from the cargo people any time and would like to do a water check before we actually have the fish."

"Ah, yes. Excellent. You may come anytime. I am here."

She wasn't sure if he'd said, 'you may come anytime I am here,' or if he'd said that as two sentences. It didn't matter now, but . . . where was her brain? *I must be more nervous than I feel,* she thought.

"Great. I'm on my way. See you in about half an hour."

"Until then."

"Okay, bye." She disconnected. "I guess I'd better brush up on my Japanese etiquette. Or check my hearing."

She texted Tig that she was going there as well, and double checked cat food and water to prevent starvation. Both cats were out on the back deck sunning as the morning fog burned off to create another stellar day.

Bye guys.

Bye Mom. Edward.

Snacks? Teddy.

I'll be back later. You have kibble.

Some non-word sound of disgust from Teddy, like *ackggh.*

You'd think they had a bowl of poison, not kibble. Elizabeth laughed to herself.

The fertile fields whipped by in a blur of green broken by bright squares of flowers on her way to town. Soon she was turning under the big torii gate that signified Mr. Tanaka's property.

She went through the side gate nearest the pump room with her bag of supplies.

Goro came to meet her from the path to the house.

"Good morning," he said with his slight bow.

"Good morning." Elizabeth bowed back.

"You are getting good at that." Goro smiled his approval.

"I think it is a wonderful custom. Better than shaking hands!" Elizabeth laughed and Goro joined in. He looked surprised that he had done so and quickly gathered his composure.

Elizabeth had Tig's cheat sheet in her bag. She knew he knew what he was doing, but had asked him to help her write notes, oh, a year ago? When she had become more involved in the business. Clients had increased but Tig still felt they couldn't pay an assistant, so Elizabeth helped if it was busy. The sheet ensured that she would follow the proper procedure to the letter and not skip any steps. It also had an equipment list which she had double checked before she left home. The problem was, what to do if there was a problem. She hadn't been around enough to help Tig trouble shoot, so only a few scribbled notes in the margins addressed that.

Just before she left, she had tossed in the fish's shipping information to be sure she didn't forget it.

She felt the whisper of anxiety stir and squashed it. "I'm going to get a sample of the main pond and then samples from all these quarantine ponds," she told Goro.

To her surprise Goro said, "I will let you do your work. I have some to do myself. Please stop by the house when you are ready to leave."

At her questioning look, he added, "If you would be so kind."

"Of course. Anything I can do." She bowed a tiny, awkward, but heartfelt bow of thanks.

Goro smiled and bowed back, then headed back toward the house.

She got out her little chemistry set and arranged it to her liking. She smiled because it always reminded her of the Mr. Science set she'd had as a child. She and Tig had that in common— he'd had one, too.

She arrayed test tubes, a stand, her chemicals and her list, then got samples from each of the ponds. She brought a Sharpie and masking tape to make labels for each of the samples. She did not want to mess this up.

She checked the temperature of the main pond, and then that of the smaller ones. Here in town it was ten degrees warmer than where she and Tig lived, so the pond was warmer than theirs, too, despite its larger size. Tig had asked about a heater on their previous visit. Only in the winter if it got very cold. Fish adapt well to cold climates, oddly enough, if is gradual, like the turning of seasons. She needed to know temperature so she could help the new fish adapt. Too hot or too cold would leave them susceptible. Next she checked PH, nitrates and nitrites. So far, so good.

She wanted to text Tig the information and saw Tig had texted her. All good at his end. She sent the information and got a text back right away that confirmed her numbers were fine.

She checked her list and packed up her kits. Done for now. She put her things in the car and headed for the front door of the main house.

She rang the bell and in a minute or so Goro opened the door.

"Come in." He opened the door wide. She knew the routine now and removed her shoes and put them in the shoe rack. Then she did take him up on his offer of house slippers.

He led her to the living room she'd seen before with the great view of the pond. She had a slight shuffling step as her slippers slid along the hardwood hall. Goro did not and she saw it was because his soft shoes had backs, whereas the guest slippers did not. Hers were also one-size fits all, which of course, is never true. She ice skated herself to a couch facing the windows where he indicated she should sit. On a low table sat a bowl of what looked like small colored buns. On a straw mat on the floor was a lovely tea set with handleless cups, a matching pot and a wooden whisk.

Goro knelt on the mat and bowed slightly to her. He held out the bowl with the buns in both hands and said, "Please have these sweets." He set the bowl back and she nodded and helped herself to a square green one. A small bite and sweetness wrapped in a slightly rubbery texture was the sensation. She set the sweet down on a small dish in front of her.

Goro did not ask if she wanted tea, but began lifting utensils and arranging items. There was much switching of hands and stirring of the water, changing directions and things Elizabeth noticed, before he scooped green powder into the hot water and whisked it to a froth. He did not explain what he was doing and she reminded herself to investigate Japanese customs. He prepared the tea without comment, although at one point he made a slight noise, and with such focus she felt she shouldn't make small talk. She alternated between watching his production and drooling at the amazing view of the pond. From this room she saw the pond extended slightly under the house, making it possible for the koi to come right up to the windows. That would be great if it were possible at their house. Then they could see the pond and the fish all the time. As it was, the pond was about ten feet from the back door so that would not work. *Close enough*, she thought.

Goro laid down his whisk and carefully poured tea into one of the lovely cups. He then picked it up with his right hand and set it in his left palm. She was about to reach for it when he rotated it with two efficient twists so that the lovely flower pattern faced her. He then set it on the table within easy reach. He nodded, indicating it was all right for her to pick it up.

Unsure, but honored at what was clearly a ceremony of some sort, Elizabeth didn't feel right just picking up the cup and slurping away. She bowed from the waist and picked it up with her right hand and set it flat on her left palm the way he'd done. She didn't turn it, but kept the cup and her hands in position and took a small sip. It was delicious, slightly bitter and earthy, like nothing she had tasted before. Of course she and Tig had been to Japanese restaurants and even had green tea, but this tea was different.

Her surprise must have shown because when she risked a glance at Goro, he smiled and nodded approvingly.

Apparently the silent period was over, because Goro said, "Thank you for this honor."

Elizabeth had no idea what to say. Way out of her cultural depth, she was utterly confused. She managed, "You're welcome. Thank you for the tea." And for lack of any other ideas, she bowed as deeply as she could, seated on the plush couch. That seemed highly inadequate to her but Goro looked pleased.

She was saved from further comment by her phone vibrating from her pocket. She was grateful it didn't happen mid-tea preparation. She didn't recognize the number.

"Excuse me, Goro, I need to take this." She stood and bowed a little and headed toward the front door for some privacy. She saw Goro begin to pick up the tea things.

"Hello?"

"Is this Precision Landscaping and Ponds?"

"Yes it is." Rats, she should start answering her phone that way.

"Airport cargo. Your pick up is ready. When can you come and get it?"

"Oh, that's great! I can come right down. I'm just a few minutes away. Where do I go?"

"Next to the main terminal you'll see a yellow sign with an arrow that says 'Cargo.' Pull in and come to the office to sign the paperwork."

"I'll be there soon. Anyone in particular I should ask for?"

"Nope. Just check in at the office and one of us will help you load if you need it."

"Great! See you soon."

She sent off a quick text to Tig and to Karl and shuffled back to the living room. Goro entered from what she presumed was the kitchen.

"The fish are here!" She couldn't hide her excitement. "Thank you so much for the tea. That was so beautiful. I have to go to the airport and pick them up. Karl will meet me here to transfer them to the ponds. Oh! This is so great." She shuffled madly to her shoes by the front door, Goro trailing her and smiling.

She knew she was a little disjointed now, but this was big. She didn't want to mess it up for Tig or the business, but picking up the fish, signing those papers, and being the first one to see them. Almost too much. *This must be what Tig feels.* She knew he loved his fish but had never really put herself in his shoes.

"Thank you Elizabeth for your care and enthusiasm in this venture." Goro was so solemn, but she noted a twinkle in his brown eyes.

"It's a real pleasure, Goro, I assure you."

"I see that it is."

"I'll be back soon with your babies!" She had replaced her shoes and grabbed her purse. She sailed out the door noting Goro's surprise at the word 'babies.'

"Oh, well. Probably not the first mistake I've made with this deal." She turned her car around and drove the short distance to the airport. The cargo area was well-marked and she had no problem parking and finding the office. The airport itself only had one terminal and one baggage claim. She loved it. Completely NOT like the big city airports.

Behind the counter she saw a small office and beyond that was a glass wall with a view of planes and hangars and bustle.

A young woman looked up from her computer when Elizabeth entered. "Can I help you?"

"Yes, I just got a call that my cargo arrived. Precision Landscaping and Ponds?"

"Lemme see." A few key board clicks. "Here it is. Cleared customs in LA and I have some things for you to sign."

Amy, for that was the name on the desk plate, brought over quite a stack of paperwork.

"Don't worry; you don't sign all of it. It's transit information, customs information and a manifest."

Elizabeth was relieved. Amy pulled the few sheets she needed to sign.

Elizabeth was hesitant. "These are fish from Japan and I'm wondering what I do if they are damaged?"

"They've been packed properly, you can probably still eat them."

Ack! "No, they are live fish. Um, valuable collectibles, not food. What if I sign for them but something happened en route?"

"Oh, no worries. This is only the first set of paperwork. You'll get the second when you actually receive the cargo. You can check it right here."

"I guess I can open the boxes." Elizabeth wasn't entirely sure how the fish were packed for shipment. She knew how they were packed when they drove them down from San Jose. A big plastic bag filled with air and a little water. Then put in a cooler and tucked behind the front seats on the floor. If they had to stop suddenly, the fish wouldn't bang their noses.

"Sure, whatever you need to do." Amy was either very flexible or didn't care. Probably a little of both.

Elizabeth signed and Amy paged someone. A stocky man came from the hangar or warehouse and took Elizabeth back to a cargo bay. Four large Styrofoam cooler-type boxes were stacked with Tig's company name written on them. They were wrapped together in a big bundle of something like plastic wrap for food, but much heavier duty.

"Can I check them before I sign?"

"Sure. Lemme cut this plastic."

Before Elizabeth could even register concern about cutting near the fish, the man had whipped out a knife and slashed through the thick binding. He peeled it away and looked at her.

"Want help opening them?"

"No, I'd better do that." Elizabeth peeled off a layer of tape sealing the first box and carefully removed the lid. An inflated clear plastic bag filled the interior. She saw two eight inch fish sitting in just enough water to cover their fins and keep them upright in transit. They were beautiful; a solid black one with a red dot on its head, and a black and white one. The markings were clear and defined and when she sent out a feeler to see how they were, she got back a wave of muddled contentment. They were still feeling anesthetized, but weren't afraid or traumatized.

She was elated. Yoshi, Tig's fish buyer, had done a great job so far. She prayed the others were healthy too. She quickly closed that box and made her way down the pile, being careful not to puncture the bags. She needed them intact until they had a fresh oxygen source in the quarantine ponds.

She moved the third box giving her access to the bottom one and her heart dropped to see that the side of the last Styrofoam box had collapsed inward. She quickly opened the box and the plastic bag was deflated and floating atop the water and the lone fish inside.

"Oh, no. Oh, no," she moaned. She quickly opened the bag and the fish was still. It was the main fish Tig had mentioned Tanaka had wanted:

the pure white one with the red dot like the Japanese flag.

She gently felt the fish. There was life. "Oh, my god."

"What happened? Is it okay?" the cargo man asked.

"No, it's not. I need oxygen. She thought fast. This was a shop of sorts after all. "Do you have an air-compressor? A small one? I need to get some oxygen in here."

"Yeah, sure. Lemme look."

She sent calming waves to the fish, that help was on the way, mostly because that's the only thing she could think to do right now. She had to get air to the fish and then get it to the pond as quickly as possible.

"Here ya go." The man had returned with a small compressor and with a hose attached.

"Sorry little guy, gonna be noisy." Elizabeth untied the top of the bag and cinched it with her hand around the hose. "There's gonna be a leak or a hole in the bag I think. Can you get some duct tape or something?"

"Sure." He took off again and Elizabeth turned on the compressor. It obediently filled up the bag in seconds, but when she turned it off again, the bag deflated from a small gash near the top.

Duct tape was thrust at her. "Can you tear off a piece and put it over the hole while I hold all this?" Elizabeth asked. She didn't wait but turned on the compressor again and the bag filled. Now that she knew where to look, she saw the hole gape. He put tape over the hole but it wouldn't hold. She wanted to cry. She didn't know how much time this fish had, but she knew she had to save it. She thought about just running for the car, but something told her she needed to buy time now.

"A bag! Do you have another plastic bag? We can put this one inside another and fill it and seal it that way."

"We've probably got one somewhere."

She kept refilling the leaking bag until he returned with a black plastic trash bag. Not ideal, but "Is it clean? Unused, I mean?"

"Yeah. It's new."

"Okay, help me lift this guy." Elizabeth didn't care if she was short with him or even rude, she just had a sense that she was running out of time.

Together they put the leaky bag into the larger one and filled it with air. She tied it closed and it held.

"Do you have hydrogen peroxide in a first aid kit somewhere?"

Jaime nodded and raced off returning with the familiar brown bottle.

She dumped the hydrogen peroxide into the water to add to the oxygen. Another emergency tactic.

"Okay, uh, Jaime," she squinted to read his embroidered name on his work shirt, "please help me load these. It's critical that I get them into fresh water. I am just down the road. If you can't give me the papers to sign right this second, I'll have to come back. I need to make sure these guys are safe.

They're valuable specimens and I can't risk losing any."

"Sure. No problem. Do you want to file a complaint with the airline?"

"Maybe, but not now." She couldn't begin to think about that.

"Okay, move your vehicle to the yellow loading zone outside the rolling doors. I'll meet you with the fish."

She raced for her car and moved it. When she pulled up to the doors he was just exiting a smaller door. He had put the fish on a flat dolly and put the crushed Styro box into a cardboard one.

"Thank you so much for your help," Elizabeth said.

"No problem." He thrust a sheaf of papers at her and she signed wherever he told her. She didn't know if she was signing away her right to complain later, but her main goal was to get the fish back to the ponds.

She took her copies and leapt into the driver's seat and raced down the road to the exit. She forced herself to calm down. Getting in an accident or stopped for speeding wouldn't help matters at all. The two miles to the torii entrance of Mr. Tanaka's took a year at 35 miles an hour.

She pulled in and Goro already had the side gate open. She reversed and put the hatch as close to the ponds as she could.

Goro saw something was wrong and moved quickly to help under her direction. Where was Karl? He was supposed to be here. Helping. Learning. She could have used his moral support if nothing else. She didn't want to tell Goro anything unless she had to.

"Open the boxes and put one bag into each pond, but leave the bags closed for the moment." She turned her full attention to the flag fish as she thought of it.

The black plastic bag was still inflated. She had no idea what she would find when she opened it. Goro raised an eyebrow at the black bag, but she ignored it. She realized her heart was racing and that she was shaking. *Get hold of yourself,* she admonished. She took a deep breath and set the black bag into a mini-pond. She untied the top and worked it off the clear, damaged bag. There was nothing she could do, so she let the water mix and prayed.

The fish lay still. Elizabeth was unsure if it was alive. She put her hand under it and supported it, then gently moved it forward and back, forcing water through its gills. She felt it stir deep within. The tail finally swished in slight, gentle movements. She worked the clear bag out of the pond while still cradling the fish. She stilled her hand and the fish slowly moved off on its own.

Elizabeth exhaled a huge breath and sat back on her haunches. "Whew." She felt her eyes tear up and fought it. How would that look? She finally looked at Goro and said, "So far, so good, but we're not out of the woods yet."

He looked puzzled at her phrase.

"I mean, we'll have to wait and see how he does. I'm not sure how oxygen deprived he was and for how long. The good news is he was kept very cold and anesthetized, so he might be fine."

He nodded.

"Okay, let's get the rest of these guys out." Goro helped untie the bags and let the fish float into their new homes.

She checked each pond and the water quality. She monitored each fish in turn, returning to the flag fish. Yoshi had bought eight to ten inch fish of the highest quality. Elizabeth, in no way a fish expert, could see that. Their colors glowed brightly, the edges of the markings were clear. Their fins were clean and whole and all scales intact; the eyes bright and anesthetic wearing off. They didn't appear to have suffered any shipping damage except the one in the collapsed box.

She took a picture of each and sent it to Tig. She would tell him the whole story later, but for now, everyone was okay.

She stood slowly, unkinking from so long at crouching and crawling. The worry, well panic, had taken its toll. She was exhausted. Where the hell was Karl?

"I'm sorry to impose, Goro, but may I use your bathroom?"

"Of course. You have worked very hard and I will see that Mr. Tanaka knows this. Please come with me."

She followed him to the door, kicked off her shoes—it was almost automatic—and headed for the half-bath Goro indicated. She washed her hands and face and used the toilet, then washed again. Her curly brown hair had escaped its bun in all the excitement and she did her best to contain it. She still looked a little witchy, but oh well.

When she came out Goro had prepared a snack and put it on a tray. "I know you have worked long and might be hungry. Here is something for you." He handed her the tray, somehow knowing she'd want to stay near the fish. "Wait; let me hold this while you put on your shoes." He smiled and took the tray back.

Maybe being psychic was a job requirement for a houseman? She did as he suggested then stood on the front porch while he handed her the tray.

"Thank you so much," Elizabeth said. "How do you say thank you in Japanese?"

"Arigato."

"Well then, ari-gato," she stumbled bit. *Gato, like cat in Spanish*, she thought. *I can remember that. Maybe.*

She set the tray in her car, still parked rear-facing the ponds. She checked everybody once more and then ate every bit on her tray. She lay back for just a minute and fell straight to sleep.

Thirteen

Elizabeth woke in the back of her car, disoriented and achy, to the muted sound of her cell phone vibrating. She had drooled a bit on her pillow, one of the pond supply kits. Her neck was sore and when she pushed her hair away from her face to look at her cell screen, she felt a big dent in her cheek where it had rested on a seam. Great.

She saw it was Tig.

"Hello?" She was a bit groggy.

"Are you okay?"

"Just sleeping."

"Sleeping? Bets?"

He only called her that when he was extremely concerned about her. She woke up fast. "I'm fine, really. I'm at Tanaka's and everything's good here. I just didn't want to leave the fish and sort of dozed off."

"At Tanaka's?"

"In my car." A moment of silence.

"Are you sure you're okay?"

"Yes, I'm fine. I'll do another check."

"I'm on my way. I'll do it. Wanna head home?"

"No, I'll wait for you." She glanced at her phone and saw it was after six. Slept the day away. Wow.

"How was Karl? Did he help out? Do you think he learned anything?"

"He never showed. He texted me that he was going to, but didn't make it. The last I heard he was going to check water quality at Masuka's. I didn't have time to follow up and then I just forgot."

"That's not like him. Maybe he got sick."

"Car accident? And couldn't text? He's probably fine." Elizabeth didn't want to spend the energy to worry about Karl right now on top of the flag fish worry.

"Okay, I'm leaving now. See you in a bit." They disconnected.

Elizabeth hated to ask Goro, but she had to use the bathroom again. She looked at each fish but didn't touch them or take water samples. They all were moving, if not swimming. Sometimes their own fish just hovered over the bottom, wagging their tails, so this behavior was normal. She likened it to dozing, but she had no idea. Keiko had been unreceptive to her query if fish napped. Keiko implied it was a rude question. Mr. Tanaka's brood seemed to be adjusting, so she slowly made her way to the front door, still stiff from her impromptu nap.

Goro already had the door open for her. How did he do that? A delicious smell wafted from the house and her stomach growled in response.

"I'm sorry Goro, but may I please use your restroom again? Tig is on his way."

Goro held the door open further. "Of course. Please."

Shoes off, she went directly to the half bath. Sure enough, she had a crease in her cheek the size of a pencil. She sighed knowing nothing but time would uncrease it.

When she came out, Goro met her in the hall. "I have prepared some food for you and your husband. Please have some."

The delicious smell had increased to the point where she could not refuse and thought perhaps she might die if she did not eat whatever Goro had made. She got a brief wave from Teddy who just said, *Ha!* or the equivalent sentiment. *I guess that's how he feels about food*, poor thing. She wanted to wait for Tig. She really did. But she did not wait. Goro guided her to a small table off the kitchen, no view of the pond but one of the rock garden. Lovely, but the food was her focus. Beautiful, small white square plates dotted the table and each held something different and pretty. *How do you make food so pretty?* she wondered briefly before she sat and Goro put a napkin across her lap like a waiter in a five star restaurant. Some things she recognized right away, like rice and teriyaki chicken, but others she did not. It was too much.

"Thank you so much Goro. You have no idea. . ." she trailed off because her salivary glands were working overtime.

"You are welcome. I have more for your husband, so eat as much as you like."

"You are so kind." It was killing her to be so polite with the food taunting her. Fortunately, he bowed and left the room.

The only thing that stopped her from choking to death was that Goro had left her chopsticks and not a fork. Otherwise, she would have shoveled until she burst. She was forced to eat more slowly as her skill was not great. It got better, though. Her first hunger pangs reduced, she sipped the green tea he had made. Not the stuff from the elegant ceremony, but a light, fragrant jasmine, a perfect accompaniment. As she relaxed and breathed, she heard Tig's truck arrive, and the front door open as presumably, Goro went out to talk to Tig.

She couldn't tear herself away from the table just yet. Tig would want to see the fish right away anyway, she justified. She'd go out in a minute and catch him up. Or, maybe better, she'd wait in here for him to eat and then she'd tell him about the cargo issue. Yes. That was better. She tweezed up cucumbers in a sweet vinegar-y marinade. Heaven. Tofu in a delicate broth. Seaweed, but light and not fishy tasting. Other dishes she could not identify, but readily tasted on the merits of Goro's previous offerings. When she really could not eat another bite, she heard the front door open again and both men entered.

Nothing for a moment and she recognized the familiar pause as Tig removed his work boots with many lacings and either put on slippers—unlikely—or just stayed in socks. Goro preceded

Tig to her table. No talking so he must have told Tig about the meal outside.

Tig bent and kissed her and they assessed one another as he sat. He looked tired to her. No smoky smell, so maybe no fire. She saw from his face she still looked a little flyaway and that her crease remained prominent. They smiled.

Goro said, "I am glad you liked my humble offering."

"Are you kidding? Humble? It was crazy good!" Elizabeth's turn of phrase drew a smile and there was no mistaking her enthusiasm. "Thank you so much."

Goro turned to Tig. "As I said, your wife did a remarkable job today. Please enjoy and I will leave you two for a moment."

Again, Elizabeth felt like they were in a restaurant and not in someone's private home.

"What did Goro tell you about the fish?"

"He mentioned the shipping box was damaged but that everything was fine."

"It was a little scary. Kind of stop and go for a bit. How do they look to you?"

Tig, much more adept at chopsticks than Elizabeth, talked and ate in between. "Good. They seem on track. Even the tancho."

"Tancho?" Elizabeth asked.

"The red spot guy."

"Oh, I've been calling him the flag fish."

Tig laughed. "True enough."

She watched him eat for a moment, and then began filling him in on the day starting with the cargo office.

Unusual for him, he didn't interrupt. She attributed it to his hunger and the amazing food, but when she got to the air compressor part he said, "Wow. Quick thinking."

She smiled at his praise and continued to the part where she fell asleep in her car.

"Yes, I can see that. How are you feeling now?"

"Pretty good. Should we do a water change before we leave?"

"You read my mind." He leaned back from the table, sated.

Goro entered on cue. "Goro, that was fantastic. Thank you so much."

"You are welcome."

Tig rose and bowed and Goro bowed back. Elizabeth, late to the party, rose and bowed too, nearly tipping over her chair.

"We have to do a water change and then if all seems well, we're taking off for the night. We'll be back in the morning to check again, all right?"

"Of course. Whatever is necessary."

"Where do you want the water to go?"

Goro looked confused. "Water to go?"

"When I pump it out of the mini-ponds, where should I put it. Or not put it? It will have ammonia in it, but no salt."

"Ah. Along the fence line is fine. All the ponds?"

"Not the main pond, but yes. Only about half the water out of each for now. I may do another water change tomorrow morning if they need it. Depends on how much ammonia the fish dump.

Then I'll refill from the main pond. Do I need to refill that as I continue to take water? Is your auto-fill engaged?"

"The auto-fill is fine so no problem. I will bid you good-night then." He led them to the front door and waited while they put on their shoes.

The long summer days meant later sunsets so it was still light when they began the water change. With both of them it didn't take long and this time Elizabeth sent out feelers to the fish as they worked. All were well. The tancho, her flag fish, was a little weak but recovering and other than feeling slow and dozy, was not ill or injured. She gave them each a mental pat and turned to watch Tig as he finished. He still wore his uniform, having rushed to help her and the fish straight from work. He looked pretty good, she thought. Then she remembered how she looked and sighed. She would never be a great beauty, but she did have her merits. Tig turned and caught her looking at him. He could be very intuitive when he chose. He came over and hugged her tight. "You did a great job today. Thank you. I know it must have been rough on your own."

She felt her anxiety drain away. "I hope Karl's okay." Her voice was muffled, tucked into his shoulder.

"I'll find out. I couldn't have a better partner than you, you know." He kissed her gently but somehow passion edged in as their lips met. Although she was tired, beyond tired, really, she responded.

"Let's go home," she said.

*   *   *   *

After tossing the cats some canned food Elizabeth and Tig shared a lengthy shower. Two angry cats filled with indignance and impatience waited outside the closed bedroom door.

This is not right, Teddy said. Elizabeth could hear him in her head after the shower was off. Not that the sound of the water was the reason. She had been distracted.

What's going on? Edward.

They've been gone all day and we've been here, all alone. What if burglars had come in and taken all the food? Then what? More in that vein. Elizabeth opened the door.

"Okay, you poor abandoned and abused kitties. Come in."

Finally.

Hi, Mom! Where's Dad? Edward went right into the misty humid bathroom to find Tig.

Elizabeth, dressed in her super sexy flannel PJs, padded down the hall to dish up more canned food. She did feel a little guilty. She *had* been gone all day, and Tig had been gone since the night before. Then they got home and didn't spend any time with the cats. Well, she had thrown down some canned food. A token, as Teddy would put it. It had been such a stressful day and she'd felt so relieved to see Tig show up, the Cavalry really, and in his uniform. There'd been no hope for her after that.

181

Teddy correctly interpreted her guilty feelings and followed. She fussed over him and gave him a little of Edward's food in addition to his diet food.

That's more like it.

She put Edward's dish up on the chest freezer where chubby Teddy hadn't been able to jump for years.

Moooom.

It's for your own good, Teddy. Save some for him. Eat dry if you're still hungry.

I'm not hungry, exactly.

I know. If you were a person you would be a stress eater. I don't know what you call it in cats.

What's stress?

I don't know how to describe it, but I can't imagine you have it. It's like worry, I suppose.

I'm not worried. I like food, though. Should I worry about that?

Not at all. She picked him up, which he disliked but tolerated, and kissed him, which he liked.

She put him down as Tig came out carrying Edward like a deflated football under one arm.

After their shower, Elizabeth was hungry and she bet Tig was, too. He was always hungry. She made a plate of emergency nachos as she called them and put them in the microwave. She always had salsa and chips, one of Tig's favorite snacks, and she added cheese and pinto beans, a sprinkling of canned jalapenos, topped with sour cream and guacamole. She was an avocado-aholic and it was a

182

sad day when she didn't have one or two ripening on the window sill.

They sat and picked from the same plate, a cold beer for Tig and water for her. Tig's phone vibrated indicating a text.

"Karl's at the hospital. He texted that he got attacked. That's why he didn't meet you."

"Oh, no. Should we go?"

"He says he's okay, but staying for observation. He took a pretty good clunk to the head, it seems, so they want to be sure he doesn't have a concussion."

Another vibration. "He says he feels fine, but is sorry he didn't get to help you. He hopes you're not mad. He wasn't able to use his phone until now." Tig smiled. "He gets mugged and is worried about you being mad."

"I feel so bad now. I was thinking he flaked but he was injured." She picked up a jalapeno. "Does he need anything? We could take it. He doesn't have any family here, does he?

"I don't think so. He says they moved him to a room from the ER earlier and that they gave him pain meds. He added a smiley face and his texting is pretty weird, so they must be working." Tig snuck some cheese under the table to the black nose. "No, no family. I'll call tomorrow and see if he needs a ride. I'll get more details then. Must not have been too bad or they wouldn't let him go."

Elizabeth scooped a big blob of guacamole onto an already laden chip. It snapped, dropping the whole mess on the table. She spooned it up and ate it. "Do you know where he was? Last I heard he was checking the Masuka's pond. It's not like we have a big crime wave here. I know it's been getting worse with meth making its way here, but I've never known anyone here to be a victim of crime. Well, beyond mailbox bashing and kid stuff."

A number of years ago their whole block was targeted by some drunk teens in a car who thought it was a great idea to baseball bat all the mailboxes into the street and beyond. Elizabeth had found theirs the next day well into their across-the-street neighbor's driveway. Blythe had been wonderful but when she'd moved, it had opened up the house for Janie and Terry to buy.

"I'm exhausted. What a day. San Jose Koi still on for tomorrow?"

"I think so. We need to check the Tanaka's pond and do a water change. Karl might need a ride home and I want to be sure he's squared away."

"Of course." Elizabeth removed the nacho plate and Tig dumped Edward to the floor to clear the rest of their snack things. "We can shop for him, you know milk, eggs, stuff like that. Where does he live?"

"Here in Los Lobos somewhere, but I've never been. I think it's a little apartment off Los Lobos Valley Road. You know that place with a bunch of little bungalows around a central park? It's more like a dirt lot in the middle, kind of run down?"

"Oh, sure. It's kind of cute. Has potential."

"I've never been to his place, but I think that's where he said. I know he makes it to the heights in record time. NetFilms?"

"NetFilms!"

The whole family headed back and dozed through a replay of *Crimson Tide,* one of their favorites.

Fourteen

Tig and Elizabeth had agreed that if they wanted to get to San Jose and back, three hours each way, they'd better get an early start. They beat the cats to the kitchen. Elizabeth prepped breakfast for everyone and Tig was double checking what he'd need for both the Tanaka's water check and the drive transporting new fish.

Over the first cup of coffee he'd expressed his thoughts to Elizabeth. She hadn't commented, just listened, because it was unusual for him to share so much. Oh, he talked a lot, but not about his feelings or concerns. He hoped they'd find nice fish. The Masukas didn't seem quite as wealthy as Mr. Tanaka, but their house was pricey and the pond job elaborate. He'd not been inside the house, so perhaps it was lined with treasures and gold bullion. Besides, he knew sometimes the wealthy didn't like to display it openly. Usually he found that to be old money, or family money. People used to having wealth didn't find the need to show it off.

Elizabeth didn't know whether to be concerned or not at his somewhat disjointed chatter. She decided he must be nervous with the escalation of events to more important clients. She supposed he thought a lot was riding on this, and it was. A beautiful pond was one thing, but live inventory, and expensive inventory at that, was another.

"The Tanaka property is well-hidden from the street you know, but once you're inside the gates and near the house, wow. I don't get invited into a client's home too often, unless it's for the initial meeting. I'm mostly outdoors and frankly, I'm usually covered in dirt, or wet, or slimy, or all of the above. Not really the guy you want inside on your plush carpets or white couches."

Elizabeth had served up a scramble and toast and although Tig was seated, he wasn't eating with his usual gusto.

"Are you okay?" she asked.

"Sure, why?"

"You're not eating much and you seem sort of anxious about the new jobs."

He spooned up some egg. And some down to the nose. "I guess. Maybe. Going all day to San Jose isn't the best thing to do right now for Mr. Tanaka's pond, but I have to get fish for the Masuka's pond. I wish Karl was back on his feet." He put jam on his toast. "Oh, remind me to call him on our way to Tanaka's. If he needs a ride home, we're right there."

A bit of buttered toast went under the table. Elizabeth glanced to where Teddy lay in the middle of the floor, emanating disapproval.

"Sure. Would you rather I stay and monitor the fish?"

"No way! I want you with me. I'm sure I'm overthinking this. We'll check the water and the fish at Tanaka's, check in with Karl, then head to San Jose. Okay? It will be a long day because we'll probably have to do it all in reverse on the way back, but it's fine."

"It's absolutely fine. I'll pack some snacks and we can stop at the Viet Namese place we like for a meal okay?"

"Sounds good. Barring unforeseen events, which seem to be happening lately, everything will be fine."

"Of course it will. Should I call Goro and let him know we're on our way?"

"Thank you. I'm just going to shave and I'm ready. The truck needs gas, too."

"No problem."

They separated to finish chores and get ready.

I distinctly heard you mention snacks. Teddy.

I didn't exactly mean you, but you're right. Just a minute.

Elizabeth called Janie across the street and explained the dire emergency requiring cat snacks during the day.

"Of course! Garrett loves the cats."

Elizabeth burst out laughing knowing how Garrett's visit to Teddy's domain would be received. "Thank you very much. I owe you one!"

In just a few minutes, Elizabeth had called to let Goro know they were coming, and all systems were go. They headed to Tanaka's after a quick fill up at Rosie's gas station.

188

Elizabeth loved road trips and each was an adventure. Often it involved getting lost, although Tig insisted they weren't lost, they were exploring. But that was part of the fun. The only setbacks might be if the Tanaka fish weren't well they'd have to stay and monitor, or if Karl had difficulty.

No traffic since everyone who was supposed to be at work already was. Of course construction as they passed the airport, but they had the right flag waver and they only had to slow.

A phone call to Karl and all was well. His girlfriend was taking him home.

"Girlfriend?" Elizabeth asked. "Did you know he had a girlfriend?"

"No, but he doesn't really talk much when we're working. You know, not work related. Guys don't really talk about that stuff anyway."

"Well, he knows about me, right? I mean you told him about my abilities, of course? After the last time?"

Tig looked slightly uncomfortable. "Not exactly."

"What do you mean? What does he know about me, then?"

"You're kind of. . . , it's just that. . . uh, you're always there."

"What?"

Quick backpedal. "I mean, you visit the site, and bring us lunch and stuff. You are really supportive, but what you do just never came up." His look of relief at what he perceived was the correct turn of phrase was evident. Elizabeth couldn't help but laugh. To be fair, she did visit the

189

heights site more than usual, because it was so close. The pond jobs that were far afield, sometimes she never saw. Maybe wives in general were non-entities in other relationships?

"Okay." Elizabeth patted his thigh and smiled. They had reached the Tanaka property.

Elizabeth again marveled at the change of atmosphere once they passed under the torii gate. Another world awaited them and serenity pervaded even into the enclosed truck cab. Crooked trees, Tig would know what they really were, fronted the lovely rock garden next to the steps to the main door.

They pulled up to the access gate, but it was closed. They parked and entered it with the pond kit. They didn't have to do any heavy lifting, so getting the truck inside wasn't necessary.

The only sounds that greeted them were jubilant birdsong and the gurgling of the pumps. Even the nearby heavily trafficked Edwina Road was muted. Goro was not there to greet them and that seemed unusual.

Tig started pulling test kits from his bag. "What did Goro say when you called to tell him we were coming?"

"He didn't pick up so I just left a message."

"Okay, we'll knock when we're done. Not too bad." Tig was looking at his water sample test numbers. "This won't take long. Can you check them while I'm doing the water change?"

This was a little bit of a departure for Tig to ask her 'professional' help. She knew he believed in her gift, to a point. He trusted what she said the cats said and felt, and he also knew her clients trusted her. But for him to ask her to check a zillion dollars' worth of fish, well fifty grand or so, was huge.

She kept her elation to herself. "Of course." As he lowered the water level in each mini-pond, she carefully observed each fish. Tig would know physically what to look for far better than she, but she observed from the inside out. Thanks to Princess Keiko, she had learned a bit about query and response. Often it got her nowhere, but she could read Keiko's non-responses now, much like she could read Teddy's. Teddy might look blank, and he might be vacant, but there was always a message and now she knew how to read it.

She was still awestruck at how lovely and perfect the fish looked. Luminescent scales shimmered in the morning sun. The lowering water level made it easy to see and detect any anomalies. She forced herself to stop gawking and really settle into her task. She recalled her morning meditation and that helped her slip into the right place for this. Although she knelt outside each plastic tub, she extended her spirit roots deep into the earth and cycled that energy through her. Slowly the negative or unhelpful trickled away and she was filled with light and a lightness as she delicately examined each fish. She checked their circulation, organs, gills, eyes and temperament. They were young and as she had supposed, unused to much in the way of human contact. What contact there had been was with a completely different culture. She had not expected that to translate to animals, well, fish, but she felt like she herself had been dropped into that culture. She allowed Goro to enter her mind and let that energy infiltrate the fish, too. There was a change in their energy, but she could not put her finger on it. Almost like an exhale. As if they had been holding their breaths and now, began to breathe again. Weird.

Her last charge was the tancho, her flag fish. He concerned her most because of his initial difficulties. Because she had already used Goro's energy to calm the other fish, she imbued it immediately in her check. He froze in the water. He stopped swimming completely. Only the most minute of fin movement showed he was in control. His gills barely opened with the passage of water. She thought he was in trouble and probed more aggressively to find out the cause. His body was fine. His energy was frenetic, despite his still form. He was afraid. She assumed it was of her, but further inquiry told her no. He knew she was there to help and protect. He sent her wave after wave of pictures, clearer than Keiko ever had.

He was an emperor fish, born of a long line of top quality koi owned and bred by the most elite of breeders to the Japanese crown. His pictures were so quick she couldn't be sure, but he was of a line before there was a prince or princess in Japan, before there was Tokyo, maybe before it was Edo. She saw not buildings and roads but a castle, like none other she'd seen. Like a wedding cake, layer upon layer of ornate roofs and circular floors. He showed her a golden fish, she saw men on horseback. Soldiers? Warriors? Wearing kimono, wielding short swords, hair tied into an intricate knot, not a pony tail but an elaborate style. Fierce faces, angry; the horses prancing, mirroring their riders' excitement. A babble of Japanese and the only word she could understand was 'shogun.'

"Elizabeth? Elizabeth!" Tig was shaking her. "Are you okay? You look pale."

She gripped the sides of the formed pond so tightly her hands ached. She slowly released them. "I'm okay. I think. . . I think, there might be a problem. I'm not sure."

"What is it? Is one sick?"

"No. They are all physically fine. I'm not sure what I saw, but it's sure weird and like nothing I've ever seen before. I. . . I don't know how to say it without sounding totally crazy."

"Elizabeth, what's wrong?"

"The tancho. He's special."

"I know, isn't he beautiful? Well, we don't really know he's a he yet."

"Yes, he is. He. . . he showed me things. Pictures. I've never seen anything like this."

"Here, let's sit for a minute. Have some water." Tig guided her to the passenger seat of the truck and opened her water bottle. "Don't they always show you pictures? I mean, isn't that how this works?"

"Yes, but um, how do I say this. He is a very powerful fish."

Tig looked like he was going to laugh, but checked himself. "Okay. How?"

"You know I know nothing about Japan, right? Other than what you've told me about the koi, and well, we watched *The Last Samurai* together on NetFilms. But that's Hollywood." He nodded.

"First of all, he can communicate. I mean, really communicate. Not like Keiko. Keiko is good for a fish, but this guy sends me movies practically. They are filled with light and sound—I know, sound. It was in Japanese so I don't know what they were saying." She felt her upper lip begin to sweat. "It wasn't like an animal, when it sends individual pictures and maybe if it's heard something important, or traumatic, like that time the owl sent the pictures of the fire and I could hear it and smell it—that was just flashes."

"Okay, calm down. I'm listening, really."

She examined his face for any sign of joking or banter or disbelief. She closed her eyes, recalling what had happened. "He is an old fish. I know he's a baby, but he's the equivalent of something reborn. He lived a long time, and a long time ago. He was in a pond near a castle. Koi are revered there *you* know, and they always have been held in the highest regard. He was like, a royal fish or something. He showed me a *gold* fish. I don't mean a goldfish, I mean a GOLD fish. It was both alive, and in some sort of statue or god-form. It was very important to him and to the people around. I don't know if it was him in some earlier life or what. It was so mixed up but so real. It was old Japan. Not a movie set or anything. The air was different. The water was different. There were men on horses like soldiers. Some kind of war was happening or about

194

to happen. I could *hear* things." She had started to tremble.

"Honey, it's okay." He took her hand. "Do you want to stop?"

"No. I got the impression that everything he was telling me has something to do with here and now, but I don't know what."

"Okay. What did you hear? You said it was Japanese. Did he make it so you could understand?" Part of Elizabeth was amazed that Tig was taking her so seriously, when even to herself she sounded like she had a screw loose.

"No, I couldn't understand the words, really. I heard. . . I heard," she let her mind drift back to the dust the horses' hooves churned up, to the mossy smell of the rocks around the pond. She was *in* the pond and not. Both at the same time. She heard the horse grunt as it turned, the wooden saddle fitted to its form, the creak of the open ended stirrups ornately gilded with a triple flower pattern. The riders were not wearing battle dress, yet. Nothing that looked like armor, but more like layers of robes—kimono she thought. The fabric rustled as they moved, the breeze pulling at them. They were definitely gearing up for something . A battle. A war? As she heard the one word she recognized, *shogun*, she thought it referred to one of the riders or even to someone on the way. She had not noticed in the flurry of action, pictures and her own shock that another person had stepped out onto the porch, for lack of a better word—she had no idea what a Japanese castle or estate called such things.

She gasped as she saw some obviously royal person—a lord of some type? Someone highly revered by the others based on their actions.

The important person looked exactly like Goro. All the pictures and sensory overload the tancho had sent seemed to coalesce in that moment. The tancho and Goro were linked. And the tancho was telling her that Goro was in danger. The tancho also looked for someone else. Someone she couldn't see. A third person who was part of this triangle of energy and history.

"Elizabeth!" Tig was shaking her rather roughly. "Did you pass out? What happened?"

"Goro! We have to find Goro!" She took off running to the front door.

Fifteen

Elizabeth pounded on the front door of Mr. Tanaka's house. Silence from within. She wasn't good with people energy, but nevertheless, she sent out feelers, looking for Goro. She got nothing. At least nothing bad, and that was good. Tig had followed her to the door. She turned back to him.

"I don't think he's in there. I hope he's okay. I hope he didn't fall and hurt himself. I mean he's not young." Actually, Elizabeth had no idea how old he was. He had a smooth, unlined face and black hair combed back. He was slight, but strong, about as tall as Elizabeth, but seemed much bigger, now that she was thinking about it. He could have been anywhere from thirty to fifty.

She yelled, "Goro? Are you okay?"

A calm voice answered from behind her. "I am fine. Why are you shouting?"

Startled, both she and Tig lurched around. Goro stood at the foot of the steps on the last large flagstone. He held a watering can, wore rubber gardening slippers, and a satellite dish of a sunhat.

"Oh, Goro! You didn't answer, and you're usually here when we arrive, and then you didn't come out and I got worried," Elizabeth said in one breath.

"I do have other tasks here, but I appreciate your concern." A smile played on his lips. "What can I do for you? Is it the fish?" His demeanor became serious.

"No, the fish are fine," Tig broke in. "We just wanted to let you know we did a water change and I tested the water samples; all good."

"I checked the fish individually and they are fine. I was concerned about the tancho but he is recovering nicely." Elizabeth was proud of her use of the correct term and Goro seemed to be as well.

They stood a little uncomfortably for a moment. For Tig and Elizabeth, this moment of nothingness was new and different. As for Goro, he seemed to be waiting for them.

Elizabeth wondered if he knew about the fish. But that was impossible, right? He didn't pick them, he didn't shop for them in Japan, Yoshi did. As far as she knew, Goro had nothing to do with the fish. Hmmm. As far as she knew.

"Goro? When you, well, Mr. Tanaka had the first batch of fish, who cared for them?"

Goro looked a little nonplused at the change of topic. If she hadn't been watching him carefully, she would have missed the shadow that passed over his features.

"We had a caretaker for them. Mr. Tanaka likes to feed them when he is home, but as you can see, that is not often."

"Well, what happened to that guy?" Elizabeth persisted. She could feel Tig mentally shushing her, it was really none of her business, but now. . .

"I believe he returned to Japan."

"Japan! He was Japanese?"

"Half. He was not what he seemed."

"What do you mean? Not a qualified fish person?" Elizabeth didn't know how to put it.

A pause. "Yes. Not qualified."

"Because your fish died? That was. . ." she dug around in her brain for what she had read on Japanese culture. Rats, she wished she'd read more. "Shameful?" That was about the worst thing a Japanese person could do, is bring shame in some form or another to himself or his family, maybe even his boss or company.

Goro nodded. "Yes." He seemed about to say more but then gestured with the watering can, effectively closing the subject. "I have much to do. Is there anything I need to know?"

Tig jumped in. "Don't feed the fish today. If they look okay by tomorrow and all the water samples check, then we can give them a little tofu."

"As you wish."

"We're off now, but if anything comes up, call me right away," Tig said.

"We're going to San Jose to look at koi!" Elizabeth said.

"Oh?" Goro's eyebrows raised.

Elizabeth suddenly didn't want to tell him the reason. She had no idea why mentioning the Masuka's pond wasn't a good idea, but an icy mental wave doused her and she flashed on the Goro-like face of the warrior leader in the tancho's vision.

"Yes. It's just something we do once in a while. Last time we went we brought back the cutest little ghost koi. I named him Casper, you know, like Casper the friendly ghost?" It was clear this piece of American culture was unfamiliar to Goro and she realized she was babbling, something she did when she was nervous.

"Have a good day, then." Goro bowed and they bowed back. The conversation was over.

Tig led the way back to the truck and Elizabeth wiped her sweaty hands on her jeans. She was scared and didn't know why. An undercurrent ran between the tancho and Goro and maybe even into the past. Something happened and might happen again. It was frustrating not knowing what was going on, but feeling it. Like being in a dark room and sensing someone malevolent was there with you.

Tig seemed to know she was out of sorts and simply drove out of the property and onto highway 101 North—San Jose bound.

*   *   *   *

The long drive helped to clear her head. They didn't talk much, but Tig turned on Pandora radio on his phone and they listed their favorite stand-up comics in the program. By the time they cleared the north end of the county an hour later, they were both laughing and Elizabeth felt much better. Tig always had good ideas. She looked at his profile while he drove and thought again how lucky she was.

200

They got into a little traffic around Morgan Hill but soon enough they were turning into the tiny, cramped lot at San Jose Koi. Elizabeth loved visiting and had her routine. She adored the baby koi and always went to those tanks first. Their cute, cuddly (yes, cuddly) energy, darting excitedly around their raised pond, playing baby koi games never failed to cheer her. Tig liked the medium and big guys better. She loved the majestic battleships, as she called them, too, but the baby energy was just what she needed. She also had to pay a visit to the resident cockatoo, Crackers, who sat loose on a perch behind the counter. He was well behaved and seldom left his perch, except when she came to visit. He immediately climbed down and marched across the floor to climb up to counter level. He then cocked his head and told Elizabeth to stick out her arm, which she did.

"Oh, don't do that," Margie, the woman on duty that day said. "He bites."

"It's okay," Elizabeth said.

Crackers climbed up sideways to her shoulder and then sat grooming her hair and murmuring into her ear. He raised his crest, a lovely U-shaped crown of feathers, so she could rub his little bald spot underneath. Then he lifted a wing and she did the same to his 'arm pit.'

The staff were agog. Even the pond workers passing by stopped to watch. Probably waiting for a crunch and for one of her fingers to fall to the floor.

Elizabeth heard all the muttered comments and some sort of wager being made, but they didn't know that Crackers had given her explicit directions on how he wanted to be attended to.

The koi store also had a small section of pet supplies--food and water bowls and some toys, and Crackers told her he'd been admiring a little rawhide chew and would very much like to have that on his perch.

Tig had long wandered off to koi shop so she bought the chew toy.

"This is for Crackers. He would like to have it near or on his perch."

Margie said, "But this is for dogs. Are you sure it's all right for a bird to have?"

Elizabeth exaggerated. "I'm a bird expert and it's fine. Has he been chewing things he shouldn't?" She of course could see the destroyed edge of the laminate counter along the back wall, and the beginning of the paneling being chewed where he'd started on the vertical seam.

"Yes, but birds chew."

"Yes, they do. Laminate has lots of chemicals in it he shouldn't have, and that could make him sick. He would really like this toy. Also, I see you had a piece of manzanita in here."

"Oh, he chewed that down to a twig and we just haven't gotten anymore."

"He loved that. Order it in bulk and your bird customers will love you for it. You could call it Crackers' special or something. But, if you attach this rawhide to his perch for now, it will buy you some time."

Margie looked dubious but nodded.

"I'm going to find my husband, because along with visiting Crackers, we're here to buy koi."

She found Tig in the back where the very expensive and largest fish were kept. The manager was with him. The large fish were never left alone with a customer. It's not as if he could scoop one out and run away with it like a football tucked under his arm, but the picture made her smile.

"Hi," she greeted them both.

"Hey, hon," Tig said, slightly distracted. Miguel, for that was on his name tag, nodded. They seemed to be mid-bargain.

The discussion carried on while she leaned over the raised edge and admired the varied fish. This tank had a four foot raised border, but went down at least six more feet giving the big guys plenty of room. They circled lazily, and she imagined music for a water ballet in her head—the old movies where the ladies in bathing caps backstroked into a circle and stuck up their legs. The image amused her, and someone in the tank picked up on her picture. Not sure who, though. Their energy was calm and the tank pristine and all were in perfect health. The problem with buying such large fish was of course in transport. They only had to drive three hours and not put them on a plane, but still. . .

Both men leaned over the tank.

"So, have you decided?" Elizabeth asked Tig.

"I think so."

"I thought you were getting them smaller fish?"

"They changed their minds. I don't know why. They want big ones and only from Japan. There are some lovely, perfect fish from Israel here, but they absolutely want Japanese koi. I even saw a double for Casper from Texas—you know their breeders are excellent, too, but no way."

"Which ones?"

Tig pointed out a white one with blobs of black and red. "That doitsu showa for sure."

"What's that mean?"

"See how he doesn't really have scales?"

"Um, no."

"Look along his spine, the dorsal fin. See how he has two lines of scales down each side, but the rest of him looks smoother?"

Elizabeth looked hard on his next pass. "Oh, yes, I see now. I didn't know fish didn't have to have scales."

"Most do, but doitsu have them only in certain places. Also, that kohaku—the white one with the bright red markings? Those deep, clearly defined red marks are unusual in such a large koi."

"He sure is pretty. How many are you getting? The Masuka's pond is a lot smaller than the Tanaka's."

"Yes. They wanted the same number, seven, but that's not going to work in that pond. I'm thinking four."

"No! Not four." Elizabeth surprised herself at her vehemence.

"Why not four? The pond won't support more of these big guys."

Yes, why not four? Elizabeth wasn't sure where that thought had come from. She just knew it was bad. Unlucky. *How to explain it when she didn't know herself.*

She thought about it. Did it come from her 'waking dream' with the tancho? Something Goro had said? The sensation seemed to emanate from this pond. Oh, boy. Listening to fish who may or may not be able to count. Teddy could count to three on a good day. Maybe she'd been underestimating fish because she didn't understand them.

Tig was watching her, caution etched on his features. "Okay, what do we do?"

The whole time Miguel just observed. He had taken a net and was skimming leaves from the different ponds under the tent-like room, but he was paying close attention.

"I think we get three big ones from here, and then see what the next size down is from this that's also from Japan and then get two. The smaller pond will keep them from getting too big, right? With that growth hormone regulator thing? Five is okay. Seven is better but that's not going to work if they want big ones."

Tig thought as he studied the koi. "Okay. I think you're right. The worst they can do is make me return them. Or we keep them." He smiled at her. She knew he felt about the koi the way she felt about the cats. She would rescue everything that came along.

205

"It's sounding like a competition between the Masuka's and Mr. Tanaka. Is that possible?"

"I don't think they know each other, but I suppose. The Japanese community is very small here. It's reasonable to expect they might have a passing acquaintance."

He turned to look for Miguel. "Okay, I think we're ready at this tank, but can you show me the next size fish down from this? They have to be from Japan and the client is going to need documentation on all of it. Can you do that?"

Miguel was dark skinned and small and extremely strong-looking. Miguel said in perfect, unaccented English, "Sure thing, man. Where do you want to start? Do you want to tell me what you want from here so I can make sure someone doesn't snap them up while we're checking out the other tanks?"

"Sounds good." Tig indicated the doitsu and the kohaku.

Tig was eyeing a black and white when Elizabeth exclaimed, "That one!"

"Which one?"

"The Halloween fish!" Elizabeth had found a huge black and orange fish that had been hovering near the bottom of the ten foot deep pond. His markings blended perfectly with the patchy sunlight hitting the pond, the orange areas could well have been sunlight bounce. He had clearly been hiding until Elizabeth spotted him. He rose to the surface directly in front of her and waited. He had been the one 'talking' to her. He had a charming black face, like Edward, and lovely orange patterns. His pectoral fins were tipped with white.

"Oh, Tig, he's beautiful! And look at the orange!"

"Technically that's red, or hi," he corrected, pronouncing it 'hee.' "He is a beaut. He's rare. I bet he costs the earth. That would probably please the Masuka's given that they gave me a green light on budget, and if it is a competition like you think, this beats Mr. Tanaka's fish!"

"How are you going to pay for all this?" Elizabeth paid the bills and knew their savings amounted to the 'baby fund,' and not much more.

"The Masuka's arranged an account for me directly with San Jose Koi. It's all set."

"How much are we talking?"

Tig glanced to see where Miguel was. He stood at the other side of the tent gazing into a pond that presumably had the smaller, high quality koi from Japan.

"A hundred grand."

"What? For fish?"

"Yes. Shhh. That's not unusual. The big winner in the Japan koi competition went for 250,000 Euros, so this is 'normal.'

"Yeah, normal for the abnormally rich and weird."

"Don't tell Miguel what I have to bargain with. I'm going to get a couple small ones. You okay to hang out?"

"Sure." Elizabeth didn't want to see any more fish that cost more than her car. Or maybe as much as their house. What a shock. She admired the "Halloween fish" and then wandered back to the babies. They never failed to make her smile.

She realized she was starving and figured Tig was too. Their favorite Viet Namese place was just across the street so she decided to order to go. No way were they stopping for anything on the way home with the Fort Knox of fish in the back seat. She could tell this whole thing was right up Tig's alley. He was completely in his element. However, it made her extremely nervous.

She called in their favorites and said she'd be over to pick them up. After ten minutes of playing with Crackers again, she texted Tig to say where she was going, and then crossed the street to pick up their orders. They'd just have to eat on the go.

When she returned after putting the food in the car, Tig was at the counter settling the bill. From buying koi here before, she knew his choices had been bagged and oxygenated and would be loaded momentarily. He always watched that part carefully, just to be sure.

The dollar amount she heard was staggering, but while it made her a little queasy, it made Tig giddy from the way he looked. Maybe because it wasn't his money. Oh, boy.

A long ride home and then straight to the Masuka's to acclimate the fish. All their quarantine ponds were at the Tanaka property, so Tig would monitor them in the deep pond. Not a problem really. They'd done it before. Just not with such a hefty price tag attached. How much were they liable for those fish? Her stomach plummeted and she felt nauseated. She probably should have asked that earlier.

She took a deep breath as Tig turned to greet her, huge smile in place. "Ready?" he said.

Nope. No way. "Of course. Anytime you are."

A quick stop for gas and they headed south. The drive passed quickly with comedy once again, but Elizabeth's thoughts never strayed far from the fish in the back seat. She kept a mental line open to them the whole time and constantly monitored them. Like a snuba air hose between diver and boat, a two-way communication that exhausted her. The fish were fine. The Halloween fish was especially happy to be with her, although he did not like the confines of the bag or the skimpy bit of water. He seemed to love having someone to 'talk' to. Just when she thought she had seen it all, something new came along in her animal world.

They drove straight to the Masuka's pond. No one appeared to be home, although it was close to eight o'clock. Daylight was waning so they worked quickly, testing water and making sure the fish were safe. Elizabeth admonished them to stay in the pond, knowing it was common for koi to jump out when in new surroundings. Her Halloween Fish seemed to be in charge, whatever that meant, and clearly understood her wish for their best health. She and Tig quickly spread a net over the pond and weighed it around the edges with rocks.

Food? drifted up from the pond. Only it was more like a sensation of hunger and not a specific named word.

Not today. Maybe tomorrow. She sent a picture of the sun coming up and moving high into the sky. Tig would have to assess them before they could be fed. She wasn't sure if that would be soon since they hadn't flown—just had a quick car ride.

Tig put back the last of the equipment. "I know it's late, hon, but I really feel like I need to check Tanaka's. I can drop you at home if you want. I can do this on my own."

Elizabeth thought. "Let me check with the cats." Tig was used to such statements and said nothing. Tig drove down the winding heights roads while Elizabeth sent out her feelers to Teddy, since he was the spokescat.

Teddy was not happy with even further tardiness, but he reluctantly admitted that they'd had a good day with Janie and Buster. Garrett, not so much. Janie had taken them all for a brief walk in the outback and stayed to play, pet, and watch TV for a while. Edward had draped himself over Janie, not terribly disturbed by the screeching and smells that went wherever Garrett did. Buster enjoyed his time on the couch and Elizabeth received an adorable picture of Teddy allowing Buster to snuggle up to him.

"We're good. I'd like to check the fish, too." Elizabeth roused herself from her meditative state and shook off her stupor, caused in part by remaining connected to the fish for hours. She felt like a rundown battery. Probably exactly what she was. She knew she'd have to connect again to check the fish at Tanaka's, so she silently gathered her energy and cycled out old and brought in new. She sent some to Tig, too, because he had had a big day as well. He'd done all the driving and had made important decisions costing thousands of dollars. And, he had to work tomorrow. Back on the twelve hour shift for two days and then his 24.

Tig asked her to call Goro and let him know they were going to drop in for a quick check. It seemed like days since they'd been there, but it was only this morning. When she connected, Goro seemed tired, too, and said he would not meet them unless there was a problem. Then they were to come to the house.

By now she and Tig were a team and little chat was needed to get the job done. Tig checked water and did a visual inspection of all fish, ponds, and connections. He also checked the big pond to make sure there were no changes. She did her 'internal' check and only the tancho even cared she was probing around. He was a truly lovely fish and she couldn't resist putting her hand in the water. He immediately came to her and rested in her open palm. She didn't want to damage his slime coat so she was very gentle, but he obviously loved the attention. With him sitting in her hand she had an even deeper connection to him, but he sent her nothing exotic like a trip into a past life. He just sent waves of pleasure.

Tig packed up once again and they both got in the truck. Exhaustion overcame them and by the time they reached home, they just showered, fed the cats and fell into bed. They didn't even notice when Edward's dexterous paws opened the bedroom door and both cats ended up on the bed. All night.

Sixteen

Both Tig and Elizabeth woke exhausted and slightly cranky from the rough day yesterday and lack of sleep. Tig was up at 6AM, late for him when he had to be at the station at seven, but it was only a few minutes' drive. Elizabeth would have liked to sleep in, but the cats had other ideas. Fortunately the summer mornings were light early, and today happened to be one of the rare bright days, making it easier to rise and be productive than on the gloomy gray days.

She staggered around making coffee, feeding cats, and getting breakfast for Tig. He could eat at the station, and probably would again, but just in case a call came in when he arrived, she wanted him to have something.

Elizabeth kissed him good-bye after promising to check on both ponds for him. She also wanted to see how Karl was faring. The sooner she could teach him a little about fish care, the lighter she would feel. She sat in her meditation chair by the window, but didn't immediately center herself. She didn't feel ready to face the day, and allowed herself a few moments to let her thoughts drift. She remembered that she should check on the Leahys and see how Ben was recovering after his surgery. For some reason, although she hadn't connected to Sadie, she thought she might have had the pup. That would be something to see. Maybe she'd visit if time allowed. That train of thought brought her to the wolf. She couldn't keep calling him OR7. That was so clinical. She decided that to her, he would be Sojourn. Traveling from place to place, not staying too long. She hoped to get him back on his journey but still hadn't come up with a way to do that.

Finally she felt ready to connect to her earth energies. Usually that connection gave her strength, but today, it was hard to get going. Maybe that was due to all the contact she'd been having with fish and the wolf--species she wasn't accustomed to talking with. It was like a foreign language you knew, but not very well. It took a lot of energy to listen to the words, translate them into your own language, and translate a response into the other language. The brain gets very tired.

She relaxed, feet on the floor, hands in her lap. Cycled energy from the earth through her roots, up and over and out again. Then she called on her ancestors, something she didn't always do, or need to do, but since her time-traveling fish incident, she felt maybe some extra pull was warranted. She felt both familiar and unfamiliar presences gather around her, including some of her spirit guides. She had several, but her big blue whale was one of the oldest and sagest. In her imagination, he hovered over her head, which was weird since he was so big, and of course, out of water. She knew that's not really how it was, but that was how her mind perceived him, this big, warm, nurturing and all-encompassing presence. He had a sense of humor, she'd found, because he thought hovering over her head in the living room was amusing. She knew his energy was somewhere else and probably in some other form, but that was how her mind dealt with it. Maybe her whale would help her with the fish problem. Whales were mammals, and fish were fish, but they did have things in common.

When she had a lot on her mind, a lot to process, she put each issue on a leaf in a river, and let it drift by. If it was something she needed to do now, the leaf would glide into an eddy near the bank and she handled it. If it was something she should let go, even temporarily, the leaf continued its journey. It was an effective method of dealing with multiple problems and weeding out the ones that could wait, but that perhaps were taking up too much of her mind.

She would physically check on both ponds later, so saved the fish for then. She sent her feelers out to Sadie, who in fact, had given birth last night. One big eggplant shaped casing of wolf hybrid pup. She checked Sadie. Having given birth before to Ben, Sadie knew what to do, and had set about eating the little casing and freeing her baby. She cleaned her off, a female this time, and both were happily engaged in nursing. The pup was high content wolf, in other words, very wolf-y, but maybe not as much as Ben. Ben was fine and noticeably calmer.

215

Sadie was uninterested in either Ben or the wolf at the moment, so Elizabeth took a chance to connect with the wolf, whose adopted territory remained within a mile radius of the ranch.

He allowed the connection immediately. She sensed it was because she was associated with Sadie and Ben. She saw him clearly this time, unlike previously when she'd had to hunt for him until he would decide to let her view him.

His energy still radiated health but he was puzzled at the distance Sadie and Ben had put between them.

Elizabeth sent out the puppy birth as one explanation, but he seemed aware of it. Apparently his sense of smell was excellent under the right conditions and at night, he shared that he had crept uncomfortably close to the ranch house. This did not alarm the cattle since they ranged far over the hills most of the time, and he had no interest in them.

It was harder for her to explain Ben's neutering to him, but suggested that Ben could not have puppies or add to or create a pack, and therefore would not be a good addition to the wolf's pack.

Underlying his puzzlement and curiosity was a platform of loneliness. The wolf had sought out a mate and thought Sadie was it. Elizabeth did her best to dissuade him and showed him moving on alone. He was resistant but did move over one ridgeline. His energy was more disjointed. Like when a person thinks one thing, but then discovers that is incorrect and that imbalance in thought reflects an imbalance in physicality.

She felt sorry for him. She tried to get him to start back north, showing piney territory and female wolves, but he was reluctant.

Elizabeth sighed and broke the connection. Her best guess was repetition and reinforcement of the danger and unhappiness that this area represented.

She dressed and fed two starving cats. While they received a much anticipated combing, she dialed Karl's number. For whatever reason, when the flea comb came out, both cats lined up, butts to her, ready for combing. She couldn't get a clear response as to why they liked it so much. Obviously it felt good, and it also allowed her to keep tabs on the flea population. She didn't like to use poisons on them unless it was warranted. When she'd probed them for a response, she got what she could best relate to as the way she felt after a massage. Sort of a non-word groan of happiness.

When Karl answered he sounded pretty normal.

"Hi, Karl. Elizabeth. How are you doing?"

"I'm good. I'm home now."

"What's the damage?"

"I'm okay. I got hit in the head, sort of beat up, so they kept me overnight. I'm bruised but okay. One guy had a knife, but they got interrupted. I was lucky."

"Oh, no. What did they want? Your wallet?"

"I don't know. The police think it was a home invasion gone wrong sort of deal."

"When was this? Where were you?"

"I was at the new client's house. I was supposed to meet them to go over the contract but they weren't home yet. I got jumped before I got too far. The FedEx guy stopped to deliver a package and that spooked them."

"So they think those guys were casing the house? Are they wealthy?"

"They have an awesome house and a huge pond with really nice koi. The client wants us to redo the waterfall and troubleshoot the pond. I mean, it *looks* like they'd have tons of expensive stuff."

"During the day?"

"P.D. says that's how they do now. When people go to work, they walk right in and steal all your stuff. If people are home, sometimes they get hurt. I was checking the pond and these guys came right for me. I can't believe I looked like I was the owner. Gardener, maybe."

"Maybe just that you could be a witness?"

"Maybe."

"Karl. I'm so sorry. I just wanted to check and see how you were doing. Do you need anything?"

"Oh, no, I'm fine now. I was going to call Tig and see what I should do. I'm not supposed to do heavy lifting for a couple more days, but I can work. I'm bored anyway. I like to be outside."

"Maybe you could help me with the Masuka's and Tanaka's ponds?"

"Sure, what do you need?"

"Tig and I both think you're ready for Fish Care 101. Interested?"

"I sure am. I love those guys. They're so neat. But, I really don't know anything about them."

"I'm going to start you today. You'll go with me and I'll show you how to take and test water samples and what to look for in the fish; things like that. Tig is really the pond and fish expert, but I do have my areas of expertise."

"That'd be great. I can be ready anytime. Can you pick me up?"

"Happy to. Ten minutes?"

He gave her an address off Los Lobos Valley Road. She checked all the pond kit supplies and noted what was running low. She decided to go to the Masuka's first since it was closer. If she forgot anything, it was a lot faster to get home.

After picking up Karl, it was just a few miles to the Masuka's home at the top of the heights. The marine layer hovered right below their house so these upper mansions seemed to float on a cloud. The little town of Cove to the north, the bay and sand spit below were invisible. Up this high however, it was magical. Elizabeth half expected to see a unicorn, or Pegasus at the very least, fly by.

Elizabeth parked on the street fronting the house and handed Karl the test kit bag to carry. A privacy wall lined the street with a wrought iron gate covered in a large design comprised of a circle enclosing two crossed swords. The swords were shorter than English-styles, slightly curved with angled blades. *A handsome design,* she thought. *Very masculine.*

Elizabeth started down the steps to the courtyard. No handrail made her watch her footing. "Should we ring the bell? Let them know we're here to check the fish?"

If Karl answered, she did not hear because she saw a body, face down in the courtyard at the edge of the pond, one arm dipping into the water. A pool of blood ran from the body along the sloping stones to the drainage tile set there to keep rainwater from causing the pond to overflow. Elizabeth felt a little queasy, like seeing a drain for an autopsy table. *Why did I think of that?* She used to watch CSI all the time. *I must be in shock.*

She stepped over the blood and knelt to feel for a pulse. She was pretty sure she wouldn't find one from the amount of blood and, oh, a lot of his face was missing. She felt her stomach spin.

Her glance fell to the arm in the pond and then she did feel bile rise in her mouth. The large koi, hungry from not being fed after their transplant trip, were happily nibbling away at the hand. She knew they were omnivores, but this was disgusting. She wanted to lift the arm out, but couldn't bring herself to touch it.

Karl was saying something from very far away. "Elizabeth! Elizabeth! Get away from there." He tugged her arm, urging her to stand. "This is a crime scene. Someone killed Mike. Stand over here."

She allowed Karl to pull her to the side and plop her on a decorative boulder. Just in time because she couldn't stand up anymore, nor could she stop herself from throwing up. Not much to throw up since she wasn't a big breakfast eater, but the coffee came back and oddly enough, tasted like. . . coffee. *What a thing to focus on*, she chided herself.

"Mike? Who's Mike?"

"He's the guy Tig and I, but mostly me, have been dealing with here. I think he's the houseman or something. He pays us and inspects the job."

Like Goro. "Who would want to kill him?"

"I don't know. We have to get out of here and call 911. We can't contaminate a crime scene." Karl took one step up from the courtyard and swayed unsteadily.

Elizabeth jumped from her boulder and guided him to it. "Are you okay?"

"Yeah. I think so. I just thought about what happened to me, you know, the home invasion? It could have been me, and not Mike. Or maybe both of us, you know?" He was babbling a little; sweat beaded his face.

"It's okay, Karl. You're fine. Maybe you're right though. We should tell the police that. I'm sure they'll check all the angles."

"What if they're inside still? They killed Mike, maybe they don't know we're here and they'll do something to us on the way out."

They linked arms, staggered up the stairs to her car and got in as fast they could. She drove down the mountain too quickly, tires squealing on the turns. Where it flattened out she finally slowed to a less dangerous pace. The neighborhood looked completely normal. Not like a murder had been committed. Not any different than any other day.

"My house is close. Let's go there," she said and turned up her street. People were out walking dogs and pushing strollers. The school yard was busy with summer soccer leagues. The clear sky didn't reflect the fear and nausea she felt. It was surreal; this exterior show of normalcy contrasted with her panicked feelings.

At home she drank a bottle of cold water and Karl sipped at his. "Do you want to call 911 or shall I?" she asked.

"You do it. You saw him first." He almost sounded like a kid. Well, he was, sort of. Maybe 25, dark curly hair, stubbled chin, but not rough like Tig's—soft and new-looking. His pale face wasn't sweating anymore, but he seemed a little shocky. Coming on top of his own assault, this was probably as much as he could take.

Maternal instincts of some sort kicked in and she had him lie on the couch with his feet up. She covered him with a blanket, actually Teddy's blanket, and started a kettle for some tea. Her Irish roots told her that a cup of tea laced with sugar could fix anything.

The 911 operator was not happy that she had left the scene but she was able to give the address and explain that they thought the burglars might still be inside. She mentioned she had checked for a pulse and had been sick. That thrilled the operator even more, but trained to follow protocol, Elizabeth figured the operator had heard worse and was certainly trained for it. A deputy would come by.

Elizabeth hung up and immediately texted Tig and then called the fire station. Tig was out on a medical call. She asked that he call home as soon as possible. She rarely called, they mostly texted, but she really wanted to hear his voice.

The kettle had long shut off but the water was still hot. She could use a cuppa herself. She brewed a pot and when it was ready she sweetened two cups and brought one to Karl. He lay, eyes closed, blanket to his chin. He was less pale now, and his lashes were very long against his cheeks. She hadn't noticed that before. Should she call his girlfriend? *I guess that's his decision. Besides, I have no idea who it is unless I rifle his phone contacts. Overkill.* She wished she hadn't used that particular phrase.

She urged him to sit up so he could drink. She sat next to him in case he fell over. Maybe she would fall over. What a horrible and strange day.

She had forgotten to mention the arm in the water to 911. That seemed like an important omission to her. Well, they'd see it soon enough. What just occurred to her was that the arm in the water had a tattoo on it. Well, more than a tattoo, what she thought was called a sleeve. A three-quarter length design, wrapping all around the arm. She could see it because the man's shirt had been torn, perhaps in a struggle and was rucked up and stuck on the rough stone edging of the pond. The tattoo extended up under the shirt but stopped short of the wrist so it could be hidden by clothing. It was a fantastic piece of art: ironically, it was a koi surrounded by foamy water. Its delicate gold, yellow and black scales were outlined in black, lined in white. It coiled around the forearm in a spiral U shape so it looked back up at its master. She also remembered that the live koi had made some progress in their nibbling. Ugh. His arm was missing not only some skin and tissue, but the end of the pinky digit. She shuddered at the recollection. She didn't know whether she wanted to have that discussion with Princess Keiko and the others or not. She knew for sure she wasn't going to think about them as the same harmless creatures again.

She jumped when the doorbell rang. She rose to answer and saw two burly deputies outside. They did not look happy.

Seventeen

Elizabeth opened the door and gestured for the deputies to come inside. They followed her to the living room but remained standing when she sat. They stood apart, feet spread, thumbs in belts. Like bookends but in an unfunny way because their faces were so serious. Karl still sat blanketed and unmoving. A distinct absence of cats that ironically had begun when she'd brought Karl home.

"Mrs. Murphy, please describe what happened when you arrived at the house up in the heights," Deputy MacDonald asked.

Elizabeth went over it again. After hearing enough of Tig's fire stories, she knew law enforcement often needed multiple retellings. It was still stressful, and didn't help that they gave her the impression she'd done something wrong. She supposed perhaps she had, but she was only trying to help in case the man was still alive. Okay, throwing up was contaminating a crime scene, too, but that wasn't really her fault. At least she'd done it in the bushes away from the body. The body. She swallowed.

"What about you?" Deputy Crabtree asked Karl.

"What about me? I followed her down the steps and saw what she saw. A big pool of blood and a guy with his head blown off."

"How did you know that?"

"When she tried to feel for a pulse, I could tell. I had to get close to pull her up and I could see the hole in the back of his head, and that half his face was gone. It was horrible."

"Come with me." Deputy Crabtree led Karl out the front door and Elizabeth's stomach flipped in alarm. Was he being arrested? Maybe not. Yet. She could see them still on the porch.

"Mrs. Murphy? Why did you touch him?"

"I told you. Maybe he needed help."

"Karl says he knew the victim was dead."

"I. . . I've never seen a body like that. I mean my grandma died, but she looked pretty much asleep." Elizabeth sipped her tepid tea. "I also came on an accident scene once. A mountain road and a truck was T-boned. There was a lot of blood there, but the people were alive. I just couldn't tell." She started to tear up and couldn't seem to stop.

"Mrs. Murphy. I'll tell you straight the problem we're having with your story."

"My story?" Elizabeth's tears slowed.

"We got to the address you gave and there was no body. No sign of a crime. The homeowners are out of the country. We checked. No sign of entry of the dwelling, legal or otherwise. No bodies, or body parts. No blood. Not even any vomit. How do you explain that?"

Elizabeth's mouth slid open. "I . . . I can't. Are you sure you went to the right address?"

"That's what we're going to find out. I have to commend you and your partner on getting your stories straight."

Elizabeth was offended. "Straight? There's nothing to get straight. We both saw what we saw."

"Good job. Small differences, like perspective, but the body of facts is the same. Let's go." She grabbed her purse from the table. He ushered her out to the porch with Karl.

"I can lock my house, right? I assume you don't have a problem with that? There have been some home invasions in the area."

"Sure. No problem." Deputy MacDonald waited while she locked the door. Deputy Crabtree had already taken Karl down to the sheriff's vehicle.

"Can't we follow you in our car?"

"Nope, sorry." He didn't seem sorry.

She slid into the back seat next to Karl, still in his blanket. She felt her cell phone vibrate in her purse. She didn't bother asking permission and answered when she saw it was Tig.

"What's going on? Cats okay?" Tig asked.

"They're fine, but Karl and I have a problem." She figured the deputies would cut her off soon so filled him in quickly and asked Tig to meet them at the Masuka's. The issue with that was he couldn't leave the station unless he had a relief come in and take his place. A certain number of fire fighters had to be on site or their station would be taken off the call list. Since this semi-rural area had few stations, even one station removed was a big deal. He assured her he'd be there soon and hung up.

She felt a little guilty about asking, because, really, she didn't know what he could do, but it was his pond. And she was his wife.

They had arrived at the correct address. The deputies had to open their doors for them from the outside and she slowly exited, afraid of what she'd see. Would the body be gone? Or would it have miraculously reappeared and she'd have to see it all over again? She took a deep shuddering breath.

Deputy MacDonald noticed her anxiety and brought down his official demeanor a notch.

"You okay, Mrs. Murphy?"

"I guess. Let's go." He opened the gate and she stepped inside. The courtyard was pristine. She slowly descended the stairs and absolutely no sign of the body remained.

The area had been professionally scrubbed. No wonder the deputies thought she was crazy at the least, or a suspect at the worst. Or both. She turned to Karl.

"Do you see anything?"

Karl shook his head.

"Can we look around?" she asked the deputies.

"Sure," Crabtree said. "Nothing to 'contaminate.'" He included air quotes. She wanted to slap him. She refrained. Both deputies stood, arms folded, blocking the stairs. *Like I'm going to run away,* she thought. *And look at poor*

Karl. He might have to be carried up the stairs. Shock on top of a recent head injury.

She closed her eyes and pictured the gruesome scene again. She made her brain slow down and examine it. At least in a memory, she had no exact smell recollection like she did sometimes with energy connections. As soon as she touched on that, she recalled the blood. There was so much of it, that there was a smell.

It was fresh, so not that rotting sort of smell she got when she hiked and came upon a coyote ravaged deer. Sometimes she felt the coyotes were all still watching her, waiting for her to leave so they could get back to it. She much preferred her 'finds' to be quite dead, not freshly dead. The cats, and particularly Buster who occasionally accompanied them, were open to anything. Once Buster found a rather large (for him) deer femur and carried it all the way back to the house, taunting the cats with it. *It's mine and you can't have it*, he kept saying. Teddy twitched his tail each time to say, *as if,* and ignored him otherwise.

"The blood. There was a lot of it." She forced herself to see his body on the pavers, the angle, the arm. "He was lying like this, with his head here, and one arm in the pond. The fish, um, they were sort of eating it." She opened her eyes to see how her news was received.

They looked interested and disgusted now. She could read on their faces that the details of her description were lending credence to her initial report.

"He was face down and other than the blood, to me, he looked sort of normal."

"Yeah," Karl added. "Until you saw the hole in the back of his head and that half his face was gone." He backed up and sat on the rock near the stairs. He looked pale again.

"Karl saw that before I did. I felt for a pulse before he told me that. I didn't step in the blood, so there isn't any on my shoes for you to test." Again, she slowly pictured the scene. "I know! The blood. There was a ton. It ran into the weeping tile," at their blank looks she amended, "clay pipe--under the drain section. Here." She pointed since the deputies did not immediately show excitement at the weeping tile.

The strip of drain ran along the edge of the courtyard and was camouflaged by landscaping. She told them it was designed for storm runoff to protect the pond from overflow. Beneath the foliage and drain was a weeping tile, a pipe with holes in it to catch and divert water.

"If there is blood anywhere for you to test, it's there. I know there will be stuff in the pond," she tried to repress a shudder, "but that's going to be too diluted I imagine. But maybe check the filters."

"Okay." Deputy MacDonald sighed. "I believe you saw something."

"Did you get an evidence crew out here? Or whatever you call it?" Elizabeth asked.

"Until now, there wasn't anything to check. No sign of illegal entry, no evidence, no body.

230

Unlike the TV you apparently watch, we can't just go into someone's home on a civilian's say so."

Elizabeth had had enough and was about to mouth off when she heard the familiar rumble of fire trucks pulling up in front. Tig! And he'd brought reinforcements. The entire crew. Her heart swelled. That's how he was able to get here so quickly. They'd brought the whole gang, so technically they were still on duty. The smaller paramedic truck pulled in behind. The courtyard swarmed with fire fighters in yellow bunker gear.

Tig's captain approached the deputies while Tig found her. Poor Karl sat on his rock, the eye of the storm.

"You okay?" Tig asked after planting a kiss. "You sure know how to throw a party."

"I am now. You sure know how to make an entrance."

"What's going on? Why are you all here?"

Elizabeth filled him in with more detail than she'd been able to on the brief phone call. He brought his captain over, who apparently was on friendly terms with the deputies. Fortunately, this captain also was fond of Tig, so her reliability went up and weirdo factor went down. She felt some stress fall off. Her brain, which, for lack of a better word, had remained clenched, suddenly released. It opened and some very interesting pictures flowed in. She wasn't sure of the source at first, but then the familiar angle and blurry nature told her it was from the koi. They had seen what had happened.

"It was Mike." Karl in his blanket spoke up.

"What?" One of the deputies asked. Hard to tell which one with all the bodies in the courtyard.

"The dead guy. His name was Mike something. He was the caretaker or houseman here."

"Are you sure?" Karl nodded. "Why didn't you say so before?"

"It's been a rough couple of days. I think I was in shock. He was face down, not that that mattered anyway. I recognized his tattoo."

"Okay, everybody out." Deputy Crabtree started shooing people up the stairs. "We've called in evidence techs so you guys need to stay out on the street. Nothing for you to do here anyway."

Tig's captain did not like being addressed that way and Elizabeth saw him, well, inflate, sort of. They got into a bit of a verbal tussle, but it was mostly bluster.

Tig wanted to stay, but his crew needed him. His captain assured him, while eyeing Deputy Crabtree, that Elizabeth would be taken home immediately. That seemed to be the tradeoff for the fire fighters leaving, that Elizabeth would also be released.

Karl was describing the tattoo to Deputy MacDonald and it was just as Elizabeth had remembered.

"Any other identifying marks, tattoos or scars?"

"Yeah. He had lots of tattoos. I didn't see them all, but he told me they covered most of his back and front in designs."

"Anything in particular?"

"Um, like fish and dragons. I think he said a lady and flowers. I never saw them, so I don't know. He was missing a finger, too."

"Oh, I saw that, too," Elizabeth added. "The fish nibbled his pinky. Like half of it was gone."

"No, that wasn't the fish," Karl countered. "He already had that. He said it was work related, but from a while ago."

Deputy MacDonald wrote all this down but exchanged a look with Deputy Crabtree at the pinky discussion.

"What?" Elizabeth asked.

"We're pursuing all lines of inquiry on this. We'll be in touch." Deputy MacDonald's abrupt close to the discussion, and his quick upgrade to believing her and Karl, made her nervous.

"Are we in danger? Karl and myself?"

"Probably not."

"Probably?"

"You didn't see anyone else, did you?"

"No," they both said.

"We'll up the patrols in your area, but you're fine."

Elizabeth didn't feel so 'fine.' Her mind jumped to the home movies the koi were sending her. They saw it all. It was only a matter of time before she did, too. She had never experienced a picture flow like this. One where she was not initiating it, was not drawing it to her and was unable to stop it. Disjointed images just ebbed and flowed and that concerned her. Something else was going on and she would have to figure it out in order to stop it.

Eighteen

Deputy MacDonald waited at the crime scene for the evidence technicians. Elizabeth didn't envy them the task of digging up the weeping tile and cleaning out the filter system. Deputy Crabtree dropped her and Karl off at her home, and then arranged to meet Tig back at the fire station for his statement. Elizabeth had heard Karl say the homeowners were rarely there, and they had dealt with Mike.

She was relieved, and then guilty for that relief, that she had never met Mike while he was still among the living. Other than elderly relatives, she had never known anyone who died. She'd come upon a car accident or two, but again, she hadn't known the victims. One odd experience when she was young and camping with her family had stayed with her into adulthood.

The family had been driving in Colorado, the lovely winding mountain road unfolding ahead. The busy scenic route and a long line of RVs, cars and even a tour bus made the journey slow. As a child, Elizabeth didn't really mind the slowness, just the curviness and resulting unhappiness in her stomach. She remembered looking out the window of their camper as a motorcyclist zoomed past the long line of traffic. A few minutes later, their vehicle passed the motorcyclist, now smashed and spattered against the cliff wall, obviously dead. His cycle tires still spun, well, the one that was still attached to the bike, and bits of machine were scattered all over the other traffic lane. Her young brain couldn't quite take it all in, that literally moments ago, he was speeding along on his way, and now he was dead. The sharp curves and high speed, not to mention his impatience with the crowd, all contributed to the sudden end of his life. She hadn't known that man, but it was a series of images that stayed with her. Alive. Dead. Alive. Dead. Just. Like. That.

She shook herself away from the past.

"Karl? How are you? Hungry?" She realized with all the activity and stress, they hadn't eaten for hours. For Karl, perhaps even longer. Suddenly she was ravenous.

"I could eat."

Me, too. I could eat. Teddy. And a little echo that was Edward.

Their first appearance in hours. She scooped Teddy up and hugged him tight. He was so solid that he gave great comfort when he permitted a hug. He must have missed her too, or sensed her need, because he allowed it without his usual stiffening of limbs and tolerant sighing.

Then she grabbed Edward who, as usual, went gratifyingly limp and purred contentedly while

235

she cradled him like a baby and kissed his head. "Oh, you guys. I missed you." She set Edward down and gave them both little servings of wet food. The dry food had a tiny indentation that meant someone was hungry enough to eat perhaps, three kibbles. Poor babies.

"Tuna sandwich?" she asked Karl.

"Sounds good."

Tuna juice?

"Yes, tuna juice," she answered before she realized that Karl was looking at her oddly. "Um, the cats can smell the tuna and I usually pour off the tuna water, you know, for them." Nevermind that she hadn't actually opened the can yet.

Karl nodded as if that made perfect sense. She mentally smacked herself. *Must be tired. Well, duh.*

"Did the deputies say when we could go back?" she asked.

"Go back? What for?"

"Well, we never actually tested the water like we were supposed to. The fish certainly seemed fine." *And hungry.* So much for not feeding them after a transfer.

She gasped as she recalled a couple things. The body was *in* the pond. Well, the arm was. The net she and Tig had put over it to protect the fish from jumping was nowhere to be seen. That's how the arm could flop into the pond in the first place. Maybe whoever did this planned to dump the whole body into the pond and let the fish have at it? Ewww. Disgusting. And undependable, but as a message. . . However, her arrival with Karl shortcut

236

that plan? If that was the case, someone did see them. Someone knew about them. Then moved the body because it would be discovered sooner than they wanted. Hmmm.

"Hey, Karl? Didn't you say the owners were out of the country for a while and that's why Mike was around to make decisions for them?"

"Yeah. I think that's what he said. I only saw the owners like, once, right when we got the job and that was on the fly. Like they just got home from work or somewhere. Or were leaving for somewhere. I don't know. It was a long time ago."

"How long?"

"Way long. Like a month? Tig will know because it was right after they okay'd the contract. Well, Mike did. He signed for the owners, like legally. What do you call it? Proximity?"

"By proxy?" Elizabeth brought the sandwiches and chips to the table.

"Yeah, that's it. Then we started the project and they were there once, I think."

"Iced tea, Pepsi, or water?"

"Iced tea if you already have it. I'm wiped, man."

"I can imagine. Hey, are you on any medication you need to get?"

"No. Just Ibuprofen if my head hurts. It kind of does."

"I have some. How about after you eat? Not good on an empty stomach."

He shrugged and took an enormous bite of sandwich and immediately said, "Ouch!"
A black nose appeared behind his plate.

"I'm so sorry!" Elizabeth rose to remove Edward from Karl's lap. She knew Edward still preferred the 'climb up the leg' method, rather than a single jump which now he was capable of. "Tig's used to that, but it's a bad habit. Are you okay?"

"Just surprised is all. He mostly got blanket. No, he can stay. He's pretty cute."

Cute my Aunt Fanny, a surly voice said from the floor.

I am too, cute. You're just jealous because there's no lap you can fit in. Edward.

I do not like laps. They are lumpy and prone to movement. I like couches and beds and floors.

Okay, you guys. Enough. Elizabeth was careful not to voice this conversation. *And where did you get that expression, Aunt Fanny? I never say it.*

Janie. She was mad. I like it. I think she was going to say something else, but that thing was there, squawking as usual, so that's what she said.

Garrett?

Whatever.

Yes, sometimes grown-ups have to be careful of their language in front of children.

But not cats. We are superior in that way.

Okay. Elizabeth couldn't help but laugh.

"What?" Karl asked.

"Oh, the expression on Teddy's face, it just made me laugh." That part was true. Teddy wore a beatific smile.

"Pretty cool." He had finished his sandwich and a mountain of chips in record time. Elizabeth poured more tea for both of them and as Karl admired Teddy's grin, he absently stroked Edward and a loud purr rattled from under the table.

"How about an Ibuprofen chaser? How to do you feel?"

"I feel great, now, but that's probably a good idea."

Elizabeth got him two capsules. "Should I take you home now?"

"No way. I feel fine. We still need to check Mr. Tanaka's place, right?"

See, cat therapy. Does it every time. Teddy.

True, Elizabeth agreed. "I would feel better about checking those fish. We can't get to Masuka's today, I bet, but those fish had almost no trauma in transport." They clearly were well enough to eat and project images. She hadn't really focused on their health, she admitted, but there had been other things on her mind. Could she do it remotely? She could try later. She couldn't do a water check remotely, but that pond had been seasoning for a while and should be fine. The ammonia dump, if there was one, might be cleared by the filters, plus they had an enormous amount of water compared to the Tanaka quarantine tanks.

Elizabeth cleaned up the lunch items and realized it was closer to dinner than lunch. Time flies when you're at a crime scene.

She got a meatloaf out of the freezer and several potatoes from the pantry to remind her of what she would serve Tig for dinner in a few hours. What a day. To the cats, she projected that she'd be back soon, well, in one naptime, which they correctly interpreted and headed back to the master bedroom.

"Oh, no," Elizabeth said.

"What?"

"The pond bag. We brought it to the Masuka's right? I saw you carry it to the steps."

"Yeah, what about it?"

"Did you bring it back to the car when we left in such a hurry? I didn't. I didn't see you with it either. I was so shook up."

Karl slowly shook his head. "No, I don't think so. I'm sorry."

"It gets worse, Karl. When we went back with the deputies and the body was gone? The bag was gone, too. I would have seen it, and for sure, the deputies would have."

Karl's mouth made an O. "You have other kits though, right? We can still check the Tanaka pond?"

"Yes, but that's not the point. In that bag, was my check list. I am not as good as Tig and I kept a check list for when I was doing the Tanaka pond myself. Also, the bill of lading for the fish was in there, with all the kinds of fish and costs. I think," she closed her eyes, "I think my name and the Tanaka's address are in that pond bag, too!" She felt hysteria rise.

Karl patted her shoulder. "Maybe it got shoved in the bushes or something and the crime scene guys found it. Don't panic yet. It might be fine."

"Okay. You're right. Might be fine," she repeated. "We have to go. We'll never finish at this rate. I'll grab another bag from the garage. You call Deputy MacDonald and see if the crime scene people found the bag. It would be evidence if we left it there, so it should be cataloged. Here's his card."

She locked the house and threw another pond kit in her car. Karl had dialed his cell and they hadn't gone a block before he was leaving a message. He left both his and her cell numbers and hung up. The rest of the drive was in silence.

At the Tanaka pond, all appeared serene and normal. That was a relief. As Elizabeth pulled the pond kit from the car, she realized she hadn't warned Goro they were coming. It was almost routine, this showing up to check the fish here, but she shouldn't take advantage of his hospitality. She showed Karl how to take samples and label them.

"Karl, finish pulling the samples and I'll let Goro know we're here." She knocked on the front door but no answer. She had never seen a vehicle in the drive and assumed they were all garaged so she had no way of knowing if Goro was here. She returned to the quarantine ponds.

"No answer. I'll just take a peek around the pond in back while you test for ammonia." She quickly showed him how and then moved along the shrubbery lined path to the larger part of the main pond. The landscaping was amazing; graveled paths dotted with huge stone lanterns or lined with what appeared to be a dry river bed. Each turning of the path hid a surprise. A tree with branches that had been trimmed into many balls shaded a stone bench with a view of a curve in the pond. She found herself moving slower and slower as she made each discovery, a small prize for her keen eye. Flat, hardy-looking grass filled in a few areas between 'treasures' as she thought of them. She heard a faint clacking sound and the next curve revealed a stone bowl filled with water and a bamboo pole serving as a pipe filled the bowl. The clack was when the pole overbalanced and poured its water into the bowl as it hit the edge. She was so entranced with this she watched it fill and drop several times before she remembered why she was on the path to begin with. Goro. She'd even stopped calling for him after the bench and Dr. Seuss tree discovery. A movement out of the corner of her eye drew her attention and she saw Goro in one of the grassy spaces doing some sort of exercise. She recognized his grace and economy of movement, but what he was doing looked very strange. It looked like karate, sort of, but alone. He was punching and kicking but no opponent met his blows. It was as much of a dance as it was karate. It probably wasn't even karate. She had no idea and flashed that she wished she'd paid more attention to the 'kung fu' movies, as she and Tig referred to them, on NetFilms.

Goro wore loose black pants and some sort of slippers but he was shirtless. She was about to call out when she realized another thing. He was covered in tattoos. His front was inked on both arms from the shoulders on down into the waistband of the pants with a central vertical stripe of clean skin, that she presumed continued. He whirled and she saw his back. That was completely covered and the predominant images which she could see all the way from here were a single giant koi and several flowers. The blossoms matched the design on the gate. The fish sprang from his lower back in curls of water and the body of the fish covered the majority of his highly muscled torso. Its face reached Goro's right shoulder. Three flowers covered the left shoulder. Goro turned again and the designs on his front were too small to discern. Her gasp made him stop mid-move, one leg extended. Even so surprised, he looked eminently graceful and perfectly balanced. It unnerved her. She felt adrenaline wash through her and she over compensated by waving her arm enthusiastically and calling too loudly, "Hi, Goro! There you are! We just came to check the fish. I knocked on the door to let you know but, um, no answer, so I thought I'd check the pond because we didn't want to surprise you."

Goro had begun to put on a loose white shirt, tucking it in as he approached. "I see."

"Surprise. Sorry about that." She bumbled to a halt. She had a habit of babbling when nervous. The adrenaline made her knees weak and she felt a little queasy. "I didn't mean to interrupt your work out."

He looked at her strangely but nodded once. "How long will this check be?"

"Oh, fast, you know. Just a water check and I'll make sure the fish are doing okay. We're almost to where we can put them in the main pond. I think Tig wants to wait a few more days to be sure. They had a long trip and that flag fish had a rough go, so. . ." she stopped.

Goro merely looked at her. He didn't seem hostile, but neither was he as welcoming, or-- she couldn't put her finger on it—deferential? She supposed that was the word she wanted. Before, he'd always seemed like a servant, sort of, if that was okay to say, but now, he seemed like more. Scarier? *Don't be silly*, she scolded herself. *They're just tattoos. Practically everyone had one nowadays.* Maybe she startled him, coming up on him like that. He's in the zone, doing his thing and then, there she is. *Maybe he felt a little exposed, shirtless the way he was. Maybe it was against Mr. Tanaka's rules or something for the houseman to be seen that way? How should I know? Jeez. There goes that cultural etiquette thing again.*

"Is there anything else?" Goro asked.

"No. I'm really sorry. I'll make sure we call next time. We need to check them every day, like I said, but we should be able to put them in the big pond in two or three days. Do you want to see them?"

"Yes. Mr. Tanaka will arrive at the end of the week from Japan and I would like the fish to be in the main pond for him by then."

"I think that will work." She really looked at his stone face. "I mean, sure, of course."

She led him back around to the small ponds.

"Who is this?" Goro sounded unhappy.

"Oh, sorry. This is our assistant, Karl. He's training for the ponds since things are really picking up business-wise. He's been pond building with

Tig for a while, but now the fish ponds are taking off we need a bit more help."

"When you said 'we,' I thought you meant you and your husband." Goro's brows made a straight line, while his lips thinned to an upside down U.

"Um, I'm sorry Goro. I'd forgotten that you hadn't met yet. Karl, this is Goro. He takes care of Mr. Tanaka's property. Mr. Tanaka is our client here." Karl already knew all of this, but she had made a mistake somewhere, and wasn't sure where. She tried formality as a way of making amends. She had reverted to short sentences and clasped hands as well as a sort of half bow without even thinking.

"Goro, this is our helper, Karl and he is very reliable and trustworthy. He's been thoroughly checked and is covered under our insurance." *What? Why would Goro care if he was insured? Jeez. Get a grip.* She bowed again, this time to hide her scarlet face. She didn't want to mess this up for Tig. *Oh, man.*

"Yes. Thank you for your assistance." She risked a peek and Goro had bobbed his head in Karl's direction.

Elizabeth's jaw fell right open as Karl bowed deeply from the waist and said, "*Doitashimashite.*"

Apparently that was the correct and life saving measure. Goro's straight brows unfurled and his upside down U mouth returned to its more neutral position. She felt air return to the world

245

and the energy around them was suddenly lighter. *What the hell was going on?*

"Goro, you're welcome to watch, but we want to get out of your hair as soon as possible, so we'll get started." She fussed with her water charts hoping to melt into nothingness as soon as possible. She glanced at Goro and recognized his slight expression of puzzlement. She assumed it was from her colloquialism about his hair, but she didn't want to start babbling again to explain it. Karl knelt beside her and she handed him the chart with the numerical and colored results of the water tests.

As rough as the last fifteen minutes had been, she didn't expect to slip instantly into communication with the fish, but she did. They had been waiting for her. Sort of like when she opened the bedroom door in the morning and two impatient cats rushed in.

It seemed this high grade of fish enjoyed 'talking' and they had a lot to say. Nothing terribly exciting, but not seeing why they had to be in this 'prison' was the general feeling. She knew they didn't know what a prison was, but these tanks were considerably smaller than their home tanks in Japan, and clearer, which they definitely didn't like. Most of their huge ponds in Japan were fairly murky and completely healthy for them. They had been moved to viewing tanks later for purchase, but those tanks were still large. Murky protected them from predators and the fish made it clear they felt very vulnerable here.

She reassured them and let them know it was only temporary. A large, beautiful pond awaited in two or perhaps three suns. She wasn't sure if they could measure time, but some of them seemed to grasp it. They were also bored. There was 'nothing to do.' Completely like kids. Or cats. She knew from Tig that was valid but wasn't sure what to do about it. It had been two days, so they could eat, but what? She hadn't brought koi food.

She texted Tig. "The Tanaka's fish are bored. Can I feed them? And what?" She didn't know if or when he could respond. She knew tofu was a great high protein food. The weather wasn't cold, so they should have no trouble digesting it.

"Goro, do you have any tofu?"

"Yes?" It was a question.

"If Tig says I can feed them, that might be the best thing. If that's okay with you."

"Yes."

"And they're super bored," she added without thinking.

Goro made a sort of rising grunt of surprise and inquiry. *An interesting sound,* Elizabeth thought.

"I'm going to ask Tig if I can add some water plants from the main pond if those water tests are okay."

"O-K." Goro made the word the full two syllables that it was. It sounded strange from him, and yet, it fit the situation the way he said it. Like, *You're bordering on super weird, here, but you're the expert.* It made her smile. Her phone vibrated and she checked.

"Tig says I can feed them some tofu, just a little, and that if the main pond reads okay, we can add a little green for them. Goro, can you help me get a plant from the pond? Not a lily, even though they'd love that, but I saw a patch of water hyacinth. Can I put a piece of that in each mini-pond?"

Now Goro looked completely out of his depth. "Of course. Tofu first?"

"Yes, please. Can I look at the pond while you get it? I'd like to check the water plants."

"Of course." Goro left to get some tofu.

"Karl, can you do a water check on the big pond while I look at the plants?"

"Sure." He took a test kit.

Elizabeth heard a clamoring in her head that was the fishes' excitement. "I know, you guys. It's coming. Just relax. I'm doing the best I can."

She knelt by the flag fish and put her hand in the pond. He settled into her palm at once and the images flowed right through her hand and up her arm. He showed her the same scene as before, some ancient lord or something, everyone looked mad and ready for a fight, although she didn't see much in the way of armor. The fish sent her the sequence that this was before a battle; that arming was to come. She heard the men speaking but it was garbled and of course, in Japanese. Then an extraordinary thing happened that she had never experienced before. The fish translated for her. There was no other explanation. She understood the group were, for lack of a better word, unemployed samurai and were planning to change the governing body of Japan. They were going to fight in a way they had never fought before.

Apparently something had changed for the samurai. She gathered there was a change in rulers? Leadership? Kings? She didn't know much about Japanese history—meaning nothing, but a battle was coming. More than one ruler was fighting for control and the samurai, who she figured from the yelling, used to work or be allied with one ruler, but were now just let loose to run amok over the countryside. They had been causing problems, to say the least, and this group was trying to support one leader and rein in the renegades. This all came in flashes of translated conversation and pictures, by a fish in a pond, no less, so its reliability of content and accuracy might be questioned. Even in her head it sounded weird. Not the fish part. He was being as accurate as he could. Whatever that meant.

Her only comparison was movies about English kings. How each one had an army but sometimes knights roamed the country looking for work. When 'hired,' they had to swear an oath of fealty to the king. In times of war, when one king lost his kingdom, his knights sometimes had an opportunity to swear to the new king. Sometimes they just got their heads lopped off. Of course, her academic knowledge was nil, and this was information was provided someplace between Hollywood and the BBC. She sighed. It had been ages since she'd been in school and other than reruns of *Robin Hood*, she hadn't really boned up on history of any kind.

The yelling brought her back. The man who looked like Goro was giving directions. Plans. The men on horseback had returned from reconnaissance and an attack was imminent.

A hand touched her shoulder and she startled both herself and the fish who scooted out of her palm. The images stopped like a movie on pause. Goro stood behind her, a small dish of tofu in his other hand.

"Are you all right?"

Elizabeth noticed he pronounced his Ls perfectly. She also noticed how weird it was that she noticed this right now.

"Yes, thanks." She rose unsteadily. She was not used to kneeling for so long.

"You were talking."

"Oh, yes. They're just so cute. I always talk to our fish. Well, all animals I suppose." There goes that babbling again.

"Do you speak Japanese?"

"Oh, no. Of course not. I didn't even know Karl did until today."

"You were speaking in Japanese." Goro looked serious.

"What did I say?"

"*Shoganai*."

"Like a shogun? I don't know anything about that except a James Michener novel. I haven't even read it!" Elizabeth felt a little hysterical.

"No. It is a different word and means, 'there's no choice.' "

Elizabeth bowed her head because she did remember when that was said. Just as the Goro-man had stepped out on his porch or whatever, the real boss, maybe in fact a shogun, had revealed himself. They were talking about war. A war in which they had no choice.

"You said something else, too. 'Tokugawa.'"

"What does that mean?"

"It is a name. The name of one of the most influential leaders of Japan. Ieyasu Tokugawa, as you would say here in the west."

"Maybe I read it in the paper?"

"I do not think that is likely. He was the first shogun of Japan and united much of the country. He went to war in 1603."

Nineteen

Elizabeth didn't know what to say. What do you say when you've had fish visions from 400 years ago? Goro looked as confused as she felt. No way she could explain it to him, since she couldn't explain it to herself. *I am an animal communicator, not 'fish psychic to the stars.'* Now she felt a bubble of hysterical laughter rise up and squashed it with all her might.

"The big pond looks great. Clean as a whistle." Karl had returned and saved her. She shook herself back to the present.

"Great. Let me check those plants. Why don't you drop a couple cubes of tofu into each mini-pond. Watch to make sure they eat it. When they stop eating, don't put anymore in; we'll have to fish out what they don't eat."

Goro handed Karl the lovely porcelain tray with the tofu already cubed small and turned back to the house.

Elizabeth felt such a wave of relief. Maybe she'd get out of here yet. She'd spent enough time with Tig and his plants to be able to check them for parasites or unusual growth that might be bad for a vulnerable fish. Really, her only concern had been the flag fish, but now she was sure he was fine. Warrior fish now, she guessed.

She didn't wait for Goro but cut small sections of water hyacinth and carefully examined them with a magnifying glass. Not as good as a microscope, but it would do. No worms or visible parasites--the plants looked healthy. Relieved she tossed a sprig into each mini-pond. The fish were ecstatic. She hoped that tomorrow they could put them in the big pond and never come back here. Well, that was uncharitable, but she was exhausted. And confused. What was she supposed to make of all the flag fish had shown her? Obviously something to do with Goro. Or Goro's ancestor, more likely. She did remember reading that Japanese koi breeding and bloodlines were carefully tracked. But for 400 years? She doubted its pedigree could be documented that far back. Were they like race horses? "Flag fish, out of Yellow Fish, sired by Super Sanke." The announcer voice in her head made her smile. Whatever. Time to get home.

"Oh, crap." She glanced at her watch. Tig was due any time.

"What?" Karl asked.

"Gotta get going. Can you get the test kits? I'm just going to check one more time. Did you pull the uneaten tofu?" Karl nodded as he gathered the kits. "Thanks. Jeez I'm tired. Did I forget anything?"

Karl looked around. "I don't think so. If you did, we'll be back tomorrow, right?"

"Right." Her whole body sagged at the thought.

"I know Tig's still working. I'll help. Besides, we have to check the Masuka's, right? Because we couldn't do it today."

Crap. Was that all today, too? "Yes. Right." She felt so worn down. So worn out. She wanted Tig and some cat therapy, as Teddy would put it. "Karl, do you feel well enough to drive? I'm beat."

"Sure, no prob." His equanimity had returned. "Since you picked me up this morning, can we go to my house? Can you drive yourself from there?"

"Oh, yeah. I forgot. Sure I can. Only a few minutes." As soon as Karl pulled out of the property, she fell into a doze. She felt like she'd *been* to Japan instead of having some sort of waking dream about it.

"Hey. We're here." Someone was shaking her. *Stop it.* "Elizabeth? Hey. I have to go in now. You okay?" Karl gently patted her arm.

"Oh. Yes." She woke groggily. It felt like a minute since she'd fallen asleep. "Thanks Karl. For everything. All your help today." *And your stolid presence. Very soothing energy.* She did not say this.

"You okay to drive?"

"Sure, I'll just keep the window down." She pulled onto Los Lobos Valley Road for one block

254

and then up a side street. Home in a minute. She could do it.

Tig's truck was in the drive and she felt a little bad for being later than he was. However, Teddy was on the porch to greet her and she felt better rubbing his large head and getting that smile in return.

Hi, Mom.

Hi, Teddy. He preceded her into the house, tail waving, stomach weaving in opposition to his body.

Tig had found the meatloaf and potatoes and dinner was already well in hand. She almost wept. He was at the stove attending to the boiled potatoes, masher at the ready. She hugged him from behind and laid her head on his strong back. She stayed like that.

"Are you okay?" he asked.

"So tired. Just need some energy. Thank you for dinner," she mumbled against him.

"I didn't do much. You already made the meatloaf. I just boiled water. And made a salad." He turned to hug her. "Whoa. You look exhausted. Here, sit down."

He guided her to the table. "I would offer you wine, but you look like you might pass out. Rough day, I know."

"Yeah. Hot tea?"

"Green? Jasmine?" She had bought tea after her experience with Goro.

"Jasmine, thanks."

Tig pulled the meatloaf out of the oven and mashed the potatoes while her tea water boiled. He

255

opened a beer for himself and brought the meal to the table. She only felt a little guilty for letting him serve her. He'd worked all day, too. Plus, he'd gotten the whole shift to come rescue her. If she wasn't so tired, she'd have thanked him properly with a cat-free time after dinner. Probably have to take a rain-check on that. She felt like she was going to fall on her face.

"Here, eat something. That will help."

Eating always helps. Teddy.

Elizabeth forked up a layer of meatloaf and potatoes. So good. Her tea had brewed and she sipped. Restorative.

See?

Yes, Teddy, you're right.

She ate quickly at first, thinking she might fall asleep before she replaced all her used calories. She noticed Tig was doing more watching than talking. *I really must look horrible.* She made an effort.

"How was the rest of your day? Any calls?"

"Easy. Couple medical. The deputies took my statement and that was about it. I feel bad about Mike. He seemed nice. Really concerned for the pond and getting fish in there."

Elizabeth saw he was eating now and she felt a little better. "Did they say it was a robbery?"

"They're not committing. You know how they are. There were some home invasions up there. It's a wealthy area."

"How do you know about the home invasions?"

"I get paid to read the paper at work, don't forget." Tig smiled. "Besides, in one other, the homeowners were there and got beat up a little. We got called out. I think it was sort of an accident, just because they were old, you know? When they answered the door the guys crashed in and the old man hit his head on the wall. The wife was shoved in a chair and she had bruises and was shook up. We got a medical call on that. Again, a neighbor heard it and it was stopped before they got really hurt. A few things stolen and broken. Could have been worse."

"This is in broad daylight? That's awful. Did they catch the guys?"

"Not yet. But what happened to Mike doesn't feel like the same thing. The other guys were a couple of punks, but Mike is a big guy. You'd have to really want to take him down. The other home invasions were strong-arm robberies."

At her look of inquiry he added, "No weapons shown or used. Just muscle. Mike was shot and it doesn't look like there was a struggle. I don't know. I'm not an expert. They don't even know if the robbers were ever in the house."

I think they might have been in the house, Elizabeth thought. She didn't want to alarm Tig but she had to ask about the pond bag.

"I think whoever shot Mike and then moved the body has the main pond bag."

"What? Why?"

"Because Karl and I know we brought it and now we can't find it. He called Deputy MacDonald to see if the crime scene people found it and put it into evidence, but no one called him back yet. I have a feeling that whoever did this has it."

"Why on earth would they take a pond bag?"

"Maybe they didn't know what was in it? Maybe they thought it was money or drugs or something. To sell? To get drugs? They came back to clean up after themselves, so maybe they just grabbed it, too."

Tig thought while the black nose searched the air above his plate. "I'll check with MacDonald tomorrow. He's a pretty good guy. I've been at scenes before with him. He might tell me."

"There's something else."

"What else?"

"My name, and the Tanaka property name and address as well as the bill of lading for the fish were all in there, too."

Tig blew out a breath. "Okay. I'd better call him now."

Elizabeth didn't want to add to the pile but felt she had to say something, given the high definition history lesson she'd gotten today. "I think we'd better let Goro know, too."

Goro probably knows more than he's telling, she thought. That little pearl wafted into her brain unbeckoned. "If the paperwork is in there, he or Mr. Tanaka might be in danger, too. Oh, Mr. Tanaka's coming in from Japan at the end of the week and Goro wants the fish in the big pond by then."

Tig just looked at her. "Anything else?"

Oh, yeah.   Let me tell you about samurai and the Japanese kingdom circa 1600. "Um, nope. I think that's it." She smiled weakly. "I'll clean up since you got everything ready.   Thank you so much. I really appreciate it." She did feel better. "Why don't you call the deputy and I'll call Goro. Divide and conquer, you know?" *Oh, good.   War references.   Super.* "I mean, it's my fault, sort of, so I'll take responsibility for telling him."

To her surprise, Tig didn't fight her on it. It was his business after all, and she expected him to want to handle it.   She watched him clear his plate and head out back by the pond--his default location for phone calls and serenity after a crazy day. Most of the craziness was on her.   She suddenly felt terrible.   She hadn't caused Mike's death, and she hadn't asked for a Japanese history lesson, but nonetheless, leaving the pond bag and potentially endangering the Tanaka household (wait, did he have a wife? Kids? Crap.) was her responsibility.

As she put away leftovers and started the dishwasher something clicked in her brain. Duh. She'd been so tired and stressed she'd missed it. Tig was afraid for her. He was quite aware that the killer might still have been on the property when she and Karl were there.   He knew what was in the pond bag because he helped her pack it, except for the bill of lading she'd put in at the airport.   He didn't see Mike's body, but he knew him, after all. That had to be hard.   Okay. First, call Goro, and then she and Tig would put their heads together and fix this. That's what they did best: work together.

When Goro answered, for a moment she didn't know what to say. Stick to the facts. "I have some bad news, I think, Goro." And she filled him in. To his credit, he waited until she ran out of words. And air. Babbling again.

"I see. Are you positive about this bag?"

"No. We haven't received confirmation from the Sheriff's Office yet that it was taken into evidence. So, we just don't know. I wanted you to be aware, though, just in case."

"Thank you for telling me. I will inform Mr. Tanaka."

"Okay. See you tomorrow for the fish check."

"Yes." He hung up.

Maybe they don't say good-bye in Japan? I think he has on other phone calls. She just couldn't remember. But, she had given him some pretty bad news. *Someone might come and break into your house and it's my fault they even know you exist.* Sigh. She really hoped this wouldn't spell the end of Tig's koi buying career. So far it wasn't off to a great start. The caretaker dead at one house, and her responsible for the robbers knowing about a second target. Great.

She showered and got in bed, Teddy joining her as soon as he heard the TV click on. Tig's signature door slam heralded his arrival followed by Edward, his little shadow. She tried to see his expression in the darkened room but couldn't.

He got in bed and kissed her fiercely. She had been correct that he was afraid for her and feeling protective. At the moment, she didn't feel

afraid or tired anymore. The cats jumped off the
bed, indignant. The TV played on.

Twenty

The smell of brewing coffee woke Elizabeth. No cats. Breakfast must have been on offer, but they were always happy to have second breakfasts when the next staff person got up. Usually she was the first up, even on Tig's early days, but yesterday had been quite a trial. She didn't want to miss saying goodbye so she hustled out in her moose PJs.

He was already dressed and shaved. He must have used the other bathroom to let her sleep. She kissed him and got a coffee mug. Unless they were eating together, he often ate at the station. Life at the fire station revolved around meals and that worked for her. However, she had said, and finally gotten him to reluctantly agree, that he needed something to eat before he got there. What if there was an early call? Then he'd have no food for who knows how long? The only reason he'd agreed was that it happened once. He'd arrived at work and they'd all been called out. A warehouse fire in Cove City, the next town over, had resulted in the whole county being called out. It had turned out to be overkill and they'd eventually been released but after that, he always ate something.

She brought her coffee to the table and watched as he ate his cereal, complete with black nose waiting for handouts. Apparently, the nose did not favor cold cereal.

I'll ask him to save some of the milk for you, she told Edward.

Okay.

What about me?

What about you? You're not in his lap. You're in the middle of the floor where we have to do extra work just to get around the kitchen. Elizabeth felt immediate remorse.

A definite snicker from Edward. Silence from Teddy.

I'm sorry Teddy. That wasn't nice. I'm really tired today. Teddy's narrowed eyes suggested he could not be appeased so easily. *All right. Some milk for you, too.*

"Tig, can you save some milk for the cats?"

"Sure." Tig had been happily oblivious to the whole issue. He set the bowl and Edward on the floor and Teddy got up and sat one inch away.

"Teddy, just wait, man." Tig scooted him a bit with his foot. "You'll get your turn." He gathered up his things and kissed her. She stood and hugged him tightly.

"It'll be okay," he said into her hair.

"I just want them to catch whoever did that to Mike."

"MacDonald said they'd up their patrols. You didn't see anything, so you're fine. I've got to go."

"I'm sorry if I ruined your koi buying business."

"Don't worry about that. More will come. You didn't ruin anything. You didn't do anything."

Oh, I'm pretty sure I did. "Okay. See you tonight."

And Tig was gone in the usual whirlwind, door slam and then silence.

Hey, Edward complained about Teddy's proximity again.

Hey yourself. It's my turn. Dad said. Teddy.

"Guys guys. Relax. Edward, I think it's Teddy's turn."

Elizabeth refilled her coffee, then sat in her mediation chair and looked out the window. It was several minutes before she felt awake enough and ready for her morning meditation. She felt stripped, raw, and wanted to create some protection for herself. The fish just leaping into her mind that way freaked her out more than a little. She had always been the one to control the interactions. Well, her end of them anyway. Like opening a door for a guest. The guest decides to come in or not. But the fish, especially the flag fish, seemed to be able to crash through the door whenever they wanted.

She grounded herself, feet flat, hands relaxed and started her cycle of energy. Purging the negative and bringing in new, bright, positive light. It took longer than usual to recharge but then she asked for her spirit guides to help her. Her whale spirit hovered comfortably near and she felt, but could not see, other energies.

What's happening to me? Do you know? Why can these fish just speak to me?

A warm blanket sensation she recognized as her whale responded. *You have opened a new door to the animal universe. You can close it again, but perhaps wait to decide. That gift is rare, and not often recognized even when it is bestowed.*

So, this is normal?

Sort of a chuckle. Her whale enjoyed her grapplings with human limitations and failings. *It is normal for you, now. But I can help you learn to control when to let them in. It would be dangerous for any animal to be able to step into your mind at its own will. Do you see that?*

Oh, yes, I'm getting that. How do I do it?

Exactly as you have described. You must be the one to open the door. You must learn to keep it closed and only open it when you want.

What about that fish? She sent a picture of the flag fish. *Why is he so powerful? Is he, or did he used to be, human or something?* A part of her could not believe she was actually asking this.

No. He was always as he is now. However, he is an old spirit and comes back often. He, like your animal friends, is tied to the human spirit he accompanies.

What human spirit? We just got him. I mean, not even us. Our friend, well, I haven't even met him, got him and stuck him on a plane...

Calm yourself. More warm blanket energy and she instantly felt calm and a little distant from the current issues. Like they were not as important. *This door we speak of. It is not an actual door, but it will be useful for you to think of it as such while you are learning. You can open it fully when you need it. You can command animals to contact you at your will, not theirs, if you choose.*

That doesn't seem right. Like I'm yelling at them to talk to me or something.

It is only a tool. Use it if you need it.

Okay. Thank you. Do you know what this fish wants? Why he's showing me ancient history?

He needs your help but beyond that, no. He does not talk to me. Only to you.

She sensed movement in the energy around her and reassurance, like spiritual pats, for lack of a better description.

Is this going to be okay? Is someone else going to get hurt?

There was no response. She was alone. She slid back into herself and felt her feet on the floor, the cushion under her bottom and the weight of two cats' stares by an empty cereal bowl.

"Hi, guys."

Hi, Mom. Breakfast? Teddy.

"You're kidding. You just ate."

Nuh uh, or the equivalent from Teddy.

I'm hungry too, Mom. That startled her. Edward was infinitely patient about being fed. She glanced at the clock; nearly two hours had passed.

"Crap. I gotta get a wiggle on." She picked up the cereal bowl and put it in the sink. She gave each cat only a spoonful of wet food, since they still had a bowl of dry they hadn't deigned to touch.

266

"All your teeth are going to fall out," she called back as she went down the hall to shower.

She called Karl and set a time for the Masuka's pond in an hour. She showered and pulled on jeans and a tee. Pond work was messy business with a lot of kneeling and crawling. *Sometimes are worse than others,* she thought wryly.

She still had fifteen minutes before she had to leave. Karl was going to meet her there since he had the other client to start work for after the water check. She probably didn't really need Karl, but she didn't want to go there alone.

"Okay, super powers, let's just see." She settled on the bed, feet flat and hands relaxed. She quickly grounded herself and 'opened her door' to Sadie and Ben. She hadn't checked the dogs for a while. Ben didn't recognize her, but Sadie did. All was well with the puppy and her health. She seemed pleased with her people, too. Ben had settled quite a bit after his neutering. Elizabeth tentatively asked Sadie about the wolf by sending a picture.

Sadie responded by showing her an empty ridgeline. She was completely absorbed in her pup and seemed disinterested in pursuing a conversation.

Elizabeth asked Ben the same thing. Ben's response was even blanker. Perhaps she had convinced the wolf to go back north.

She took a big breath and slowly let it out and 'pushed' for the wolf. She searched the way she normally did, but no response. He was no longer near the ranch properties. What a relief. She just wanted to be sure he was okay. She didn't want him here, but she didn't want anything bad to happen to him either.

She recalled what it felt like to have the fish jump into her mind. It didn't seem like she did anything; they just appeared there. Okay. She pictured a door with a handle. She saw herself turning it and projected, no *told,* the wolf to be on the other side. The door opened and the wolf was there all right. Right on the ridge. Behind their house.

Twenty-One

She didn't mean to, but Elizabeth slammed the mental door on the wolf. Even in her meditative state, she realized what a ridiculous move that was. It wouldn't change his physical position one iota. She did get a wave of surprise from him. He was willing to talk to her. She didn't know if it was due to her new ability, or superpower, as she decided to call it. Seemed less scary that way. And it certainly was scary.

Maybe he was just ready to talk. She reopened the door and he was still there. It was like a movie with a door to another dimension. He stood just below the ridgeline behind their own home, head lowered, watching, just as she first seen him watching Sadie's ranch. He was as non-threatening as he could probably get. He exuded waves of curiosity and familiarity, she supposed from her previous encounters. She had done nothing to him, not forced him or coerced him in any way. Perhaps he felt safe with this parasitic entity that was Elizabeth.

Why are you here? she asked.

I needed to be.

No, not here. I just needed you to move away from Sadie and Ben. For your safety as much as theirs. You were in danger there. You're still in danger since you've moved where even more people are.

I needed to be, he repeated, and sent a picture of her.

You found me? Followed me? How?

You told me.

I did not!

You have been with me and protected me and stayed with me.

Stayed with him? *I don't think so.* Unless, it was her superpower kicking in—leaving the door ajar, as it were. She wouldn't have known about it. Crap.

Okay. Well, maybe, she allowed. *This place is not safe for you.*

For you either. That is why I am with you.

What do you mean? Safe?

The wolf sent her a picture of the flag fish. She almost laughed because a koi was the last thing she was afraid of, but then goose bumps ran up her arms. How would he even know about that fish?

Why do you have this fish in your head?

No answer.

Okay, but you can't stay here. It's too dangerous. Besides, don't you have a pack to find? A home to go to?

Hesitant. *Yes. But you are part of my pack now and I have to protect you until the danger is gone. Then I can leave.*

Gee, that's all. I'm part of a wolf pack now and in danger from a fish. Not from a murderer, but a fish. A fish with basically no teeth, so it's not like Jaws... she started to smile, but remembered the Masukas' koi enjoying a nibble on Mike's arm, and her stomach flipped.

I see you understand now.

Clearly she didn't, but the wolf felt strongly about her. If anything happened to him, it would be her fault now. He was gorgeous. She felt him moving down the hill toward the back gate. He knew exactly where she was.

Fear sliced through her, not for herself because she believed she was his pack, but for Teddy and Edward who had no idea of this kind of predator. Even ancient Buster couldn't imagine this.

Stop! she shouted. *I have a pack, too. You can't be near my pack.* Pictures of Teddy, Edward and Buster flew from her mind. She didn't mean for that to happen, but she couldn't help it. She didn't know if it was like sending out targets for him.

He stopped half way down the ridge, in a grove of pygmy oak trees, just off the main trail. No one would see him there, but he could certainly hunt anything along the trail. Any small dog some owner left off-leash. A dog would smell him, though. Right? It would sense danger. Right?

Now she felt really ill. *If you kill anything here that belongs to a human pack,* she sent pictures of as many of the neighborhood animals as possible, *you are dead. Do you hear me? Dead. They will hunt you and I won't be able to stop them.*

He considered. *Those are pack animals? They seem like prey.* He was really entertaining the idea, turning it over. .When did he become so adept at communication? Then she remembered the koi translating for her. Perhaps she was doing that for him? Allowing him to communicate fully with her through her superpower.

Yes. A very important pack. You can't. She thought fast. *If you do, and they come after you, you won't be able to protect me. You have to protect me, right? That's what you said.*

What about this? he sent pictures of squirrels, deer, rabbits, mice. *Is this prey or pack?*

She sighed. She hated this. *Prey. They're prey. Just hunt over the ridge, okay? Far from human dens.* She sent a picture of the houses from up on the ridge trail. She and Tig had hiked there enough, she knew exactly what to show him.

Yes.

Something was nudging at her. She needed to break the connection. She closed the door. She'd said all she could for now. She slowly returned to herself, in her chair. Her phone was ringing and cut off abruptly. That was what must have brought her back. A time check revealed that she had to meet Karl. She grabbed her bag and phone and headed out. Another buzz indicated the

272

caller had left a message. She didn't recognize the number.

First, the fish.

*　　*　　*　　*

Karl was already at the Masuka's but since she had the only pond bag at the moment, he waited in his car.

"Hey," she said, grabbing the bag. "How are you today?"

"Good. Ready for this?"

"I think so. Any word on the other bag? Did the deputy get back to you?"

"Nope. I think we're not a priority." Karl followed her through the ornate gate.

"Tig was going to try and find out, too, but let's assume the worst."

"Well, you have other bags. No big deal, right?"

She hadn't told him about the Tanaka's information and her own personal info left in the bag for the killer to find. Maybe having a wolf guardian wasn't such a bad thing.

"Right. No big deal." She knelt at the pond's edge. The fish rose to the surface, hungry. "Oh, I forgot to pack food for them. Shoot." Not like anything else was happening to make her forget.

"I got some. I figured if I'm going to learn pond stuff, I should start my own bag." He held up a smaller version of her spare bag. "I didn't know what kits to get yet, so I haven't done that. Maybe I

273

could write down yours today and start getting stuff together?"

Wow, he really did want to learn. *Or take over business*, an evil voice in her head added. Oh, for Pete's sake. Karl was a good guy. Jeez. All this was getting to her.

"Sure. Great idea. You want to feed or check water?"

"I'll check. The more practice I get with you or Tig, the better I'll be on my own. I promise to call you though if I'm ever, you know, not sure of something. After seeing how much these babies are worth, I don't want to take a chance."

They were valuable babies. Thousands of dollars. And the Tanaka fish were worth even more. She briefly wondered at the value of Mr. Tanaka's first batch of fish. The ones that died.

A clamor of fishy comments drew her back to the bag of koi food in her hand. "Okay, guys, here you go." She sprinkled a few bits on the surface and watched them carefully as they rose to suck them in. They were really cute. If you didn't think about them eating you. Stop it!

She would have to move on from there if she was going to be any use at all. She tossed in a few more. Speaking of eating people, she figured she might as well ask them what they saw. She giggled as she imagined saying those words aloud.

"What?" Karl asked from over by the waterfall where he checked for leaks.

"They're just so cute," she improvised. Well, they were.

"I know. Makes me want some, too."

Okay, you guys. Show me what you saw. In seconds and she was under the water, looking up from the perspective of the koi. She knew she was in a big *showa* koi, black with red and white markings, one of the few names she remembered. Probably because it was a short word.

He was not as adept at pictures as the flag fish, but he knew what she wanted. He replayed someone coming past the pond to the front door. A human shape was all she could tell. All the fish were curious. Curious about everything in this new environment. They all gathered around the *showa*—the pack leader. *Pack. Ha. Focus, Elizabeth. At what point would all of this be too crazy and her brain broke? Jeez, focus.*

Now she seemed to get pictures from multiple fish, since the same picture came but from slightly different angles.

The door opened and Mike stepped out. He held a gun and backed the other person into the courtyard. The other man grabbed for the gun and they wrestled, collapsing on the pavers in a struggle for control of the gun. She could only tell it was two figures rolling. The second man got control of the gun and forced Mike to kneel. A clear view from the fish. The *showa* also provided sound, but garbled. The men were talking. She 'pushed' the *showa* and the words became clear, although a bit muted due to the waterfall, pumps, and other noises within the pond.

She heard "killed those fish," "priceless," "obligation," "shame." Mike lowered his head, seeming to accept the inevitable. The *showa* rose to the surface and the voice became clearer.

"Tokugawa-san will not accept anything less than this. A finger will not suffice this time. The clans are at war and will stay at war. You never should have come here, Mamushi." The gunshot sent the fish to the bottom of the pond, but she knew what had happened.

Mike Mamushi was murdered, his body falling along the edge of the pond. The fish quickly overcame their fear when the arm fell into the pond. Curiosity won out and she again saw and heard from their point of view. She heard her own car pull up and her voice. She saw the second figure pick up the gun and dart around the back of the house.

The fish began to nose at the fingers and she was inordinately relieved that what she had taken for them eating the finger was a digit already missing the last joint. However, the fish made it clear their intent was certainly to taste this new thing in their world.

Nothing more was forthcoming.

"Hey, you okay? How do the fish look?" Karl was matching test samples to the water chart. "The water looks great. We did a good job of clearing the concrete before we put them in."

Karl referred to the new concrete leaching into the pond and possibly harming the fish. Several water changes had ameliorated that.

"Oh, the fish are just dandy." Elizabeth tossed a few more koi kibbles in and resealed the bag. "I'll replace the food we used today. Unless you want me to keep this and just buy you a new bag?"

"Sure, whatever." Karl was easygoing, that was for sure.

"Okay. You want to write the test kits now?"

"Already done. Did it as I went. I also wrote down the order and my notes, in case it's a while before I do this on my own."

"Good idea. Ready?" Elizabeth had packed up her few remaining things, Karl having neatly stowed what he had used.

"I'm good to go." They mounted the stairs to the street level. "Need help with the Tanaka's pond today?"

"No, it's just a quick check I think. If I can get Tig there to confirm, we can put the fish in the big pond tomorrow. We might need you for that. You free?"

"Sure. You bet. That's exciting. I haven't seen that part before. Tell Tig I'm working at the new client's today. Making the materials list and whatnot."

"Okee doke." They both got in their cars and Karl drove away. Elizabeth decided to check the voice mail. Maybe she forgot a doctor's appointment or something. It had been a few crazy days. No such luck. The message was from a detective in the city police department. He wanted a word. Please call him back. Oh, boy. Now what? Los Lobos was in the county, an unincorporated part of limbo, not a city. No P.D. That's why crime was under the Sheriff's jurisdiction. They also had highway patrol here too, but no city police.

She dialed the number he left. *This just keeps getting better and better.* As she waited for the line to be answered, another thought occurred to her. Mamushi sounded like a Japanese name. But he didn't look Japanese. Maybe he was only part, but that was why he was a houseman for the Masuka's. Like Goro.

Twenty-Two

Elizabeth waited on hold while the receptionist got Detective Dominic. The police department was big since the city had over 100,000 people. More during the week when the outlying areas emptied and commuters came in to work. She wondered what he was detecting about her, since the Sheriff's office also ran the crime lab, so what was left? Didn't they have enough of their own crime?

"Dominic."

"This is Elizabeth Murphy returning your call?" Nervousness made it a question.

"Oh, yeah, thanks. I need to talk to you about the body you found? In the heights?"

As opposed to the many other bodies she found lying around on a regular basis. "Sure. How can I help?" Elizabeth relaxed a little. Just another statement. Clarification. But why?

"When can you come in?"

"In where?" Back to being tense.

"Station. I need to talk to you."

"I can talk on the phone now." She sounded squeaky even to herself.

"I can come to you, but it's better if you come here." He didn't sound threatening, but if coming to her meant going back to the station in cuffs, that was different. Her heart rate was definitely up.

"Okay." What did she have to do today? She had no idea. Her mind completely emptied of all useful information except that she had to tell Tig. "I can drive in now if that will work."

If that will *work*? It wasn't a coffee date.

"Yeah, good. Tell them you're here to see me. How long?"

"How long what?" Her brain really was on hold.

"How long 'til you can get here?"

"Fifteen minutes or so?"

"Okay." He hung up.

It must not be too bad if he's letting me come in myself. Well, it's not like she was turning herself in. But it felt like it. She broke one of her rules and made a call while she drove. She did put the phone on speaker in her lap, so she was not illegal. It was hands-free, so technically. . . technically she wanted to throw up. Authority made her nervous and she had no idea why the city detective wanted her statement about the body. Why didn't she ask? He probably wouldn't have told her, that's why, she answered herself. But she hadn't even tried.

Tig's phone went to voicemail. She left a message about what was going on. She hoped she didn't need bail. For what? She didn't know. Clearly she watched too much crime television. By the time she parked on Walnut Street and walked into receiving on shaky legs, she was a complete mess.

A waiting area very similar to a doctor's office greeted her. A speaker on the wall with a sign indicated she should press the button. She did and a woman's voice answered. "Yes?"

"I'm here to see Detective Dominic? Elizabeth Murphy. He's expecting me."

A buzzer sounded and she heard the door lock release. She pushed through and was in a hallway. She didn't know where to go so she stood there. A moment later a man in plain clothes loped down the hall toward her. Very long strides made him look like he was running at her, but she figured she was just nervous. Duh.

"Thanks for coming. I'm Tony Dominic." He stuck out a hand for her to shake. So far not much like an arrest. Early days yet. "Let's go into an interview room. Too noisy in the main office."

And they could record her conversation. There was no expectation of privacy in a police station, no matter what room they put her in. Unless she had her lawyer with her. *Shut up, just shut up*, she told herself.

"Coffee? Water?" He indicated she should sit at a small Formica topped table that had seen better days.

"No, thank you." More squeaks.

"I'm sure you're wondering what's going on." He opened a file folder she hadn't even seen him carrying.

God, relax already. "A little." And the understatement of the year award goes to. . .

"Let me back up a little. I'm on the Gang Task Force and some information has come to light."

Elizabeth knew gangs were active in the county, but beyond that, she didn't know much. Every once in a while a meth lab would blow up on some remote part of the mesa, and didn't the head of the Hell's Angels live in Cove City? She was getting ahead of the detective who had resumed talking and she'd missed it.

". . . cartels splitting the state and we're in the middle."

"I'm sorry, what?"

"We have the Nortenos and the Sudenos, and we are the territory to fight over."

"Who's we?"

"The state of California. The cartels are trying to get a real foothold north of L.A. but this new development is a little alarming."

She really must have missed a chunk. "What new development?"

He sighed, she assumed because he'd already covered this bit. "The yakuza."

"You're kidding!" That was not in the realm of reality.

He sighed again. "No, I'm not kidding. We've been watching this for a while and so far we thought we were in the clear. The cartels take up our time and energy out here."

"Yakuza? Here?"

"As far as we could tell, they were not operating here. Now we're not sure. We're investigating your murder."

"My murder?" The blood drained from her face.

"Sorry, sorry. Poor word choice. Not the murder of you, but the murder you found. Well, the body. The body we couldn't find."

"I'm sorry. I'm sort of shocked by this."

"Seeing a body is hard. Especially if it's someone you know."

"I didn't know him. I only knew *of* him."

"Okay. You're husband and his assistant knew him, right?"

"Right. Are you going to talk to them?"

"Yes, but you're one of two people who found the body, and who saw the crime scene before it was cleaned."

Elizabeth thought. "Okay, start over with the yakuza. That's Japan, right? Like the Japanese mob?"

"Right. There are differences but most people call them that. They started in Japan and then got a real foothold in Hawai'i. It's the perfect place for them because they blend in and Hawai'i is a gateway to the east for all things illegal. Mostly drugs and the sex trade, but up 'til recently, Hawaii was about as far east as they went."

Elizabeth felt she'd been dropped in the middle of a thriller plot. Crime to her was fiction, but now it was very real.

"You sure you don't want water or something?"

Suddenly, she did. They could have her DNA if they wanted, she just wanted some water. She nodded. "Water, please."

The door opened and a uniform put two water bottles on the table.

I knew it! I knew they were watching me. Small satisfaction. She opened her bottle and drained half.

"Okay," she panted slightly. "Go on."

"So, they spread to Los Angeles and San Francisco, the next two biggest Asian communities. Now we're seeing them spread further east. Fresno, for example."

"Oh, my God. That's crazy." She flashed to a gang war in Ohio or somewhere in the middle when the Italian mob and the yakuza met. What was happening and what did it have to do with her?

"Not so crazy. I know you're wondering where you come in." She nodded. "Our county is smack in the middle of all of this. We have cartels already here, we have some nasty biker gangs and now we are the center of the golden triangle of the yakuza strongholds."

Elizabeth really didn't swear much, but now she said, "Oh, shit."

"I know, right?" His face was grim, but she saw his enthusiasm. He was dialed in and ready to go.

"What can I do?"

"Tell me everything about everything. How you got involved in this and how you discovered the body. I know, I know," he held up his hands, "you've said all this before. But now I'm involved and I need to hear first-hand."

"Why are you involved. How?"

"I'm going to tell you some things I might not ordinarily, but family, eh? Your husband works with my brother, Honu."

That's why his name seemed familiar. She'd met Honu Dominic at some fire department events. Tig spoke fondly of him. A large, round man with a ready smile, his nickname Honu, meant turtle in Hawai'ian. So, maybe their family had connections to Hawai'i which was another reason Dominic was willing to talk to her.

"But no discussing this outside of this office, okay?"

She nodded.

"Mikio, A.K.A. Mike, Mamushi was a high ranking yakuza lieutenant. A hitman, among other things. We've looked into the property he managed and discovered it is owned, via layers of shell companies, by the second highest yakuza family in Japan. We need to know why he was here, and why that house was purchased. Are they moving in here? Starting up business? If that's the case, we need to be ready."

"How do you know that Mike. . . that Mike was. . ."

"Yakuza?

"The missing pinky. And the tattoos."

"That's it? Everyone has tattoos. He could have cut off his finger in an accident!"

"Those two elements are enough for me to look into it, but there's more."

Wait. He knew Mike's last name. And she only just found out about it herself. And he said, 'couldn't find the body.' Meaning, did they find his body?

"You found his body, didn't you?"

Detective Dominic raised his eyebrows. "How did you guess?"

"You knew his last name. I didn't, but you did." Technically, she didn't know his last name until the fish let her hear it, but tomato-tomahto.

"You probably wouldn't know that unless you'd found him. So, you found him."

Dominic leaned back in his comfy plastic chair. "You're observant, I'll give you that. Mike is Mikio Mamushi, the right hand of the Sato family, the second most powerful of the families in Japan."

"Is he like a half-son, or step-son or something? He didn't look Japanese at all." Well, maybe that was because when she saw him he was dead and face down in a pool of blood. Maybe. But Karl and Tig saw him and they never mentioned it. It makes sense, she supposed, that the Masuka family would have a Japanese houseman/caretaker.

"The yakuza aren't like the mob in that 'family' thing. They don't go by blood connection. The yakuza adopt their members and there is a type of father-son relationship. It is very real and the

286

honor of the family, the obligation, is serious and genuine."

Obligation. She'd heard that before. The man talking to Mike before he shot him. He mentioned obligation.

Dominic was still talking. "It is a ritual and connected with the Shinto religion so it's not something you can change your mind about once you're in. The 'child' might literally have to take a bullet for the 'father.'

"I see." She didn't, but she couldn't think of anything else to say.

"So let's go over your statement again." He shuffled his papers and got out a small recorder.

"Wait. You found Mike. Where was he? What happened to him?"

"Some hikers found him out in California Valley."

"Okay. What happened? Why so far away?"

"We think he wasn't supposed to be found for a while. He was in the salt flats out by Soda Lake. It's been so hot that he was mummified by the time he was found. He was buried in salt, so if the hikers hadn't come upon him he wouldn't be discovered for a while."

"Ewww. Sorry."

"It's okay. We don't get many mummies out here."

"Why would they do that? Wouldn't it be better if he was never found?"

"We're not sure. I'm the de facto expert, but without talking to the killer, my guess is that it was to disrespect the body and the family.

Remember I said that the Shinto religion is part of this?"

She nodded.

"They cremate their dead and the ashes are placed in an urn, like we do. Some of the ashes are often given to family members and kept in a place of honor. The gravesite has a big headstone, sort of like we do, and only the urn with the ashes is there. It's very a complex ritual with a lot of steps, but what was done to him is about as disrespectful as you can get according to their beliefs. My guess is that he was expected to be discovered at some point, but probably not this soon. As a way of thumbing their noses to the Sato family."

"You say Sato, but the Masuka's supposedly owned the house?"

"Not a real name. A shell corporation, Masuka International, actually owned it."

Elizabeth thought about everything she had seen and heard. Of course, a lot of it she could not repeat to Detective Dominic.

"Who are the Satos then?"

"Remember I mentioned the second most powerful crime family in Japan? That's the Satos. Okay, keep going." He nodded at her.

She repeated her statement as best she could. He asked a few questions for clarification, but basically let her talk.

A few moments of silence while he finished some notes. Then she said, "What's next?'

"I have to figure out if this is going to start a gang war here. A yakuza gang war. I'm sure word has got out to the Sato family, and that one of the

288

other two prominent families is to blame. Slights of honor and disrespect do not go unretaliated. I just need to make sure none of our citizens are harmed in the process."

"Do you think I am in danger? My family?"

"You didn't see the killer, so no, I doubt it. We have patrols in the neighborhood so just go on about your business the way you would."

"What about those other two yakuza families you mentioned. Are they here, too?"

Dominic closed his file. "Truthfully, I don't know. I didn't know for sure any of them was here until this. They cover their tracks pretty well, and they haven't started any businesses here to trigger our investigation. Like I said, between the street gangs, the bikers and the cartels, our plate is pretty full."

"We don't have a big Japanese population here. Wouldn't it be easy to find out?"

"I can't just investigate people because they're Japanese. That's called racial profiling and is frowned upon."

"Oh, yeah. But, Mike, he had a regular name didn't he? And he didn't look very Japanese. What about that?"

"It doesn't help us if they are using people who are not Japanese or who are part Japanese and don't look it. In Hawai'i, everyone is mixed, so everyone blends in. Here might be more difficult."

"I guess so. Should I do anything?"

"Don't take chances, no basements or late night meetings in the dark. The usual."

"Funny."

"Realistically, you're a pretty bad witness, so I wouldn't worry about it. If this is between the two or even three families, you're a non-issue. The Satos are all back in Japan and we don't have anything by way of evidence--of anything in our jurisdiction, yet. But," he held up a finger, "if anything unusual happens, call me right away." He jotted a number on his business card and handed it to her. "This is my cell. If you think of anything day or night, let me know."

He stood to let her know it was over. Her bum was completely numb from the plastic chair and she moved a little stiffly out of the room. So much to think about. He escorted her to the lobby.

Just as she sat in her car, her phone rang. Tig. Boy, she had some 'esplaining to do.'

Twenty-Three

Elizabeth answered her cell while she still sat in her car parked on Walnut Street. Her time at the police station had left her a little confused and even more nervous. She had seen the killer, sort of, through the fish's view, but she didn't know who it was. She did know the killer still had been on site at the Masuka's, Sato's? house and might have seen her. He might not know she didn't know who he was. If he was a hitman for some other yakuza family and had taken out Mike, she had no reason to think she might not be on his list.

As she spoke to Tig, all these thoughts ran simultaneously on a loop in her brain. She wasn't making the best sense to Tig and she heard the frustration in his voice.

She couldn't tell Dominic how she knew some of these things. She'd end up in the state hospital for mental patients. The only thing that cheered her, sort of, was that thing she'd heard bits of: this was an honor killing, shame and obligation involved and she had nothing to do with that on any level with any of the three families. How could she find out if she was at risk in that arena? The only Japanese person she even knew was Goro. How would *that* conversation go? She decided maybe the internet was her best choice.

"Bets!" Tig only called her that under certain conditions. Apparently, this was one. "You're not making sense. You're at the police station because you saw the body?"

"Yes."

"That's not their jurisdiction. That's the Sheriff's Department. Why? What's going on?"

"You know Honu from your station?"

"Yes. Now you're making even less sense."

"His brother is a cop."

"I know." He used his super-patient voice.

"I'm sorry, Tig. I think I'm more worried than I realized. He is a detective on the Gang Task Force and asked me to come in to talk to him about it. So I did."

"What does that have to do with Mike? Was he in a gang?"

"Sort of. Uh, the yakuza."

Major silence. "The Yakuza." Not a question.

"Yes. Apparently, the Masuka family doesn't exist and that Masuka International, a shell corporation, bought the house. The task force doesn't know why."

"You're saying the yakuza is on the central coast and Mike was a yakuza guy. What did he do?"

"Um." She picked at a loose thread on her seat. "A hitman."

"What?" He yelled that. Immediately he said more normally, "I'm coming down there."

"No, don't do that. I'm done. I'm not even in the station anymore."

"You come here then. I want to talk to you."

"Really, I'm fine. Mike's dead and they, well Detective Dominic, doesn't even know if the yakuza is active here or not. He did mention L.A. and San Francisco, and. . ." her voice got smaller, "Fresno, but so far, they just bought this house."

"Well, hell. I was working for the yakuza." He blew out a breath. "Where are the Masukas now? Are we in danger?"

"Oh, no. There is no Masuka anyway, that was just a cover name for the Sato family in Japan. Apparently there are three big competing crime families in Japan and this was probably some internal thing that ended up with Mike dead. I don't think we have anything to do with it. Except, you know, accidental. Circumstantial? Whatever the word is."

"Jeez, you seem to know a lot about this."

"When Dominic said he knew you worked with his brother, he got a lot more friendly. You know, Honu?"

"Oh. Yeah. But he thinks we're okay?"

"Pretty much." Elizabeth hated to lie to Tig, and she really wasn't very good at it.

"Pretty much?"

"There's something else I couldn't really tell him."

"Great. Let's have it."

"The fish showed me Mike's killer." Nothing. "Tig? Tig, I couldn't tell Dominic that. I have no proof or anything. And I really didn't see who it was. Just a figure. The fish couldn't see him well."

"The fish couldn't see him well," he repeated.

"It's okay, Tig."

"That means the killer *was* still there when you and Karl were."

"Well, yes, but that doesn't mean he knows I saw him. Sort of saw him, anyway."

She started her car, switching the phone to speaker. "I'll drive to your station, okay?"

"No. Nevermind. I have training, I forgot. We can talk tonight."

"I can't identify him or anything. He would know that. We really arrived after he'd gone behind the house. He doesn't know about the fish-vision or anything. I am perfectly safe."

"Okay." Tig was a talker, so when he reverted to one word answers or worse, none at all, he was upset.

"Don't worry. I'm fine." She did feel better. Just sharing with Tig was helpful. The killer had no way of knowing she'd seen anything. And what did she see? Nothing really. She'd heard stuff, though. That was bad. Again, the killer could not possibly know she'd heard anything either. "I'm going to check on the Tanaka ponds, okay? I think the fish are good to be transferred into the main pond tomorrow. I'll double check the main pond too."

"Okay."

"Please, Tig. It'll be fine. I'll see you tonight. Anything special you want for dinner?"

"No, anything is okay. See you tonight."

He sounded really down. Who could blame him? This was straight out of a Jack Reacher novel. Only, she was no Jack Reacher. She remembered when meth was getting big. That was a big city crime and then suddenly it was here, in their little community. Even other crimes were up.

She would stop at the store on the way home and make him something special. Right now, she wanted to finish at the Tanaka's and get home. She'd spent too much time on this lately. She still had the wolf to worry about, some potential new clients of her own, and Millie! She'd totally forgotten about Millie. She had to check and see if her doctor's appointment had gone okay. Poor Jato, the dog, wound up out of his mind with worry.

By the time she finished berating herself for not caring for her own clients, she was pulling into the Tanaka property.

"Crap." She'd forgotten to let Goro know she was coming, as she'd promised. "Boy, I'd better get my head in the game." She dialed the house from her car. She didn't want to surprise Goro again. If he didn't answer, she'd just check the ponds and the fish and be out of there. He picked up.

"Hi, Goro. It's Elizabeth Murphy. I've come to check the ponds but I wanted to let you know."

"You are here?"

"Yes. In the drive. I'm sorry, I was distracted and forgot to call you ahead. I can come back if it's a bad time. Tig agrees we can put the fish in the main pond tomorrow if today's check goes well."

"Yes, that is fine. Mr. Tanaka arrives tomorrow evening, so that will please him."

"Oh, good. I'm just going to do this and be out of here, okay?"

"Thank you."

They disconnected and Elizabeth unloaded her pond bag and got to work. The mini-ponds needed a water change. Although they had pumps, the amount of water was not enough to adequately serve that size of fish. She could do a water change, no problem, but it would take her longer than she'd wanted to be there. Oh, well. What was best for the fish was what she had to do. She looked forward to the day when she got back to her own life. It had been ages since she'd seen Janie or watched a Garrett dinner show. She sighed as she finished the ammonia and PH tests. *Poor me.* She smiled a little at that. She was on a beautiful property, on a gorgeous day, taking care of animals, which she loved. Things could be worse. Now that she was out of the station, she felt she had a little more perspective on Mike's murder. It was a 'family' thing and nothing to do with her. She knew nothing and furthermore, she had nothing whatsoever to do with crime on the other side of the Pacific. Besides, she'd never even been to Hawai'i. It was on her list of places she and Tig wanted to visit, but now, maybe not so much.

She drained each mini-pond leaving only enough water for the fish to remain upright and stable. Then she refilled each using the main pond as a water source. It took time since she did them one at a time. While the water level was shallow, she did her visual check. She tried not to touch the fish in case it damaged their slime coat, but that flag fish was irresistible. She put her index finger out for him like she would for one of the cats. He immediately came and nuzzled her, gently bumping his little nose against it.

All the fish told her they were hungry and she went to her kit to get the koi food she'd gotten from Karl. It wasn't there. "Rats." She thought she had put it in her own bag after Karl had said, "Whatever," but maybe she'd dropped it in his. His looked like hers only a little smaller. She'd been pretty distracted by the movie the fish had shown her.

She finished refilling the ponds and told them to "Hold your horses." She really didn't want to ask Goro for more tofu, but she couldn't think of a faster, simpler solution at the moment.

She rang the doorbell and waited. The door was so solid she didn't hear anyone approaching, but it swung open and Goro stood expectantly.

"Hello, Elizabeth."

"Hi, Goro. I'm sorry to bother you, I know I said I'd only be a little while, but the fish are hungry and I thought I had some food with me, but I don't, so could I. . ." she stumbled to a halt.

"Tofu?"

"Yes, please. I promise I'm going right after this."

She suspected he too would be relieved when her daily visits stopped.

Manners dictated that he open the door, inviting her in. She loosed her sneaker laces and stepped out of her shoes, deftly slinging them into the shoe rack by the door.

"Getting good at that," Goro said with a smile.

She was happy to see his demeanor soften. "I'll wait here. No need for house slippers, okay?"

He nodded and left in the direction of the kitchen. She sat on the bench next to the shoe rack and looked down the long hall to the wall of glass facing the pond. So lovely. Suddenly, she had an urge to see the pond from here.

"Goro?" she called.

His head appeared around the corner. "Yes?"

"Can I please go down the hall to the window? I'd like to see the pond."

A flash of emotion passed over his features, too quick for her to discern. "Of course. I will join you in a moment."

Forgoing house slippers, she walked down the smooth dark wood hall to the window. The floor squeaked slightly with each step, even in her socks. To the left was open, with access to the kitchen entrance and the living room. To the right were closed doors, to bedrooms she presumed. One door was open and she gasped when she glanced inside. The floor was covered in straw matting and the room was nearly empty. A cushion, a small table meant to be used by someone sitting on the cushion, and a flower in a vase in a wall niche were all she could see. It was so beautiful, clean and simple. She wanted to lie down in this room, head on the pillow and sleep. The far side of the room was not a solid wall, but looked to be sliding doors built of floor to ceiling squares. She was out of her league with Japanese housing construction, but the room itself exuded peaceful energy, and she was an expert on energy.

Goro slid the doors to the room shut from behind her. She was embarrassed he'd caught her peeping, but it wasn't like she was going through papers in a desk.

In one hand he balanced a tray that held a tea pot and two ceramic cups. This pot was slightly different from the previous one she'd been served: cerulean blue, and square, with a metal handle wrapped in bamboo strips. The handleless cups were blue on the outside and cobalt on the interior.

Goro guided her to the window where she'd said she'd be. Another wave of embarrassment washed over her. She'd been caught snooping and he was serving her tea. So, not only was she caught, she couldn't escape anytime soon. At least this didn't appear to be a tea ceremony again, just tea.

He placed the tray on a tree stump table she'd taken for just a decoration. Now that she saw it, it was amazing. Dark, rich wood, with layer upon layer of lacquer that gave the knobs and whorls in the wood such depth. He set two small padded stools on either side of the table and indicated she should sit.

Silently he poured tea and she finally looked out the window she'd been so hot to get to. It was worth the wait. The pond stretched and looped and she saw eddies and coves that had been invisible from the path. Lucky fish to live here, she thought. Lucky Goro. The back of the house faced the hills and the landscaping hid any neighbors. She was a little turned around but thought that the back of the property faced a vineyard. She saw the dry hills stretching beyond but heard no sounds from the neighbors or the nearby airport.

"To the fish." Goro raised his tea cup.

"Absolutely. To the fish." Elizabeth sipped her tea and sighed. If she could spend her life drinking tea by this window, it would be perfect. Slightly guilty, she amended, with Tig.

Goro sat very upright and she thought about what this meant to him and to her. For her, it was a treat. To be invited into this house for tea. But that was her western bias. For him? He was a houseman, a servant, so was he having tea with someone of his social class or even someone he viewed as beneath him? Was he being a good host in his 'master's' stead? She suddenly felt uncomfortable; judged and perhaps found wanting. He certainly hadn't wanted to talk. He initiated no conversation beyond the toast.

"I should probably feed the fish. Thank you very much Goro, for the tea, and the view. It was lovely," Elizabeth said.

He nodded and rose. "I will meet you at the door with the tofu. Please leave the dish out on the porch when you are finished."

"Sure." He didn't want her to bother him again. She felt herself start to slip into 'overthinking mode' as Tig called it.

By the time she'd put her shoes on again and tied the laces, Goro was back with a small dish of cubed tofu. He held the door for her.

"I'm sorry to have bothered you. I know you must be busy getting ready for Mr. Tanaka."

"Yes, that is so." The house had not appeared to be in a flurry of getting ready. She saw no landscapers, gardeners, housekeepers. In fact, the house looked exactly like it had every other time she'd visited. Immaculate. Quiet. But the energy was different, now that she thought about it. She bowed and let him close the door behind her. As she carried the tray, she realized the energy didn't come from the house. When she'd looked out the window or at that obviously special room, the energy had been serene, but energizing at the same time. The energy, the anxiety or darkness of it, had all come from Goro.

No further pondering was allowed, since the fish 'yelled' for their tofu. "All right, you guys, here you go."

She tossed a few into each pond and they ate ravenously. Again, she thought of how relieved she'd be when her duties were over. Tig only had two more days until he was off, and then he could check these guys himself.

She made good on her promise to herself to stop at the store for a special dinner for Tig. He loved to BBQ, so she bought chicken breasts and would make her special marinade. A huge salad and those squishy sourdough rolls he liked so much rounded out her meal plan.

As she pulled into her drive, her two greeters, big and small were on duty as usual. A glance at her phone told her how late it was and beyond tossing down some canned food, she completely ignored the cats while she prepped.

She and Tig might have a heavy duty conversation ahead of them tonight, so she wanted him as full and happy as she could get before that happened. *Good luck to me,* she thought.

Twenty-Four

Elizabeth heard Tig's truck in the drive. The two cats went to greet him, as per their contract. Elizabeth had just finished setting the table and girded her loins. She wasn't sure exactly how mad he would be. She popped the top off a beer and set it at his place.

"Hey," she said when he came through the front door, dropping his work stuff right on the floor. Well, that was normal.

"Hey," Tig said back and immediately came to kiss her hello. He seemed cheery enough.

"Hungry?" she asked.

"Starved." So far, so good. He picked up the beer and took a sip. "So good. What's for dinner?"

"I marinated chicken breasts and we have salad and those rolls you like. I pre-heated the barbeque but if you're too tired, I can broil them. They're thin cut so they shouldn't take long."

"No, that sounds great." He put his beer down and wrapped his arms around her. "You scared me today, you know."

"I'm sorry. It's okay, really. In fact, since the Task Force is taking over, I feel like we're out of it entirely."

"Yeah, Honu's brother came by the station to get my statement. I never saw anything weird about Mike ever. I barely saw anybody else. He asked me to describe the one time I saw who I thought was the Masukas, and I came up blank. When I'm working, I'm working."

"I know." Elizabeth decided to treat herself to a rare glass of wine. This was going much better than she'd anticipated. "Want some?" She held up the pinot grigio she'd stuffed in the back of the refrigerator and forgotten about.

"Nah. I'll stick to beer. Where's the chicken?" She handed him a platter.

"I'll get a clean one for after the meat's cooked. No contamination here." She'd gotten a little paranoid after reading an article on raw meat.

Tig took the platter out the back and Edward followed. Elizabeth knew at least fifteen minutes of watering would ensue, so she took her glass of wine to her meditation chair. Teddy accompanied her, but then saw she had no food, and made a U turn out the back to the chicken holder.

Elizabeth allowed herself to relax for the first time all day. Tig was home, and apparently not too angry, and the investigation seemed to be veering away from them. The wine was icy and not too sweet or bitter. Not much of a wine-person, she would not be able to describe it in wine-y words like bouquet and whatever twigs and flowers they used. She either liked a taste or didn't.

Millie jumped into her mind again and she dialed. No use putting off again what she really had meant to do days ago. Some friend.

After the initial greetings, she got down to it. "Did you listen to Jato? Did you get a check up?"

"Yes." Hesitant.

"It's not my business, but if I can help. Please let me."

"I have a mass. Jato was telling me I have cancer. They biopsied it; came back malignant."

"Oh, no. No, Millie. Where? What did they say?"

"The good news is it's in a good position and surgery is an option. Then of course chemo and radiation. My other health issues notwithstanding, they think I will make it."

"Jeez, Millie. I'm so sorry. What can I do? Do you need rides or someone to be with Jato?"

"No, I've got that covered. After the surgery which is scheduled for next week, I can come home if they get it out clean. They won't know until they get in there."

"Is Toby taking care of Jato? I can talk to Jato for you—let him know what's going on."

"I think that would be a great help. He seems to have calmed down some. Since he's a service dog anyway, he came to the appointment. Toby came too, to be with Jato while they were poking around, but seriously, Jato seemed to grasp what was going on. I was really surprised."

"I'm not. He's smart. He knew those folks were there to help you."

"The hospital smells didn't seem to bother him either. He's been to tons of doctor's appointments with me, but not hospitals. In fact, he wanted to visit some other patients." Millie chuckled. "They turned a blind eye in the oncology ward. I mean, they didn't let him go into patient rooms where people were vulnerable, but he visited the waiting room where people go for appointments, and then he decided to visit the chemo suite. All these recliners with people hooked up to IVs and Jato just marches in and says hello. Brought tears to my eyes how compassionate he is. And you should have seen people's faces light up." Silence. As Elizabeth was going to sign off, Millie added, "I'll be there soon enough. I'm bringing Jato, too."

"Okay, you let me know if Toby can't be with you, or you need anything. I'll be waiting to hear how the surgery goes, so tell Toby to call me."

"I will. Thanks Elizabeth. Really." She sighed. "I think maybe you and Jato saved my life."

Elizabeth immediately teared up. "You just get better soon, okay?" They disconnected.

Teddy, in his connectedness to Elizabeth appeared at her feet.

Okay, Mom?

In one minute I will be. She reached down and scooped him into her lap. He felt so good. The softest, fullest coat in the world.

Oh, Moooom. But he let her squeeze him. She rubbed the little flat spot on top of his head and down to his forehead where the stripes made an 'M' and then under his chin. He purred and smiled. She set him down.

Thanks, buddy.

Anytime. Well, not to pick me up, but to scritch. You know that.

I know Teddy.

She rose to see how Tig was doing with the chicken. He removed it from the grill and put it on the new platter. She placed the chilled salad and warm rolls on the table.

Tig set the platter down and was about to seat himself when she threw her arms around him and squeezed him.

"Hey, hey. It's okay, what's going on? The case is done for us, right?"

Her tears returned and she sniffled. "I'm sorry. I'm okay. I just talked to Millie and she has cancer. I feel so bad for her. They think she'll be okay, though."

"Well then," he steered her to her seat. "We'll do everything we can to support her. Especially you with your superpowers. Between us and the cats and her dog, she has to get well, right?"

Elizabeth was a little startled at his use of the word superpowers. He didn't know, right? Not really? She was pretty sure she hadn't mentioned time-travel in their previous discussion. She wasn't sure that she ever would. It was weird enough that she had seen things from the fish's point of view, but that wasn't totally unprecedented. She'd done it before when she'd 'talked' to some animal residents of a warehouse fire. An owl in particular had been helpful in showing her what he'd seen. But, samurai and speaking, or at least understanding, Japanese was a whole other ball of wax, as her grandma would say. Or kettle of koi.

Tig served up the salad and passed her a chicken breast. She hadn't been hungry but watching Tig, and Edward's nose, then seeing Teddy's rather sour expression from the middle of the kitchen floor, brought normalcy back for her. She was famished and tried to remember if she'd eaten lunch. She didn't think so. She'd gone from the police station to the Tanaka pond and then to the store. No wonder. She dug in and let Tig's recap of his day wash over her.

". . .and the best part is, I traded days off so I can do the fish transfer at Tanaka's tomorrow! It means I have to work the next day, but then I'll be back to regular schedule. Well, regular modified schedule." He smiled and passed a chicken morsel to the nose. He continued but she spaced out a little. They'd spend the day together tomorrow. That was the best news in quite some time.

*   *   *   *

The next day began sunny and bright, unusual for the coast. That promised good things for the day in Elizabeth's mind. Everything was normal and boring. She was thrilled. No calls from the police, no more bad medical news, the cats were healthy and happy. She double checked that during her morning meditation. She sent healing energy to Millie and explained the situation to Jato who took it very well. He was at his best with a job, and

Millie was his job. She told him to 'call' her if he needed an explanation or interpretation. Jato's command of words and comprehension of humans was exceptional due both to his training and his nature.

She roused herself from her meditation and made a special breakfast for their big day. Transferring the Tanaka's fish from the small ponds to the larger wasn't particularly difficult, but did require care and finesse. Tig wandered out in his PJ bottoms and crouched over the coffee pot. She slid a cup in front of him. She had let him sleep in given the previous busy and stressful week, and also the day ahead.

In reality, she figured being married to her was way more stressful than running into a fire. Well, maybe not exactly, but she was more of a long-term stress. She smiled and gave him a smacking kiss on the cheek just as he tried to sip his coffee. He slurped and heroically did not spill a drop.

"Blueberry pancakes and sausage when you're ready. I've been up a while and I'm hungry, but if you need to wake up a little more, that's fine." Elizabeth was someone who could not eat upon rising. She needed about an hour to assimilate before her stomach caught up. Tig was almost always hungry, so she tried to be prepared.

He nodded. "Just a few minutes." He took his cup and went out the back to see the pond. When she glanced out a few minutes later, Tig stood by the edge and Edward sat next to him, tail neatly curled around his feet. He had extraordinarily long extremities. His legs were long and deer-like and his tail was its own snaky entity. His body seemed long and even his pointy chin made his face long. However, a sweeter, more cuddly creature did not exist. The fact that he'd taken to Tig in particular was just icing.

She sat and poured syrup on her pancakes and sausages. Just one of each for her. She had a stack and a pile respectively, for Tig when he was ready.

She had just about finished when he sat at the table. She got his warmed plate out of the oven and set it before him, refilling her coffee and sitting, too.

He ate automatically and passed bits to the little black nose without missing any of his own bites. Pretty good.

"What's the plan today?" she asked when he came up for air. He'd consumed a startling amount in a short time.

He sighed contentedly and sat back. "I told Karl to be ready by eleven. We'll all meet there and do this thing."

"Did you call Goro? I sort of got into a bad habit of forgetting to tell him when I was coming over."

"Yup. We're good to go. We'll check everybody one more time and then if they're all well, we'll lower the water in each mini-pond to make it easier, and then transfer them to small tubs. The less touching of them the better. Two people on a tub, we'll lower it into the big pond and let them swim into it. Easy peasy."

"Thank goodness they're not that big." They'd had some dicey transfers when the koi got to be a couple feet long and very heavy. Water supported them best, so after a certain point, they tried never to net them except as a 'corralling' measure. Damage to fins and gills was a real possibility if the weight of the fish was out of water. Plus, the fish hated it. Their fear rolled off them and they thrashed and twisted. Elizabeth likened it to people being held underwater without knowing why or for how long.

"Sounds good. I'm going to clean up breakfast and then I'm ready."

"I'll double check supplies after I shave."

They each dispersed to separate tasks but met at the truck. "I packed waters and snacks, just in case this goes long," Elizabeth said, adding a small cooler behind the seat.

"Ah. You know us well." Tig smiled. "Ready?"

"Ready."

The drive into town was fast and the broccoli fields bright green as they whipped by. Their distinctive, rather unpleasant smell wafted into the cab. "It's a wonder anyone eats broccoli at all," Elizabeth mused. She liked it well enough, but it was one of Tig's favorite vegetables.

"I know, based on the smell, who would ever eat it?" he agreed. The city limit was an invisible line where townhomes magically sprouted instead of flowers and food. Elizabeth always felt a little twinge when she passed it, wondering when their beautiful valley would cease to be an agricultural belt and transform into an extension of urbanization. She didn't have time to ponder because the light traffic meant they reached Edwina Valley and the Tanaka property in record time. Even the airport traffic, such as it was, didn't hinder them.

They drove under the torii, the beautiful stylized Japanese gate, and parked. Tig had no qualms about leaping out to knock on the front door. She waited in the truck and watched as a brief discussion with Goro ensued. Goro apparently declined to watch since the door closed and Tig returned, but went to the back of the truck and lowered the tail-gate. She joined him.

"All good? Goro okay today?" she asked.

"He seemed happy that we're doing it today. Mr. Tanaka arrives tonight and he wanted them all in the pond. I did explain I'd need to come and check them tomorrow."

"Aren't you working tomorrow? Didn't you switch days with someone to get today?"

"Yup. That means you." He stopped pulling strapping out. "That's okay, right? You knew that when I switched days? You're me and I'm you as far as Precision Landscaping and Ponds goes, right?"

"Sure. I knew that. Just double checking." Actually, she had forgotten in the excitement of having Tig to herself for the day. Speaking of 'to herself,' Karl's little truck pulled in next to theirs. "No problem. Then you have your regular 24, right?"

312

"Yes, ma'am." Tig had resumed throwing straps onto the gravel. When they packed up the mini-ponds, they would strap them into the back of the two trucks again, the way they had brought them.

"Morning Karl," she called. He looked a little worse for wear. He was still young enough that eleven in the morning might still be considered way too early.

"Morning all," he answered cheerily enough. He brought his little matching pond bag with him.

"So cute," Elizabeth mumbled. Maybe not quietly enough because Karl shot her an odd look. She pretended not to notice but followed Tig to the mini-ponds. Karl trailed after.

Tig reviewed the procedure for Karl, who had never done this before. They all set about testing the water one more time and Tig went down and checked the pump room. Since he didn't go back to the house, Elizabeth assumed Goro already had unlocked it for him. They met back by the new fish.

"Okay, here we go. Everything looks great. We'll feed them later. I want them to be a little hungry so we can see how they do when they come for food. There are probably a lot of yummy things in there for them to eat anyway. Bugs and plants and anything fallen in."

Elizabeth flashed to Mike's arm in the Masuka pond and blanched.

"Sorry," Tig said to her. "Karl, you watch how Elizabeth and I do this first one, and then you help with the next, okay?" Karl nodded.

Tig lowered the water level while Elizabeth checked the fish from the 'inside.' She explained what was about to happen. The fish were eager. Tig double checked for flukes or parasites, misshapen anything that might indicate a health issue. All was well. Elizabeth picked up a small, shallow plastic bin that easily fit inside the mini-pond. Tig lifted the edge of the pond sending the water and the fish to one side. She deftly scooped them into the bin with enough water for comfort. Tig set down the pond and grabbed one end of the bin with her. Together they lifted it out and took it to the main pond access point they'd decided was best. They carefully knelt and lowered the bin into the water. They didn't 'pour' them out, but just kept lowering the bin until it was fully submerged and the fish rose to the surface of the bin and scooted into the main pond, instantly disappearing into its depths.

"That's sweet," Karl said. Elizabeth had heard him say this often enough to know he didn't mean sweet like she would, that it was darling or cute. It was the new incarnation of great, or even awesome.

"Pretty easy," Tig agreed. "Very little trauma to the fish. You need two people or even three if the fish are really big, but the hard part was all those water checks leading up to this."

"You got that right," Karl said.

Elizabeth very charitably didn't mention that she'd done most of the checking. Karl had found the body with her, and that was trauma enough to cut him some slack.

"Getting them out of the big pond would be the hard part," Elizabeth added.

"Why would you do that?" Karl wanted to know.

"If you have to isolate one. If it's sick and needs quarantine," Tig answered.

Karl processed that. "Oh, man. That would be so hard. How would you do it?"

"This is a huge pond. Sometimes people build in sections so you can contain fish in one area. I didn't check to see if this one has it. Like a corral for horses or cows. It keeps getting smaller until you get the one you want and scoop it."

"What if it doesn't have the corral part?" Karl asked.

"Draining some of the water is a technique, but this is a giant pond, so that would take time. One this big should stay pretty healthy. It becomes its own ecosystem unless something changes. We do water changes on most ponds, but this is practically a lake. It requires other measures. Anyway, let's do the next one."

Tig and Karl worked while Elizabeth knelt by the flag fish pond.

Hello, Elizabeth asked.

Hello.

How are you?

Ready to get out of here.

I can imagine. Do you want to tell me anything before you go?

Like what?

Elizabeth sighed, exasperated. *You gave me movies and a history lesson before and now you have nothing?*

Blankness from the fish. Maybe that was out of his vocabulary. She knew better than to let frustration speak for her. Animals didn't understand much in the way of sarcasm. Teddy was the exception.

She sent back some of the pictures the fish had originally sent her.

Oh. That. I was excited. My world is returned.

Elizabeth did not understand that comment. The fish didn't say 'world' but that was the sense she got. Whatever the fish wanted, it was content and felt it had received it.

Darn fish. Confusing. She tried again. She sent the picture of the men in dressy kimono-like clothes and focused on the one who reminded her of Goro.

Yes! The fish sent jubilant energy flying at her. Her whale had said that this fish was connected in time to its people, or person, so maybe, karmically speaking it was Goro's fish? Or Goro's ancestor's fish? Now it was getting really confusing. The fish was happy and healthy so she gave up.

Tig and Karl stood ready behind her. "Alley-oop," Tig said as Karl hefted this last pond.

"Tig, let me," Elizabeth said.

"Sure." He handed off the bin. She scooped the pure white fish with the perfect red dot.

Tig helped her carry him to the pond and they knelt keeping the bin level. This time when they lowered it in, the fish didn't race off like the others. He hovered at the surface facing Elizabeth. She put her palm under his body. It felt comfortable and comforting, like Teddy's solid body did. He rested there, his weight fully in her palm.

See you soon, he said, and in a flash he was gone.

"Whoa, that was weird," Karl said. "Did you see that?"

She assumed it was rhetorical but nonetheless answered. "Sometimes they do that. You know, if they're used to people. Maybe someone in Japan used to do that when he was little. I'm pretty good with animals."

"I'll say," Karl said.

"Me, too," Tig added, but she knew he was being funny. He knew about her gifts. Well, this particular one. "See any of them?" Tig asked.

"Nope," Karl said. "This must be paradise for them after all they've been through."

Tig and Elizabeth exchanged a glance. Pretty compassionate for a beginner--thinking of the fish like that. An excellent quality for a company who wanted to expand into fish acquisition.

"I think they'll be very happy here," Tig said. "I would."

"So would I," Elizabeth said, but she was thinking more of the house. She had been in it more than Tig had and couldn't forget the feeling of peace that emanated from it. She'd like to bottle that for their own home.

Karl and Tig began collecting the ponds to load into the truck beds. Elizabeth knew they'd be a while strapping and checking. She wandered the path again, keeping close to the water's edge. She didn't see a single fish. She didn't really expect to, but she sent out her feelers and all she got was the fish equivalent of *"wheeeeeee."*

She laughed and enjoyed their happiness with them. "I'll be back tomorrow," she said.

I know, came from the pond. She recognized the flag fish's energy.

She sat on the bench near the Dr. Seuss ball tree and waited. The flag fish appeared at the surface.

How is it?

Just as I remembered.

Right. That's not weird or anything, Elizabeth thought to herself.

Weird? It is weird, or it is not weird. You have confusing ways.

Rats. She'd forgotten to close her 'mental door.'

There are rats. They come to drink.

Fine. I can't keep you out. Is it nice in there? It looks lovely.

It is. . . home.

"Elizabeth? Where are you? We're ready to go," Tig called.

She didn't want to shout back and perhaps disturb Goro. She stood and glanced at the plate

318

glass window facing the pond. A figure stood there. More of a shadow. Unsure if it was Goro, but who else would be inside the house? Housekeeper, cleaner, perhaps? Never the less it creeped her out and she hurried back toward the parking area.

The fish had sent her calming energy as she hurried--ran back to the trucks. He seemed okay with whatever was going on, so maybe it was. She let his energy reduce her heart rate and by the time she reached the men, she almost felt normal.

"Good job today, everyone," Tig said. He and Karl had been discussing the new client because his next comment was for him. "I'll meet you later then and go over the suppliers."

"Sure thing." Karl drove out first.

Elizabeth clicked her seatbelt as Tig backed around the gravel area. "How about lunch at the Cove Cafe and walk by the bay to look at boats?" he suggested.

"Sounds perfect. I could use that."

"Seems like we haven't spent much time together lately that hasn't been work related. I'm meeting Karl's client at four, but that gives us a few hours."

"Perfect." And it was.

Twenty-Five

Elizabeth and Tig's private time went by so fast. They had a lovely lunch on the restaurant deck under colorful umbrellas. The view of the tiny marina opposite was always entertaining with people wandering by with dogs and kids, renting kayaks; watching lovely boats, myriad sea birds, and on a few lucky occasions, a sea otter floating on his back.

Stuffed, they opted to drive the few miles to the larger marina in Cove City that fronted an embarcadero filled with interesting shops and galleries. A very tourist-oriented place, never the less it was fun and relaxing to hold hands, talk about nothing important and admire the over priced items they could not afford but loved to check out.

Soon it was time for Tig to meet with Karl and the new client and he dropped her at home. Teddy and Edward had really missed her company the last few days and she spent time with them, reassuring them that staff and service would improve.

Lying on their wooden deck, just a raised area for the hot tub, sun warming all three of them, her mind wandered to the wolf and she decided to check in. Technically, she could connect with animals anytime anywhere, as she had with the deer and fawn, but she had always found it much more difficult than when she sat, calm and still, in her meditation chair.

Well, she thought, *I should really put these superpowers to work.* Eyes closed against the sun, back warmed by the planking, she let herself drift and called to him.

She still used her 'door' picture to help her, but she sensed she didn't really need it. Except maybe for the nosy fish who seemed to think they were welcome to rummage around in her mind whenever they felt like it.

She opened the door and the wolf was there. She didn't recognize where he stood, though.

Are you still behind my house?

No. I can protect you here.

Where's here?

He looked around him but for some reason, she couldn't see beyond the door way and his form. It was like looking into a dark house when the front door is opened. You can see who is standing there, but not much beyond, she thought.

I can't see where you are. Are you all right? Injured in any way? She wondered if something had happened to him and that was why she couldn't really see him.

I am not hurt.

She was a little confused by this, since it had not happened before. A lot of things had not happened before. She knew part of it was that she was not literally seeing the wolf. She didn't literally 'transporter beam' the animals to where she saw them. It was their energy she saw, manifesting in a form she knew, that they both knew. She wondered what her energy looked like to animals she had not met. She'd not considered that before, either. Yet another learning experience.

I am not sure where I am now, but I am not near your home or your pack. I can't seem to find my way, but I know I am where I should be.

That doesn't make sense. You can't find your way, but you are where you should be?

She thought perhaps things had gotten lost in translation, him being wild and not linguistically inclined. He'd done a good job so far, and if her superpowers were helping her, then she could translate for both of them.

If you look around, can you show me what you see?

The wolf turned his head and she saw a green, unfocussed jungle. No distinguishing landmarks, nothing stood out.

I came to this place. I don't know why. No females are here. You are not here, but I know I am supposed to be here. I will wait.

Okay, but remember what I showed you about human packs. Stick to hunting what we talked about. Just because you're not near me anymore doesn't mean you can eat human pack animals. It will still not go well for you. We have a lot of coyotes here—she sent him a quick picture— *and they eat a lot of human pack animals. They are hunted because of it. They bring danger to you. Do not be seen.*

He flashed her energy of understanding and showed her many pictures of coyotes along his own journey. *I dislike them. They are not wolf. Their ways are strange.*

Elizabeth remembered the coy-dog at the wolf rescue place and how the workers thought something was wrong with the animal until Fish and Game pointed out it was coyote, not wolf. That explained a lot.

Do you still feel you have to protect me from something?

Yes. Soon. Danger is near.

Great. Do you know what it is? Even if it wasn't real danger, if he perceived it as such, things could get messy. That was something she learned early on about animals, and she supposed it applied to people too. It didn't necessarily matter what something was, it mattered what it was perceived to be.

He flashed her some muddled energy of shadowy people and she thought, of fish. She had koi on the brain, so she might be wrong about that. Maybe she was going to get mugged like Karl. Or her home invaded like the Masukas.' Satos.' Whatever. That spooked her a little.

She and Tig had discussed getting an alarm system when several burglaries occurred and then the mailbox bashing. That was outside, but still, it was damaging and invasive. They hadn't done anything yet, of course, life being what it was, but perhaps it was time to revisit that topic.

Is there anything I can do to stop it?

The wolf in the doorway sat and looked squarely at her. She felt his eyes as well as his energy. A strange feeling to be sure. Usually she was on the outside, like a movie, but he had connected with her on a deeper level. Like the cats. He certainly thought of her as his pack for whatever reason.

No.

That was definitive.

I will be there with you.

Okay. I'll wait for you. She had no idea what to say after that. An invisible body guard, against an unseen and unknown enemy. She would love to tell Tig, but there was no way she could put it to him that he would believe. Or understand. She didn't understand it herself, but she sure believed it. The wolf made it clear and that somehow, he would be there. Wherever *there* might be.

The wolf turned and left the doorway and was immediately lost in the green-black fog beyond him. She rose to the surface of her mind and felt the deck beneath her, which had been warm and comforting before. It was now like concrete.

Two very round sets of eyes watched her, side by side, from about a foot away.

"What's wrong? Why do you guys look like that?" She asked the cats.

What's wrong with you? Why was that thing here? Teddy sent a picture of the wolf.

324

"I'm sorry, sorry guys." It hadn't occurred to her that the cats might sense her exchange with the wolf. "It's okay. He's not here. Nowhere near the house. You're perfectly safe."

You're not. We heard him, Edward said.

Mom, what's wrong. What's going to happen to you? Teddy was very agitated.

Nothing. Nothing's going to happen to me. I don't know why, but this wolf is here and he's helping me. I helped him, so maybe he feels an obligation, like a favor. I don't know. I've never talked with an animal like that before except you guys. He was here. He promised to leave and he did. She reverted to words, pictures and energy so she could soothe them. *He's somewhere in the county, I guess. He doesn't even know. Something is driving him, some instinct. Maybe the same one that brought him here looking for a pack mate. I don't know. But really, you guys are safe and I'm safe. Okay?* She pulled Edward into her lap and scritched Teddy under the chin which he could not resist. Rumbling purrs from both cats.

"Hey, how about a snack?" She stood and draped Edward, scarf-like around her neck. Teddy followed her into the laundry room which was the cats' dining room.

"Here you go." Teddy was instantly distracted by the full fat, non-diet treat. Edward sat for a moment.

I will be with you too, Mom.

I know sweetie. She loved how possessive the cats were about her and Tig. Edward sent her a bolt of energy so strong that it forced her a step back. "Whoa. Where did that come from?"

I. . . I can do things. I am learning things. I can't control it sometimes, but I found out that when you are in danger, a part of me goes with you. I don't mean to, but it does. It used to scare me, but not anymore. Now, I know, I am supposed to be here. I am like a wolf! His last statement was said just like little, excited Edward, and not like some great wizard or prophet which had begun to freak her out.

She hid her shock as best she could since apparently her cat was psychic. Fan-tastic. She decided immediately to get to work on her mental open-door policy. Meaning, there wouldn't be one. How about a lock? And a portcullis? And a moat?

Now Edward daintily lapped his treat, while Teddy, having long ago inhaled his, hovered by Edward's ear.

You gonna finish that? Teddy leaned in just a touch more.

Yes, I am. You better back off, bud. Edward sent without pausing.

Miracle of miracles, Teddy backed off. In a slight huff, but he did, flopping dejectedly in the middle of the floor.

"Aaah! The time!" Elizabeth had lost all sense of time and had no dinner thoughts. They'd gone out to lunch so she didn't want to rely on take out. Cheating, sort of, two meals in a row.

With Tig as her meal partner, there were seldom leftovers unless she made a double batch of something. Wait. She did have tofu. They kept that

326

on hand for the koi. The vegetable bin yielded miscellaneous treasures. Inspiration! She prepped the rice maker and started a quick stir fry. Lots of rice and veggies and there would be enough even for Tig. Saved.

Tig arrived full of news of the new clients and they enjoyed a fairly normal dinner. She declined to share her day with the wolf, or Edward's proclamation of newfound wizarding skills.

She and Tig shared a much needed cat-free time, but opened up again for a NetFilms episode. She was drowsing ready to drop off, Tig already snoring when a voice in her head screamed.

They're taking us away! They're going to kill us! Help!

Sleep was very long in coming.

Twenty-Six

Elizabeth woke groggily after a hit and miss sleep. After the screaming in her head, she had tried to send out energy to see who it was. She knew it was animal in origin, rather than human. She didn't have much luck connecting that way with people. Animals were her specialty. She worked her way down to her oldest clients, and one time clients, including Yuki the abandoned and then rescued tuxedo cat, with no success. She even sent out feelers to the flag fish since the energy felt a little 'fishy' for lack of a better word, but according to him, life couldn't be better.

Tig had already left for work, she could tell. The house was too silent. Shoot. Tig's side of the bed had two cats sprawled on it, which was another clue. She must have been really tired to miss him readying for work. Today was his last twelve hour shift, and then tomorrow would start his 24 hour shift. She both looked forward to, and dreaded that. The 24 hour shift meant he would be off for several days in a row, but it also meant he was gone for a whole night and day.

She sighed and got out of bed. No point in rushing to get dressed. She had to visit the Tanaka pond, make sure the PH was okay, and check in on the fish, but that wouldn't take long. All the hard part was over. It was a long way to go just for that. She should be happy about it, but she just felt worn out.

The voices bothered her. Animals seldom sought her out. She couldn't remember an animal actually asking for her help. She felt she was letting something or someone down, and her melancholy affected the cats.

They lay on the bed, limp and unmoving; only their eyes opened and met hers.

"Hi, guys. I'm sorry I'm down. Do you know what's going on?" Why not give them a shot? Edward, or Edwizard, as she almost called him, might be able to do something. She mentally replayed the call for help from last night.

They remained unresponsive. *I don't know,* Teddy said.

Me, neither, Edward agreed. *They sound scared.*

You guys are not helping. So much for animal intuition and Edward's new skill set.

Sorry.

Sorry. Little echo.

How about some breakfast? Teddy asked.

I know daddy already fed you guys.

That was ages ago.

Elizabeth checked the clock and he was right. A couple of hours probably, and for Teddy, in cat-time, that was ages.

"Okay. Up you get. Coffee for me, disgusting salmon for you. How's that?"

Two plops as they jumped off the bed and waving tails suggested this was acceptable.

She got her coffee brewing first and then scooped out a little from the pink can. For whatever reason, this kind smelled particularly icky to Elizabeth. The cats had the opposite opinion.

She was almost too tired or too bummed to meditate. She reminded herself that she always felt better after renewing her energy, but she didn't look forward to having some animal rampage around in her brain. Too early for that.

After half a cup of Peet's French Roast, she felt ready to cycle her energy and ground herself. Maybe it would help.

Feet flat, hands relaxed, she released old energy, pulled in energy she had expended and then cycled earth energy through her. She felt her batteries recharge. She still felt a little depressed but her energy drain had stopped.

Okay, she told herself, *here goes.* She let the call for help play again in her mind. She really listened and felt, not only for the voice or voices, but the source. It *was* fish in origin.

Suddenly a picture flashed into her mind. The pond at the Masuka property. Of course. The only other fish she really 'knew.' She had forgotten about them because her attention had been consumed by other things. They had helped her when she asked, and now they needed her.

Once she got the pond picture, she sent out feelers to them. Nothing at the pond so she knew they were no longer there. What had happened? Where did they go? Running away on their own was probably not the case.

She sent out more general feelers, but other than the *showa* who had really been the leader and the most helpful, she didn't know who to 'talk' to. She got nothing. Wait. A very faint something. Not a voice, but sort of a line of energy came from far away. It looked a bit like a line of gold glitter, but with meaning attached. *Cool. Stay focused.*

She repeated her request and the 'glitter' line got brighter and stronger. It was the *showa*.

Where are you?

Not sure.

Are you okay?

I think so.

Are you. . . dead? She had no idea if she could talk to dead animals. Heck, she was talking to animal spirits now, or reincarnated animals, so what was next? Maybe that wasn't so impossible.

No. We are weak. In a pond.

Were you the one who called me last night?

Last night? Confusion in the question. Time-related aspects often eluded animals.

Well, did you call to me at all?

Yes, but it is too late. We are not there. She assumed 'there' was the Masuka pond.

I know. Do you know where you are? What kind of pond? Send me a picture.

331

She got a fuzzy image of black walls and a rectangular shape. Not really a pond, more like a box. The fish were scared, their energy fractured. Some of them would become ill soon; she could tell when she moved around inside the box with them. After their drive from San Jose and transfer into the Masuka's pond, and now another removal to an unknown and perhaps hazardous location, they could all be lost.

Okay. I will help. You have to keep them all calm and relaxed. Can you do that? You are the leader, right?

I can do that. She sent calming energy and 'pushed' into him, forcing the energy through him and out to the others. They immediately slowed their frantic circling of the box. She realized something else. Even though the pond box was rather large, there was no pump. No air source. That load of fish would need air and a pump—a filter to cycle their waste.

She felt sad. They were a beautiful group, hand-picked by Tig and valuable. She didn't know if whoever took them realized that. Perhaps stole them to sell? Surely, if their value were recognized, better care would have been taken? She just didn't know.

I promise I will talk to you later today.

A fishy sigh in return and the connection was broken.

She knew he trusted her, but didn't have much faith she could do anything. She wasn't sure herself since she had no idea where they were.

She roused herself and didn't feel much better than when she started. Although she had cycled and cleansed her energy, that had been drained by the exchange with the *showa*. Now, mentally, she was sad and frustrated that they could die and there was nothing she could do about it.

Wait. She thought of one possibility and padded back to the bedroom. The cats had already re-retired to the king sized bed. She unplugged her cell from the charger and dug out Detective Dominic's card where he had written his personal cell number.

He picked up on the second ring. "Dominic."

"Detective Dominic I have a question about the Masuka property."

"Who is this?"

"I'm sorry. Elizabeth Murphy. I heard the koi were gone and I wondered if they had been reported stolen."

"How did you hear about that?"

Elizabeth was not a good liar, but she gave it her best shot. "Uh, a friend went by the property and saw the pond was empty."

"Yeah, sure. Animal control has them. Why? You want them?"

That had not occurred to her. "I might. Where are they now?"

"Main holding. Kansas Street."

"I didn't know you had facilities for fish there."

"Well, they don't, but they threw something together. The house is evidence and is being seized pending investigation."

"Can you just take it like that?"

"We can take property used in the commission of certain crimes. It's a jurisdictional mess right now. We have an extradition treaty with Japan, but we don't know who actually committed the crime and they're not going to hand over a citizen just because he bought a house here where a murder occurred. We have no proof right now that a Japanese citizen was even involved in the murder. Mike Mamushi was yakuza, we know, but beyond that, we've got nothing. We can have video depositions made for our records of the corporate house purchase but no one will ever come here in person. I mean, why would they? We're at a dead end. We're never going to hear from the right people anyway. We can't just steal the house, but we're trying." She heard the smile in his voice. "Anyway, we asked about the fish and they said to keep them. Well, their lawyers did."

"Oh. So, they can be adopted, or whatever?"

"I guess. Not my department. Go down and talk to animal control. Have them call me if they have questions. They'd probably be thrilled to get rid of the responsibility."

"Thanks. I guess from what you said, nothing new on Mike's murder? No more yakuza popping up?"

"For all we know it was a vacation home and their only tie to the area. He was yakuza, the

Sato family is yakuza, but his murder might not even have been related to that. Maybe local drugs, money. We're keeping our options open. Just stirring the pot, see what floats to the top. I gotta go. Good luck with the fish."

"Yeah, good luck with the investigation." She hung up.

Now she knew what else she was doing today. Drive to Animal Services, with an air pump at least, and see what she could do about those fish. Their own pond couldn't support them all. They were lovely though. Tig had taken such care in choosing and transporting them. He'd be heartbroken if they died from neglect. She had become attached to the *showa*, and she knew Tig probably had a favorite, too. Maybe they could keep a couple. What to do with the rest?

The Tanaka pond was certainly big enough. Maybe she'd ask Goro when she went there later.

Armed with purpose, she dressed and dug out a pump. To Animal Services and another mission of mercy. She 'told' the fish, through the *showa*, that she was coming. She felt the best she had in a couple days.

Twenty-Seven

As the crow flies, Animal Services wasn't that far. However, the roads and mountains didn't cooperate and it was 30 minutes before she pulled into the parking area. The facility was a little too close to the jail for her comfort, located right across the lot. And, a huge prison sat across the highway. She'd never had a reason to come to Animal Services before, odd as that sounded. When she helped clients, she only called here, or visited the website.

She entered the building and a cacophony of barking greeted her. A counter separated her from the office area, and a door to the left led to the barking, and she presumed some cats. She sensed them, knew Animal Services catered to them, but the dog noise was overpowering. Maybe that was for the best. If she was going to bring home fish, it probably wouldn't do to surprise Tig with a new cat. Or kitten. And certain other members of the household would have something to say as well.

A harried but kind-looking woman came to the counter.

"Can I help you?"

"Yes, I understand you have some koi here and I'd like to see them?"

"Koi?"

"Like giant gold fish?"

"Oh, yes. How did you hear about that?"

"Detective Dominic told me. He thought it was okay for me to come and see them and he said for you to call him if you had any questions."

The woman obviously wondered why Dominic would tell someone to come see the fish, but also, she had a lot going on and opted not to pursue it. Elizabeth saw two uniformed Animal Control deputies at desks, phones rang incessantly, and other women typed and filed madly.

"James!" she hollered over the din. "Come here." One of the deputies abandoned his desk. "This is Deputy James. He took the fish and is working on the report. He can help you."

"What can I do for you?" he asked.

"I was told I could see the fish and I, uh, brought a pump for them."

"Who told you that?"

"Detective Dominic."

"Oh, he did. Hmmm." James eyed her specutively. "Why do you have a pump?"

"He said that you folks weren't really equipped to handle exotic fish, so I thought, maybe you didn't have one for them." She didn't mention that from her vision, she was sure they didn't know the first thing about fish care, and from the current state of affairs, it wasn't likely they had time to learn.

"What's it to you?" He didn't sound hostile, but curious, even though the phrase brought out the NetFilms equivalent of a bad mafia movie.

"My husband's business specializes in these fish and I work with him." Stretching the facts a bit. No problem. "Dominic thought maybe I could help and if they were available for adoption, I know some places." *One of them being my house,* she silently amended.

"Okay, let's go." He flipped up part of the counter and came into the tiny lobby. She thought he would lead her outside where she'd seen some large corral areas, but he punched in a code on the dog barking door and indicated she should enter.

She had about two seconds to block herself from the onslaught of canine conversation. She could do nothing about the noise level of the barking itself, but she could not bear to think what the dogs would say to her. She double locked her mental door. It was one of the hardest things she'd done. She felt them there, pressing on her, energy mixed of despair and hope. She thought she might cry.

Head down so she wouldn't see any of them, she quickly followed Deputy James down a long hall to a back door. That door led to an open compound and she saw the fish box right away. It had been hastily thrown together with unmortared cinder block, and heavy black liner had been draped inside. The whole thing was unstable and unsecured.

"Oh, my gosh." She rushed to the box and looked in, calling to the fish the whole time.

I'm here, guys, I'm here.

Their health had declined in the interim.

"They need air. Please, find someplace to plug this in. Hurry!" she added when he just stood there.

He took forever to find an extension cord that would reach from the outdoor socket of the building to her six foot corded pump. Her frustration mounted as she waited. The fish didn't talk to her, and worse, they barely swam. Small fin movements kept them relatively upright, but they didn't move around the box. One of them, a black and white with gorgeous metallic scales, listed and only occasionally righted himself.

She got the pump going, all the while consoling the fish. She wanted them all now, but had no way to transport them. She also thought one more transfer in their current condition might spell the end of them.

"Can we please add more water?" She cursed herself for not bringing her pond kit. Wait. It was probably in the car. She'd been testing water every day and was supposed to go to the Tanaka's today. *Please please please be there.*

"Sure." Deputy James pointed at a hose bib.

"Can I please test the water? I would hate for these fish to die and they don't look good."

"Well, we just picked them up, so it's not us."

Elizabeth didn't mention how she had purchased them less than a week ago, and they had been in perfect health all through that and their transfer to the new pond.   It would serve no purpose and she needed him on her side.

"No, I know you guys just got them and aren't really equipped for this. I'm just here to help, okay?"

Huge sigh. "Okay. I've got stuff to do, so I'm going to let the volunteer coordinator know you're here and for her to check on you, see if you need help."

"Great, thanks." She preferred it if he left her alone with them anyway. He took her back to the lobby and she ran to her car. In her haste she'd forgotten to lock it. Oh, well. But yay! The pond bag was there.   Also, something else that sent shivers down her spine. The *original* pond bag was behind the passenger seat, on the floor, partially covered by her cloth shopping bags. The county plastic bag ban meant she always had several cloth bags in the car. She looked around the parking lot but no one else was there and all seemed normal. Except the whole jail-prison thing. Who could have put the bag in her car? Who knew she was here? A van pulled in and a lively family piled out, the children racing for the front door. Someone was getting a home tonight. She hoped.

She slowly opened the bag and tried to see if there was something bad in there. A knife. A grenade. Anything dangerous. She didn't see anything. This was the 'good' bag. Her own was sadly lacking in several things, one being food, another being a variety of medications for fish. She dumped the whole thing in the parking lot, even unzipping seldom used side compartments. She was sure she looked weird, and was positive there were security cameras but she didn't want to risk bringing anything inside that would get her in trouble. She was thrilled to see a bottle of hydrogen peroxide, a quick oxygen fix.

Nothing scary. Her heart lifted a bit as she saw she could help the fish more than she had first thought. She carefully put it all back. As she zipped it closed and made sure to lock her car, she realized the bill of lading and her own information were no longer in the bag. She refused to think about that now. Plenty of time to panic later.

She forced herself to focus on the current problem. Back in the lobby, she was met by Abby, a sweet-faced older woman who introduced herself as the volunteer coordinator. She punched in the key code and Elizabeth followed her down the same hall and out the door to the back.

"My, we're lucky you stopped by," Abby said.

"Well, I'm glad I could help."

"Is there anything you need?"

"No, I think I have it all now. Thank you."

"Deputy James said it was all right to let you work, so I've got visitors to show around. You should think about volunteering here. We could use someone like you."

What did she mean by that? A spurt of panic rose. *Can she tell I understand the animals? How would she know? How could she tell? How awful. Maybe she's a psychic?* Elizabeth felt her face redden.

"Oh?" was all she managed to sputter out.

"We don't have anyone on staff who really knows about fish, so it would be lovely to have you. Do you like dogs and cats, too?"

Elizabeth's relief was immense. Man, her exhaustion and stress were really making her weird. Sheesh. "Oh. Yes, well. I am pretty busy, but I do like helping," she hedged.

Not a chance in a million years, was what she thought. *I would be insane inside a week hearing all the animals' stories and trying to help them.*

"I'll let you get to it, then. I'll leave a wedge in the door so you can get back in." Elizabeth hadn't even noticed a keypad on this door. "Come find me if you need anything."

"Okay, thanks."

Elizabeth leaned over the fish. She dumped in the hydrogen peroxide. *Can you hear me?* She figured the pump had been running for about ten minutes now. Did they seem more lively? Maybe a little. She grabbed the hose and turned it on, washing the end as best she could. She wasn't going to put it in contact with the water, since she didn't know what contaminants might be on it, and did her best.

She tested the city water and it was okay. She draped the hose over the side so it didn't touch the water and turned it on. She checked the PH levels. Off the charts. They were poisoning themselves in there. They probably dumped a huge load of ammonia when they were netted and who knows how they were brought here. The water level was not high to begin with so she didn't want to dump any. Diluting and a chemical re-balance would have to do for now. Also, that little guy who was floating on his side. Could be his swim bladder was damaged or he had parasites. She couldn't fix it if it was a swim bladder issue, but if it was parasites, she could treat for that. The exposed pond liner looked none too clean and she hoped nothing toxic had been on it.

She calculated the pond's gallonage as best she could. She was terrible with that sort of estimation, and dumped in Prazi—a parasite treatment, erring on a little less just in case.

Hey, guys, guys, she called. She received mumbled responses, as if they were waking up from a stupor. She guessed they probably were. Fresh water, an infusion of air and medication. It had to feel good.

Are you hungry? What can you tell me?

A little hungry. I am better. She recognized the *showa*'s energy.

Can you tell me how you are feeling?

I could not swim. I could not breathe. But here you are and now I can do both. A wave of gratitude.

The others, they can't talk to me the way you can. Will you please ask them for me and then tell me what they say?

Yes. She figured their energy was entirely taken up now with just survival, so answering her questions was a low priority.

It was as she suspected. The move had been traumatic and physically demanding, a brutal netting process with bruising and some damaged fins.   The good news was that nothing was permanent. Still unsure about the listing black and white, Elizabeth noted that he seemed more comfortable now.

She stayed for hours monitoring them. Even the listing fish was doing better, responding to her gentle queries with fishy murmurs.

She had to get to the Tanaka pond.   That was also critical, their first day in the new environment.

She made a promise that she would take them all tomorrow. Tig could help during the day since his 24 hour shift started at 6PM.   She remembered that these fish would have to be quarantined again, no matter what pond they went to, but no problem. She would not see these guys stay in this horrible cinder block prison one more minute then they had to. They were too weak to transport or she would do it herself, today.

She explained her plan to the *showa* and he would tell the others. All but the black and white metallic fish ate a little before she left. If he didn't want to eat, one day wouldn't hurt. He probably knew what he wanted. She got no real information from that fish, he was too ill, although showing improvement. She got very little from any of them in fact, except the *showa*.

She packed up her stuff and left a note on the pond saying not to feed them, to leave the pump on all night, and that the caregiver would return tomorrow.   She hoped it would be read and followed.

In the main hall she met Abby coming out of a side hallway lined on both sides with dog cages. She beckoned for Abby to follow her to the lobby.

"Everything okay out there?" Abby asked.

"It's all good for now. I'll come back tomorrow and check, but I'd like to remove them to a controlled environment so their health will keep improving. Can I do that?"

"I don't think you can just take them. I guess you could adopt them."

Elizabeth wasn't sure if a bribe was being requested. Abby blinked at her from behind large lenses. Nah.

"Sure. I'll adopt them. Do you work tomorrow? I'd like to take them then if they're stable."

"No, but I'll leave word that you're adopting them. Between me and Deputy James you're our new hero around here."

Elizabeth was sure she was overstating, but it felt nice to be appreciated. She felt a little guilty thinking that Abby might have been putting her on about adoption.

Abby turned and hollered over the counter. "Hey, Melissa, fix up some paperwork so Elizabeth here can take the fish tomorrow."

"Why can't you do it?"

"I don't know how. We've never had fish here. Besides, I'm not in tomorrow."

"Fine. Come back around 11. Bring your own stuff. You can't use ours." Melissa sounded a little cranky, but Elizabeth gave her some credit since the office was a zoo. The family from the

345

parking lot came bursting out the door from the cage area, the middle-sized kid being towed by a boxer-looking dog with a sweet face and wildly wagging stumpy tail.

"We might get her!" the little one shouted to no one, but Elizabeth answered anyway.

"That's great. Where are you going right now then?"

"Out to the lawn to play. To see if she likes us and wants to come home with us!"

Elizabeth knew instantly it was a perfect match. She held the door for the family and watched them as they played. She tossed her pond kit into her car and let the exuberance of the dog buoy her flagging spirits. More cars had filled the lot in the interim and she hoped for more happy adoptions.

She sighed, completely wiped out. She had done a good thing. Animals were hard, even when all went well. As hard as kids? She and Tig had talked about starting a family. If kids were harder than animals, she wasn't sure she was up for it.

Then she remembered her joy when she spent time with Janie and Garrett. The surprise she felt when Garrett had communicated with her, or she with him, she wasn't sure which, while Janie was still pregnant.

Would that happen if she and Tig had a baby? Would she be able to communicate with it? A terrifying thought. But, upon reflection, she felt a small smile form.

Twenty-Eight

Elizabeth *had* to eat something, or she might die. Her stomach growled audibly as she pulled out of the Kansas Street lot onto the highway. She headed south toward Tanaka's but knew she needed food before she tackled that. Another half an hour wouldn't make a difference to the fish.

As she hit the first traffic light and the highway turned into a city street, she thought of Fattoush, the Middle Eastern place where she often got take out. Tig was particularly fond of the chicken shwarama plate and she loved the hummus and falafel.

Suddenly she didn't know if she could make it even one more block. Of course she did, and pulled into the corner lot moments later. She was such a frequent customer the owner greeted her by name. His family owned another restaurant in town, but this one was his alone, a tiny cafe with some outdoor tables. He seemed to appreciate her loyalty and often offered her a bonus, a free drink or extra grape leaves, while she waited. She rewarded this by passing on his little menu to everyone she met.

She ordered and decided to eat at one of the cafe tables facing the main drag. She rarely minded eating alone and could use the rest and diversion. He brought out her drink and a little paper dish with two rolled grape leaves on it that she hadn't ordered.

"I thought you might need this. You look extra hungry today." He had a warm smile.

"Thank you so much. You have no idea."

"Your order will be right out."

Elizabeth took a bite of the dolmades. Bliss. Tangy, textured, perfect. The grape leaves were stuffed with seasoned rice and lots of lemon juice. Not too oily like some she'd had. She ate them both in seconds.

Her lunch appeared in front of her, delivered by a college-age employee. "Enjoy," he said. She appreciated that the owner hired personable help. Another reason she returned, for even if he wasn't there, his staff was always polite and efficient.

Pleasantly stuffed, she threw out her trash and brought the remains of her iced tea to the car. Feeling much better about life in general, she skirted the main town and headed toward the airport and the Tanaka property.

Traffic had picked up as the day waned and it took longer to get to the Edwina Valley property. She didn't mind. The whole day seemed to have been rush rush rush and she enjoyed the forced slowing of life for a bit.

Her first surprise was that the gates under the torii were closed. Locked, maybe. "Oh, crap." Once again, she had forgotten to call Goro and let him know she was coming. She would be very surprised if Tig's company was retained after this project. She mentally apologized for that. She had learned from Goro that respect and manners meant a great deal to him, and perhaps to his culture in general, so she figured he probably thought she was the rudest, most uncultured lump he'd ever encountered. Even if he gave her points and didn't think she was rude, he had to feel that she was an idiot for this to happen again and again. Really, where were her manners? She never did this. She always called clients, said please and thank you, kept her napkin in her lap at meals. Her mother raised her right.

At least the gate was inset enough that her car fit off the busy road. A buzzer and keypad were mounted on a stand near the drive. She had never noticed them before, because the gates had been open. Of course, she had pulled in too far to reach it from the driver's seat. She sighed, got out, and pressed the button.

"Yes?" a metallic version of Goro's voice.

"Hi, Goro, it's me, Elizabeth. I'm here to check the pond. I'm sorry I forgot to call again. It's been a crazy day."

Something in her voice must have conveyed her sincerity, because he merely said, "Of course," and buzzed the gate open. He even sounded not too mad. Hard to say for sure through the speaker. She decided to be as unobtrusive as possible and scoot. She prayed nothing was wrong with the water or the fish and she'd be out of here in minutes.

She pulled into the usual spot, close to the side gate that led to the pond access point, the pump room, and the path around the pond.

She grabbed the big pond kit; all its resources making her feel competent and efficient. She knelt at the edge of the big pond and took her samples. The pond was huge so she really should take samples from more than one spot, but she didn't want to be seen further into the property or discover Goro doing his karate dance.

"Oh, grow a pair," she said to herself. "I'm just doing the best job I can." Before she relocated for more water samples, she looked for the fish, but of course, none to be seen in this vast sea.

Hey, guys, she called. I'm here checking in. How are you? Anybody out there? It was so peaceful here; quiet and serene. She waited for a response. Nothing.

She specifically called to the flag fish. *Come on. I need to know if you're okay. Answer me.*

What if they were all dead? A spurt of panic. What if whatever had killed the first batch was still in the water and they hadn't found it? Tig might have if he'd had more time, but she was a complete novice. If it wasn't in her water chart she had no idea.

Hi.

Oh, thank God. You're here.

His little red spot bobbed in the clear water. He was adorable. Had he grown a little? She did a little health check since he just waited there. He sent her a wave of impatience.

I'm hurrying.

Not that. He sent a picture of her hand in the water and she laughed. She knew what he wanted. She placed her hand, palm up, just under the surface and he swam into it. She could swear she heard a sigh of contentment. What an odd little fish! She was very careful to let him control where he touched her palm. She didn't want to disturb his protective coating, but he didn't seem to care. She couldn't resist. With her other hand she gently rubbed his red dot with her index finger. Waves of contentment rolled toward her.

"That is very interesting," said someone who was definitely not Goro.

She startled and the flag fish leapt out of her hand and disappeared into the deep in a flash.

"Oh, jeez, you scared me," Elizabeth said, wiping her wet hands on her jeans. She stood and faced a very tall, imposing-looking Japanese man. Oh, boy. This must be Mr. Tanaka. She had completely forgotten that he had arrived. That's probably why the gates were closed. Just how she wanted to meet him, kneeling in the gravel, wet jeans, dirty shirt, fooling around with his million dollar fish.

"How do you do that?"

"Oh, Mr. Tanaka, it's so nice to finally meet you," she managed to get out. She bowed as well as she could and when she rose, he had a slight smile.

"I see you know something of our customs," he said. He seemed amused by her attempt, but maybe it was just that she was pretty awful looking at the moment. Her curly hair had a mind of its

351

own at the best of times, but after her day and then with the pond stuff, it was probably a fright wig more than a hair style.

"Let's continue this inside, shall we?"   It wasn't really a question, but she tried.

"Oh, Mr. Tanaka, your home is so lovely and I'm kind of a mess."

"No matter." He turned and led the way to the house, the long way that would take them past the picture windows and the main rooms. She opted to collect her equipment later.   She thought she heard laughter bubbling up from the pond. "Easy for you, buddy," she mumbled. Tanaka didn't slow his step, but something in the shift of his shoulders told Elizabeth that he'd heard some or all of that. No way to explain, so pretend it didn't happen.

She studied him as they walked, and he was not only tall for a Japanese man, he was just tall. Maybe six-two?   His broad shoulders filled a custom suit and he moved easily and gracefully down the path.   His jet hair was combed straight back and lightly gelled in place. No glasses.

Her brief look at his face, when she wasn't completely freaking out, said he was handsome. Strong features, and didn't look like he laughed often, or perhaps even smiled.   Of course, Goro didn't smile much either.

He preceded her into the house and Goro met them there.   Shoes were exchanged and Goro presented her with a pair of pajama bottom sort of pants, black with wide legs and a drawstring waist.

"Mr. Tanaka would like to talk with you and your clothing is a little. . ." he struggled for a polite word.

"I know. I've been working all day and I didn't expect to be inside. Sorry."

Tanaka had left them the moment his house slippers were on, and Goro allowed a small smile. "No problem. Expect the unexpected."

"So true." Elizabeth smiled back.

"Please follow me." He showed her to the small bathroom she customarily used and the place to put her dirty pants. "Come to the living room when you are ready. Feel free to make use of the guest toiletries here." He slid the door closed.

She must look worse than she thought. A look in the mirror confirmed that.

"Great first impression, Murphy, just great."

She didn't wear a lot of make-up, but the little she had put on seemed to be resting under her eyes rather than where it belonged. A smear of dirt over one cheekbone, and another on her forehead trailing into her hairline.

"Oh, my God. It's a wonder he didn't have me thrown off the property," she mumbled as she scrubbed her face. Her light foundation covered her despised freckles, but she figured it was better to show them than to look like she'd escaped from Dickensian London. She found a wide-toothed comb in the toiletries collection and dampened her hair, wrestling it into a bun again. Maybe it would stay if she didn't fall in the pond or do something stupid. Her shirt was damp and had an interesting smell from the water at Animal Services. It didn't look terribly dirty, so it would have to do. *Those poor fish,* she thought again, before her focus came back to her appearance. She took Goro's offered pants and they were comfortable and surprisingly soft. Her socks were disgusting from her work, pond, mud, sweat and who knows what else, so she removed them and saw another open shelf with yet more wrapped house slippers, exactly like the ones at the front for guests. She liberated a pair. She rolled her socks into her dirty pants and tucked them on the slipper shelf.

One more glance in the mirror. It was as good as it was going to get. She slid open the bathroom door and crossed the wide hall to the living room. It was empty so she went straight to the windows to see the pond. So gorgeous. From this vantage point, Mr. Tanaka had a clear view of her as she tested water. She figured the same view could be seen from the kitchen windows around the corner from this room. The pond curved around the house maximizing the vantage points to view the water. And the fish, if they ever showed.

Goro entered silently behind her and she nearly jumped out of her skin when he asked if she would like tea. By now she knew the 'three-rule,' and said no thank you. He insisted, she resisted, and they finally agreed on tea.

He gestured she should sit near the windows and he left her alone, she assumed to make or get the tea. She had no idea how that worked. Did he have it ready? What if someone really didn't want tea? Or the opposite. What if someone was really hungry and needed to eat. Do you still have to say no three times? The etiquette was a mystery to her but she really did want to be polite and respectful. Except about calling ahead. Apparently there, she was a rube.

Oh, well. She took a deep breath and exhaled, automatically putting her feet flat and relaxing her hands in her lap. The energy from the pond itself and the fish in it was very strong and flowed directly into her with little prompting. She felt the flag fish 'push' at her, much the way she did to him.

"I see you are enjoying my pond. I am glad."

Startled, she opened her eyes. How long had he been watching her? Mr. Tanaka sat opposite her and he'd changed into more casual attire, pants similar to hers, but with a regular button-down men's shirt. It was very plain and simple but she bet it cost a bundle.

"It's the most amazing pond I've ever seen."

"I had it designed especially. I flew in the top designer in Japan to do it. When I am here, I want a little piece of home with me."

"It must be hard, being away from home. And here is pretty far," Elizabeth added. "We don't have much in the way of a Japanese community here, so I can see it might get kind of lonely."

She couldn't get up the nerve to ask about a Mrs. Tanaka, so she waited. He nodded once, acknowledging her comment, and then lifted his cup in a toast. "*Kampai,*" he said.

She figured it was like bottom's up, so she said it back. They sipped.

"How did you do that with the hinomaru?" he asked.

"The what?"

"The koi. How did you get it to come to you?"

"What did you call it?" She didn't think that was the name Tig had told her for that special fish.

"Hinomaru. It is one of the names for our national flag. It means circle of the sun. It is a prized fish."

"I've been calling it the flag fish, too." Elizabeth smiled to think she had something in common with this man from the other side of the world.

He smiled back and it changed his face completely. He went from strong featured to extremely handsome in a heartbeat. "So, did you train it? Did you have food in your hand?"

"No. I didn't really do anything." *Anything I could tell you about.* "Perhaps someone trained it back at the breeders. We have a specialist in Japan who selected your fish for you. He will be honored that you are pleased." Now she sounded like a character in a movie. Get a grip. "I have noticed from my experience," *none from koi, of course,* "that animals can read us often better than we can read them. You could train it to come to you. Probably all of them, in fact. They are high quality koi from the finest lineage." There she went again. "I could tell you how to do that if you want."

He sipped for a moment. She sipped, too, for lack of anything else to do.

"Yes, I would like that. What do I do?"

356

"The first thing to consider is where you will feed them."

"Where?"

"Yes. Where did you feed your other fish from? Or your pond in Japan, if you have one. I don't really know."

"Yes. We have an automatic feeder in both ponds."

"Okay. I see you have a need for that, but if you want them to come to you, which is a very wise decision which I'll get into later, you will have to feed them by hand."

He rose and went to the picture window, flipped a latch and the whole thing swung open making a door onto a little deck over the water. "Here. I will feed them here."

She joined him. "Where is your automatic feeder?"

He pointed to the right where the pond met the drive as it wound around the garage to the back of the property. She saw a small machine with a small nozzle-like device aimed at the pond. It was camouflaged in the landscape and almost invisible.

"Okay, that's good. Is it adjustable?" He tilted his head in inquiry. "The, um range of the pellets and the angle and such? Can it be moved?"

"Goro will know."

Elizabeth presumed he'd bought, or rather his pond guy had bought, a top of the line feeder so she went with 'yes-adjustable' for now.

"What you want is for the pellets to disburse about the same area you are going to feed from.

They will learn quickly to come to this area when they are hungry, or if they see you here."

"I see."

"Also, what I mentioned before about this training being a good idea, is because when they feed, they are usually at the surface. You can check them and see if they seem healthy and are behaving normally. Also, to count them. Make sure they are all there every day. For a while we had an egret around our pond and we were always worried he'd get a koi. Our fish are too big for it to pick up, but that wouldn't stop it from puncturing one. Then it could get sick or even die."

"All of this is excellent. I wish I had more time to spend here. Can we try it now?"

"Sure. They really like tofu so that would be a good training tool. Turn off the auto feeder while you do this. That way only you or Goro are their source. These little guys are new to the pond so showing them where food is will be quicker."

Goro had magically appeared again. "Goro, tofu please. And turn off the automatic feeder if you have already programmed it."

"Of course." A bow and he melted away.

She presumed they spoke English out of courtesy. She wondered if the flag fish, hinomaru, would translate for her if they spoke Japanese.

She began calling the fish. She promised them tofu. They hadn't been fed since the transfer, so barring how many bugs they found or water plants they nibbled, they should be hungry. Of course, Mr. Tanaka or Goro wouldn't be able to 'call' them, but she could help this process along if she explained the situation to the fish. The more she learned about koi, the more she thought they were like cats. Even when they knew what you wanted, they only did it if they felt like it. Teddy's face popped into her mind. She smiled.

"What is it?" asked Mr. Tanaka, noticing.

"Oh, I think I see one coming." She prayed for the tofu to arrive.

It did. Goro passed a tray with small-diced tofu to Mr. Tanaka and bowed. Tanaka gave the tray to her. She tossed a few cubes of tofu out and they floated for a few seconds before slowly descending. She called again and waited.

"Should you throw more? Perhaps they cannot see it in such a big pond."

"That's true but they won't eat it as well off the bottom for some reason, so it will just pollute the pond. We skim out the uneaten tofu from our pond to make less load on the filter, but yours is so big, that would be impossible. It's better to put less in. Something you can do to help attract them is to make noise."

She squatted and gently slapped the water, then tossed in a few more cubes, also while calling them.

"Can they hear that?"

"Absolutely. Water transmits sound well. What you want is for the splashing or slapping to become a dinner bell for them. You know how some cats or dogs are trained to come running when they hear a can opener? Because they know food is on the way?"

He looked at her blankly. *I guess not.* Probably his 'people' fed any animals he might have, but she suspected he might not be an animal person. A fish person was still acceptable.

"Anyway, eventually, if you feed them at the same time and place each day, they will know to come."

"How will they know?"

"Usually by the sun." *Or some magical unknown reason she had been unable to pry out of Princess Keiko. The hinomaru probably wouldn't tell her either.* But she was the 'expert' here and had to come up with something.

Finally! she scolded the hinomaru as he swam up trailed by his pod. Whatever you call a herd of koi. God, the landmines she was avoiding, she thought.

She slapped the water and tossed them tofu.

You don't have to do that. I knew you were here. We all did, hinomaru said.

I know, but I'm not going to be the one feeding you, and they need some way to get your attention. Sometimes it is a little lacking, you know.

More, came from the crowd in general.

Elizabeth gestured to Tanaka to toss some tofu. He seemed tickled when they scooped it right up and remained at the surface. His face lit up and she saw shadows of the little boy he'd been.

"When they slow their eating, when they let the tofu drift past and don't go after it, then stop. Just throw a little at a time and watch them. You'll know who is a pig and who is a dainty eater very soon and you can track their behavior." She shot a

360

meaningful wave of energy at the hinomaru, much as she'd glare at Teddy if he was being too piggy toward Edward.

All she got was amusement in return. He was a rascal. She had to admit, she liked him. Pretty only went so far, but a rascal was entertaining.

"How do I get them to come to my hand?"

"That will probably take some time. Not all of them might. Some just don't like to be touched, which is more natural for a fish, really. Others seem to enjoy it." She thought of their own fish. Princess Keiko allowed it, but didn't seem to want it like hinomaru. Elizabeth was 'training' Casper, their ghost koi, as much as one can train a koi. He seemed to like it, especially the top of his head and his whiskers. He liked to 'snuffle' her hand, as if searching for food, which he knew wasn't there. She equated it with Teddy rubbing his jaws against corners, the reason why many of their white walls had little dark smudges about eight inches off the floor. She washed them off periodically, but she didn't really mind them. She knew they made Teddy happy so they made her happy, too.

"Your first step is to get them to come for feeding. Once a day is plenty and the key is same time-same place. Once they do that reliably, you can have them come closer and closer to you to get the food."

He grunted in assent and rose from his uncomfortable squatting position.

"Thank you. For all your assistance. I am grateful." He gave her a real bow, and she recognized that as true respect.

She bowed back, slightly lower, as she'd learned, and said, "It has been my pleasure."

This seemed the logical place to take her leave, so she made her excuses and returned to the bathroom where she reluctantly put on her dirty pants. She kept the house slippers on until she could get to her shoes. She stuffed a sock into each front pocket, which felt weird, but thought it was better than walking around with them in her hands.

When she slid open the door, Goro was there. She was relieved she hadn't been doing anything else in the bathroom. His ninja-like appearances were unnerving.

"Thank you, Goro, for your hospitality. Those pants were amazing."

"Bamboo."

"I beg your pardon?"

"They were of bamboo cloth. Among the softest cloth fibers."

Well, you learned something new every day! She and Tig had at least half a dozen varieties of bamboo at the house and she knew it was eaten and used in construction, but fabric?!

"Well, they were great. Thank you. And for the tea."

"*Doitashimashite.*"

Her brain whirled. "I forget."

"You're welcome."

"Oh, yes! Um, *domo ari. . .*" something to do with cats. . . "*arigato!*"

362

"Very good. I will walk you out."

She knew by now it would do no good to protest that it wasn't necessary, so she followed him to the back door, put on her socks and shoes and went around the path with him to where she'd left her kit.

She decided not to test more samples. She'd been there long enough. Tomorrow was another day. If Tig said the chemicals were fine again tomorrow, maybe that would be it for a while. She hoped so. It certainly had been a learning experience for her, exposure to a whole new culture. She was exhausted, both mentally and physically from all her interactions, both on the energy plane as well as the real world, in English and in Japanese.

Twenty-Nine

Elizabeth's attention faded on the drive home. Traffic was backed up on Los Lobos Valley Road, not only because she had hit 'rush hour' such as it was in this area, but also because Cal-Trans was repaving one lane at a time. She was informed by roadside LEDs to 'expect up to 20 minute delays' and that made her even more tired.

Obviously she projected her commute and frustration, because Teddy sent her a picture of him and Edward waiting on the porch for her. That made her feel much better. When she reached home, there they were, and she gave each one an extra scritch and thank you even before unlocking the front door.

The house emanated peace and quiet and it enveloped her with instant improvement of mood. Until she remembered dinner. Rats. That always seemed to roll around too soon, and lately she'd not been prepared at all. What was happening to her? Normally she was organized and efficient but lately she was falling apart. Even when she'd worked at the fire station doing temp work last year, she'd managed her time better.

Open a can, Teddy said.

Yes, please, added Edward.

Sure, okay. A can. That's not going to help me, now is it?

You could at least help those you are able, Teddy said sagely.

Elizabeth laughed and did as she was bid. It did help. When she opened the pantry to get cat food, she saw spiral pasta. That prodded her brain and she thought of homemade macaroni and cheese. They always had cheese and that wasn't too hard to throw together quickly.

Thanks, guys, she said to the cats.

Told you, Teddy said as he inched nearer to Edward who still ate slowly.

Teddy! she scolded.

Fine. He backed off the tiniest bit and Edward shifted so more of his back was to Teddy, an insult to be sure.

She set water to boil, turned the oven on, and then began her roux, a butter, milk, flour base for her cheese sauce.

Not a lot of salad ingredients, since she'd been neglecting her grocery runs, too. The other day she'd just bought what she'd needed for that meal and hadn't stocked up on anything else. She did have tomatoes, a kind neighbor had left home grown cucumbers on the porch, and onions were a staple. Vinaigrette-marinated three vegetable salad. That took her just moments to whip up while the pasta water boiled.

While she made the salad, she'd pulled the white sauce off the heat, but now she put it back on low and gently added grated cheddar and then some tangy cream cheese.

Perfect. She drained the pasta and rinsed it, then dumped it in a big bowl, stirring in the cheese sauce. She added a little garlic powder and lemon pepper. Sometimes she added fresh garlic to the roux, but she'd forgotten this time, so the powder would have to do. The mixture went into a large glass baking dish and she topped it all off with Panko, Japanese bread crumbs. Those were not because of her new-found discoveries into Japanese culture, but because her mom was on a low sodium diet and on some previous visit, Elizabeth had scoured the grocery aisles looking for options for her. The Panko had almost no sodium, plus they all liked the bigger pieces that were more like breadcrumbs and less like powder. She would bake it covered for thirty minutes and then uncover for five or so. She and Tig both liked it brown and crunchy on top.

Time check. Tig should be home soon. A quick shower for her while the casserole baked. She felt pretty sticky. Heading back to the shower, Teddy followed but Edward went to the closed front door and sat. That must mean Tig was near. Tig and Edward's connection was similar to hers with Teddy, only Tig wasn't aware of it. He knew Edward favored him, but he'd yet to experience it directly. Elizabeth felt that would come. They spent time together watering and if Tig sat for even the shortest amount of time, Edward was in his lap.

Maybe that came because when Edward was very little, he'd taken to climbing up Tig's leg for attention. Then Tig would reward this bad behavior by carrying him around, or tucking him in a pocket, literally, because he was that small. Now, even though Edward was too big for pockets, he still sought that closeness. Tig liked it, was flattered by it, but Elizabeth knew he didn't understand how much Edward loved and needed him.

Now that Edward was a wizard, or whatever, she wondered what else it meant. Too much to think about now.

The shower felt so good. She washed her hair and put on clean clothes and felt human again. Teddy was on the bed when she came out. She didn't hear anything, but the house's energy had changed and she knew Tig was home. She peeked out the bedroom blind and sure enough, he was out back watering, a small black fur ball rolling on its back nearby.

She felt a rush of love for both of them and a little prickle of irritation from Teddy. "You're still my guy," she said and gave him an extra good belly rub. His lips curved up in a smile and his paws stretched out.

He was so cute she gave him a kiss and he was less pleased with that, but allowed it. He understood that it was human affection, but no matter how Elizabeth explained it, he didn't understand why it was necessary.

It's not necessary, she'd tried to tell him at one point, *I just can't help it. You're so cute and I love you so much.*

A sigh and a *whatever,* sort of response. She tried again.

You know how if I rub your tummy or the base of your tail a lot you get really excited and your claws come out and you can't help it? It's like that.

It's not like that at all. That had been the end of the discussion, but she'd had to give him another kiss for it.

She checked the casserole and took the foil off. She grabbed a beer from the refrigerator and went to greet Tig, Teddy trailing.

He gave her a one-armed hug and a big kiss. She gave him the beer and patted Edward who had shifted to his on-guard position near Tig, feet close together in a tiny square, long long tail wrapped around him.

"How was your day?" she asked.

"Busy but not exciting. He went into a story about an elaborate practical joke they were setting up involving an old resuscitation doll, a uniform and the bathroom stall, when the chief made a surprise visit to the station and they'd had to put it on hold.

"I'm sure you'll get to pull it off soon," she reassured him.

"Yeah, but it was just so good. When will Terry be at this station again?"

Janie's husband Terry and Tig were best friends but they worked at different stations. Apparently he was just swinging in to cover someone's shift that day, so of course, Tig and Terry made the best of it.

"Gives you something to look forward to. Hungry?"

"Starved." The usual response. "It smelled so good in there I thought I'd die."

"It's almost ready. You want to shower first or eat?"

"Eat. I have a little more to do here. The upper bamboo bed," he gestured with the hose.

"Okay. I'll finish while you finish." Teddy followed her back to the kitchen and flopped in his customary spot, the middle of the floor.

"Really?" she asked. "You can't be to one side or the other? The middle where I have to step around you all the time? I could hurt you. I wouldn't mean to, but I might."

No, you won't. You would never do that.

They'd had this conversation six thousand times before, so she gave up. She pulled the casserole out, browned to perfection and set it on a hot pad in the center of the table. Serving spoon, salad and place settings and she was ready. She had just gotten a glass of water when Tig and Edward came in.

Tig washed his hands at the sink while Edward sat near his chair.

See, I'm *out of the way,* Edward said. All Teddy did was narrow his eyes, but didn't otherwise respond.

"This looks great," Tig said.

"Thanks." Elizabeth dished out a large helping of mac and cheese on his plate and a smaller one on hers. Tig helped himself to salad and then passed the bowl to her.

For a few minutes there was only eating. Edward had disappeared from view, so she knew he was in Tig's lap. When they were working on second helpings, smaller and slower, she finally picked up the conversation again. She realized she had a lot of catching up to do, so she condensed it.

"I got a 'call' from the fish at the Masuka's pond. They thought they were going to die and sent me a distress call. They had been picked up by Animal Services since the house is empty and may be seized as part of the investigation. Not sure what's going to happen to the house, but it's empty now and the fish were taken. I took a pump and checked the water and did the best I could. I told Animal Services I would pick them up tomorrow. Can you help me?"

Tig looked surprised at all this. "Why are you picking them up?"

"Animal Services isn't really equipped to handle exotic fish. They didn't have them set up well. They did the best they could, but it seemed they didn't know who to call for help. I mean, even a pet store wouldn't really know unless koi were their area, right?"

"True." Tig's chewing had slowed way down. Maybe he was full and not mad. Sometimes he was hard to read.

"So, since we have the quarantine ponds back, I figured we could keep them here until suitable homes were found. They were in bad shape or I would have tried to move them myself."

"I'm glad you didn't. That was probably a good call."

Elizabeth found his support reassuring so she went on. "I know you spent a lot of time and money on them at San Jose Koi, so I know you'd want the best for them. One doesn't look too good. Remember the black and white with the shiny scales? He was sideways. I treated with Prazi and checked the water. They had no pump or filter so I put in a pump and diluted the ammonia as best I could. Everyone ate except for him by the time I left. He seemed better though. Not completely upright, so maybe it's his swim bladder. I don't know what to do."

"I guess we'd better rescue them tomorrow, then." He smiled. They both had soft hearts and although she felt that way about all animals, she knew koi were Tig's Achilles' heel. They'd rescued fish before, so this was not unprecedented. "I'll set up a pond right now. I know there are five but they've been together; I'll put them in the frogateriam." That was their pretend word for their largest plastic pond that remained filled most of the year. It was too big to move and didn't go on rescue missions.

"Do you need help?"

"No. It's already in the outback. I'll get some water checks and a pump going."

"Okay. I'll clean up dinner, but text or yell if you need help."

She knew he was tired, but Tig on a fish-mission was unstoppable, and it made him happy. He opened the yard gate to the 'outback'--the rough, undeveloped area behind their property that connected to a twenty-five thousand acre state park. Edward followed, always happy to supervise anything Tig did.

371

The large preformed plastic pond was there, filled and seasoned and often operated as a frog nursery. For a while, it was filled with water hyacinth, but lately it was a drinking station for deer that wandered through. The seasoned water, meaning it had been in the pond for a while, harmful chemicals removed and had figured out its own cycle and eco-system, would be perfect for the traumatized fish. Strictly speaking, it wasn't large enough for long term care, but she and Tig could easily monitor and medicate them until they could be moved.

Rats. She'd forgotten to ask Goro or Mr. Tanaka if they would want any of those fish. Of course, if they agreed, it would have to be the ones of the highest quality. Tig would have to weigh in, since her main criteria was 'cuteness,' as Tig liked to tease her. It also happened to be true.

She wrapped the meager leftovers and started the dishwasher. She was suddenly so tired. She rested her hands on the counter near the sink and looked out the window to the large bamboo grove. Nestled in the center was a golden baby Buddha, who's charming expression never failed to lift her spirits.

She was definitely ready for some NetFilms. Tig returned with his shadow and locked the back door.

"Shower time," he said.

"Go ahead, we're right behind you."

By the time she'd changed into her PJs, the center mass of the bed was taken up by two cats. A mathematical impossibility and yet, two smallish cats took up more acreage than two humans on a king-sized bed.

"Give me a break, Teddy," she begged as she tried to scoot him over from the exact spot she needed for her feet without breaking a hip or straddling him like she was riding a horse.

He scooted but not without a dirty look. Tig came out of the shower and put on his PJ bottoms and a tee shirt while she watched and wished she had the energy to do something more than admire. Edward was scooted easily and when Tig lay down, he crawled up onto his chest, arms extended and paws resting on Tig's cheek.

Elizabeth clicked on the TV and NetFilms box and while they waited for it to 'check network connection' and decide to do what it was told, she remembered her other big news.

"I met Mr. Tanaka today," she said.

"How was it? What's he like?" Tig's questions were slightly muffled by Edward's paws.

Elizabeth described her adventure and closed with, "He seems nice. He has a very powerful energy, though. At first he was so stern, very off-putting. I can see why he runs huge corporations in Japan; you wouldn't want to mess with him. But I like him. I think he loves his fish as much as you do. He just doesn't know as much about them. He sure wants to learn, though."

Elizabeth had had enough of a brush with actual crime recently so she didn't feel like watching her usual choices on TV. They agreed on the new season of "Psych," and although that was technically a crime-solving show too, it was so masterfully written and so full of humor, it didn't count. Soon enough they were both laughing hysterically to the disgust of the cats, who personally hated comedy. After two episodes they called it a night. Too tired to remove the cats, for once, they let them stay.

It wasn't the cats that woke them in the middle of the night. It was Elizabeth's cell phone, the shrill ring startling all of them. Goro in a panic. The fish were sick. Starting to do what the last batch did. He'd been keeping an eye out. He thought it might be something with the pumps. Please hurry.

For the unflappable Goro to call in the middle of the night, showing that much emotion, it had to be bad. They hurried.

Thirty

Tig drove deserted streets to the Tanaka property. Small town living had its perks. They had thrown on their old clothing, figuring they'd get dirty and probably quite wet. Elizabeth had the foresight to grab the 'good' pond bag from her car and transfer it to the truck. When Tig saw it he asked, "Sheriff's return it from evidence?"

"Not exactly. I found it in my car."

Tig grunted. It wasn't that unusual for one or the other of them to find a lost item right where it belonged or in some place they'd thoroughly searched.

She let him think that. Now was not the time to come clean and worry him. Traffic picked up a little near the airport, not that people were traveling—the airport shut down at night—but it was the warehouse district as well and shift workers and early morning deliveries made the rounds.

It was close to three in the morning by the time they pulled under the torii into the gravel. Tig hit the gravel at a run, Elizabeth right behind him. They made straight for the pond, each bearing a kit.

The area was lit up with enormous flood lights Elizabeth had never seen before. Both Goro and Mr. Tanaka stood at the edge of the water, gazing at fish at the surface, struggling to breathe. When fish gasped for air, *in* the air, it was bad. Something was taking the oxygen out of the water.

"When did this start?" Tig asked.

"I noticed the fish acting this way a little before I called you," Goro said. "I called right away. It is just like last time."

"This is what happened last time? Exactly like this?"

"Yes, but they died. I knew of no one like you to call."

"It was awful," Tanaka added.

"Oh, Tig, this is Mr. Tanaka. I told you he was here, now," Elizabeth said by way of introduction.

"Hi." Tig ignored all formalities, as did Tanaka and Goro, so absorbed were they in the fishes' condition. "We have to remove them. I didn't bring any ponds with me. What do you have around we can put them in as we catch them?"

"I will find something." Goro took off at a run.

"Bets, start taking water samples. I'll throw in a pump, maybe get some air going. As soon as Goro gets back, we're transferring them to anything else."

Elizabeth dropped her kit and rapidly gathered and tested water. All her days of pond checks finally paid off and she was able to move quickly without having to refer to directions and charts.

"Tig! There's almost no oxygen in the water at all. Something has sucked it out and they're suffocating. Ammonia level is okay, it just seems to be oxygen."

The bright floods allowed Tig to find an exterior outlet near them and he tossed in a pump. She called to the fish to come as close to the pump as possible. One by one, they slowly made their way to the pump and air. Tig had only brought one extension cord with him, so the pump was close to shore. It broke her heart to see them struggling to get close, their proximity to people not a factor. Hinomaru was last. He had taken it upon himself to make sure all the other fish got close to the air source, so he was the last to receive it. She 'pushed' all her energy into him to help him along. She pictured herself carrying him in her palm to the bubbles. He felt it and let her, receiving the energy wholly and finding an area of air with the others.

Tig was doing additional tests of his own while she used her gifts to see inside them. "There is a high level of methane in the water," Tig determined. "Do you have a well on the property? Anyway methane could be introduced into the water at high levels? Is there any drilling nearby? Natural gas or anything like that?"

"No," Goro panted. He must have heard the last bit as he was jogging up with two plastic bins. "I think I know where there are more of these. I will see."

"Elizabeth, tell the fish we need them to do what we want in order to save their lives. The amount of exposure is in direct proportion to their internal damage. Help me catch them." He didn't stop for a response, but ran back down the path.

She immediately closed her eyes and cycled energy from the earth, through her and to them, telling them what was happening. The fish had responded favorably to the oxygen and heard her. Tig returned with two fish socks--giant nets with small-weave, on poles.

Tig had already tested the water from the nearest hose and told her it was safe. It would need some treatment but was methane free. "Mr. Tanaka, fill these bins as quickly as you can."

She and Tig did their well-practiced fish catching dance. Since the fish were so sluggish, it was quite easy. They knew she was here to help but they also didn't want to leave the oxygen source.

He guided the fish with his net, she blocked with hers, he scooped and she lay her net atop his to keep the fish from jumping back into the pond. That last step was habit, because these fish just lay gasping in the net. Tig dumped them into the bins and by the time Goro returned with two more bins, six of the fish had been removed.

The flag fish, hinomaru, had paid a price for protecting the school and coming last to the oxygen. He struggled to remain upright and breathe. She sent energy inside him and breathed with him. His gills were burned and each breath seared like fire. He wanted to give up. She told him to hang on.

"Tig. His damage is the worst. What can we do?"

"I don't know now. Let's just get him out of there and into clean water." They scooped and dumped.

"Tig, put the pump in here, first."

He complied. "Jeez, what a mess." He scraped back his hair with a wet hand. "Any idea what happened here?"

Mr. Tanaka stood staring at the bins. Elizabeth didn't have to have abilities to know what he was feeling.

"No," Goro said. Something in his tone made her look up at him. He was lying. She was sure he hadn't vandalized his own pond, well, sort of his pond, but he had a clue.

Mr. Tanaka asked, "What did you mean, exactly, when you told Elizabeth to call the fish?"

Tig shifted uncomfortably. "Uh," was all he got out.

Elizabeth was too tired and too worried to be discreet any longer. "I have a gift for communicating with animals. All animals. The hinomaru comes to me because I ask him to. Not all the time of course, I can't control animals. They have free will, but often they do as I ask because I am helping them. He just happens to be a strange little fish that craves human touch.

"Ask him what happened. Ask them all." Mr. Tanaka was very angry. She was mildly surprised that he took her at her word, without question.

She asked. She got pictures of someone in the pump room, which the fish could see from the water through the picture window installed there.

"Someone did something to the pump room. They couldn't see clearly, and of course they don't understand technology, but they showed me someone in there."

"Have either of you been in there?" Tig asked the men.

Tanaka shook his head negative.

"No," said Goro. Since I gave you a key to check down there, I have had no reason to go."

"You said it was something with the pumps when you called?" Elizabeth said.

"I assumed that, but I didn't know."

"Why did you call Elizabeth and not me?" Tig asked.

"She usually calls to say she is coming to check the water. Sometimes she calls when she is already here to check the water." A small smile. "Her number was on the top of my call list. It was fastest."

Elizabeth checked in on the fish. They were doing better in the clean water. Except hinomaru. She knelt and lay her hand under the surface. *Come to me.* He did and rested in her palm. She felt from him, that if he was going to die, he wanted some contact when he went. She started to cry.

"Go. Check the pumps. Both of you. Fix this," Tanaka said gruffly. She heard Tig and Goro crunch off along the gravel path, but she kept her full attention on the fish. She felt Tanaka kneel beside her. She had her full force focused on keeping the hinomaru alive. He wanted to leave. She did not want him too. He was in such pain, though. Was that fair? To put her wishes above his? She didn't know at that moment, but she trusted her instincts. Hang on.

She felt Tanaka's hand on her shoulder, and then his other hand moved next to hers, his palm aligned so that the hinomaru rested on them both.

She felt power, raw power from Tanaka flow to her and to the hinomaru. Where his hand rested on her shoulder, it burned slightly and felt so heavy. Hinomaru jolted as if receiving a shock and collapsed into their joined palms. Elizabeth's tears dripped into the bin.

Thirty-One

"No!" she cried but Tanaka shushed her. "Wait."

She still cycled energy automatically and she felt Tanaka's in sync with hers. She had been on the verge of hysteria, but Tanaka had halted that and drawn her attention back to feel that hinomaru still lived. She looked inside him and saw that their combined energy was healing his burned gills. She didn't know how, she had never healed anything before. It had to come from Tanaka, but how he knew how to do that, when he didn't know how she talked to the fish, was a mystery. No time to ponder. She focused her all and she felt the little fish recover. He righted himself and she stayed inside him, feeling his struggle to breathe lessen, and the pain dissipate. He was still weak, but would not die. He sent waves of gratitude.

They pulled their hands from the bin and sat back. She felt weak but exultant. Tanaka must feel the same. She heard crunching on the gravel and tried to rise but her stiff legs didn't help. She started to tell Tig and Goro about their success when she was pushed violently from behind and clubbed, but her fall made the blow a glancing one, and not lethal as was probably intended.

Tanaka was on the other side of her and she saw her attacker come at him as she fell. He was older but faster in his reaction time and managed to stand before the man, she was sure he was male, was upon him. The area was lit well-enough, but the blow to her head affected her vision. She watched horrified as her blurry eyes made out a gun pointed at Tanaka. Tanaka was made to kneel, just like the fish had shown her Mike had done.

However, this attacker underestimated his older opponent. Tanaka grasped the gun with two hands in a twisting arc that brought them both to the ground. Tanaka kept hold of the gun and torque on the wrist. the man yelled in pain as the gun was yanked away. She heard a bone pop and a thump and she assumed Tanaka had hit him. The man did not get up.

This happened so quickly that by the time her bruised brain and bleary eyes took it in, it was over. Terror and nausea rose in equal parts as she thought of Tig and Goro. Why hadn't they come? Had the assassin killed them first? Alone and trapped in the pump room? She knew Tig would die to protect her, so what happened? Goro was trained in some martial art, and she had seen that Tanaka was as well. Maybe Goro couldn't protect them both against a gun in the cramped space.

Not knowing drained her of the ability to rise and check on them. She didn't have long to decide. A dark figure came down the path toward them, and she knew it wasn't Goro or Tig. The presence of a second assailant answered her questions.

"Tanaka!" she called.

Tanaka turned just as the man raised his weapon. He was not going to make the same mistake the first had.

They fired at the same time, but only the unknown man hit his target. Tanaka fell, his gun falling into the shallows at the edge of the pond. Elizabeth managed to get to her knees to help Tanaka. Maybe she could reach the gun in the dark water. The man had other ideas. He moved quickly forward and she saw he was Japanese. She'd never seen him before. His tattoos ran up his neck from his shirt, and out the sleeves of his sweatshirt down to his wrist bones. Yakuza. Somehow, this was a hit. Like Mike was a hit and Tig was now probably dead like Goro and Tanaka. Part of her didn't care if she was next and she met his gaze. He was still a little blurry but she saw surprise and maybe respect on his face. He hesitated just a moment, and that was all it took.

A dark shaped launched out of the night, a whirling, snarling, snapping form that she knew even without clear vision was Sojourn. Her wolf who had sworn to protect her, and had promised to be here. Somehow, he knew.

Seeing him in real life was so much more powerful than in vision-form. He was much larger than the wolves at the rescue place; his muscles honed from miles of travel and fights with opponents she could only imagine. When he hit the lighted area, his fur glowed a rich copper brown. His head was huge, the teeth clamped on the attacker's wrist which dropped the gun the moment the jaws closed. The man had no choice. Sojourn was determined to remove that hand. The man tried to punch and kick at the wolf, but Elizabeth saw that even years of martial arts didn't prepare you for a fight with a wild animal that weighed almost as much as you did--an animal filled with anger, hate and fear. She felt all of this coming off Sojourn in waves. She was terrified but awed at the beauty and grace of her savior. She tried to send him a message that he didn't need to be afraid, but it turned out he was not afraid of the man who had passed out, or at least gone limp, in his jaws. He was afraid for her. Just as he'd said. She was his pack and he would die to protect her.

"Stop!" she said aloud, and in his mind.

He froze, but didn't let go. She didn't know where the gun had gone, but from the attack and the shaking the man got, it probably wasn't anywhere she could find now. The wolf turned his face to her. Amber eyes, surrounded in a dark face, glowed in the lights.

"Enough," she told him. He dropped the arm and the man lay where he'd fallen. The wolf stepped toward her and she wasn't afraid. Not even a little bit. His head came to her waist. She put her hand on the great skull and found it hot, the fur incredibly soft.

She dropped to her knees and took his face in both her hands. She looked into his amber eyes. *Thank you. Thank you for coming. For saving me.*

He dropped his gaze and lowered his body, acknowledging her as an alpha. That surprised her, because in all their interactions, she'd felt he was the alpha.

No, she said. She lay beside him and put her arms around him, between his great paws. *We are the same,* she sent. *We made promises and we kept them. We are the same.*

The wolf let out a sigh.

Are you injured?

No. I am tired. I have traveled long for this. I thought. . . I thought it was to build my pack, but it was not. It was for this. Now I must go. I do have a pack to find.

Yes. You're not safe here. I will never forget you, but please, never come back. Go back where you came from. She showed him traveling north, the sun traveling east to west, guiding him.

They rested together. She cried as she realized she would never have a moment like this. Never have a wolf in her arms again. A magnificent creature that had risked all for her.

I will always be your pack, she added.

"Elizabeth? Where are you?" She heard Tig's voice, weak but moving closer.

"Oh, my God. What is that?" He had seen the wolf.

Steady, she told the wolf. She shakily got to her feet.

"It's okay, Tig. He saved me. I know him. I'm his . . . friend, I guess you'd say. He says I'm in his pack. I would have died without his help." The wolf had slowly risen and now stood cross-wise in front of Elizabeth, head low, eyes on Tig. She kept her hand on Sojourn.

He is my pack mate, she told him. She felt the wolf relax under her hand. *Can he touch you? You are special and we will never see you again. Can he please feel what I feel?*

Yes. Then I must go. Someone is coming.

"Tig? Are you hurt?"

"A little. Goro is worse. I have to call an ambulance. I don't know where to begin. I rushed to find you. I thought you would be dead. Is Tanaka dead?"

"I don't know. Call 911. Then Sojourn," she indicated the wolf, "has to leave. He says you can touch him if you want. I think you should. He is wild, but will allow it because you are my pack mate, and by extension, that makes you part of his pack, too. He's leaving, Tig. I told him he has to go, but I'll never see him again." Her crying got the best of her. She was torn. She wanted to go to Tig. She wanted to check Tanaka. She wanted to hold this exotic creature longer.

Tig pulled out his cell phone and made the call. She dropped to her knees once more and cried into his fur. He sent her energy that felt a lot like love, but what do wild wolves know about love? Maybe that was a question for the wolf rescue people.

He gently licked the tears.

"Okay," Tig said. "Cavalry's coming. I should check everyone." Elizabeth met his gaze. "He's a little scary," he admitted.

"One chance. It will change you."

Tig slowly came forward and held out his hand. "I can touch him?"

"Sure. He feels amazing."

Tig's face changed as he stroked the top of Sojourn's head. Finally he ran a hand down the length of the wolf's body. "I've never felt anything like this in my life."

"Softer than you'd think, right?"

"Yeah, but something else. Not physical. I feel, I don't know. Hope? Something. I think it's coming from him."

Elizabeth tuned in and Sojourn was indeed sending Tig a message.

"Oh, shit!" Elizabeth said. She didn't mean to, it just popped out.

"What? Are you okay?"

"Sojourn is telling you, yes, hope, but hope for the future. We're having a puppy. And that's a quote. I think he even has a sense of humor."

Tig's jaw dropped and he looked from Elizabeth to Sojourn and back again. "Oh, my God."

"He also said Tanaka is alive, so we'd better do something."

She hugged Sojourn tightly. He allowed it. Then she kissed him right on top of his head which surprise him. Tig patted him one more time and Sojourn leapt off into the darkness leaving nothing to say he was ever there. Nothing but the energy

388

and feeling he'd implanted and they'd both remember forever.

Thirty-Two

Tig's training kicked in. He had not done anything for Goro except to see he was alive and not bleeding out. At the time Tig had left the pump room, Goro was unconscious and Tig had raced to find Elizabeth.

Now Tig checked Tanaka. Elizabeth hesitantly went to the man Tanaka had taken down. He lay in a pool of blood. She felt for a pulse and didn't find one.

Tanaka was coming around. "What happened?" he said.

"You got shot," Elizabeth said.

"It's not too bad," said Tig. "He missed the important stuff. You're going to be fine." Tig had padded his over-shirt onto the wound to stanch the bleeding, leaving him shivering in his tee shirt.

Elizabeth rarely got to watch him work, and was both proud and worried. It was cold in the pre-dawn and although Tig was young and strong, he might be shocky himself from his own injuries, the fear of losing her, then her being saved by a *wild wolf,* and of course, the little matter of her pregnancy. She hadn't even known. She wasn't far enough along to notice a missed cycle. Wow. Sojourn was good. Assuming he was right. Somehow she thought he was.

Sirens announced that help had arrived. Her vision had cleared so she went to the gravel drive to wave them in. In seconds the area was filled to bursting with fire trucks, EMT vehicles, police cars, Sheriff's cars, and a CHP officer with nothing to do. *Well, that wasn't fair,* she thought. When a fellow officer was down, whether it was law enforcement or fire department, everyone turned out. She was actually a little flattered for Tig, since it was that awful time of night when nothing good happens and everyone just wants to stay asleep. A faint orange haze behind the pond indicated the sun was thinking about showing up.

When she returned to Tig after showing them the pump room and saw Goro being tended to, he was mid-statement to the Sheriff's deputies. Once again, they were outside the city limits.

Tanaka was also being cared for and was sitting up and talking. Gurneys were wrestled along the gravel path. The man who'd attacked her and Tanaka was dead and the pond was being searched for the weapon.

She looked for the second assailant and didn't see him. He'd gone down, maybe even with a gunshot wound, and definitely a broken wrist courtesy of Sojourn. Maybe the EMTs had taken him? She didn't see another gurney.

"Excuse me," she asked a man working on Tanaka. "There was a second man over there," she indicated the other side of the path. "Did someone take him already?"

"I don't know. I don't think so."

Elizabeth stepped to Tig who was still talking with a Sheriff's deputy. "Tig? Where's the other guy? Did they take him to the hospital already?"

"No. I don't think so. They saw that guy was dead and Tanaka's here."

"What other guy?" the deputy asked. "The man who assaulted you isn't that man?" He pointed to the body by the pond.

"No, there was a second man. We were both incapacitated and he came up here," Tig said.

"But he didn't attack you?" he asked Elizabeth.

"Well, yes, he did, but then his partner or whoever, the second guy from the pump room came out and attacked Mr. Tanaka and me."

The deputy looked confused. "Okay. So there were two attackers?"

"Yes," said Elizabeth. "The man at the edge of the pond attacked us first, and Mr. Tanaka fought him. He was very brave. Then a second man came out, and he must have been in the pump room with Tig and Goro." Here her eyes welled up a bit. Tig put his arm around her.

"It's okay. We're all fine. Go ahead," he said.

"Mr. Tanaka got the gun from the first man and he and this second man shot at each other. I think Mr. Tanaka's shot must have missed. Mr. Tanaka just fell over." Elizabeth heard the gunshots in her mind again. So loud. The smell from the guns was very strong. "The other man was going to shoot me, too."

"Why didn't he?" asked the deputy. He seemed a little skeptical about a second man, given there was no body. Maybe he thought she was hysterical. Maybe she was. She started to shake.

"A really big dog came out of the dark at him. I guess it was a neighbor's watch dog or something, and it grabbed his wrist and the man couldn't shoot me."

She felt Tig stiffen next to her, but she refused to look at him and draw the deputy's attention to what promised to be a super big lie. Tanaka had been unconcious, so he didn't need to corroborate anything.

The deputy took notes. "Okay, so a dog saved you?"

"Yes. That's right. We don't live here, but I assume it was a neighbor's dog. Anyway, the dog was big and I think it broke the man's wrist or arm. The man went down and didn't get up again. But now I don't see him. He must have escaped in the confusion."

"Must have," said the deputy. He didn't seem very happy with her account. She would never talk about the wolf to the authorities, and she hoped Tig wouldn't.

"I don't feel very well," she said. It was true, and she wanted the deputy to stop talking to her. Everything Tig would say for the report was true. She had no idea what had happened with Tanaka or what was going on at that end, but a lot of things were starting to make sense. She and Tig had wandered into a yakuza family feud. Somehow, she figured Tanaka was part of it. Goro must be, too, and when they took him to the hospital, they would see the tattoos. At least he had all his fingers. It would be about a second before they connected this to Mike's murder.

She *knew* nothing for sure. But now, almost being executed brought things into the light. The figure the Masuka's fish had shown her was Goro. He fit their vision physically.

Her pond bag! Again, she didn't *know,* but she was sure Goro must have put it in her car during a water check at the property. Magically appearing at the jail complex probably had nothing to do with it, even though that's where she discovered it. Goro took it from the Masuka's that day when he cleaned up the crime scene. Maybe to buy time and build some doubt about her story. It was unfortunate for him that Mike's body had been discovered so quickly. He probably *had* seen her and Karl at the property. If that were true, he knew they were no threat to him, not having seen him themselves. Thank goodness she didn't mention fish-vision to him. Or had she? Tanaka knew. But how much did he know? She 'communicated' with the fish. He didn't know they showed her things. He didn't know hinomaru took her back in time. Tanaka obviously felt connected to hinomaru, but only she and the fish knew it was historical in some way.

Genetically, genealogically? She didn't even know what to call it. Do fish have souls?

Wow. She must have a head injury. Now she really didn't feel well.

"That's enough for now," said Tig. "We'll make ourselves available for questions or statements later, but for now we're done. My wife's pregnant and I want her checked out at the ER."

The deputy looked like he wanted to argue right up until Tig said she was pregnant. *She* wanted to argue with Tig that it wasn't necessary, but she rethought. Best to be safe, and that would get her out of here, which is what she wanted to do more than anything right now.

Tig drove her to the ER after the two ambulances left with Goro and Mr. Tanaka. The body would remain until the crime scene folks got there. She idly wondered why the attacker was dead. He wasn't shot. What would cause the pool of blood she saw? He hadn't hit his head on any rocks, and besides, the blood wasn't coming from his head.

The ER wasn't as bustling as she thought it would be. She came in the walk-in side, not through the ambulance bay, maybe that was it.

She was checked in rather quickly and taken to a bed. They didn't fool around with pregnant people. Everything was normal. Well, for her. There were only so many curtained cubicles and she didn't hear anything that sounded like emergency stuff happening. Where was Goro? Mr. Tanaka?

"Tig? Can you find out what happened to Goro and Mr. Tanaka? I don't hear anything. This is a small emergency department. Unless they've been assigned rooms already, they're not here."

A nurse came and asked more questions about what happened and her pregnancy. They took blood.

"Are you going to do an ultra-sound?" Elizabeth asked.

"It's about the size of a poppy seed right now, so no. But we're going to confirm through a blood test that you're pregnant."

"Okay. So, the poppy seed is okay, probably, right?"

Tig entered just as she asked that and threw a concerned look at the RN. The nurse laughed.

"You're probably fine; it's really well padded in there. If you'd been in a car accident, maybe, or had a huge physical trauma, that might be different. We're not going to discount mental trauma, either, though. You'll have strict protocols to follow to make sure you don't miscarry due to stress. You'll need to follow up as soon as possible with your own OB-GYN."

"Absolutely." Elizabeth grinned. She was a little surprised at how happy she felt.

"What's a poppy seed?" Tig asked.

Both women laughed. "Becky just told me that's about how big the baby is right now, so I don't need to worry about it being hurt in there when I got hit or fell or anything. I actually feel really good right now. Okay, tiny headache." Elizabeth said. "What did you find out?"

"Doc will be right in to go over your discharge info." Becky left, whisking the curtain closed.

"Goro refused treatment when he arrived. The deputies got a statement from him at the scene and were going to follow up, but by the time they did, he was out of here."

"Hmm. Interesting. I think he's yakuza, too, like Mike."

"What?"

"Detective Dominic, remember Honu's brother? He told me Mike was yakuza, and I saw Goro's tattoos one day, and remember the first batch of Tanaka's fish were poisoned, too?"

"Um, you're not making much sense," Tig said.

"It is kind of confusing. I forget how much I've told you over the past couple weeks."

"Okay, I know Goro said the first fish were poisoned, so they needed replacing."

"Yes, well, I think that Mike Mamushi, who belonged to a rival crime family in Japan, did it. I think he found out that Tanaka had a safe house or something here, tracked them down and did it. Then he orchestrated through shell companies and the Sato family, the second to the top Yakuza gang in Japan, the purchase of that house so he could keep an eye on them without them knowing it."

"Which 'them' are you talking about now?"

"Tanaka and Goro. They must be yakuza, too. I don't know what family, but look at this house here! Dominic was thinking the Yakuza was setting up shop here on the Central Coast, because it's right in the middle of all the territories they're moving into."

"Do you have any proof of anything? Anything at all more than a great story?"

"Not really. I just put things together from what Dominic said, what I've seen and what the fish showed me. And, uh, what I read on the internet."

"You're kidding. The internet?"

"So you believe my fish-vision more than sources on the internet? *That's* the part you're questioning? There are reliable sites. I mean, I didn't get it all from Wikipedia."

"What's fish-vision? What do you mean by that?"

She explained that it was like when the owl showed her things from his point of view, when she was helping Tig during an arsonist's streak.

"There's something you're not telling me. What?" He watched her carefully.

She was a terrible liar and so she explained as best she could that for some reason, hinomaru was connected to a place in history in Japan and could take her there, too.

"That's kind of cool. How do you know it's real?"

"I wasn't sure. But then I started researching. There's too much to be coincidence. I saw some guy who looked like Goro in the vision, but I thought that could be because he's the only Japanese person I really know. But, then I realized something tonight. Mr. Tanaka was the main lord, or the leader in the vision, too. He was the one all the other lords were coming to. I know he was a shogun, and I had never seen him before my vision. Then tonight, he helped me heal hinomaru and I knew."

"Who's hinomaru? What did you know?"

"Hinomaru is the flag fish. I was calling him the flag fish because he looks like the Japanese flag. Tanaka says the fish is hinomaru because that's what they call the flag. It means circle of the sun."

"Explain the healing part. You don't heal. Do you?"

"No. I never have. Hinomaru was dying, it was terrible. He wanted me to touch him so he wouldn't die alone. Then Tanaka came and touched him, too, and," she shivered, "it was creepy, magical. I don't know. Our energies mixed and flowed into hinomaru and helped him heal. It was Tanaka, he did that."

"Are you sure?"

"Yes. Tanaka and hinomaru have a connection beyond here and now. My visions of the past were from that fish's point of view. I know that. And the man in charge, even then, was Tanaka—well, his ancestor, I guess. When hinomaru arrived, he said he was supposed to be here. At first I thought his person was Goro, but it wasn't. It's just that Goro and Tanaka are always connected and when the fish saw Goro, he knew Tanaka, his person, was near too. So, hinomaru knew that he had found his person again. Well, something like that. And when Tanaka touched me and the fish, my subconscious realized that he was the Tanaka from way back. He shared his soul or his energy with that shogun."

"Like reincarnation?"

"I have no idea. This is so far out of my usual weird wheelhouse, I can only guess."

Tig was remarkably calm. *He probably thinks I have a concussion,* she thought. "There's another thing."

"Oh, good. I was worried we were running out of 'things.'" His smile softened his words and he took her hand. "Go ahead."

"When I was 'back in time' with that fish, the kimono of the shogun had a distinctive pattern. Each lord has his family crest on his clothes and on his things. Well, that same thing is all over the Tanaka property. I even saw it on a pillow inside this amazing Japanese-style room he has. It's three hollyhock leaves. We don't have a lot of hollyhocks around here. In fact, I've never seen one."

"They're in Tanaka's yard," Tig said. Now he looked serious.

"That pattern was also on the gate at the shogun's house. It was everywhere."

"That pattern is on the torii here, too."

"When I first made the connection, Goro said I said some Japanese words. One of them was Tokugawa."

Tig looked blank. "Who's that?"

"The shogun who is reputed to have changed Japanese history and rearranged the hierarchy of the samurai, who are the roots of the modern day yakuza."

"That's pretty amazing. A fish showed you that?"

"Yes. The connection is more than energy, it's generational or even something else. Tokugawa went to war in 1603. This goes back at least that far. I don't think Goro or Tanaka know, but the fish does. To me that means Tanaka is either a descendent of Tokugawa or somehow shares his energy or spirit." She dropped her head back onto the pillows. "I need to clear some things up. I want to talk to Tanaka," she said. "Did you find him? Did he get here?"

Just as Tig was going to answer, the curtain ripped back and the ER doctor entered with her discharge process. Tanaka would have to wait.

Thirty-Three

Tig insisted on taking her home to rest. She didn't put up much of a fight, she was so exhausted. Tig was off that day anyway, supposed to start his 24 hour shift that night. He said he'd switch with someone and stay with her.

She thought about telling him not to, but she decided to be selfish and let him. They needed an evening of just them. And the cats. Perhaps without an emergency in the middle of it.

Tig rearranged his schedule with Karl, too. They were to work on the new client's place today, but Tig wanted to stay around the house.

"You must really trust Karl to let him take the lead on this," Elizabeth said.

"He brought the client to me, so it's his find. He proved himself on the Masuka's pond--I know, that's not their real name, but that's how I think of them, so that's what it is to me."

Elizabeth smiled, propped up in bed with two cats providing comfort. "Hey, can you find out how Mr. Tanaka's doing? He didn't come to Sierra

Vista Hospital, so either he ran away like Goro, or maybe he went someplace else? He seemed too injured to run. He's not as young as Goro. Maybe he's worried about the authorities because he's not a citizen and he killed someone? I mean it was self-defense, but that guy was dead with a lot of blood, and he sure didn't shoot him. Find out about that, too, okay?"

"Yes, ma'am." Tig kissed her. "You need to rest. You can sleep, but I'm supposed to wake you every hour to be sure your brain's not exploding or anything."

"That certainly will be restful. I am tired, though. How long do you have to wake me up every hour?"

"Eight hours from release. So, mid-afternoon. If you sleep all that time."

"All right. When you wake me up, I want to know what's going on, okay?"

He shook his head in mock frustration. "I will be watering. Text me if you need anything." Edward woke up as Tig was leaving the bedroom. "Correction, Edward and I will be watering."

Elizabeth smiled and snuggled down into her pillows. Teddy rested along her side, his downy fur and strong purr a comfort. She immediately dropped off. Seconds later, Tig was gently shaking her.

"Hey, time to check on you."

"Oh, my God. This is awful."

"What? Are you in pain? Dizzy?"

"No. Wiped. It seems like I just fell asleep."

403

"You sound normal to me, go back to sleep."

She wanted to tell him to give her an update, but that wasn't as important as falling back to sleep right now. She let go.

Several more hours of checks and brief sleeps occurred before she decided to stay up for a bit.

"I think I'm hungry. Grilled cheese sandwich?"

"On its way." Teddy followed Tig out to the kitchen.

Elizabeth flipped on the TV while she waited. The noon news was on. *Journalists were as good as detectives at ferreting out information sometimes,* she thought.

The whole yakuza thing had hit the airwaves. They really sensationalized it, but she couldn't blame them. I mean really, here on the Central Coast? It truly was unthinkable.

They had the gist of Mike Mamushi's murder, but that had happened ages ago in media time. No suspects however. It had been confirmed that he was yakuza and the Masuka house was bought by a yakuza family through a shell corporation. They didn't know why.

They also had a sketchy report of the events of last night--a 'home invasion' they were calling it. They didn't mention her or Tig by name, but spoke of 'friends at the home' at the time of the crime. She wondered who was able to keep their names out. Maybe Dominic? His brother worked with Tig, so as a favor, perhaps. Or to hold back info

404

pertinent to the case. She knew about that from her many CSI episodes; however, she knew all that happened on the show wasn't real. Rats. If it were, the case would be solved in 45 minutes by the crime scene guys and gals on DNA alone!

They also mentioned that both the owner and the caretaker were injured during the fracas, they actually used that word! Elizabeth was tickled. Some fracas. The story ended with the usual, "The investigation is ongoing."

Nothing about Goro running away or where Mr. Tanaka was now.

Tig appeared with her sandwich, a cup of tea, and two cats. She clicked off the set. "Thanks. Did you find out anything? Where did Tanaka get taken, Tolosa General?" she mentioned the other hospital in the city.

"I called Tolosa and they don't have him. So, I called Honu at home and asked him to find out for me from Pete. I just heard back a little bit ago."

Elizabeth was hungry so she just ate while he talked. She nodded, indicating he should continue.

"Okay, this is all hearsay, and I don't know how much is really true, because Pete wasn't able to comment on an ongoing investigation. That's a quote. Having said that, he told his brother what he could, understanding it was for us and would go no farther. Right?"

She nodded again.

"Okay. Goro is in the wind. They think he's probably on his way back to Japan. He either went north or south immediately where he has

405

connections to help him get home. Tanaka was taken to Tolosa because he said he had a heart condition and he requested it. He's older and had obviously sustained some injuries. However, he disappeared from there, too, like Goro. They think he requested Tolosa, not for his heart, but because he had friends there. They helped him escape and the Gang Task Force is sure he's on his way back to Japan, too."

"Wow."

"According to Dominic, we could, well *they*, could extradite him since he was involved in that man's death on his property. They don't know how much. We'll both be called to give extensive witness statements, but they have no one in custody. Everyone who might be a suspect of anything is either dead or gone."

"That must be so frustrating for Dominic!" Her tea had cooled to the perfect temperature. Green tea. It reminded her of Goro and Tanaka. She somehow couldn't reconcile in her mind that they both belonged to a huge criminal syndicate.

"So, Goro and Tanaka are yakuza, too."

Tig nodded. "Seems so. Weird, huh?"

She replayed last night's attack in her mind, and no, she hadn't seen Tanaka kill the first man. She hadn't witnessed anything but him defending her and himself. Tig hadn't seen anything either. Goro and he had fought their attacker, but had been overcome. Goro might have been shot too, she didn't even know that. Tig had been knocked out and wasn't able to add much. The second man must have escaped after Sojourn's attack. If he had any

406

brains at all, he was back in Japan with the rest of them.

"What about the dead guy?" Elizabeth asked. "What happened to him?"

"He was stabbed and bled out. No weapon found." Tig eyed her. "You didn't see anything like that, did you?" She shook her head, shocked at this information. "You'd tell me, right?"

"Sure, but I didn't. I was banged around pretty good last night. Tanaka fought to protect me and took the gun away from the man at his own risk. The guy fell down and didn't move. I never saw a knife or anything. Maybe he did a suicide whatchamacallit? Hara-kiri or something?"

"I have no idea what you're talking about."

"You know, you read about it in the papers even now. The Japanese commit suicide to prevent shame from falling on themselves and their families. Some big corporate head did it last year. I didn't know they still did that. It sounds so medieval."

"It sure does. I don't know about that suicide part. Maybe Dominic does and just isn't telling."

"So the case is stalled?" Elizabeth put her sandwich plate aside.

"It's probably moving forward, but Dominic just can't talk about it. For now, we're out of it."

"Any word on what happened to the pond? The methane poisoning?"

"Methane was introduced to the pond from the pump room and from a tank they found in the vineyard behind the property. A hose ran from there to the pond. There's so much foliage it wasn't seen. That's probably what happened the first time."

"Is that part of that yakuza family feud?" Elizabeth asked.

"Dominic thinks so. A way to bring shame on one family, stealing or damaging property. Apparently it's well known that they love their koi, so that became a weapon."

"What's going to happen to the fish now that Tanaka and Goro are gone?"

"I don't know about that either. I'll ask Honu. I bet they're not a priority."

"The fish at Animal Services! I'm supposed to get them today at eleven. Oh, no! It's way past that." Elizabeth dialed her cell. "Will you go if I can arrange it?"

"I want to stay with you."

"But they need us. It won't take long. I'll tell them you're coming. Please? You already have the quarantine tank ready."

Tig thought. "Okay, on the condition that Janie can come and sit with you for an hour or so while I'm gone."

"Oh, yes!" Elizabeth said to both the person who answered the phone at Animal Services and to Tig. She told them about the change in pick up, but not why. She got a little lecture on punctuality and the use of the phone when plans change. Melissa was not happy with her. It was just as well she was sending Tig. No woman could resist when he decided to be charming. She warned him as he changed into 'pond clothes' as he put it. Not his super grubbies, since he had to impress them, but clothes he didn't mind getting wet and dirty.

"I'm going to load the truck," he said and kissed her. "Remember I'm not going unless you have a sitter." Teddy and Edward looked slightly indignant. "A human sitter who can dial a phone in an emergency," he added.

She nodded and was already calling Janie. Fortunately, Janie and Garrett were free and arrived just as Tig was ready to leave.

Janie came straight back to the bedroom. "Anything you need?"

"No. Thank you so much for coming."

The two cats had evaporated like morning mist the second they'd heard Garrett squawk at the front door. He loved the cats, but it was not reciprocated.

Clicking toenails meant Buster had come, too. Elizabeth was happy to see him. It felt like an age since they'd all visited.

Garrett was toddling a little now, and Elizabeth had not child-proofed their bedroom. In between chatting, Janie dogged him and removed things from his grasp. She whipped a plug protector from her pocket and stuck it in the one exposed outlet.

"Man, you're good," Elizabeth said.

"This little guy keeps me hopping; I'd better be."

Buster had managed to get on the bed and lay next to Elizabeth, in Teddy's usual spot. She rubbed his rough graying coat and listened to his wheezy Pug breaths. He was content. So was she.

Her eyes felt heavy and she needed a real nap. "Sorry," was all she managed before she fell asleep.

Janie tiptoed out with Garrett and that's all she heard until Tig's truck pulled into the drive.

Thirty-Four

Elizabeth woke slowly and heard Buster's snores turn to awake wheezes. He declined to check on whatever was going on. Elizabeth lay relaxed, while she heard Tig chat with Janie in muffled tones. She saw a voicemail left on her phone. Millie. Her surgery had gone well. All prognoses were positive. Good news. She sent reassurance to Jato. She made a mental note to call after Millie came home.

She finally got up and used the bathroom. The tea had caught up with her. Plus, she wanted to see the fish.

By the time she reached the driveway, Janie had gone, taking Garrett and Buster with her. She was sure because both Teddy and Edward supervised as Tig removed five large plastic bags filled with water, air and a koi each.

"How are they?" Elizabeth called from the front door. She held it open. "Here, go through the house, it will save steps. Can I carry one?"

"No," he said firmly. "Just open the back door and the gate." He referred to the gate from their yard to the outback. He had a large, probably heavy bag in each hand.

"You got it." She was still in PJs, but had her slippers on; practically dressed for anything. She felt fine. Not even dizzy.

Tig carefully placed the still closed bags in the frogaterium pond, and returned for two more. In moments all five floated in the water, bags bumping, filling the surface.

Elizabeth assessed as Tig did his checks. What she thought of as 'her' black and white fish seemed fine. They all did.

Tig started to untie the bags and she helped. The faster the fish got into clean, well-oxygenated water, the better. She felt their contentment at being 'rescued' and put into a new pond.

"How was it?" Elizabeth asked. "Did you have to wrestle the clerk to get in? Get a lecture on your wife's terrible manners?"

"No. They were really busy. I gave them my bonafides and showed my FD I.D. and that reassured them. I don't know why a fire department employee has anything to do with fish, but maybe I wouldn't steal them? I don't know. Maybe they checked with Pete Dominic before I got there. I think he's probably too busy to vet a fish thief, but at any rate, they let me do my thing."

"I bet they're happy not to have to worry about these guys anymore." She watched them swim. No listing, tilting, flashing. Tig tossed in some koi pellets.

"How do they seem?" Elizabeth asked.

"All in all, pretty good. Anything at your end?" He meant her 'energy check.'

"No. They've recovered really well since yesterday. I guess the damage wasn't permanent. Even Spot there doesn't seem to have any swim bladder issues."

"Spot, huh?"

"Um, the black and white one."

"It's always a bad sign when you name something."

"I've been thinking what to do about these guys. I know we can't keep them all, but maybe one or two?"

"They're still pretty small. We can manage that, I think. I'm sort of fond of that orange and black there." He pointed to a lovely streamlined fish.

"I love the Halloween fish, too! Can the others go to Karl's client's pond once they pass quarantine?"

"That's a great idea. That pond won't be ready for a while, and by then, we should be sure about these fish. Karl's got them expanding the pond, as well as the waterfall repair. I'll talk to him about it."

They watched the fish eat all their pellets. Elizabeth promised them a tofu treat later. Together they covered the pond with netting, and then a foot over that, a fine metal mesh to prevent raccoon's curious hands from dipping in and damaging the already fragile fish. Elizabeth told them about their new environment and warned them about predators. They seemed remarkably relaxed but she figured that was because they had no idea. At least they were physically protected from claws and beaks.

413

They had food and oxygen and room to swim; heaven for them.

"How are you feeling?" Tig asked as they passed through the gate into their own backyard.

"Pretty good. Still tired, but no headache or anything. I could eat, though."

"Me, too," Tig said. *Me too,* echoed two other voices.

Elizabeth laughed.

"What's so funny?" Tig asked as he held the kitchen door for her.

"Some things never change. The cats are definitely just like you in the food department."

The cats waited expectantly for a yummy wet food treat, and Elizabeth obliged. Tig called from the refrigerator, "Not much here. How about pizza and NetFilms?"

"Perfect," Elizabeth said.

Cats love pizza, Teddy said.

Yes, they do, Edward added.

Tig called for delivery as the whole family headed back to the bedroom.

As they settled in to watch a movie, Elizabeth sent a wave of gratitude to Sojourn, whom she found had already traveled about thirty miles north. She saw him near a small town with a deserted mission and knew exactly where he was. He acknowledged her presence, but kept moving forward.

Good idea, she thought. *We should all keep moving forward.*

A couple excellent references used in this creation are:

Hickling, S. (Ed.). (2002). *Koi, Living Jewels of the Orient*. Hauppage: Interpet Publishing.

Kaplan, D., & Dubro, A. (2003). *Yakuza: Japan's Criminal Underworld* (Expanded ed.). Berkeley: University of California Press.

Also, please visit a couple more friends who helped make this possible!

The real travels of Sojourn (OR7) can be found at: http://www.dfg.ca.gov/wildlife/nongame/wolf/

Wolf Hybrid And Rescue (WHAR):
WHAR.org

Great koi can be found at:
Clarke Koi of Toronto, Canada
www.clarkekoi.com